What they're saying about *The Rites of Passage*:

"Jonathan A. Taylor's *The Rites of Passage* is marketed as the first in a series of novels; it also ably stands on its own. The story follows Jamie Goldberg from elementary school to college, as he grows from an abused boy into a self- possessed young man. His life is a symphony of pain, humor, filth, and beauty as he struggles to come to terms with his identity in homophobic America." **Foreward Reviews**

"Heartbreaking and hilarious, provocative and romantic—in *The Rites of Passage*, the first book in *The Goldberg Variations*, debut novelist Jonathan Taylor drills down till it hurts in a coming-of-age and coming out story tailored to our times." **Linda Watanabe McFerrin**, author of **Namako, Dead Love** and **The Hand of Buddha**

"When I read the searing tale of Jamie's journey from childhood through adolescence and young adulthood, I lived it as if it were my own. It chronicles his anguish as he finds himself on the outside, increasingly isolated from family, school and college, his coming to terms with transgressive fantasies and his authentic self...set against the backdrop of political upheaval that defined the Seventies." **Kunal Mukherjee**, author of **My Magical Palace**

"*The Rites of Passage* is like encountering a gay *Portnoy's Complaint* in its distinctive blend of Jewishness, sex, moral panic, and maternal dominance. And it's painfully realistic in its depiction of what 'coming out' is, its alternation of moments of euphoric liberation with moments of renewed shame and sorrow, as if life were a coin God is flipping and can never be better than half right, but not always the same half. I've spent many pages and many hours with Jamie, and I still want to know what happens to him." **Patrick Mulcahey,** seven-time Emmy Award-winning screenwriter of **The Bold and the Beautiful**

"Reading *The Rites of Passage* reminded me of the fragile time in one's youth when one may or may not mistakenly believe that all information is somehow related to one's self. So, rather irrationally and hilariously, I started to assume the book was about me and was frankly upset about that. This is when the genius of the author's trick hit me. Through Jonathan's writing style and his character's problematic self-driven gay psychosis, he managed to bring me back to that most vulnerable part of myself: youth. Reading it then became addicting. If *The Rites of Passage* doesn't remind you of yourself, it will certainly remind you of someone you love." **Rene Capone,** gay figure painter and author of many graphic novels including **The Legend of Hedgehog Boy**

THE GOLDBERG VARIATIONS:

THE RITES OF PASSAGE

THE GOLDBERG VARIATIONS:

THE RITES OF PASSAGE

Jonathan A. Taylor

ARNOLAND PRESS

ArnoLand Press, Publishers
74 Pond Street, San Francisco, CA 94114 USA

CATALOGING DATA:
The Rites of Passage
By Jonathan A. Taylor
Library of Congress Control Number: 2018910022
ISBN: 978-0-999-53363-5

Cover design: Michael Arent
Cover illustration: *Tremble Again* by René Capone

Excerpts from *Narcissus and Goldmund* by Herman Hesse, translated by Ursule Molinaro. Copyright © 1930, 1957 by Herman Hesse, Montagnola. Translation © 1968 by Farrar, Straus and Giroux. Reprinted by permission of Farrar, Straus and Giroux.

Excerpt from "The Wave" by Antônio Carlos Jobim, Copyright © 1967 by Antônio Carlos Jobim. Reprinted by permission of Corcovado Music Corp.

The lyrics to "Die Trockene Blumen" from *Die schöne Müllerin* by Wilhelm Müller (1794 – 1827) are translated © 2005 by Dr. James C.S. Liu. Used by kind permission from the translator.

Dedication

In honor of the enormous genius of
Doctor Morris Lyle Taylor (1931-2016)
the late husband of the author and this book

In commemoration of lives cut too short:
Steven Maldaver and Leonard Taylor

Perhaps such secrets, the secrets of everyone, were only expressed when the person laboriously dragged them into the light of the world, imposed them on the world, and made them a part of the world's experience. Without this effort, the secret place was merely a dungeon in which the person perished; without this effort, indeed, the entire world would be an uninhabitable darkness.

—James Baldwin, *Another Country*

Theme: Delusion, Guilt and Sexuality
1970

Allegro moderato
(Moderately fast)

Chapter 1: Jamie Goldberg

Detroit, Michigan, Spring 1970

"I am sorry, Mrs. Goldberg, it is against the school rules." Mrs. Bradford's temples were pulsating. I, Jamie Goldberg, was her least favorite student. I was as annoying as a precocious ten year old student could be. Too smart for my own good, but not smart enough to make life easy for myself. She regularly humiliated me in front of my classmates, leaving me to wonder when I would ever feel like I belonged somewhere.

Mrs. Bradford enjoyed thwarting me with brute strength, if not mental superiority; but my mother was a force for which she was unprepared.

"You can't let me take my own son out of school?" scolded my mother. Her small five-foot-one frame, bobbing red hair, and outrageous blood-red designer coat with the black tentacle fringe, made her look more menacing than her size.

The tall, gray-haired Mrs. Bradford towered over my parent. "He's not sick; he's perfectly well. There is no reason to take him out of school, Mrs. Goldberg."

"Stopping a war isn't a reason to take my son out of school?"

"No, it isn't."

"You won't let me take my son out of school?"

"No!" Mrs. Bradford barked.

I saw my mother relax. I could not suppress a smile; I knew Mrs. Bradford had lost.

"Okay, just try and stop me then." With that my mother, Mrs. Ruth Esther Goldberg, demanding wife, defender of the people of Detroit and mother of the school's most unpopular student, walked over to my chair and picked me up by the arm. I almost stumbled out of my chair.

"Go, Mrs. G!" cried Brian Germaine, one of the school's first black students—courtesy of my mother's political machinations.

"We're going," she said as she hauled me out of class.

Amid hoots from the other kids, Mrs. Bradford ran to the school intercom, yelling something I could not hear because, in an instant, I was out of the room.

Mom whisked me into the car where my older brother, Steven, was already sitting.

"What Neanderthal schmucks," she fumed. Off she drove with us downtown. The ride was jerky, but for us it was normal. Mom's foot didn't quite reach the gas pedal so she resorted to giving it a good kick in order to maintain speed.

In the back I was breathless from the tension in the school. I was thankful that the fight was over and settled in my mother's favor, my terror of the later consequences notwithstanding. I was certain Mrs.

Bradford would take revenge on me in front of class in some dark and horrific way, while my mother, who was trying to save the world, was more than ready to sacrifice her son just as Abraham willingly offered up Isaac. Whether God would stop her at the last minute, I was unsure.

Mom was driving Steven and me to an anti-war demonstration, and it wasn't the first time her political activities had gotten me in trouble with authorities and my pressuring peers.

When I was seven years old she had maneuvered to desegregate the local school district. She succeeded in getting only one African-American child, the aforementioned Brian Germaine, into our school. Mom's accomplishment turned all my friends against me. Not at first, but as the kids compared notes with their parents, they ended up hating my guts, calling me "nigger lover" and other names my mother would never allow me to repeat, let alone complain about.

The only real close friend I had after that episode was this very same Brian Germaine, the single African-American whose family had the courage to choose the all-white school.

Unfortunately—that is for me, not for the United States—around my eighth birthday my mother tried again. Any remaining sympathizers disappeared when she and a local civic organization successfully sued the school district for discrimination. The presiding judge ordered the school board from the neighboring African-American township to resign. Then the judge fused the two school districts into one. Instantly my school went from seventy-five percent Jewish and twenty-four percent Catholic to fifty percent African-American and forty-nine percent "beleaguered" Caucasian. The latter group couldn't get out of town fast enough—except my family; we were in it for the duration.

The school became an integrated/segregated school. The African-Americans stayed among themselves and took my only friend, Brian, with them. This left me with no one. Neither side thanked me for my association with the ruining of both schools. I was alone, but not left alone.

At first the new world order shocked me.

"Hey, Jamie."

I heard a familiar voice. I looked up from my gym locker. I smiled. It was Brian. I thought my lost friend was coming back. "Oh, hi, Brian. How is it going?"

Then, he was joined by three more unsmiling kids. "Brian?"

"Get up, Jamie."

Brian's voice resonated with that friendliness I associated with our former relationship. I even thought this was a discrete moment for us to declare our mutual friendships with new friends to boot. It wasn't until he kicked me in the groin and his new buddies kicked my legs from behind that I realized something was amiss. The feelings of friendship quickly blended with howling pain and humiliation, creating a cognitive dissonance from which I was never to recover.

I came home bruised and my clothes dirty, chiefly

because they were thrown into the garbage by Brian's friends. My mother gasped, but she was on the phone.

"Mildred, you have to realize desegregating the schools is the most important—wait a sec, what happened to you?—nothing Mildred, my son just came home a mess. Anyway, keep me posted on Oakland County. I'll come up there for a strategy meeting … knives? Mildred, that's no excuse for cowardice … Millie, we have to start somewhere … pragmatism breeds poverty … What do you mean who said that? I did—look I gotta go; I'll call you right back … Okay, then I am calling the mayor … Fine. Goodbye." She slammed down the phone, then glanced at the damage. "What happened to you, Jamie?"

"I fell." She accepted the excuse with a surprising ease.

"You fell? Again? Honestly, how can you be such a klutz. You have to be the most uncoordinated kid in school. What am I supposed to do with you?" It was a question she often asked but never answered. "Can you stop looking so sad all the time? Why not invite Brian and his new friends over to play sometime?" She stared at me and heaved a disgusted sigh. "Oh, go wash up—and change your clothes before your father comes home."

I wasn't just the butt of the black kids' fury. I had become an equal opportunity target; both whites and blacks felt a compulsion to bully me.

But by then, I felt I deserved this fate, even the

furtive beatings that followed. My situation lightened inadvertently when Jeremy, a high-voiced sissy tried to come to my rescue. Poor Jeremy. His weakness attracted the malicious beatings of our schoolmates with a fervor unmatched by those associated with my political views. On the one hand I felt a vague kinship for Jeremy. This kinship extended just enough to make me feel guilty about his torment, but not so far as to join his side. Though I suspected even at that early date that his was the side on which I really belonged.

At the Kennedy Square demonstration, by comparison, the action was orderly. We marched resolutely around the square in a vain attempt to stop bloodshed in a distant land. My mother's passion failed to allay my fear of the intimidating police. On horseback with grim unfriendly faces, they circled the marchers. Other sneering policemen in riot gear stood ready to pounce at a moment's notice. I was shaking. My mother was defiant. For all their scary intimidation, the police did nothing. To Mom's disappointment, there would be no arrests this time, unlike the 1968 Poor People's March, the highlight of my youth.

Then, I was in a sea of strangers, the only white kid. My mother and father had run ahead so Mom could hobnob with Martin Luther King, Jr.'s second in command, Ralph Abernathy. I was marching down Woodward Avenue mouthing what seemed like the words to songs I did not know. We all walked hand in hand, my eight-year-old white hand clasped by larger black hands. It was a beautiful experience. I was not afraid at all … until the march ended at the waterfront. There, white policemen on horses knew how to deal with people who marched in peace. Without warning, the men on horseback charged the crowd. A terrifying chaos ensued, during which I was pushed away, threw a tantrum, and was subsequently whisked away by Eileen, our house cleaner, who had somehow lost her shoes in the fracas. It was a nail-biting wait for my parents to return.

It was not until much later that night that my father and mother reappeared with a small African-American child named Ladon. He was maybe two years younger than I was. He lived with us for barely six months. Why, I am not exactly sure, though I was quite angry when he left. He was my last real buddy, someone who looked up to me. Ladon's departure made me realize how alone I was in my own home.

This anti-war demonstration in Kennedy Square was pretty tame by comparison. Still, in spite of the solemn chants—"What do we want? Peace! When do we want it? Now!"—and our orderly marching with placards, I braced for the police to come and destroy us at any second. I was, for some reason, waiting for the hammer to fall. My brother Steven, looking completely unperturbed, shook his fists at them. My mom, noticing this, followed suit. Luckily, all to no avail, Mom's only achievement was to heighten her youngest son's fear.

The police surrounded the demonstration but left

us alone, much to Mother's disgust. "What a bunch of cowards," she muttered. "If there were three more blacks here, we'd be getting trampled right now."

I stared at the policemen on their horses. They seemed belligerent and proud. I swallowed. I began to chant, "Trample me! Trample me!"

Fortunately for me, they did not comply.

Chapter 2: Secrets

Summer 1970

"The in-bound pass to Jamie Goldberg, he fakes Lanier, and he's alone in the lane … HE DUNKS IT! What a comeback. Pistons down by one, Kurt."

"It's Incredible, Tom, the Pistons should have put Goldberg in earlier—"

"Sorry to break in, Kurt, Catchings inbounds to Lanier—and my God!—Goldberg strips the ball away. At the buzzer—IT'S IN! DETROIT WINS!"

Actually, the game ended because I had thrown the last chess piece into the wastebasket. I was fantasizing a cold winter sport in the stifling summer heat, not to escape the temperature, but rather, to get my father's attention. But he was steadfast in his dedication to Saturday sports. I hadn't even the sense to know that in the summer baseball was his game of choice, not basketball. As usual, he paid me no mind. He was more intent on watching the Detroit Tigers destroy the Minnesota Twins than me destroying my chess set. Instead, the chess set was dispatched with unheeded fanfare, the chess set I knew my dad didn't like.

Although I was hoping for some fatherly approval,

I also threw away the set to help erase a memory. The chess set troubled my sleep. It was 'no game for a kid.' From the moment Steven's friend gave it to me, my father was suspicious of the expensive present from such an older boy. I played the game anyway and for that I felt ashamed. I needed to forget the chess adversary along with the crime, or maybe crimes, I had committed for the sake of a game of chess. Those crimes I was not able to face so I promptly tossed them into the wastebasket just like the chess set. However, unlike the chess set they wouldn't go away so easily, whatever they were. Still I was worried about what my dad would think about me, and now by throwing out the chess set I wanted to show I was doing what he wanted. I needn't have bothered as my father sat securely behind the television set. I was ignored even as I loudly stomped the delicate wood of the chessboard to smithereens. The approval I had longed for was not forthcoming. Indeed, something told me he purposefully ignored me. He never forgave me for running away during the riots in 1967. My father accidentally separated my elbow, stopping me from what he thought was running away from home. I was actually eager to see the tanks drive down Woodward. Dad ran after me. He pulled me by the arm a little harder than necessary. His embarrassment over the accident turned into a shameful secret that only he and I shared. It wasn't really Dad's fault, it was an accident, but our mutual silence on the subject turned it into something dark and shameful. So he ignored me. He ignored my playing chess with this friend of Steven's, which also turned into something dark and shameful.

Deep down I knew that Dad wasn't giving me the silent treatment. Even before the elbow separation, my dad was a man who spoke few words. He was a construction electrician and came home tired and often took a nap right away. After the accident, he dropped down to zero words in my presence and withdrew into his own world. A world of losing sports teams (except the 1968 Tigers, "God bless them all, the long, the short, and the tall"). Dad's idea of parenting settled into growling disapproval when I did something patently wrong—and ignore the rest. I could only inhabit his world by watching a baseball game and cheering on the home team with him. His joy in life seemed to be the momentary hits and dunks in what was typically a losing battle.

If we stuck to sports, we had a relationship. The trouble was that deep down inside I felt all sports were pointless. I was a poor liar about that fact, my "It's only a game" refrain further arousing his suspicions. So we went our separate ways, and I often padded into my room to play chess by myself, thinking of the last person who seemed to care about me. Until I could stand it no longer and threw the game away: that person was never coming back.

That person, I can say it: Gary was someone who cared about me. Even taught me something, chess, it's true. I didn't care if it was inappropriate. I didn't think of him for too long, because if I did, a flash with a trace of a tortured memory would make me shiver and loathe him. In the past, I had even thought he was my real dad. But he tricked me into stealing, and I got caught. That ended everything: he got kicked out of the house. And there was other stuff. But still, he took an interest in me. Inappropriate, apparently. To compensate, I tried rejecting him and idolizing my real father—a fruitless endeavor if ever there was one. So I lost my fathers all together. Obliterating the chess set once and for all for my oblivious Dad left me with an empty felling. It was a good thing mom rushed to fill in the gap.

"Jamie! Get in here and finish your book!" Mom angrily yelled at me from the living room.

Chapter 3: An Urban Fugue

Her anger was aimed at me, but I knew she was still bristling from my father's refusal to install air conditioning. In the heat, her temper was like a loaded gun. Mom didn't lose her cool often. She carefully picked her battles, but those battles were always fought to the finish and she always, always won.

That's when I stepped into the room with my homework. It was the summer; the homework wasn't from school but from Mom. She'd assigned me: *The Autobiography of Malcolm X*. She didn't so much assign it to me as leave it on my bed, carefully placed. A day later, she'd told me to write a book report on the book and deliver it—unrequested—to my class in the new school year. "That'll teach 'em," she said, pleased to deliver another lesson through the medium of a ten-year-old child.

The heat made her especially bossy. My brother Steven, home from Michigan State for the summer, was wiser than I was. He had retreated into his room. Before I settled into the book, the doorbell rang. Without waiting for someone to open the door, my cousin Harold walked in. Harold had now become a super-tall, long-haired hippie. Both Steven and Harold were desperately trying to grow bushy, if spotty, beards.

"Hello, Hal," said my mother, looking up from the television. "Sorry it's so hot in here."

"No problem for me, Mrs. G." My mother called Harold 'Hal' and Hal fell into the habit of all of Steven's friends of calling Mom 'Mrs. G.' "What you should do is get air conditioning like my parents did. They are cool as cucumbers in the house." My mother smiled broadly and my father glared intently at the television. "Steven's in his room?"

"Yes, but I don't want you smoking—cigarettes—in the house either."

"Sure thing, Mrs. G." Harold paused as he sauntered by me. "Hey, little man. You're growing bigger and bigger. Give me five."

He held out his hand. I slapped him five. Ever since Steven's friend, Gary, was kicked out of our house—Steven claimed I had him kicked out—Steven would always painfully slap my hand, claiming to 'give me five'. Not able to get over his resentment, he would also perform other random acts of unkindness. Just stupid stuff like biting the ends off my hot dog because he knew those were my favorite parts.

Harold, on the other hand, was gentler and kinder; he gave a friendly five back. He patted my head. I rarely saw him, but he was always kind.

Harold walked back to Steven's room, and I went back to my daunting assignment. *Malcolm X* was a hard read for me at age ten. I needed a dictionary.

Reading was particularly difficult at the living room table as there was heavy competition for space. The table had become a desk overflowing with books, old newspapers, and bundles of political campaign literature ready to be distributed or forgotten.

I was reading about Malcolm's work as a waiter at a restaurant called Small Paradise. Trudging along through the chapter with Malcolm X was painful. Malcolm did not have many kind words for white people. I assumed as a white person I was both responsible and guilty. My mother's ongoing battle with the television news further complicated the chore. Still, I tried to read:

All of us—who might have probed space or cured cancer, or built industries—were instead black victims of the white man's American social system. In another sense. The tragedy of the ...

"This is Fred Harris, live from Washington. The last American ground troops have left Cambodia, leaving a full day ahead of President Nixon's scheduled—"

"It's about time, the jerk—of course, leave it to Nixon to pull off this PR," decried my mother. "Now he's gonna be the peacemaker not giving any credit to the real heroes. Like Kent State and Jackson State didn't force his hand! Moron," she barked with contempt.

I tried to concentrate on my book:

It was my first schooling about the cesspool morals of the white man from the best possible source, from his own women. And then as I got deeper in my own life of evil, I saw the white man's morals with my own eyes. I even made my living helping him to the sick thing ...

"Federal Judge Harold Cox has issued a statement praising the police against the revolutionaries and anarchists who provoked the killings at Jackson State College—"

"Do you hear that?" she yelled at me. "Those bastards! First Nixon claims he got us out of Cambodia. *We* got us out of Cambodia, and then they shot and killed those innocent students. Now we get called 'anarchists and crazies' by some schmuck judge in Godawful, Arkansas!"

"But at least they pulled out of Cambodia. That's good news," I said.

"Don't be so naive. Do students like you have to die for freedom of speech? How did we wind up in this Neanderthal world?"

The enormity began to sink in: Those students could easily be me—age difference notwithstanding, I was only ten after all.

"Can we take the people who shot them to court? It was murder, wasn't it, Mom?"

"Yes, it was definitely murder. But no, there is no justice in this country. Instead we have some cockamamie judge who thinks anyone exercising their freedom of speech should be shot."

"It makes me feel ashamed to be an American."

"It should!" said my mother, turning back to the

television. "We can love this country but still be ashamed of our actions."

"Mayor Roman Gribbs is meeting this week with officials from General Motors to see if a standoff with the United Auto Workers can be avoided—"

"Like that will help anything," she quipped.

Hearing Mayor Gribbs made me think of the man he replaced, the forlorn Mayor Cavanaugh. I still felt sorry for the former mayor. I met him when I was four years old. The Mayor was bright and sunny then. Then after the riots, my mother's political ambitions shot, I saw Mayor Cavanaugh on television. He was sad and beaten. Second banana to a Republican governor, who took control of the city.

"What ever happened to Mayor Cavanaugh?" I asked Mom.

"You know, Jamie. The riots ruined what little chance he ever had."

"Little chance? But I liked him. He was nice to us, wasn't he, Mom?"

My mom thought this over. "He was. He was very decent and gave me a chance. Ha, I fared about as well as he did."

"You're still in office," I pointed out.

"Thank you, but the Wayne County Democratic Central Committee is hardly a political office. Goodness it is hot in here, isn't it, Jamie?"

"And Sports comes back after the following break," blared the television. Dad perked up.

"Do you know how hot it is in here?" my mother

asked my father.

"Yes, I know how blasted hot it is. I choose not to think about it." My father responded in one of his rare moments when he lost his cool and showed it.

"It's broiling in here, Irv, and I want to know what you are going to do about it."

"Can't stand the heat, get out of the kitchen?" He alone chuckled. I wanted to get out of the room as fast as I could. "All right, how about we go to a movie? … We can get another fan."

"Terrific, we'll be sweltering in here, but at least we'll have a fan collection that will be the envy of everyone on the goddamn street." My mother, already seething, wasn't about to let my dad out-anger her.

"What's for supper?" he asked softly.

"I asked, do you know how hot it is in here?" she demanded again. "What are you going to do about it?"

"How about a ceiling fan!" my father offered.

"Don't be ridiculous."

That did it. They were having a full-on fight. Did I have to see my father verbally beaten into submission again? Nor did I want the feeling that I was taking sides, though I wished my father would stand up to her just once. But on the other hand, it was dreadfully hot and humid in the house, so my mother was right. As their voices raised, I decided to retreat to my bedroom.

Chapter 4: Room Without a View

I headed to my room, aka the fallout shelter. On my way, I heard loud noises coming from Steven's room. That was all the excuse I needed to interrupt whatever Steven was doing. Steven and Harold were working on my brother's bedroom door.

"What are you doing?" I asked.

"We're installing this." Steve held up a metal contraption. "It's a lock, dummy. I am getting a little privacy—from you. Long overdue, but since you got Gary kicked out of the house, I had to go into business for myself. And that means I need a little privacy, get it?"

"I get it." I said, eager to change the subject. I thought I had just gotten rid of the topic by destroying the chess set.

"You have to stay out of my business," said Steven.

"Please can't we forget it," I pleaded, panicky.

"You want that, don't you," Steven barked. "It's your fault."

"Steven, it wasn't my fault. He made me do it," I said.

"No one made you do anything; you shouldn't have gotten into mom's stuff. Now he's gone, crybaby."

"I am sorry he's gone," I whined dishonestly, but wishing to appease Steven. "He was my friend, too," I lied.

"Fuck you. He wasn't nobody's friend. He was my business partner—supplier, if you know what I mean, you spoiled brat. Wah wah wah he made me do it wah wah wah."

"Hey, cool it, Steven," snapped Harold. "What are you getting so upset about anyway?"

"Gary stopped a fight, did you know that?" It leapt out of my mouth; I immediately regretted it. But I couldn't take it back. I realized the danger and somehow Steven did too.

"What does that mean, 'Stopped a fight'? You mean stopped from getting your baby ass whipped again. I don't want to talk about it."

"He stopped a fight?" asked Harold.

"He did. He stopped a fight. I … I was about to get beat up in school. Billy and those racists cornered me because mom was for bussing. I was alone … and that's when … when Gary pulled his car to a screeching halt—I heard it. He did it just to stop a fight. He was a real hero—then. But that was before he … and before he sort of made me steal mom's ring. When Dad caught me."

Steven turned red. He looked to the ground. Then at once it seemed like he was going to punch me. Harold bear hugged him.

"Chill, Steve, chill. He's your little bro," said Harold. "What's going on here? Well, I'm glad we're rid of Gary. He was a creep. I don't understand why he was in Jamie's room to begin with."

"He was my friend," I snapped defensively.

"He was? What did you do together?" Harold asked.

"What difference does it make?" said Steven. "Gary was desperate for money. His house and restaurant were burned down; that's where he got most of his money. Jamie, you should have just ignored him."

Steven stared at me, anger in his eyes. His anger felt like a slap. My face burned as if he had hit me. I thought of saying something else but decided it was safer to just shut up or I would end up back in my own room. Harold looked at me sympathetically.

"I just don't understand what he was doing in your brother's room all the time."

"He taught me how to play chess," I snapped defensively.

"He did? Aren't you kinda young for chess." Harold's voice was kind, questioning.

"I am ten."

"Of course," said Harold. "We'll have to play sometime."

"I don't have a chess set anymore."

"You can come over to my house and play."

"You have a chess set," Steven snapped. "What about the one Gary gave you?"

"It's missing," I said gloomily.

"Go, dig it out of that pit you call your room; now beat it."

I noticed another small metal contraption on Steven's desk. I tried one more delaying tactic. "What's that on your desk, Steve? I've never seen that before."

"If you must know, it's a scale to weigh things."

"We have a scale in the kitchen; its bigger than that."

"Yeah, this is a special kind. It's for weighing … small amounts—oh, forget it, Mr. Clueless. It's for a science project we're doing for a chemistry course." Steven laughed. "And why don't you beat it and go back to your room; you're really getting in my hair."

"How does this fit in the door?" asked Harold, holding a big piece of the new lock.

"You put that in the door; that's what I am drilling here."

"That whole thing has to fit in the door?"

"Yes, it has to be strong enough so this little twerp can't get in here." Steven turned to me, "Now get out of here, wimp."

"Leave him alone," Harold said. "Can't you see? He's lookin' kinda sad."

Steven rolled his eyes. "I see, all right. I'm tryin' to get him to be hip, but look at him." Steven softened up a bit—at least by his standards. "Jamie, don't go mopin' around all the time. Jesus, if you stop acting like a baby, people won't get so frustrated with you. Really, you're like a frightened puppy. Come on,

Jamie, go to your room. Hal and I wanna talk—about stuff you won't understand."

"Are you upset?" Harold asked me.

"Mom and dad are just having one of their arguments," Steven answered for me. "Jamie, try and be a little tough, for crying out loud. Here, this will help. Take it with you." He handed me a rolled-up magazine. "Don't peek at it until you are in your room and don't let anyone catch you with it either. Go on. That'll make you happy."

"Go ahead, little man, see you in a moment," Harold said softly.

I walked out with the magazine.

"He just mopes all the time, a real drag," I heard Steven say as I headed back to my room ... moping.

I dragged my feet over to my dreaded room. I opened the door. There, against the wall, below the window was my bed. My bed and the window both seemed so sick. I slumped in. Immediately the bed stood there like an accusation. I got up and closed the door. I looked at the magazine. It was gross. Steven, the practical joker, I didn't see why he had given me a *Playboy* magazine. I lifted my bed mattress, and with revulsion, I threw the magazine down on the box spring. The mattress covered it, and the whole problem that magazine posed—if any—went away.

Alone in my mess of a room, I sank down to the floor on the seemingly archaeological layers of chaotic mess. It all had accumulated since Steven's friend was expelled from the house. I was caught stealing my mother's ring for him. Even if it was a while ago, it was like yesterday for me and apparently for Steven too. I felt ambivalent but also mysterious when I thought about Gary, which was rare. One moment I would miss him. Then the trace—just the trace of the memory of him and I'd get the shivers again and be glad he was gone. My dad, Steven, and Gary it all seemed so confused. Although it was unclear how, there seemed some connection between this guy and a recurring nightmare I had. A nightmare, or nightmares of hawks or some other magnificent birds. They would plunge toward me. Somehow I knew these birds wanted to devour me. I was pecked by their sharp beaks. It scared me, but I was also terrified that they would go away. I'd wake up and my face would be damp with tears.

I wanted to stop these nightmares I also wanted to be more comfortable in my own room. I'm not sure why, but I hit upon the idea of rearranging my room as the solution. Against the window was my bed. Next to it, my desk. Opposite the bed, my dresser. The dresser was big enough to block the window—at least a bit. I decided to switch the place of my bed with my dresser, but my dresser was too heavy to budge. I started to take the dresser drawers out and stack them on the floor. The drawers were so over-full of junk like dirty clothes, discarded books, torn stories, and broken toys that the stuff fell on the floor as the drawers clapped to the ground.

Suddenly the door swung open; my father stood at the door. Maddeningly, he never knocked for his biannual intrusion.

"What the heck are you doing?" he asked.

"I am trying to move my bed and my dresser," I said, hoping my dad would help me.

"Jamie, you are making a mess," said my father. "Put all that stuff back immediately; this place is a pigsty. For gosh sakes, Jamie, you pick up after yourself. Don't move any furniture. Clean this mess up first."

I moped, hoping to get another reaction out of him or at least make him feel sorry for me. Instead my father walked away shaking his head in dismay. Rare though they were, I learned to be grateful for these gruff encounters; at least I got some attention from him. The problem was, if I wasn't careful, I would sometimes do bad or stupid things just to get his attention, the smashing of my chess set being my most recent failed attempt.

When my father left, I lost all hope. I plopped down on the floor, papers crunching underneath me. Then, Harold surprised me by appearing at the door. "Hey, kid, what's up? Mind if I come in?" He had to bend at the doorway a little since he was so tall. "What have you been doing here?"

"I want to ..." Suddenly I couldn't talk. "I want to ... move my bed and my dresser. I have to, but I can't ..." I stammered.

"Geez, Jamie, don't cry. What's wrong?"

"Please ... help me ... move this?" I asked in front of my dresser.

"Of course, I'll help. Look, Jamie ... I don't know how to tell you this. But you're okay."

"No, I am not."

"Jamie, believe me: You're okay."

"I want to move my bed from underneath the window, to where the dresser is. I have to. Please?"

"Hmmm, maybe we need some extra help here; I'll be right back."

Harold somehow convinced Steven to help me. I feared he would think I was being a baby, but Steven, under Harold's direction, actually seemed to enjoy moving the furniture. In no time my room was transformed. My dresser was blocking the bedroom window. It was comforting seeing that first, and not my bed there under the window, which gave me the creeps, like someone could crawl through the window and attack me. Additionally, my clothes were down the laundry chute and my papers in a single heap as an added bonus.

When all was finished, Steven triumphantly strutted out of the room. Harold stopped and turned around. "You'll be all right. Things are tough now, but you'll be fine. Maybe I understand you better than you think." I looked away, felt awkward. "Look. Look at me, Jamie." I looked and saw his soft, understanding eyes gazing into mine. "Give me a call sometime? When you're lonely and need someone to talk to, give me a call."

I couldn't think of a response to his simple request. Finally, I nodded my head. Harold smiled, winked at me, and left the room. Despite the hint of a future talk, there seemed something final in his departure.

First Variation: Guilt
1970-1976

I Kräftig bewegt, doch nicht zu schnell.
(Strong movement, but not fast.)

Chapter 5: Nightmare Oblique

Alone, I closed the door to my room. In the evening twilight, I sank down onto the floor and leaned against my bed. I felt happy. I felt relieved with the new furniture arrangement. I started laughing, laughing for the absence of something. I started to laugh so hard I remembered something else, my friend Brian Germaine, and then I realized I wasn't laughing at all; tears were rolling down my cheeks.

Quiet, I felt something urgent inside about Brian Germaine, my long-lost friend. My friend who beat me up with his buddies. I still wished we could become friends again, yet I was sure he never thought about me anymore. I wish he knew I forgave him. Still, as I thought about him, this inner glow radiated within me. I dared to think about him, imagining him somewhere safe. Thinking about his smile made me smile.

Then, I thought of that stupid magazine Steven gave me. The women inside the magazine were, of course, very beautiful. Beautiful enough that people from all over the world, people—humans—like me, want to see them naked. We all consist of flesh and blood, covered in skin and fed with a network of veins and nerves mounted on structures of bone and muscle. I'd learned in my biology class, we're 70-percent water. And I know that some flesh is endowed with special inalienable rights to be beautiful. That flesh, those people are a treat to behold. Steve was doing me a favor. Yet, I dared myself to think about Brian's naked body. There was something so beautiful about him. It was hard to explain. The sleekness of his legs. The color of his dark skin, my squeamish interpretation of 'Black is beautiful'. If his leg was next to my leg we'd look like night and day, black and white. Together, we would make up a whole. I could see this clearly even though I had never seen him naked. I was so sure I knew what his naked body would look like.

Without thinking, I reached for the radio. Soft voices, singing a nameless love song, encouraged me. A flash of shame shivered through me. A tear. Gary was in this room and then the ring. He used to stay here. He was on the bed, I was on the floor. No! I forced myself to think of Brian. Then, my arm went mysteriously behind me. It was supposed to be an indifferent move, but I had to fish around between the mattress and box spring until my hand caught the magazine. Humbled by the effort, I meekly grabbed the *Playboy* from my bed. I looked at the woman on the cover. She was suggestively holding up her "Student Power" T-shirt, though she did not look like a student to me. Brian was a student. The magazine model had a Playboy bunny tattoo on her stomach.

But Brian needed no special adornment. Nevertheless, eager to get to the heart of the matter, I opened the magazine straight to the center section. The woman was indeed very beautiful, though her breasts seemed too large for her size.

Instinctively, I knew the drill: Look at the magazine and do not think of Brian. Yet, the magazine seemed wrong and Brian right.

My mother taught me about how bad pornography was—not from a moral standpoint, but the more important political one. Pornography equaled the objectification of women, she'd pointed out. Treating humans as objects was about the worst thing you could do to a construct of blood, nerves, muscles, and bones—and don't forget the 70-percent water. Mom also explained how women were more vulnerable than men. I looked at this pretty woman in the magazine. She was smiling at me. I wondered if it was a forced smile. I felt a little sorry for her because she had to do this objectification for a living. An easy solution to the whole problem would be to limit pornography to men. They weren't vulnerable like women, so there would be no objectification.

The woman's bare flesh was interesting to look at. I wanted to touch her, wondering what it would feel like, but my mind wandered back to Brian, thinking how different his chest was from hers. As I looked at the magazine, I balanced it with my left hand. My right hand went absentmindedly to my crotch.

I caressed the area between my legs. My pants

were soft. Underneath the fabric something was stiffer than usual. I petted my pants in a certain way, which felt good and safe. There was something comforting about the barrier between my hand and what was underneath, as if the pants were protecting me. But I was afraid I would not be content with that as I turned the pages of *Playboy*. I feared a bizarre compulsion would get the better of me. The cover model was beautiful, and I could swear at first I felt something like love.

However, I also felt it creeping in, this irresistible sense of shame. My hand had already migrated to underneath my pants. Inside my pants, my hand pulled my stiff penis over the soft underwear. I tried holding my cock, just holding it very still, comforting it, trying to calm it down. But this cock was greedy. It had hijacked my mind, and it would demand more. Still I had to softly—just softly—caress the tip, the way I imagined I'd caress Brian's hair or the almost naked woman's back.

The beat of a jazzy song encouraged me to stroke my stiff cock a little longer. The exquisite shame I felt rubbing my cock with my hand confused me yet forced me to go on. The penis begged for more, regardless of what I wanted. I tried to force myself to stop. I withdrew my hand. But Brian, the woman's picture, and even the jazz song, wanted me to continue.

"*...even lazy jellyfish do it...*"

I put the magazine down. I unfolded the centerfold

flat. I could look down at the picture of the scantily clad woman stretching her body. The stiffness in my pants throbbed. I dared to imagine what Brian's penis looked like. I even pictured what his buttocks looked like. His would be dark, strong, and smooth, while the buttocks in the magazine was white, soft, and supple.

Disobeying my every thought, my hand veered out of control. It unbuckled my belt. I sighed. It first unbuttoned and then unzipped my pants. My hand jumped into my underwear. Direct contact: skin to skin. Hand to cock.

When I touched my penis, I became insane.

The world starts to narrow to my room. The hand grabs the cock. Why? The cock is rubbed. I feel a rush of shame, a rush that is hungry for more shame.

The world continued to shrink. The room closed in. There was the magazine, the music, the friend, the hand, and my paralyzed mind. I satisfied that shameful hunger by pulling down my pants and underwear around my legs, a humiliating position worse than any school beating. Moving my hand—no matter how slightly—made me flush. I tried to let go, but the penis demanded to be touched and stroked again.

This feeling was compulsion. I did not understand why this was happening to me. And it terrified me that my hands could decode something my brain could not. My hand would move up my cock, and it was no sooner up than my cock begged for the hand to go back down, bypassing my brain completely. The world shrunk to that magazine, Brian, and my dick.

I tried to pretend it wasn't happening by thinking of Brian, but my cock dictated this addiction for more and more rubbing. My hand complied.

The music disappeared. Now, the world was just me, Brian, and the picture. I started to rub the taut skin with my hand. I kept doing it while looking at the woman. Then she disappeared and I was just left with Brian and the urgency. Rubbing harder and harder, even Brian left me, and I was left with only my penis. The world disappeared. Humility disappeared. I became an animal. I thought of nothing but satisfying that hunger.

Then a burning flash and a jarring sigh. My penis hurt. It was over. I had to stop. Then, I had to cover my tracks. Guiltily, I pulled up my pants. Not so strong or arrogant anymore, I could safely tuck the limp cock back into its underwear.

Sanity returned.

I had no idea what had gone on as the world started expanding again. What had happened while I was doing this shameful thing? Had someone called my name? Were they waiting for me? Was I caught? I didn't know. The guilt started to flood in. Why had I done this dirty thing, and how could I be saved from it happening again?

I felt intensely alone. The naked lady had already disappeared back into her hiding place under the mattress. Brian was never there to begin with. I could not avoid the sense that I had become—at least temporarily—a sort of unmentionable subhuman creature. I had done something no one else had ever done before, I was certain. Certain because it was so grotesque, and I'd never heard anyone say anything about this to me. Even in the school where there were classes about such stupid things as home economics, there was no course about something so sick or disgusting as compulsively rubbing your cock. I had to be sick. God's damnation sounded in my soul.

"God, help me," I prayed. "Rescue me from this sickness."

A singer's mellow voice suddenly emanated from the radio, a soothing voice I had never heard before:

So close your eyes, for that's a lovely way to be;

Following the lyric's instructions, I closed my eyes.

Aware of things your heart alone was meant to see;
The fundamental loneliness goes
whenever two can dream a dream together.
You can't deny, don't try to fight the rising sea
Don't fight the moon,
the stars above and don't fight me
The fundamental loneliness goes
whenever two can dream a dream—

"Stop it this instant!" shouted my father from the living room.

"I'm not stopping!" countered my mother.

I buckled up my pants as fast as I could. I was returned to the larger world of intimidating vastness.

Two worlds, but nowhere was I really at home. This third world, the one inhabited by music, however, intrigued me. I had closed my eyes, and listening to the sounds, it was like a different world. Perhaps there I could find a real refuge.

"We're getting a-c and that's that. I'm not cooking in this steam bath, JAMES!" shouted my mother.

Groggily, I stood up. I had to force myself to forget my shame, obliterate its memory. I straightened up. I prayed to myself, "Please let's forget this ever happened."

I could hear my father's voice cry, "Perhaps."

Chapter 6: Uneasy Rider

"It's decided!" shouted Mom from the living room.

To cover up my sins, after tightly tucking in my shirt, I decided to puff up my shirt a little bit to look like I had not just put on my pants. Then, I returned to the chore of reading *Malcolm X* to clear my brain of what I had just done. Unfortunately Malcolm was in the midst of even seedier criminal activities. I read more about the evil the white man had visited upon the black community. According to Malcolm X, there was plenty for the whites to be ashamed about. Pulling on one's dick couldn't be as bad as selling drugs, beating people up, and being racist, could it? Anyway the desired effect was achieved: I thought of politics, crime, and racism instead of my sins and my sickness.

"Come on, James, we're going out to eat!" I jumped up. I'd forgotten my mother called me to come to the living room. I always became 'James' when she was upset. I stopped at my door. I didn't want to go. It was round two in their fight: heat vs. air conditioning. The fight actually had never stopped; I had merely blocked it out, along with just about everything else when I did my sick thing.

"James!" she yelled.

If I responded, I would appear to be siding with my mother against my father. But there was no alternative side to take. My father didn't say, "James stay where you are" or anything like that, so I put down the book and joined the fray.

I raced into the living room to watch the same fierceness that had intimidated Mrs. Bradford also triumph over my father.

"We're staying home," insisted my father, in a pathetic whine. "We can't afford it."

"Oh, yeah? I am not cooking in this hellhole. James Macaiah Goldberg, get your shoes on! And tuck in your shirt, you slob!"

"We can't go," Dad repeated, addressing my mother as if I were not there, getting ready to leave with mom.

"So stay home."

I hated their quarrels. Why wasn't my brother Steven dragged into the mess? But I knew what I had to do. I went to the front door to put on my shoes. Doing as my mother wanted wasn't taking sides, I told myself, it was obeying the only instructions I'd been given. My poor father, how pathetic he seemed. I wanted to somehow show my father I wanted to be on his side, but I couldn't. He said nothing, demanded nothing, when Mom ordered me to fetch Steve. My father, frustrated, stomped off to their bedroom. When I returned with Steven, my father emerged from the bedroom, looking sad. He had capitulated, having changed into his black pants and white shirt. Without making eye contact with anyone, he marched out the door.

My family walked outside into a brick wall of humidity, reminding us all that summers in Detroit were horrific affairs. The humidity mirrored the escalating temperatures and tempers. We piled into a broiling car, which was soon as frosty as the emotional atmosphere. In the air-conditioned restaurant, the icy conversation melted from divorce-enticing hostility to neutrality and then to reconciliation, a healing forgetfulness induced by the powers of pastrami, cole slaw and fried kreplach. In my family you could always count on a mountain of food to soften the mounting malice. After the meal all seemed right, if nauseating, with the world. Outside the restaurant, even with the sun down, it was still hot and muggy.

"It's great weather for a movie, isn't it?" my mother said.

"Yay!" I knew just what to see. "Can we go see *Kelly's Heroes*? Everyone wants to see that one!"

"No, Jamie, it just opened; it will be expensive and impossible to get a seat besides," Mom said.

"Oh, please, all the kids on the block have already seen it," I pleaded.

"There's a revival film I want to see: *Easy Rider*," my mother replied. We mostly saw what she called 'revival' movies. These were essentially cheap second-run films, and rarely something to talk about with other kids my age.

"Oh, yes, Mom," enthused Steven. "We have to see it! You will love it!"

Easy Rider it was.

Dad turned on the radio, which blared a news story about plans for Mayor Gribbs to meet with the executives of General Motors.

"Mom, why does the mayor side with General Motors?" I asked.

"He's not taking sides. The union wants to avoid a strike, but General Motors is being greedy, as usual."

"Why are they greedy? They live in Grosse Pointe, they have huge houses and cars, they're conservatives; what more do they need?" Grosse Pointe, I thought, got its name from the gross people who lived there. And I thought the word 'conservative' was an insult similar to 'jerk.'

"They want, more, more, and more, and they'll never get enough," said my brother Steven perfunctorily. "Shoot, I wouldn't mind having a little more myself."

"The mayor's just trying to talk some sense into their thick skulls," said my mother. "If they're smart, they'll listen to him."

"I think they're stupid," I said. I simmered in the injustice of their greed while others suffered without food or, as in our case, without air conditioning.

"Oh, they're the smart ones," my brother Steven piped in. "I wish I lived in Grosse Point instead of our brick-oven shack."

"Oh, stop that!" Mom snapped.

"You called it that, Mom," I said, coming to Steven's defense.

"I suppose you want another chess set," quipped

my brother, who then unplayfully pinched my arm. I squealed in pain. Steven laughed. Pain flashed across both my arm and my heart.

"Be thankful for what you have, both of you," said Mom.

"Yes, listen to your mother. If you have to step on the backs of people just to live in a huge house…" My father's voice trailed off.

"Then they can keep their huge mansions," my mother finished. "We may not live in the lap of luxury, but we have a clear conscience. We can sleep at night."

"It's hard to sleep in this heat," I said, instantly realizing what I said and then trying to correct myself. "I mean, I am used to it now, of course, Dad. But uh … you're right, Dad, it's better to sleep with a clear conscience."

"I wouldn't mind a few restless nights, just to live in Bloomfield Hills," Steven quipped.

"I know you would," said my mother. "And I would still like to know how you can afford that Corvair just by selling pizza sandwiches."

"They're popular, Mom." Steven turned to me and winked. I knew where he really got his money. "I sell pizzawiches."

Mother rolled her eyes.

Steven had started a small 'business' with his friend Gary. He owned a pizzeria, which was burned down during the riots. Afterwards, together with my brother, they made sandwiches baked in pizza dough instead of bread. They sold these sandwiches to stores, bars, and apparently quite a few parties, but unknown to my parents, Steven also sold pot along with the sandwiches. After Gary was eighty-sixed from the house, Steven went into the same business for himself, though I never saw him make a single sandwich.

"Great, Steven, but are you boys doing anything to help make this a fairer world to live in?"

"Come on, Mom, I bought a car; that keeps people employed," replied Steven defensively.

"I went with you to the Civil Rights March," I offered weakly.

"Yeah, who's that helping?" said my brother sarcastically. "The poor people's campaign failed; every candidate you've passed out literature for has lost."

Mom laughed. "We don't have a very good track record, I'm afraid. But we're doing something right. We're organizing early for George McGovern's run for president in seventy-two."

"Already? It's two years away," said my brother.

"We won't get sold out like we did in sixty-eight."

"What happened in sixty-eight?" I asked.

"You know, I was a delegate for McCarthy , and Humphrey stole the nomination while your brother was getting pummeled by the Chicago police outside the convention center. And that bastard Humphrey didn't say one word about what was going on. What a Neanderthal schmuck. We're gonna make sure seventy-two is no repeat of sixty-eight. This time the will of the people will prevail over back-door politics."

The political discussion ended when we pulled into the theater parking lot. As soon as we entered I thought I was saved: *Easy Rider* was rated X by our local theater.

"I am sorry, the boy can't go in; he's underage."

I could barely contain my glee.

"Underage? Don't be ridiculous."

"It's rated X."

"Oh, it is not; it was rated R everywhere else for one thing, and for another—just let the kid in; it isn't pornography or anything like that," my mother demanded.

"Let him in for free?"

"Of course, then there's no paper trail."

The cashier was not buying this explanation. But the tenor of the conversation wiped the smile off my face.

"Why are you making a big deal of this?" Mom grilled. "Are you the owner? Is my seventy-five cents going into your pocket?"

The cashier was not so much convinced as exhausted. With a heavy sigh, she waved me in.

The film was not a children's classic. The movie had all sorts of images I could not shake out of my mind afterwards. First I could not help but notice that the hippie-biker character, Billy, with his bushy hair, mustache, and brown leather fringed jacket looked like my brother Steven; while another hippie-biker, named Wyatt, tall, slender, and handsome with a large head of brushed-back hair, looked like my cousin Harold. The bikers meet one particularly nice, handsome man, an ACLU lawyer. The lawyer seemed amazingly wise. I remembered his observation that Americans like to talk about freedom, but they are deadly afraid of anyone who actually acts free. Americans would rather kill that person. In fact, in the very next scene this sweet, smart man is butchered by cowardly bigots in his sleep. More horrifying still, at the end of the movie, the nice guy named Wyatt is blown away by a dumb hick with a shotgun, who then chases down Billy and shoots him too. It was like watching Steven and Harold getting murdered by company men from General Motors. When the movie ended, I was morose and shaken. The animated conversation on the road home passed me by while I pretended to sleep.

Once back home, the source of the fight with my parents made a second coming.

"Can I have some tea?" my father asked innocently.

It was their custom to have tea and some kind of cake before going to bed.

My mother poured some water in a kettle. Then she put the kettle down to wipe her forehead. Suddenly she yelled, "I am not putting up with this shit anymore!" Picking up a heavy metal spoon, she began whacking the teapot, banging it and bending it into a misshapen vessel.

My father dared to say, a little too sharply, "You're acting like a child; we can't afford air conditioning!"

Without thinking, I screamed, "You leave her alone!"

Seeing the pain on my father's face made me feel even worse for taking sides. I ran into my room, sat down in the darkness, and waited. The voices erupted and I reached down and picked up *The Autobiography of Malcolm X*. I felt so sorry for Malcolm that after a few pages I couldn't read anymore. I seemed to share something in common with the teenage Malcolm Little. He had done something forbidden. So had I. He was a criminal. What had I done? What was my crime? Reading the wrong books? Going to the wrong movies? Having the wrong friends? Playing chess? Harboring a *Playboy* magazine in my room? I didn't understand why I was so bad; rubbing my penis couldn't explain everything. Where was all this guilt coming from? Like an opportunistic infection, the guilt that dared not speak its name was eager to attach itself to something.

Four years later that opportunity arrived.

Chapter 7: Nixon and Bussing Gone

Summer 1974 (four years later)

The television blared the good news as my mother and I sat on the couch:

"With the Supreme Court taking decisive action, there really seems nothing in the way of President Nixon's impeachment. Speaking for Chief Justice Burger, a spokesman for the Supreme—"

"Turn him off," my Mother barked. I reluctantly shut off the television. In the new silence I heard the hum of our air conditioner chilling the room.

"Don't you want to listen? It's great news! Nixon's finally getting impeached." I thought it would cheer up my mother. She had been uncharacteristically sad for almost two days.

"No, Jamie, a failure of the political system is never great news. The things he did to destroy the presidency, the misery he caused—not good news. It's a sad day for democracies everywhere."

"At least he's gone," I pointed out. "What the hell." I was a little impatient with my mother's sorrow in a day of long awaited good news.

"It's a tragedy, Jamie. The Supreme Court killed

us, you specifically, and I don't even want to see Burger's face."

"Me? They all voted against Nixon—"

"They voted against Detroit." She sighed heavily. "I don't get caught by surprise. I know better than taking anything for granted." She put her head in her hands, then looked up at me. She caressed my cheek in a foreign expression of affection. "Oh, Jamie. What's going to happen to you?"

"Huh?"

"We had such good plans for you."

"You mean I won't be bussed." My mom was hoping the cross-district busing, the plan shot down by the Supreme Court, would get me bussed to another school, thereby allowing me to attend an integrated school again, a prospect I was not keen on.

"Mom, I don't want to go to another school with their cliques and who knows what," I whined sheepishly, avoiding any mention of my fear of new bullies. "I am *comfortable* at Mumford."

"How can you be?" She saw right through me. "We have very few with our background. It seems things go from one extreme to another."

Her attempts to integrate our school had been a success for only a few fleeting years. Since the years of the riots, our white neighbors had fled for the suburbs as if gold had been discovered just north of Eight Mile Road, Detroit's northern border. Mom was used to bad news. It seemed we were on the wrong side of almost every political debate or candidate. This blow, however, sucked all the oxygen out of the house.

"There's no hope anymore." Mom looked defeated. "Now you have to go to Mumford."

For me personally, I didn't see the need to change schools at all. With the white kids mostly gone, things eased up on the bullying front. I much preferred being a "honkey" to a "nigger-lover." Moreover, any racism I encountered because of my skin color I wrote off as affirmative action-like reparations. It also helped that our newer neighbors were friendlier than their lighter-skinned counterparts.

"Anyway, you have work to do before you go out tonight." She smiled.

"Sorry, mom?" I couldn't imagine what she meant.

"I want you to clean your room before you even think of leaving the house," she said, her forced smile sadder than her silent tears.

"All right, but I wasn't going anywhere anyway."

"Yes, you are. Have you forgotten, Jamie?"

"Forgotten what?" As soon as she asked, I remembered a stupid neighborhood party.

"Tonight you are definitely going to that barbecue in the park."

The barbecue would be attended by a who's who of the cliquish high school crowd and I would be as welcomed as wet toast. Having failed to integrate our high school, Mom was now trying the equally daunting task of integrating me. For my part, I assumed I would be lonely no matter where I went. I felt different, not just because of my skin color, but because my secrets set me apart and surrounded me in perpetual weirdness. Just how weird I was about to discover.

"Why would I go there, Mom?" I asked.

"Maybe to meet someone? Jamie, you have friends, but you never go out. You don't ask anyone to come over. How can you expect to find a girl for the prom if you are always in front of the tube?" This was pure denial on the part of my mother. She still imagined I could meet a nice Jewish girl not yet banished to the suburbs.

"You have to start somewhere. Look, you're a grown kid, you look great—you do. There's no reason why girls aren't fighting over you."

"Really? Maybe to kick me."

"Hardy-har-har, you're not unpopular."

She was right. My mother's local politics also had a moderating effect on the new student body. My former Jewish neighbors threatened that I would get "beaten up and stabbed by the blacks." The reality is I was allowed to go about my business, albeit alone.

"Jamie, you're an attractive young man. Go out; you'd be surprised. I wish you would, the sooner the better. You can wear that new shirt I bought for you."

The shirt was a fancy 'designer' shirt I dreaded wearing. "They'll laugh at me," I said.

"They will not; it's the latest fashion."

"No one wears fringe on their shirts, Mom."

"It's 'in'; it's in all the style magazines. Anyone

who laughs is a square anyway. You don't know what's 'in' because you need to get out more. Go clean your room and go to the barbecue. I have to go to the schoolboard meeting, but Irv'll take you."

"Sure, Mom."

"Go, clean your room."

"What is this new fascination with cleaning my room anyway?" I asked suspiciously.

"It's a pigsty; go! And then go tonight; they're expecting you."

Chapter 8: The Good Book

I sauntered reluctantly over to my room. Every step was heavily laden with teenage passive aggression. I had no intention of going out anytime soon. I opened the door. True, the room was a mess, but that did not explain my mother's eagerness for me to return to it. In true Ruth Goldberg fashion, she had placed the book on my recently made bed. At first, I thought it would usher in a new chapter in my life, a new intimacy with my parents. I thought the book would prove my savior. But the book—a book meant to save me from destruction—was no savior. No one talked to me about the book—ever. There was no introduction. No discussion. No anything.

The title of the book was titillating enough: *Everything You Always Wanted To Know About Sex.* The author was one Dr. Reuben. Was my mother daring me to have sex with a girl at the barbecue? Maybe she assumed I already had. My parents and I had never discussed the typical 'birds and the bees' topic. I assumed this was the substitute.

I looked immediately for pictures. Skimming the pages, I was disappointed that there were none, not even a scientific drawing or two. Then, one word in the book caught my eye: 'masturbation.' I'd never heard of it and wondered what it was. The section on masturbation was a godsend. It allayed one of my worst fears:

Masturbation is most common in early puberty when sexual objects are unattainable and social prohibitions are enforced ... Young boys usually masturbate by grasping the erect penis gently and with the hand and stroking it repeatedly from tip to base.

All this time I had been rubbing too hard and fast. Who knew? All kids did this. Even after sex ed, I had no idea children or anyone did this, let alone that they had a name for it. I masturbated ... compulsively ... and without knowing better, I was convinced I was truly sick and perverted. After reading a whole chapter on the topic, I felt a great relief. I even fancied that Brian did this, possibly at the same time that I did, and that maybe that gave us a mystical spiritual connection. My gratitude to the book and my parents was extreme.

The feeling did not last.

I read on. Then I came to a chapter that described a group of perverts, disgusting individuals whose behavior was truly abominable.

"Whenever I feel like sex, I drive down to the bowling alley. I walk into the men's room, find an empty cubicle, go in, take down my pants, and sit on the toilet. Then I wait; it never takes long."

My jaw dropped.

"Pretty soon another guy sits down. I watch his feet. If it's a gay guy he'll slide his foot over and nudge mine ... he moves over to my cubicle and sucks my penis. That's how it ends. Sometimes I suck his penis, but usually I just go home." No feelings, no sentiment, no nothing.

As I read, I became more alarmed and frightened. It wasn't masturbation I should have been worried about, it was the thoughts during masturbation, specifically thoughts of my mystical and spiritual friend, Brian. Of course, I had no fantasies of meeting Brian in a bowling alley. Not yet anyway. Just to be sure, for safety's sake, I probably would be better off not thinking about Brian. That should be simple. He really did not like me, nor was I ever likely to be friends with him again. Besides, I had amassed about a half-dozen of my brother's *Playboy* magazines. Done. That was settled. It was ridiculous to think that I would be one of those homosexuals. I read the rest of the chapter with contempt, ignoring for the moment my more horrifying physical reaction—I had an erection.

The next chapter was even more distressing.

Most [homosexual encounters] are more impersonal ... a homosexual walks into the washroom and spots another homosexual. One drops to his knees, the other unzips his pants and a few moments later it's all over.

No names, no faces, no emotions ... There are dozens of variations but they all have this in common: the primary interest is the penis not the person.

I had never done any of those things in my life, yet strangely, I felt accused. Kneeling on the floor in front of a quavering, oversized penis seemed a very real and threatening image to me, a nightmare relived. Surely, I was mistaken that this could ever have happened to me. I read on for some reassurance. Instead of making me feel better, it got worse:

Those who combine homosexuality with sadistic and masochistic aberrations are among the cruelest people on earth. In ancient times they found employment as professional torturers and executioners. More recently they filled the ranks of Hitler's Gestapo and SS.

Playing the Hitler and Nazi cards succeeded in dissolving my erection at once. Yet, at the same time, I knew exactly the people Dr. Reuben was describing. I racked my brain for how or why I felt this. The book went on.

They specialize in luring other homosexuals to their apartments, trapping them, and torturing them ... Terror, intimidation, gratification with the victim's pleading, usually satisfy the "S and M." Unfortunately, the outcome is unpredictable. Occasionally, the torturer gets carried away, the evening escalates and ends in mutilation, castration and death. Sadly, that's all part of the homosexual game.

Terror, intimidation, gratification—these words weighed heavy on my mind.

Darkly, I thought that through this book, my parents were accusing me of something. Gary may have been this type of pervert but surely I wasn't. But the book did not discriminate who did what and under what circumstances. What if one of them just wandered into meeting the other person, without intending anything, and it happened by accident. I had to find some way to stay normal by just concentrating on what I learned was penis-vagina sex. Then I thought idly of men again—nothing specific, just a naked male body. I stopped myself in terror. This wasn't happening. Just reading a book couldn't do this to me—or could it? Never again could I take anything lightly; the slightest hint of favoring the masculine over the feminine had to stop.

Suddenly, watching my favorite show, *Happy Days*, a series about teenagers in the 1950s, became an ordeal. I found myself looking a little too long at Fonzie's face, too intently at Richie Cunningham. Why was I looking at them *like that*? Did I really like the shows or was I watching it with ulterior motives? In the days that followed I worried if my eyes lingered too long on the faces of television actors like Henry Winkler, James Garner, and Michael Landon. I felt helpless. How could I stop this behavior from getting worse, from developing into who knows what? I had to find some way to make sure I never thought about bad things again. I resolved to do two things: first develop a strategy, and in the meantime, grow a mustache.

Chapter 9: The Reign of Terror

I had resolved to call my cousin Harold. Somehow I knew he knew something about this. It had been years since his offer of help, but I needed to take him up on it now. The evening I resolved to call him, my mother called me into the living room. She wanted me to watch an old movie on the French Revolution called *The Black Book*. It was a predictably not-age-appropriate drama about a Frenchman named Robespierre during the period called the Reign of Terror. Robespierre wanted to be elected dictator, but people were trying to stop him, especially a man named Charles Da-boney (D'Aubigny). I was fascinated, but Mom quickly tired of the film. She turned it off.

"Mom, I was watching," I complained.

"Jamie, it's just nonsense. A little black book, honestly!" Her contempt was searing, but I wanted to know how the movie ended.

"But I just want to know if Robespierre became the dictator or not."

"Of course he never asked to become dictator."

"Okay, but in the movie he did; I want to know what happens."

"It never happened, Jamie."

"But, does he get away with it, or does this Charles Da-boney stop him?"

"Jamie, there is no Charles whatever-his-name-is."

"But in the movie there is."

"Jamie, you want to know something about the Reign of Terror? That movie doesn't do it justice," she said. "In real life, things like the Reign of Terror started with censorship. You know, banning books because you think they are pornography, books by great writers like Henry Miller."

"That's not the French; that happened right here. I remember you talking about how Zero Motel and Lenny Bruce—"

"It's Zero Mostel, but that's just the start. There are those who want to be dictators and exploit people's fears, people like Joseph McCarthy. You remember, I told you about him."

"Yes, the guy McCarthyism is named after."

"Exactly. The Reign of Terror was much like that, except instead of a witch hunt in the Senate, they had roving teams of prosecutors. Whenever they heard someone talking about subjects that were forbidden, after a phony trial they put the poor person on the guillotine."

"What's a ghee-o-teen?" I asked.

"It's an execution machine, like the electric chair is today. It is a large blade affixed to a high post. A man puts his head underneath it."

"Murder?" I asked.

"Exactly."

"We'd be killed during the Reign of Terror, wouldn't we?"

"And I am sure every one of our friends would too. You can't outlaw thoughts unless you are willing to kill us all."

"What were the forbidden subjects?"

"Saying things against or threatening the government."

"So these people were attacking the country?"

"Not exactly. The ideas that were forbidden shifted as one politician struggled for power over another. One day Robespierre was the leader and everyone who supported him was promoted; the next day supporting him became forbidden and all those people were murdered. It was a terrible page in human history, which we have relived in our smaller versions, with destroying lives like McCarthy did passing for our own guillotines. All in the name of power and trying to kill people's thoughts."

"You can kill thoughts?" I asked. The idea fascinated me, even as the story of the Reign of Terror horrified me.

"Especially when you can never make up your mind which thoughts you want to kill. You end up killing everyone and anyone."

"That's so true."

"Yeah, let's watch something interesting, like Lou Gordon." She switched on a local news talk show. I walked back into my room, like I was about to cry.

Back in my room, I started laughing. I laughed harder and harder. I was extremely happy. I realized that I had stumbled onto the solution to my problems, all of them. I knew what I had to do. I could start my own Reign of Terror. The thoughts I wanted to end would not shift, they'd remain the same and constant. These thoughts would be killable. My guillotine would not murder people, it would murder thoughts.

So, I became my own internal Reign of Terror. Guilty thoughts went to the guillotine. Good thoughts were let go. In this way I'd make sure I would not become one of those contemptuous people the sex book described.

The terror strategy produced some early victories. First came censorship: I stopped watching offensive television shows: *Happy Days* gone, *Little House on the Prairie* gone, and *The Rockford Files* eliminated. I even broadened this ban to include shows with no apparent value except to show attractive male leads, which pretty much knocked out television completely. I ceased watching movies with actors I blacklisted— handsome actors like John Ritter, Marlon Brando, and James Dean. Instead I forced myself to watch movies with repulsive guys like Clint Eastwood, Charles Bronson, and Charlton Heston. Other things were even easier to give up: soap operas, television trading cards, and *People* magazine. The Terror then went through my room, shredding posters, tearing up pictures and inappropriate (attractive male) images.

Joyously I realized I could win the battle. I was not too late.

At first this procedure succeeded. My fourteen-year-old mind did not think of men all that often. And I had no desire to do what the sex book described: going to bowling alley toilets, getting maimed, and so on. As long as I was ruthless, I could easily keep these small issues in check.

I had more proof of success: I learned other things about homosexuals that had nothing in common with me. I found out from the television that most homosexuals were social outcasts and spoke with effeminate voices. True, I was a social outcast, but I never spoke like a girl.

Finally I felt it was time to talk with my cousin Harold. That plan was permanently upended when I overheard my parents talking with my Uncle Max. Uncle Max first started in about my mom's support of cross-district bussing.

"Personally, I am happy. I don't want any of my kids going to Detroit schools. And if it's so bad here, just because there's no bussing, why don't you move, Ruth?" said my uncle Max. "Detroit isn't for us anymore."

"What? Are you out of your mind?" Mom asked.

"Think of Jamie, Ruth." Max stood closer to my mother, my father looking away, afraid to speak. "Ruth, is he gonna find a nice Jewish girl at this school?"

"Max, for better or worse we're stuck here. I made

a commitment, and now the commitment's made us."

"What does that mean?" Uncle Max asked. My father's face went red.

"Max, can you please just drop it?" snapped my father.

"Oh, you can't afford it anymore. I am sorry, Irv." Uncle Max turned to dad. "Don't feel bad; I am in the same boat. I could only afford another store here in the city. The property values in Southfield or even Oak Park are incredible. Look, if you need help maybe you wanna ask Morrie for a loan, he's pretty flush with his stores. This neighborhood's changed. If you know what I mean." My parents did not speak. "It's not just the *schvartzes*, you know. The funny people are movin' in here as well."

"Funny people?"

"You know they caught a bunch of them down at Palmer Park, the other week ... you know, *faygelas*. Between the *faygelas* and the *schvartzes*, it's not a good place for children, know what I mean?"

"Max, for God's sake." My mother regained her fierceness.

"I mean it's bad enough with Harold—you know, Morrie's kid—he's there all the time."

"Oh, will you stop it, Max? Have you nothing better to do than gossip?"

"It isn't gossip. How can you stand that kid in your own house, Ruth?"

"Max, there is nothing wrong with Harold."

"I'm tellin' you, he's a *faygela*."

"Oh, he is not. Do you see him walking around in women's clothing or getting involved in heroin, like most of them do?"

"I'm telling you he's as queer as a three-dollar bill, Ruth."

"How do you know?"

"How do I know? I am telling you. You may be interested to know my new shop isn't far from one of those fairy joints, and I saw him nearby."

"Nice to know McCarthyism isn't out of style. Max, don't give me that look. Even if he was, what are you gonna do? Shoot him?"

"I am just saying, he's a bad influence. Steven's got that long hair already—"

"Oh, stop it. First, Harold isn't like that. And certainly no son of mine is. Even if Harold was ... he may be sick, but it isn't contagious. And by last count, Steven had three girlfriends."

"All I am saying is be careful. I saw Harold going into one of these fairy joints with a *schvartze*."

"Can we change the subject?" demanded Mom.

"Sure we can, but do you think it's okay, Irv?" asked Uncle Max.

"Max, I think what's really bothering you," said my mother, "is Louise and Morrie, and nothing to do with Harold at all."

"What have I got against them? They're a bunch of crooks. They stole my business away from me, but I don't care. Keep the damn Southfield store; I relocated in a really sweet inexpensive place. I am just sayin' their son's a fag."

"All right, Max," said my father.

"That's enough!" said my mother.

They changed the subject, but a certainty settled in my mind. I was not and could not be what Uncle Max called a *faygela*. Suddenly the idea of calling my cousin Harold was out of the question.

Chapter 10: Requiem

A few weeks later, I was on my own for dinner, so I was walking home from school carrying a planned three-course meal consisting of boil-in-bag buttered noodles, frozen pizza, and a Hostess berry pie. I entered the house with a guilty hunger when my dinner plan was abruptly thwarted by the unexpected presence of my mother. The lights were not on, so everything was dim in the early twilight.

"Mom?" I asked. She did not respond or even move.

I switched on a light next to her. She was hunched over the living room table, her head in her hands. I'd never seen her like that before. She was silent. For a moment, I didn't dare to say anything. I was afraid she was ill. Some time passed.

"Mom, are you okay?" I ventured to ask. "I can explain the bag, it's not what you think … er, for dinner I …"

She turned to me. All the fierceness was drained out of her body. Her eyes were not alert; instead they were tired and bloodshot red. Although I hadn't heard it, I was sure she had been crying. She tried to cover it up, but did a poor job. She opened her arms to me;

another gesture I had not seen before. I walked toward her. She hugged me and I hugged back, hoping some of my physical strength could transform this person back into my powerful mom. Instead, she looked meekly up at me as I looked down at her. The unequal view seemed very strange.

"Jamie, dear ... yesterday," my mother's voice retreated deeper and deeper into her throat, "your Aunt Lou ... Jamie, your cousin Harold ... died." She looked away.

My life collapsed. Immediately, I realized how stupid I was for not calling him earlier. Suddenly, I realized how much I was counting on Harold's assurance. He'd said to me, "You'll be all right. Things are tough now, but you will be fine." I remembered those words. But now that reassurance meant nothing—worse, it meant Harold was wrong. I would not be all right.

The flash of panic made me feel guilty—thinking of myself—because my only source of hope had died. But I could not help myself. I had not spoken to Harold since he helped move my bed. He reached out, and I waited until it was too late. Disoriented, the only thing I could think of was that I'd never know what he wanted to say, what he understood about me. I pulled up a chair and sat next to my mother.

"I can't talk to him anymore?"

"No, you can't." She could barely speak, but determined to do so.

"He can't do that!" I suddenly lost control. "That fucking asshole has to come back!"

"Don't, Jamie, don't. He's at peace now."

"I am not! I am not at peace! — Sorry, but he was my favorite cousin." That outburst shot guilt through me, extinguishing the anger. Couldn't I have said something to comfort my mother? "How did it happen?" I asked.

She just shook her head. "Poor boy." Then she stood up. "Poor Louise. She'll never … I am going to your Aunt Louise. You stay here." She walked toward the door. She turned around, suddenly seeming quite vulnerable. "Your father is coming home. He'll bring you to Aunt Louise's in a little while, okay? Have your father take you out to eat—wherever you want. Steven's at your aunt's already." She turned around and left the house.

I looked down at the wastebasket. It belonged in the kitchen, but here it was in the living room. The local community newspaper was in it. I don't know what made me think of it, but I picked it up out of the trash. The paper was wrinkled with my mother's tears. I should not have looked.

In the lower right-hand corner of the page was a photo of my cousin Harold on the floor in fey flowery clothing. There by the picture was a headline, "Local Student Overdosed on Drugs." The story went on to relate the death of a sad "degenerate" 22-year-old man who "accidentally" took an overdose of heroine. I pressed my teeth into my lip. I bit very hard. I could not connect the newspaper story to Harold. Harold, the one who wanted to help me. Could I have prevented this? I could have called him. If I had called, this wouldn't have happened.

In a strange analytical moment, I unfolded the paper. The article was buried in the front section, page eight, inside the fold. I read and reread the article. It was clearly about someone other than Harold. But there was the shameful photo. It would become most people's final memory of Harold; that photo now defined him.

I longed to have one last conversation with him. I imagined him assuring me that I was not going to turn out like—like what? Like he did? Now, I would never know. A couple times, hoping for help, I'd picked up the phone, but I could not bring myself to dial his number.

I took the newspaper and returned it to the trash.

After the news came out, we all converged on Aunt Louise's house. A tall dark-haired woman, usually a lively person, the older aunt who once merrily told me life was shopping and eating, stood like a stone statue; her humanity seemed sucked right out of her body. No smile. No energy. It was as if Aunt Louise had been cordoned off by an invisible police line.

At Harold's funeral, I was suddenly whisked away by my parents when one of Harold's friends, dressed in women's clothes and makeup, began to cry hysterically. I recalled the shameful sight, especially the black-gray streak of mascara and tears falling down a hysterical man's face. Everyone believed he was misbehaving, though now I'm not sure if he was crying from grief or because my Aunt Louise was having him forcibly removed. Everyone felt so embarrassed in their sympathy for Louise. While I harbored a private mortification for the man, I also joined in the group condemnation.

Harold had not just died, he evaporated. During the next two weeks we "sat *shiva*" or mourning with the entire extended family. No one talked about the newspaper article or any of the circumstances it insinuated. Harold's name was never mentioned. The incident at the funeral was never discussed, the newspaper article never explained. The issues Harold's death had stirred up in my mind never surfaced in normal discourse again. Uncle Max never again mentioned *faygelas* or fairies walking with *schvartzes*.

My Aunt Louise did make an offhand comment she never explained to me. At the end of *shiva* she took me aside. She said to me very quietly, "He was depressed. It's not what you think. It doesn't matter, he's gone. But maybe later it will."

The profound loss of Harold from my life triggered all sorts of guilt feelings. I believed that if I had accepted his helping hand it would have made him feel less depressed. It also made me quite lonely. I found myself doing some pretty crazy things.

"Hello? Hello? Who is this?" asked the familiar African-American woman's voice on the phone.

"Ha—he—he ..." I wanted to speak to Brian, but I didn't dare.

"Look, whoever this is, will you please stop calling. I hear you on the phone, your pervert! ... It's that caller again ... I don't know."

Then Brian's hostile voice came on: "You better stop calling here or I am gonna find out who you are and beat the crap out of you!" Then a loud click sounded in my ear as Brian Germaine slammed down the phone. I was paralyzed. I didn't want to repeat my mistake with Harold and wait until it was too late to talk to Brian. I felt my life depended on talking to him. But once I called him I had no idea what to say. I tried five or six times, always with the same result: I would say nothing. I would hear a heap of abuse from Mrs. Germaine, who had no idea it was me, and then the phone would slam-click, and I would feel like the pervert she accused me of being. Before, I had only read it, but now I heard it for fact: I was a pervert.

Chapter 11: Faust or Brian

It was a year after Harold's death that Brian came back into my life. I thought for sure I had alienated him forever. I had lost his friendship ever since the school became integrated.

He had changed. He became very popular in school and almost always had a girlfriend. Perhaps with the distance of time, Brian felt less threatened by whatever triggered his hostility. Maybe he felt bad for bullying me in the past. Whatever the reason, when we took the same English class, he decided to sit next to me.

Within a couple classes it almost seemed like old times when we were together. The 'almost' is the internal policing of my thoughts, which kept me from acting truly relaxed around anyone. Unfortunately this made me appear stiff and stuck up, and with Brian this was no different no matter how hard I tried. Cautiously I could chat with him about the weather or the books we were reading. But even these books turned out to have hidden minefields in them.

We often read in class. Sometimes I would idly desire to just touch Brian. How I would rail against the injustice. Why couldn't I touch him? Just put my hand on his arm; that would be so awful? I tried to reason with myself. He's right next to me, three feet away. Just a simple touch. How bad could that be? The simple answer was: I would go straight to hell. I would be damned forever just by touching him. *No, you can't touch him.*

Quickly and uncontrollably, mental dams began to breach. Immoral scenarios were so loud and noisy in my mind, I became convinced they were leaking out, and Brian knew all about them. Yet I could not stop them, nor stop looking at him. My eyes drank in his image like a greedy, thirsty desert crawler. The palpable prospect of again befriending Brian more and more sent thrilling chills of horror down my spine and waves of incredulous bliss into my hopeless heart.

In the midst of this emotional turmoil, the class was assigned to read *Narcissus and Goldmund*, by Hermann Hesse. The book was both a gold- and a land- mine. In the book, my feelings for Brian were printed before my very eyes and for all to read. Yet the love between Narcissus and Goldmund was pure and chaste—so mine for Brian also had to be.

Our English teacher, Mr. Bantam, even made a point of it.

"That's enough reading, Sandy," said Mr. Bantam, face deep into the book. "Jamie, why don't you take over at the top of page thirteen."

I glanced at the page. I didn't dare to read it.

"Jamie?" Mr. Bantam asked again.

I swallowed with dread and launched into page thirteen.

"Narcissus's thoughts were far more occupied with Goldmund than Goldmund imagined. He wanted the bright boy as a friend. He sensed in him his opposite, his complement; he would have liked to adopt, lead, enlighten, strengthen, and bring him to bloom. But he held himself back, for many reasons, almost all of them conscious. Most of all, he felt tied and hemmed in by his distaste for teachers or monks who, all too frequently, fell in love with a pupil or a novice. Often enough, he had felt with repulsion the desiring eyes of older men upon him, had met their enticements and cajoleries with wordless rebuttal. He understood them better now that he knew the temptation to love the charming boy, to make him laugh, to run a caressing hand through his blond hair. But he would never —"

"Stop there, Jamie, a moment," Mr. Bantam interrupted.

Thank you, God! I thought, as sweat beaded my forehead, internal heat inflamed me, and an ugly smell wafted from my underarms.

"Thanks for doing a good job reading, Jamie. I know some people mentioned that they thought certain passages—like this one—in the book could be construed to be homosexual."

The mere mention of the word sent mean snickers through the room. Still, Mr. Bantam dared to say it.

"Rest assured, obviously, this is not the case. The whole beauty of this book, why it is regarded as such important literature, lies in its noble struggles, its idealized strivings. This is really high romanticism—remember this, it will be on the test—in the Faustian sense of the word."

Mr. Bantam, despite all his high school drivel, finally delivered a truth that spoke to my soul. There was one thing that stuck in my mind, something noble and pure: "the Faustian sense of the word." "Faustian" was extremely comforting, especially since neither I, nor anyone else, had any idea what it meant. Nevertheless, it gave this longing I had a newfound legitimacy, and confirmed and redefined my base lusts for Brian into something romantic and lofty, regardless of the greedy sensual images that accompanied them.

Mr. Bantam continued, "This higher romanticism, if you will, is not at all something like you read about in the papers about homosexuals ..." I knew exactly what Mr. Bantam had read in the newspaper, too. Ashamed, I recalled Harold's shameful appearance in the local paper, one year ago. "...There is nothing seedy or unseemly here—"

"Or degenerate," popped out of my mouth.

Heads, including Brian's, swirled around and stared at me.

I shouldn't have said that, I thought.

"Yes, Jamie, Narcissus and Goldmund are very devout and pious, that is obvious. They clearly love each other as brothers, so let's not have anything more about this, okay?"

The fact that no one wanted to stroke their brother's hair was irrelevant; Mr. Bantam's speech was liberating. If Narcissus could do it, then why not me? It wasn't degenerate. It was Faustian. The relief was immense.

The next day just before class, Brian was reading over his notes. He caught me in a deep stare and pleasantly asked me, "Is there something, Jamie?"

"Oh, Brian, you know, I was … I was just thinking about you … and me —you know, kind of like *Narcissus and Goldmund?*" I looked deeply into his eyes; they seemed to soften with the reference. "Can I read something?"

"Of course, Jamie." He smiled.

Confirmed, I confidently got out my book to read an underlined passage. "I was just thinking, about you and me, you know how at the end of the book, on his deathbed, Goldmund says to Narcissus before he dies—let me find it—we're good friends aren't we?—what I mean is—here—" I read from the page. *"'[You] mean a well in a desert, a blossoming tree in the wilderness. It is thanks to you alone that my heart has not dried up, that a place within me has remained open to grace.'"*

I guess I shouldn't have said that, because when I looked up, it seemed like someone had spit in Brian's face. I looked around. There was no one eavesdropping; the only spit had come from my own words. His disgust was all because of me.

Brian gave a kind of half laugh. Then looked around quickly. No one was looking. Class had not yet started.

"Funny kid," he muttered.

Someone walked in and sat in the back. Brian stood up without looking at me. He walked to the back. The two said something I could not hear. They snickered. I did not dare look. An overwhelming compulsion to apologize to Brian came over me. The compulsion turned to panic. I had to say it wasn't what he was thinking—even if it was. I got up and turned to him. He glared at me. Suddenly, a flash of fear and panic got the better of me. My face started to burn. I couldn't breathe well. Gasping, I ran out of the room. But worse fears started plaguing me out in the hall: that I was being ridiculed and unable to defend myself. In the hallway, consumed with another kind of paranoia, I turned back. In the room, all was quiet. Brian was seated in the back of the room. Feeling humiliated, I sat back down in my usual seat. Gaze now fixed on the floor, I poisonously felt the vacant chair next to me. Every second of its emptiness was a terrible accusation.

The next day, my isolation was complete: there was no one in a two-chair radius of my seat. If they hated sissies, they ignored me. I guess that meant a victory of some kind.

Brian never did say anything to me. Despite my traumatic need to apologize, he ignored every overture I made to talk with him. Intuitively, I realized it would be wrong to push it. Helpless, vulnerable, and so powerfully paranoid due to an overwhelming sense of guilt, I swallowed the pain, the misunderstanding, and the hurt.

Back home, humiliation and shame rained down on me. I was desperate for help. It was then that I remembered Mr. Bantam's "Faustian sense of the word." It allowed me to find my true boon companion. That this companion was considered rude, arrogant, mean and anti-Semitic did not matter to me in the least.

Chapter 12: Guilty Pleasures

Fall 1975

My search for a lofty expression of my dark and suspect desires needed to go higher than *Narcissus and Goldmund* if they were to maintain their purity. I first thought of Goethe's *Faust*. Its obscurity had worked for Mr. Bantam. The problem with books, though, was the words. Words were intelligible to people and open to interpretation, or worse, to being misconstrued, or even worse, seen through, as Brian had seen through me. I needed something that was unintelligible—even to me—and while open to interpretation, the interpretation would be opaque to all but the initiated. I needed some way to speak in a secret code with hidden meanings.

I devised a plan to translate these very palpable desires into theoretical ones. Inspired by Mr. Bantam's obscure reference to *Faust*, I decided to maintain my purity through obscurity.

I did a much better job than Mr. Bantam in discovering the obscure. I decided to flee into a world where, under the cover of asexuality, I could savor my forbidden desires. I submerged myself into philosophy and opera.

While looking for a tome on Goethe, I stumbled across a book about Friedrich Nietzsche. The attraction was immediate: the consonants to vowels ratio alone made his name unpronounceable and esoteric. Little did I know a kindred spirit lay behind the impossible name. Nietzsche was a man who lived a tortured loner's life, who expounded a philosophy people misunderstood, and who had a reputation that unjustly repulsed most people. In short, he was made to order for me. It also helped that Nietzsche came up with easily digestible aphorisms that were both confrontational and comforting— sayings like, "If you seek followers, get nobodies;" "Why do you run ahead? To be alone? To be different? Maybe it's just to be an actor?" and my personal favorite, "That which does not kill you makes you stronger." I found these quotes very challenging, and they more than made up for the dense prose encouraging me to overcome decadence. Although he never clearly defined decadence, sometimes that barrel swung around and seemed aimed at me, but even then I was still fighting myself to overcome it.

Nietzsche's philosophy, a mixture of uncanny compassion and brilliant outrage, fascinated me. I retreated, burying myself in him. My book reports, class presentations, even classroom discussions centered on Nietzsche's ideas of overcoming our weaknesses and decadence. No one cared anything about this decadence. I, however, was fascinated by it. Nietzsche also added a certain measure of pseudo-intellectual snobbery that was the icing on the isolationist cake. No more Brians would tempt me. Even bullies started to feel uneasy around me. This discomfort spread to teachers as I spoke precociously over their heads. Nietzsche protected me like no Reign of Terror ever could.

But my favorite hiding place, the refuge that substituted for my social life, was opera. It started out with a chance comment by my father, who hated opera. Then I read a glowing endorsement of opera by Nietzsche, in his book *The Birth of a Tragedy*.

From that moment onward, opera fascinated me, especially the work of Richard Wagner, the composer and notorious anti-Semite whom my father described as the proto-Nazi. At first, I took Wagner's music like medicine. Then something strange happened. Listening to the music in small chunks, like in the "Best of" collections or opera highlights albums, I discovered that Wagner's music could be mesmerizing. The melodies and lietmotifs could throw me into a deep meditative state. It seemed to be talking to me on some deep secret level—a place of nameless sounds, music, and words in German, a language I did not speak. I had found my secret code.

Slowly, the music began to untangle and spoke to me on an emotional level. Its abstract associations brought me to emotional realms a concrete association would never afford me. Wagner's music portrayed joy, heroics, and ecstasy, which were all missing from my life. But it could also luridly depict my worst nightmares. Not knowing what the words meant kept things abstract. The plots were incomprehensible, the German text even more so, even if translated. For example, one Wagnerian hero, Tannhauser, declares emphatically he would sing the praises of his girlfriend, Venus, to everyone for the rest of his life. Then to the first people he meets he denies ever knowing her.

Tannhauser was the first opera that worked this magic on me. It opened up a guarded world of ecstasy and excitement. I knew the story only vaguely. It vacillated between a celebration of sensuality and/or romantic Narcissus-and-Goldmund-like love. The opening bars of the overture depicted abject loneliness. Not just loneliness but also hopelessness and futility. The lonely brass, the unadorned seeking melody, echoed my own solitary yearning. Then sad cellos added to the misery, roaming aimlessly in a spiritual desert. The pain grew as the violins echoed and confirmed the solitude. The music conjured up a vision of a musical figure walking all alone in a barren and endless landscape. He tries to comfort himself by looking for something impossible: happiness or something to distract him. But the music builds to a bigger and bigger sense of overwhelming isolation. There is no help for this poor main theme, which I identified as myself. Then at once a sound of hope comes. The hope—a strong moralistic choral passage for brass—accompanies a crying theme. There is some hope, but not for me—other people, possibly, but not me. I heard the hope marching off into the distance, and again I was left to my own heartbreak.

This music knew me better than my parents, teachers, books, or anything. The music returns to the unhappy solitude, nothing of the hopeful music left to help, nothing to comfort, no hand on my shoulder, not even a lap to cry on. The misery continued, and then, all of a sudden comes the magic! After the thick moralistic strings and brass come the scintillating violins and then dancing woodwinds. Oboes and clarinets deliciously seem to laugh like the start of a lascivious party. Lighter, energetic strings come in and add a wave of overwhelming joy and happiness. Then the full orchestra conveys musical images of people dancing and jumping, and coming together in sensual fun. The main character seems to hesitate. Does he dare? Yes! The ecstatic music imbues everything— what is it—love? Fun? Sex? It is a party, and everyone indulges in the joys of wild abandonment. They even beckoned me to join them. They didn't care who I was; they liked me. We all enjoyed ourselves and let go.

We were free! The gladdening music splashed and engulfed me in wave after wave of joy and delight. The waves rose ever higher to laughter, to ecstasy. If this were water I would have drowned in it. I was swimming in a pool or a river of delight. I lost myself. I was no longer in control; it took over. I turned into an animal, but so has everyone else—wild dances, lascivious gestures, freedom. Nothing existed but joy, and the joy seemed without end. Just when I thought it would never end, the music slowed and then began to build and build to a huge orgasmic climax, an explosion of ecstasy. Then the joy is followed by a terrible moralistic decrescendo, a letdown, a stabbing pain of regret crashing down and exposing the thoughtless abandon. As in my real life, joy and delight now yielded to waves of self-conscious loneliness. Pain and regret chased everyone away and the monolithic brass blows away any vestige of happiness by recalling isolation. At once I returned to the state of pain and wonder in which I started. Longing returned, impossible longing because the hope of fulfillment had vanished. My life was exposed. I was brought to tears in ways no books, no words could ever replicate. Wagner, anti-Semitic Richard Wagner, took me in his lap, put my head on his shoulder, and let me weep. His music seemed to whisper, "There, there, kid, weep. Go ahead and weep. I am staying right here with you." No ridicule, no belittlement, serious comfort for serious pain.

I ran from Brian to *Tannhauser*. Brian was dangerous. My desire for him was a pitfall. But this music was pure. It was beyond reproach. To everyone else it was arcane and intellectual. Only I knew the world of delight and ecstasy that lay hidden within it. No one could take it away. No one would call me names for it. No one would beat me up for it. My mother would not worry over it. My father may have objected to the music, but he wouldn't be as contemptuous as he was over Harold.

The music was also obscenely sensual to me. Ecstatic thoughts could freely float in and out of my mind, unattached to anyone or anything. The music had no gender. Alone in my room, I even masturbated to it. Homosexual, heterosexual did not exist. I became a tonal-sexual for which there was no moral reprobation nor condemnation. Quite the opposite: to love music was sublime and lofty, exactly what my *Narcissus and Goldmund*-inspired mind was aiming to achieve. As Tannhauser's own best friend announces at the end of the opera, "Jamie! You have been saved!"

The sense of salvation delivered from a Wagnerian prophet was for me a sweet victory. What I did not realize was that this world too could crash.

Second Variation:
Innocence's Funeral March
Veterans Day 1975 to Memorial Day 1976

II Trauermarsch. In gemessenem Schritt. Streng.
Wie ein Kondukt.

(Funeral March, in measured steps. Strict. Like a processional.)

Chapter 13: First Steps

Of course, I was the mastermind of the crash. I wanted to make the world turn its back on me. With my dual weapons of philosophy and opera, no one in high school, neither students nor teachers, wanted anything to do with me. I wanted to make the world turn its back on me. Subconsciously, I had entered into a plan that was bent on my own annihilation.

As my fifteenth year trudged on, my vigilance waned. I kept up the punishing loneliness, my operatic sexual delusions becoming more and more fragile, my predilection for the male body more and more impossible to smother. Slowly, my subconscious yearnings eclipsed my conscious censorship. Eventually, my clean fantasies of opera became muddied with dirty male thoughts. It became evident that I was struggling against an increasingly potent hunger. To my horror, I seemed helpless in stopping myself from becoming what I did not want to become. If I kicked men out of my life, they still invaded my mind. I had to admit it: I was losing the war.

One Saturday afternoon, the struggle reached a climax. At home I felt agitated, full of strange feelings. I was breaking out in a sweat. I felt a compulsion to suddenly run out of the house. I told my parents I needed to walk around just to think things over. I needed to be alone.

Outside it was one of those strange Michigan spring days, very warm, so warm you didn't need a jacket, and the heat was melting the snow that had accumulated just the week before. I went for a walk, an aimless walk to nowhere in particular. Magically, I found myself at the West Side Lanes—a bowling alley! I somehow just happened to have walked there. Panicked, I begged myself, *Isn't this enough that I walked here?* Some mean internal voice answered, *No!*

I stole into the men's bathroom. There was no one at the urinals, no one in the three adjoining toilet stalls. I stepped into the middle stall. I pulled my pants down. I felt a flash of accusing humiliation. I waited. My penis stood awake, waiting. I felt dizzy. I was burning inside to leave, but still I waited. I felt nauseated, but I still waited.

Someone walked in.

He went into the stall on my right.

I looked intently at his feet. They shuffled.

Please don't slide over, I prayed. *Please don't. I will go home like a good boy. I swear I will never do this again, never, ever, just don't slide over.*

His foot did not slide over.

Suddenly there burst a rush of the most intense scatological odor. The fetid smell attacked my nostrils. Then the toilet brayed, announcing this guy was leaving. Or if he wasn't, I was. Then his stall door opened. Holding my shirt up to my nose, I heaved a sigh of relief. I froze, not daring to move until whoever it was left. The man took forever to wash his hands. I could not wait to leave. It seemed like he was drying his hands with a Q-Tip.

Sitting on the toilet, it all began to dawn on me: What a fool, what a joke I was. Pants between my legs, I flushed with frustration, disappointment, and condemnation—the worst internal condemnation— that rained down. Who was I fooling? I had become just like the sick perverts I thought I could fend off. The door to the men's room opened and crashed shut.

In one disgusting act, my carefully constructed hideaway came tumbling down. Wagner, Nietzsche, Hesse—all discredited. My feelings were no more romantic than the sewer I was sitting above. I felt ashamed and immobilized. It was over: I was lost. I could not stop myself from becoming a degenerate.

I walked out of the toilet as slowly and with as much dignity as I could muster. Outside the bowling alley it started to rain. I sprinted all the way home.

I can't be what that book described, I reasoned. But what else could explain my behavior? I thought I was so above it all, and instead I was worse than the worst.

I arrived home soaking wet.

"Jamie, where have you been?" My mother had no idea what a wretched question that was.

"I got caught in the rain."

"I can see that. Honestly, you don't even have enough sense to come in out of the rain?"

"Sorry."

"You'll catch cold. Come on, get on some dry clothes. We're going door to door dropping off literature for Jack Paxton. You remember Jack; he had dinner with us last year. Anyway, he's running for the State House."

"Going out in this weather?" I asked bitterly.

"Properly dressed!" Mom snapped back. Then kinder, "Come on, we'll go out to eat with your father afterwards."

"Uh … no thanks, Mom. I have to … study; I really do."

"Study what?"

"I'm writing a book report on … Watergate. It's due Monday."

"Okay, but stay inside, for crying out loud."

My parents left without me. I heard the car doors close. A motor started and trailed away. I was alone.

I walked into my room. A Nietzsche quote, once a source of comfort, now accused me:

> *"It is a self-deception of moralists to imagine*
> *that they escape decadence by opposing it …*
> *one later discovers they were among the*
> *most powerful promoters of decadence."*

Desperately I put on a record. Wagner even seemed to abandon me:

You have enjoyed such evil desire,

Burned with passion in the fires of Hell,
You wanted to have sex in a toilet,
so you are now eternally damned!
Just like the staff in my hand
Will never grow fresh green leaves,
So, never can your salvation bloom!
You will rot in hell.

I was not fooling myself anymore. I could not avoid the fate I had feared so much, but I also could not live. Harold's end would not be mine. Best to end things now while my parents could still claim ignorance.

Everything at home was quiet. I knew exactly what had to be done. I went to my room. I started to undress. I felt a tingle of sensuality as I peeled my shirt off. I felt my chest. I felt my groin begin to stiffen. I let them in: thoughts of Brian, as naked and as perverse as I could make them. I started to remove my pants as slowly as possible. I caressed my right leg as I drew the trousers over it. Then the left. I let out a long sigh. It felt good. All that remained now was my underwear. Protruding from my underwear was my penis. I dared to pet my penis and let the tainted thoughts flow. It was okay now.

I walked naked into the bathroom. I looked around and saw the medicine chest. I opened it, glanced around. Pills, medicines, dangerous looking things all over. My cock twitched. I envisioned an evil young man holding my mother's ring stretched out on my bed, leaning back in the pleasure that I was commanded to give. In the medicine chest I saw a small package of my father's razor blades. I took one of the blades out of the package. I was surprised. They were thin and bendable. I was expecting something much more substantial. I held the razor blade up to the light. Then I drew it down, close to my wrist. I trembled. I was angry at being so weak. I looked away. The blade slid against my wrist. I bent my wrist downward and away from me, as I had seen in a movie. I felt the delicate metal cut into the skin, which made me feel nauseated and afraid. I could not stifle a scream of shock.

Obstinately, I continued. A flash of pride. The deed was done. I was courageous enough for this calling, I thought.

The blood did not pour out. It trickled. One drop fell on the floor. The blood was darker than I thought it would be. I tossed the blade into the wastebasket. *I have done it*, I thought. Irrevocable.

I jumped into the bathtub. I lay down in a kind of ecstasy. I folded my arms. I waited for death to come The warmth of my blood trickled over my chest, down my side like a tear from my eye. Thoughts of shamelessly petting Brian's body soothed my wait.

Soon I realized blood was not flowing like it was supposed to. I heard my parents return home.

Quickly I turned on the shower washed away the tablespoon of blood and put on an inconspicuous bandage.

The miracle of miracles was: I got away with it.

They never noticed the bandage. Dad did not miss the razor blade. No one even ask me why I was taking a shower in the middle of the day.

A week later I had my chance again. Returning naked to the bathroom, I opened the medicine cabinet. This time I hastily swallowed every pill I could find; surely enough of them would poison me. I went to the kitchen cabinet and swilled some liquor.

I began to feel dizzy. I went to the bedroom to lie down for the final big sleep. And then … nothing happened.

Several days later, in a general way my mother asked my father, my visiting brother, and me who had thrown away her pills. I was silent, but so was everyone else. The case was closed without a suspect. There were no repercussions.

But I was zero for two, no better off than when I had started. This was clearly not my forté.

I had to do something to kill myself, but I was at a total loss as to what.

Just at my deepest, darkest moment, I got this brilliant idea. It was a beautiful, elegant plan. It would take time, but I would get someone else to kill me. And the best part: I knew exactly who would do it.

Chapter 14: Processional

I walked into Westside Sam's Delicatessen, just off Woodward near my neighborhood in Northwest Detroit, savoring a feast: soup, sandwich—maybe even a latke—and Dr. Brown's Cream Soda. This was to be a day of excess. I was going to order my last meal.

The deli was a loud blustery place. The walls were plastered with playbills of Broadway shows that never played there, and music crooned out of the jukebox. Brightly lit, smelling of garlic and pastrami, the delicatessen was a constant source of comfort to me. How fitting for it to be the site of my last dinner.

A familiar, yet anonymous waiter showed me to a booth at the back. Along the way we passed a deli case hosting a huge pickled tongue, gefilte fish, kishke, and other comfort foods. The smells in the room changed from garlic to pastrami to fresh rye bread and back to garlic again. Along the serving ledge, plates of gigantic pastrami sandwiches oozing with Russian dressing lounged along with plates of chopped liver and my personal favorite: fried kreplach, scantily clad in gravy. I was handed the menu. I clutched it expecting my killer to appear any minute.

On the menu, a plethora of specialty triple-decker sandwiches made me wonder what my murderer would select. Maybe he wasn't Jewish. He'd order something like corned beef and mayonnaise. The name, Jake Kurtz, sounded Jewish, but maybe he was German. He was, after all, 'a post-bearer of the gestapo' according to Dr. Reuben, the sex book author. The thought upset me, but I'd put too much work into arranging this ultimate meeting to chicken out now.

Pulling the meeting off had taken time, commitment, and a grim determination to do away with myself—or rather, to have someone else do it. Months ago, I had crept into a dirty bookstore and stolen something called *Gay Liberation* magazine. 'Stolen' is a relative word; the magazine was free, but I was underage and promptly kicked out of the store, but not before I grabbed the magazine. I wanted to find the S&M homosexual executioners that Dr. Reuben had written about. I thought this magazine would guide me. I was not disappointed. In a section called "Personal Ads", among the cryptic ads for meeting people, I saw "sm active" and "leather/sm" in several ads. I responded to all of those. I wrote, lying about my age, that I wanted to experiment. According to Dr. Reuben, this was how most homosexuals met their end: experimenting with homosexual sadists. It took a while and some correspondence before I could arrange a meeting with anyone. In the long intervening months, I managed to keep my life miserable and lonely enough that the end was still an attractive outcome. Yet now, with the moment close at hand, I was no longer so sure. Moreover, the violence it would take was off-putting. The final act probably involved knives, whips, chains, leather straps, canes, sticks, and the like, but that was none of my business.

It took about three letters before I received Jake's offer to meet me. He was open to experimenting, but he had rules that had to be followed. One was that I had to call him 'Sir'. This seemed to fit the bill of a gestapo-executioner-crazy. I offered to meet him somewhere. He insisted somewhere in public. The delicatessen was the only place that came to mind.

I started to feel uneasy and regretted the entire arrangement. Why did I arrange this meeting in public, where I was known, or at least recognized? I wanted to meet at my house. My parents were away in New Orleans for a political convention. At home the deed—or deeds, for I had no idea what it would take—could be done quickly.

Looking at the empty space across from me, I fidgeted in my seat. I began to feel a kind of anticipatory embarrassment. I should never have invited someone I didn't know to a place where people knew me. I shifted in my chair. I was afraid this guy would hate me; actually I was counting on that.

Dark panic seized me. *Get up and leave*, I told myself. *Don't do this.*

I fantasized the horrible ways "Jake" might kill me. A vivid picture filled my imagination. I saw him hacking my head off right there in the delicatessen, blood pouring out from the booth as my dismembered skull rolled on the floor like a lopsided bowling ball, a waiter kicking it down the aisle in disgust. I got up to leave.

Too late.

Jake walked in.

Chapter 15: Step for Step

I sat back down, head lowered. I'd never seen Jake before, but I knew it was him.

Even though I could barely look, I could swear that as he crossed the room everyone in the deli stopped and stared. He was tall and sauntered through the restaurant like Gary Cooper in *High Noon*. He stuck out like a smoking gun. I could feel everyone's jaw-slackened expressions as he approached my table. My death would not go unnoticed. Waiters would tell the police.

My personal grim reaper noticed me. He marched toward my table, his presence proclaiming me guilty forever. He was very old—at least thirty—but a sharp-looking man, muscled, severe, penetrating eyes visible through predictable gestapo-like eyeglasses. He looked every bit the role of the criminal sadist the book described. Dressed in black leather, he was gross, disgusting, sexy. Dr. Reuben would have approved.

The dark creases in his face made him all the more fearsome and attractive. He had a crew cut. He appeared to be a total square, definitely a Christian pervert. According to the movies I saw, all perverts were Christians. He was exactly what I'd asked for.

The job would be done; all would go according to plan. I calmly resigned myself to my grim future. *Time to meet your fate. Jamie, this is the man who will kill you this evening.* Inexplicably, I had this extremely hard thing between my legs, forcing me to cross them.

Jake sat down silently at the table. He looked right into my eyes. I gazed down at an imaginary hole in the middle of the table, the one that led straight to hell. Jake fished a pack of cigarettes out of his pocket. He lit up, blew smoke in my face. I suppressed a cough. Cigarette? I could swear I'd specified non-smokers.

The stink from the cigarettes was the last straw. How many bad decisions could I make in a single evening? My tongue, nose, eyes, and brain were assaulted by everything; I could not look at Jake or his clothes, not the leather jacket covered with metal studs, nor the tight shirt hugging criminal muscles.

Bizarre sexual murder fantasies continued to race through my mind. He would strip off my clothes and hang me with my own Levis. He would tie me to a bed, take out a knife, and draw fanciful designs all over my body until I bled to death. He would sit on my face and bounce up and down until I died of … something.

"You know you did not make it easy to find you." His voice was at once comical and horrifying. From this grim macho *man* issued the highest, most effeminate voice I had ever heard. I had to stifle the urge to laugh out loud. *I knew all homosexuals spoke like this! Maybe I'm not one after all. What was I thinking? Harold didn't talk like that either. This was a mistake, a huge mistake. Waiter, check!*

"Boy, do you hear? You did not make it easy to find you. You are not wearing the hat we agreed on."

"Oh, sorry, I forgot. I was … nervous." I was still trying not to laugh.

"You know how you were to address me when you first saw me. You read my letter." He looked angry, his tone effeminate but mean. I was a cornered savage.

"But here?" I asked helplessly. He didn't say anything. I swallowed. "I am sorry, Sir."

He didn't respond. I then gathered up all my strength, trying to sound as normal as possible. "Good evening, Sir Jake."

He smiled approvingly. Relieved, I couldn't help flashing a small relaxed smile of my own.

"Now that we have that out of the way, I will tell you a little secret." He hunched over the table until his smoky breath poured right into my face. "If you don't freak out about it and just say 'sir' in a normal tone, no one will suspect anything. They will think you are just being polite."

He seemed nice. *This must be how they lure you in*, I reasoned.

"Sorry, Sir Gary, I just …"

"I didn't hear you, boy. What did you say?"

"Sir Jake," I repeated, upping the volume.

"What is my name?"

"Sir Jake, Sir—"

"Then stop calling me Gary. You think I'm Gary Cooper or somethin'."

I swallowed.

"I was calling you Gary? Sorry, Sir." I flashed heat from my face.

His eyes took straight aim at me. I was in serious trouble. Maybe dying wasn't all it was cracked up to be.

"Sorry, Sir. I just wasn't expecting you to come dressed like that."

"It wasn't my idea to come here, and I always dress like this. And now that you have seen me, if we meet again, I expect you to rise the moment you recognize me."

"Yes, Sir Ga—Sir Jake."

"That's better. Settle down, boy. That is a dark color of red you got there. Take a few breaths."

I was sure if I stayed another minute I would die of embarrassment. I had to run. But then I remembered my mission, so I took three deep breaths. I felt myself relax with each inhale. I knew I was in good hands and everything was going to okay, whatever that meant.

"That's better, boy. Say, how old are you anyway?" I was wondering when he was getting to that question. I lied that I was twenty-one, because any lower numbers never got any replies to the ad. I looked down and didn't answer. He seemed to think better of following up that line of questioning. "Have you ordered anything yet?"

"No, Sir Jake."

"Good. You're getting the hang of it. It's starting to sound natural. You're a fast learner. Now listen, boy. In a moment the waiter will come to take our order. When I give my order, you can excuse yourself and leave. Otherwise you are staying until the end of the meal, understand?"

"Yes, sir." Repulsed and fascinated, I sat frozen, unable to move.

"Do you agree? ... I asked if you agree. This is one of the only times I will ask this question."

"Yes, sir," I replied sharply.

He scowled. "Good. You can ask me anything you want until my order is taken. After that I do the asking, understood?"

"Yes, sir."

"Good. Now what questions do you have, boy?"

I was too overwhelmed. I could not think of what to say or what to ask except to be excused.

Slowly, through the silence, I started to feel a kind of regard for him, as if he would take me gently to that other side. I began to feel some other indescribable warm feeling. A sickly familiar longing matched with a familiar feeling and unspeakable desire. Was it that desire I wanted or was something to be demanded of me? I felt so confused. It made me ashamed to be in his presence. No, I wanted deliverance from this hell I was living. Only he could do it by bringing me to the other side.

"I am not afraid, Sir Jake; I am prepared."

"Well, you should be afraid." I was so glad to hear that.

"Yes, I should. But I am ready, Sir."

"Yes, you seem ready."

"Why should I be afraid?" I asked.

"Good you asked. You are afraid. That's healthy; but nothing bad will happen to you. You have to make some choices. I am not going to force you to do anything."

"Then why should I be afraid?"

At that moment I felt his foot in between my legs. He applied pressure. He smiled. It hurt. He studied me with his eyes. They softened, and he looked at me quite sweetly. Inside, I was getting really scared, as any shadows of doubt disappeared about what Dr. Reuben said these people were up to. Jake took his foot away from my crotch and smiled.

"You passed the first test, kid. Sit over here." He patted his side of the booth and I felt sick, but I got up and sat on the edge of the booth. He put his hand violently on my knee and squeezed.

"Why should you be afraid? Ever get *fucked* before?" I shook my head "no," not even knowing what it meant with another man. The words were clear; I had read Dr. Reuben after all. But in my mind I still imagined something wretchedly violent. Whatever it was, he would not fuck the kind soft way that men would gently have intercourse with tender women. I was going to be fucked to death.

"No, Sir, I haven't." I swallowed.

"You've never done this before, boy?"

"No, Sir Jake, I haven't."

"Relax, you won't be harmed. I promise you that."

That was disappointing. "Then why should I be afraid?"

"In my hands, I will show you who you really are. What you really want."

Anything but that! This was not turning out as I had planned. One thing was sure, I was in over my head. I no longer had the confidence that this guy was going to kill me, but instead do something far worse.

I got up and left. *Molto allegro.* I heard Sir Jake's voice behind me as I left, but I blocked the words out. As the sound faded, I knew I was not being followed. If I was quick, I was going to be safe.

I walked out without looking back at my dinner companion or the restaurant. I walked directly to my parents' car and took off toward home.

Driving down Woodward Avenue I felt a bit queasy, so I pulled over to the side of the road. The corner looked familiar and safe, an oddity in Detroit.

I stopped the car just in front of a lighted alley. I thought of taking a deep breath, as I had been instructed earlier. I took one. Abruptly, I broke down into unrestrained wailing.

A knock came at my passenger window. I thought instantly it was the police. I stiffened. I tried to wipe away the tears. I rolled down the window.

"What's up, dude? What are you crying for?"

I looked up. It was a scruffy young guy in a dirty

green shirt and tight blue jeans. I realized this must be one of those male gigolos I'd heard hang around the corner of Seven Mile and Woodward. Before I could answer he climbed into my car. He shut the door and then he heaved a huge sigh of relief. I waited for him to say something or do something, but he didn't say or do anything.

"Excuse me, I was going home," I explained.

"Fuckin'-a, man, I'm tired," he said, and he closed his eyes. It was my turn to sigh a deep exasperated sigh. Before I could think of what to say or do, he fell asleep. I sat there behind the wheel feeling like an idiot. I had just gotten myself out of a mess. How did this happen?

I looked at the passenger's rough, beautiful, sleeping body. Another Gary, I just knew it. I wished I was back in the deli with the ugly man, doing whatever he wanted me to do. That man was comforting in an odd way, while this one was definitely more dangerous, At least Jake had said that nothing bad was going to happen to me. So much for that theory.

Sitting in the car with a sleeping prostitute, I didn't know what else to do. I turned the ignition. The car started. Tears still flowing down my cheeks; my sobbing did not awaken my passenger. I drove home wondering how much this night was going to cost me.

Chapter 16: The Body

Daylight streamed through the familiar louvered windows. I smelled the familiar mixture of Old Spice cologne and Faberge perfume and felt relieved. I was home. I opened my eyes. The green plush blanket and green paint on the walls told me I was sleeping in my parents' room. I saw the white painted ceiling with the imitation gold chandelier-cum-ceiling fan. Against the wall next to me was my father's tall faux-wood dresser. Very orderly, only two pictures stood atop it, one of a dashingly cute man—my father in the Navy— and another ancient photo, an old idealized grayed image of him on his "Wedding Day" with a woman who looked like one of the glamorous Andrews Sisters (that was my mother). Yes, I was in my parents' bedroom, but I was not alone.

Next to me was the guy who had climbed into my car, a sheet partially draping his intimidating naked body. I, on the other hand, was fully clothed under the covers. While I was wide awake most of the night on my father's side of the bed, the guy slept on my mother's side. His open mouth had completely slimed her pillow.

He snored. He wasn't dirty, but he was not exactly

clean either. His skin had a gray tinge to it. His body was covered with dark tattoos of axes, guns, and knives cutting flesh. He had painful-looking scars on his back and stomach. In his snoring open mouth, I could see some missing front teeth. He was a brute with an amazing body and a vaguely unpleasant odor. I felt nauseated thinking what terrible things he'd endured to get those scars, what combinations of knives and dirty fights. He'd probably been beaten up for being a faggot. *Faggot*: coming soon to a theater near you.

Thoughts whirred through my head: evil, hungry thoughts, so horrible I didn't dare find out what they were. I let them rage through my heart. I found myself drawn closer to this man in bed with me. But why? There was not a single attractive thing about him. What was I doing? I drew closer, my mouth right up against his skin, my eyes looking at the nape of his neck. Now my mouth was near his shoulder; I felt his breath blowing onto my skin. Afraid to wake him, I drew back.

I looked as he turned his head, still asleep, spittle dripping down his cheek. It was gross, or was it?

When he awoke I knew he would be a big problem, a lot of trouble. Last night his excessive drunken state saved me from any problem apart from sliding his naked body over so I could sleep on the bed too. I didn't dare leave him alone here. I was already shocked how he staggered naked into my Mom's room. I needed to sleep there because I had to be there when he woke up. My heart pounded as I tried to think of a way to get rid of this criminal before he robbed the house blind, beating me to a pulp and leaving my bloodied, dead body for my parents to find when they came joyously home from New Orleans. I recall reading in a book on G-man Elliot Ness that the Mafia would cut off your balls and stick them in your mouth. That fate seemed far-fetched at the time. Now it seemed a real vivid possibility.

Yet there he was. What a bundle of human contradictions. Repulsive, but beautiful. Desirable, but dirty. He smelled bad, yet was somehow alluring. Then, I felt a compulsion to taste him—but it passed.

I felt so sorry for him. He needed to be comforted. I wanted to give him that comfort, but that's all. I knew he would make me pay if I comforted him. It seemed unfair. I didn't ask him to get into my car. I didn't ask him to come into the house. Yet here he was.

I roused myself. I just wanted him gone. I was under attack. I was already fleeing from one *situation*, only to find myself attached—no, glued—to this new ... what do I call it? Imbroglio.

I just wanted to get rid of him, but waking him up would be rude. I was unsure how he would react to that. Besides, maybe he was hungry. Maybe if I just fed him like a hungry lion, he would be nice and crawl away? The fact is, I really didn't know what he was doing in my house, why his clothes were off, why he got into my parents' car, and then why he climbed into my parents' bed when I specifically asked him not to do so. Him—him—never had a pronoun felt so intimidating before.

Then he had the audacity to fall asleep. For him, falling asleep was an act of aggression. Apparently he was milking the connection, whatever it was, for all it was worth—sleeping long and luxuriously in my parents' bed, his head on my mother's now damp pillow. No doubt he knew a good thing when he saw it. I was young, naive, stupid, and he was taking advantage by deliberately sleeping.

Then I remembered that last night he drank all the beer in the refrigerator. Luckily it was only three bottles (my parents' annual supply). How he found them in that over-stuffed fridge is anyone's guess. It was safe to say those bottles wouldn't be missed anymore than Dad's razor blades.

I continued to watch him. At one moment I thought he woke up. Instead, he swung an arm violently over me. Clothed and suddenly captive to a naked arm, I began to cry. I turned and cried, sliming my father's pillow. Somehow I fell back asleep.

Chapter 17: The March

I awoke with an arm slung on top of me. I opened my eyes. There was an ugly nose and closed eyes in my face. His eyes opened. They were brown and blood-shot. He woke up. He looked at me as I was trying to get up from under him and out of bed. He held me back.

"Hey, fuckin'-a, man, we haven't done anything yet." He held me tighter, the first blow about to fall.

"Good morning. That's okay. We can just leave it at that," I said, trying to sound bright and cheery as I squirmed for my life. Then he did something astonishing. He let go.

"No, kiddo, I need some money. Let me do you."

"No, that's really okay." I could still get out of it for free!

"Well, do me then."

"What?" I said with a small trace of panic. I had no idea what he was talking about, but it sounded awful and violent, maybe the same thing as Sir Jake suggested: being fucked to death.

"First take your clothes off," he said with a kiss-me-or-kill-me grin. "Take 'em off, and then do me."

Wait one moment, who's the prostitute here, I

thought, *and what does "doing me" mean?*

"That's fine. It's okay. I don't need to do anything," I sputtered.

"No, man, I do; I need the money … and a case of beer."

"What?"

"Yeah, you had me the whole evening. I could have made some bucks."

I didn't know what to say. Did I have any choice? I was silent, hoping the issue would go away. I was lying in bed with my eyes wide open, staring up at the ceiling, hopeful that this guy had something else he needed to do. It must have been around noon.

His voice popped the balloon of silence. "Hey, dude, I'm hungry."

"You gotta go; I have things to do," I said, trying to be courageous.

"Yeah, sure, dude, but I am hungry, and I need my beer. And I want what's coming to me, you know." He was waiting for a reaction from me. I felt like an innocent deer frozen in the oncoming headlights. "I usually get twenty, but I have been here all night so let's make it forty and a case of beer, okay?"

Just giving in to him seemed wrong and weak. I couldn't be so easily intimidated, like some spineless worm. On the other hand, he was stronger than I was. And I wanted him out of my house quickly and easily. A fight would be messy. Of course, he could kill me, which, I had to remind myself, was the whole point of this wayward plan.

"All I have is twenty," I stated.

"Okay, twenty and a beer." He went to pounce on me, but I slid away and slithered out of bed.

I walked into the kitchen and made salami sandwiches. He followed me into the room, still embarrassingly naked.

He stared at me and smiled. "I like you, dude; you're nice. Don't go crying on me again, though; I hate that. Some bad shit must have happened to you last night."

You!

My personal Cat in the Hat walked over to the sandwich I was making. I was still going to put lettuce and tomato on it, but he just took the plate with salami and bread and greedily stuffed the sandwich into his mouth. I wanted him to just go away, but still a lump formed in my throat. *He must be really hungry*, I thought to myself. Still I had to tell him he had to leave.

"Are you still hungry? Do you need another sandwich?"

"Aren't you gonna eat?"

"Take my sandwich," I said as I made another sandwich and put it in a baggie. My bleeding-heart liberal self showed through even in the most trying of circumstances.

Talking with his mouth full, he said, "So let's get some beer and party."

Party? Are you out of your mind? I just want you to go away; but first, out of the house. "Well, maybe

… actually … *dude*, I can't party. I gotta go … I gotta go to a meeting downtown."

"Cool, man. Just take me to my place; it's right near downtown."

"It is?" I asked eagerly. The first good news I had heard all day.

"Yeah."

"Where is it?"

"I'll have to show you; it's on the south side."

A pall fell over me. I had committed to taking him home way too soon.

"That's nowhere near downtown," I said.

"Hey, chill. Be cool, dude; you had your fun. Besides, how am I gonna get home? You picked me up, dude. I can't stay here tonight." I was completely offended by the misrepresentation of the facts. Then he dropped a little bombshell. "I gotta meet—my—girlfriend," he said while taking a triumphant bite from the sandwich. 'Girlfriend' fell like a slap in the face. I thought up until that moment, he was … one of 'those' and not only that, one of 'those' and … well, attracted to me. Now, because he had a girlfriend, I felt like the whore.

After devouring his sandwich, he finally covered up his body and got dressed. I opened the door to the outside. I peeked to make sure the coast was clear. I ran to the car. He slowly sauntered over and climbed into the passenger side.

"Before you start, bud, rules are rules."

"What?"

"Don't play dumb; that annoys me."

Then I remembered the twenty dollars. I took out some crumpled money from my pants pocket. I tried to count out twenty. He must have been a better counter, because in a moment he grabbed the bills.

"That's twenty. I'd like a case of beer, so give me another ten."

Keeping score—that was twenty dollars for leaving me alone, and ten for the beer and to be rid of him. All I had to do was first, drive this Gary to the store; second, drop him off; third, run home; fourth, clean my parents' room; and fifth, take a shower. Five simple steps and the whole thing never happened. It was going to be easy after all.

Chapter 18: The Funeral

I dropped him off at our local convenience store. I stayed in the car and hunkered down behind the steering wheel. I couldn't risk being seen with him by anybody— not that anyone cared.

I was weighing the pros and cons of just driving off when he emerged from the store with his case of generic black-and-white labeled beer. He climbed back into the car.

"We're good to go. What's your name, dude?"

"Jamie," I said, and he grabbed my hand and shook it with a sadistic squeeze.

"Fuckin'-a, you're a good guy, Jamie boy. Let's go party."

Party? What happened to his girlfriend?

"Party? We can't party. I really like you, but I told you I need to go to my meeting."

"Sure. First drop me off," he said, seeing right through me.

"It's true. It is. It's a meeting of the Democratic ... Caucus."

"Yeah, sure. Just drive to I-75 South. I can tell you how to go from there, dude."

He put his hand on my thigh. I felt a shiver of

something really disturbing. Then, I thought of the man I'd abandoned at the deli. I imagined his firm hand on my thigh. He would have said, "Nothing bad is gonna happen." No matter, we were off to South Detroit, and finally I would be rid of him, I hoped.

We finally entered the freeway.

"Should I be afraid?" I spontaneously asked.

"Don't be stupid, kid," was his disquieting reply.

We drove and drove on southbound I-75. We kept driving south past everything I knew. We ended up on a street named Melville near a street cruelly called West End.

We arrived at Gary's dilapidated home on the south side, a bad neighborhood even by Detroit standards. He lived in this dreadful old house. Looking at where he lived, I could not keep the lump in my throat from returning. Was it pity? I forced myself to remember I just needed to drop him off and the odyssey would be over.

I stopped the car. He did not open the door.

Oh, God. What now?

As if answering for the Almighty, he said, "Come on, I want to show you something."

"You do?" I asked.

"Yeah, I feel I owe you something," he said with an evil grin. "Come on; I want to show you my place." The insistence in his voice was unsettling.

I hesitated. He owed me thirty dollars, and that was all.

"Don't make me."

"What? Come on," he said sharply, losing his patience, but still smiling. He wielded some weird authority I could not resist.

I looked at his house again. It looked like it would collapse at any moment. The lower part of the structure had burned out. He was living in the upper half. There was a ladder to his 'home'.

I knew in my heart of hearts this was the place he wanted to trap me. His gangster buddies were probably waiting inside, ready to tear off my clothes, gang rape me, beat the crap out of me, stuff my dead face in the toilet, and take the car and leave me for a newspaper headline to top my cousin Harold's. I realized that on some level this was the point to the whole plan last night, but somehow that point had lost all its appeal.

"I want to live," I said.

"I hear you, man, me too. Come on, sweetie."

Sweetie! "Okay, but it can't take long. It can't take long because I have the Democratic Party … meeting, you know."

"Sure, come on."

I got out of the car.

Walking as slowly as I could to the house, I bid my parents' car a farewell. The end had come. Let this be a lesson to all of you: This is the way freaks end up—bludgeoned on the top floor of burned-out buildings in crummy neighborhoods.

He climbed the ladder, balancing the case of beer. I waited to be sure he could make it all the way safely before setting a foot on the ladder.

When I started to climb the ladder, I realized my end could come much quicker than I thought. This ladder was waterlogged and bent with every step. The stench from the lower floor was terrible. The worst part was vaulting over the upper window into Gary's place. He did this easily. I, on the other hand, landed right on the greasy windowsill. Brownish grime got all over my clothes. Even when they found my mutilated body they would never get the stains out. I was stuck over the sill, frightened to death to move at all, let alone go inside.

A firm hand grabbed my back and, holding me, dragged me gently into the room. I braced myself. *Here it comes, my moment of death. Just let it come.*

"Here you go, friend—something I have been meaning to give you!"

I braced for the end of my life.

Then I felt his face, his breath, his mouth ... his tongue, then his tongue in my gaping mouth.

What the fuck?

He held me in a death grip, his mouth sucking all the life out of me. But then he released me. I didn't dare open my eyes.

I heard beer cans open. I knew we were not alone! I just knew it!

I winced, my eyes not fully adjusted to the darkness after the bright sunlight outside. I braced for the first rip of clothes, the first baseball bat swing to my stomach. My body wrenched back at the first metallic sensation. Then I realized there was something hard in my hand. I straightened up. Someone was putting something cool in my hand. A gun? No. I felt a vague feeling of disappointment when I realized it was a can of beer for me. As for the others—I shot a glance around the shadowy room— there were no others.

Feeling the saddest I have ever felt, I guzzled that bitter beer. I then realized an old cliche: you always remember your first kiss. And this would be no exception.

"Fuckin'-a, man, have another." He gave me another beer.

"Thanks, dude," I said, 'dude' rolling off my tongue like a brick.

At his insistence, I drank more.

He took my head in his hands. He carried it to his face. I realized I was a little woozy from the beer. Again he aggressively stuffed his face into mine.

"Hey, dude. Take off your clothes."

Hadn't we done enough?

He was smart, smart in a way I never was. Knowing about Immanuel Kant's moral imperative, Nietzsche's theory of the *ubermensch*, or even the date of Kierkegaard's death did me no good here.

"Take 'em off."

He was going to do it after all. The place stunk. It was dirty. I could barely see. Woozy and full of bad judgment, I started to unbutton my shirt. I under-estimated how ashamed I would feel. I shook trying to undo a button. He couldn't see the tears I felt coming down my silent face.

"Take it all off! Don't be dumb, faggot! Jesus! Just lay down. No, first take off the rest, dude."

I gritted my teeth and prepared myself to be ravaged, raped, and hopefully killed. I lay my naked body gingerly down onto a sandy bed. I tried to lie lightly on the bed, so no creepy-crawlies or sandy dirt would get on me. He came in closer for the kill, lying on top of me, pushing my back unforgivably into the dirty mattress below.

At first I thought it would be okay; he just wanted to masturbate me. Then he said, "Feet to Jesus, dude."

I didn't move. I didn't know what it meant.

He suddenly grabbed my legs and lifted them over his shoulders. He pressed his penis against me. I panicked. *He can't do this. It won't go in. It's too big. It will hurt. It's a sin. It's against God's laws and the laws of nature. My mom won't like it.*

He held me tightly in his arms. He wouldn't let me go. But it wasn't a stranglehold; it felt friendlier but still bad. As he held me, I realized his cock was right up against my asshole. My legs were wrapped around his.

"Please don't," I pleaded with him, unsure how audible I was, afraid I was going to cry.

"Jesus, just relax, dude. It's cool. You're gonna get what you want, and I'm gonna get what I want," and he smiled. Then he leaned into me. I braced. He seized the moment and pressed into me. His penis would not go in; I was too tight. I could win this fight. He pressed harder. Next, I felt a finger protruding into my air-tight ass. After some forceful insertions, my ass went soft and wet. The finger won. My asshole let me down and capitulated.

My ass started to give. My body betraying me, I relaxed. He tried the big insertion again. An excruciating pain came between my legs. He pulled out. It was over.

"Oh, thank you," I said, glad he stopped.

He spit in his other hand and put it underneath him. He tried again. It slid in. He was going in for good this time. Violation complete.

He started to move his body back and forth in me. Slowly, in spite of myself, I shamefully began to enjoy it. It was an odd feeling of horror and compulsion at the same time. Then I heard a damning heavenly verdict in my head: I was that kind of pervert.

The pain had dissolved into something I liked. He gave a few shoves and my own erection actually got harder. The enjoyment only added to my shame and excitement. He leaned in to me and kissed me sloppily. A man kissed me. He kissed me while doing this. His saliva, gross tasting, slid into my mouth. It was at once grotesque and glorious.

Improbably, I said, "Yes," as if agreeing to the whole ordeal.

He stroked me. Then, it ended quickly. At one moment, he started breathing hard and began a weird hallowed chant. "Oh God, dude, that's right," he chanted over and over again with every odd thrust. He started to behave like an animal. He seemed no longer human. Saying weird things, making weird noises, and this pumping inside me speeded up as my feelings were quickly being tossed aside for something more urgent.

"Whoooa!" he started to whoop.

The incessant pumping in my numbed asshole was sensually dehumanizing me. I was finally being treated like the subhuman I suspected myself to be. It was my turn to go down the route to being an animal. After he made a hard firm thrust, he shouted, "Ahhh!"

Suddenly I felt his penis pulsing inside of me. Quickly though, with minimal touching, my own subhuman spasm came and shot goo all over my chest. He looked down with a stupid grin, pulled his weird looking, uncircumcised penis out of my anus and collapsed a little too hard.

"Ooooph!" that was me. His penis was wet and more wetness secreted from it on my belly. I was squeamish, until I looked at his face.

He lay there looking so happy. So happy because of me. What followed was a cloud of ecstasy and horror. I calmed. I felt the pain of his weight on me. I didn't know what to make of it.

"Thank you," I said, hoping that would bring it all to some conclusion.

He rolled off of me. He wiped my cum off my chest with a stiff rag. Actually he smeared it around more than anything else. He put his heavy arm around me.

"I know you needed it," he grunted.

There I was, lying down in sandy grit. Time must have passed, as my own cum had crusted on my body. His arms were slung around me. His elbow pressed painfully into my belly.

I became disconnected from myself. The pieces were broken. Did I like it? Did it hurt? It felt like I was forced. I felt like a submission. I seemed to have enjoyed both. Did I do this willingly? There were no answers. Only a spontaneous "thank you."

Did Gary love me or hate me? Did he really have a girlfriend? He became larger than life. At that moment, he could have done anything he liked to me, and I would have solemnly taken it. Instead, he did nothing but sleep.

He slept soundly, peacefully. He looked happy. Was I responsible for that? Was it worth giving away all my humanity to make this male prostitute happy? Happy in his unhappy house? Was this the reason why God had put me on the planet? And if so, maybe that wasn't the worst thing.

I lay there, awake, exasperated. Suddenly all the gross things, the millions of creepy-crawly things in his bed, the smell of his breath, the foul musty tastes in my mouth, the sore feeling in my butt, and my overstimulated genitals converged into a collective revulsion, a shower of shame and self-hatred. I had to get out of there at all costs! He could still kill me.

I gently pushed his bulky body off me. I got out of

bed silently and crept out of the room. I put my clothes on near the window exposed to the empty street, feeling as if Detroit itself was watching in judgment.

I was dressing when I realized I was putting on his underwear. I glanced around quickly and tripped over the half-on underwear. I hit my head on the windowsill. I was afraid I woke him up. Holding my breath, I looked away and put his underwear on anyway. Dressing quickly, I climbed down the ladder, falling before the last step to the muddy ground, landing on my butt, and my back striking the ladder. I limped and jumped into the car.

Back in my car, finally alone, I assessed the damage. A miracle had occurred. There were no creepy crawlies on my body. The shit all over my clothes was just a small grease stain. The pain in my ass was gone and moved to my back. I had been saved. This whole thing never happened.

Chapter 19: Measured Steps

When I arrived home, my parents' Impala was parked in the garage. My heart sank. They beat me home. By the blueish cloud of smoke inside, I knew they had been home for some time.

I was greeted with the stabbing motion of a cigarette.

"Where were you?" asked my mother in lieu of a hello, her black-sequined dress flashing like a disco ball at me with her head framed in red ruffles. Her red hair made it look like she was a flower on fire.

"I'm sorry, I was attending a civil rights meeting—with the Democratic Party, downtown, you know." Why I said this I don't know. If a male prostitute didn't fall for it, why would she? I realized I also stank from my earlier whatever. I choked back the desire to tell my mother she looked like a flower.

My mother stared at me but kept silent. Somehow she knew better than to call me on an obvious lie. "Don't ask a question you don't want to hear the answer to," she often said.

My mother took another puff from her cigarette, her hair jumped as she tilted her head upwards to blow the smoke out. My mom was a political visionary, but parenting was not one of her higher priorities.

"We were worried about you. Worried sick … Did you hear me? We were worried sick."

"I'm sorry; I didn't think you would be back …"

"That I can believe. The place is a mess. Who knows where you were? Why can't you pick up after yourself? Or clean up our bed? Jesus." The J-word sounded odd; this was new so she must have been really worried. Then she looked closely at my face. "What happened to your forehead?"

"Oh, that? I'm sorry, I must have fallen. Yeah, I fell."

"You fell? Honestly, you're such a klutz. Where did you …" Her voice trailed off and she looked at me. I was undeniably dishevelled. Silently, I begged her not to continue this line of questioning. "Where? Where did you fall and hurt yourself like that?"

Luckily my sins were so many that it made concentrating on any one difficult, making any kind of confession impossible.

"I'm sorry." I sputtered.

"Why can't you be more dependable like your brother," my mother lashed out.

"I am sorry. I *am* sorry," I sputtered again. She knew the comparison to my brother would hurt. My spoiled brother, Steven, was not my favorite topic of conversation. He was always used as a paragon of virtue, despite the fact that he was a small-time marijuana dealer. Mom was oblivious to his negative side and I was constantly being held up to account against a fictitious version of my brother.

Undeniably, I had erred. Even if I blew what

happened out of my mind, its physical evidence was undeniable.

I had destroyed my life in a different way than drugs, but destroyed it, I had. Luckily, I learned how one could change the subject on Mom to distract her.

"How was your trip to New Orleans?"

"Oh, don't ask. It's over with, and we can get back to work. The political backstabbing—I'll tell you about it later. The Latin Quarter was amazing … Look, I don't want you out of the house anymore today. We were worried sick, did you know that? You have school tomorrow. You don't get enough sleep. You don't study enough. You don't eat enough, and I want you to clean up your room."

She walked back over to the couch, joining my father in front of the television, picking up her notebook from an end table. Her work as a parent was done for the day. She started writing while my father watched TV.

I just stood there, feeling stupid and guilty. Then something shook me awake. *Jamie, there is something wet coming out of your behind.*

I walked as slowly and normally as I could to the bathroom. This was surely a sign of uncontrolled diarrhea, the obvious wages of the unthinkable sins just perpetrated. I entered the bathroom and could not stop myself from slamming the door.

"Don't slam the door!" cried my mother. Just as I was slamming the door, the house shook with a clap of thunder outside. A storm was gathering.

I pulled down my pants and sat over the toilet. Nothing happened. I felt something drip into the toilet. I got up and looked.

It was blood.

I wiped my behind. There was more blood—rich red blood. My pursuit for the end had come after all. Resolutely, I flushed the toilet and walked out into the living room as calmly as I could.

"Everyone, I am sorry, but I have to go back to the meeting; I left my book there."

"What? You just got home," mother replied.

"I know. I know you want me to stay in, but I just have to. I have to. You see, I left my book, and I need it tomorrow for school. Someone might steal it. Sorry. I'll just go."

And before my mother or father could say anything I grabbed the keys and went out the door.

I ran in the pouring rain amid another lightning strike and clap of thunder. The rain coming down in sheets soaked me even before I got to the car. In the car, I saw out of the corner of my eye on the passenger seat *The Nietzsche Reader*. What luck. There really was a book I could bring back. I'd have to remember to bring it in when I got home. I needed Nietzsche now. "That which doesn't kill you makes you stronger." But this time I'd gone too far.

I drove like a maniac to the only hospital I knew of, convinced it would be a one-way trip. The place of my birth might as well be the place of my death.

Chapter 20: Strict Formality

"Excuse me, young man, you have to tell me what is wrong, otherwise I can't register you."

"I can't tell you." My underarms were drenched.

The nurse looked at me hard. I had already tried her patience. She had essentially agreed to fudging my date of birth so I didn't need parental permission. Surely she wanted me out of her office to get to the rest of the people waiting in the hospital emergency room.

"There is something wrong," I demurred.

"Yes!"

"Err … with my …" I could barely say it. "… butt."

"What exactly?"

"I am dying."

"I am sure you are, young man. What is the problem with your anus?"

"It's bleeding."

The nurse heaved a sigh of relief.

"Now, that wasn't so bad. Anus is bleeding." She spoke as she typed. "What are we talking about? Drips? A stream? Is blood pouring out? Do I need to wash the chair. What?"

"I don't know. I am here; doesn't that say enough?" I said as calmly as I could manage.

"Stand up. Go on. Now turn around. Turn around … all the way, thank you." She started typing. "Drips. And what about your forehead?"

"Oh, that? I fell, but it's okay … it was … an accident, ha ha. It's okay. I'm good."

She looked at me very strangely. Then, as if finally putting two and two together, became alarmed.

"It doesn't look okay. Who did that?" She demanded an answer. "Look, James, if that's your real name, who attacked you?"

"Why do you want to know?" Wrong thing to say. I felt cornered and panicked. "I mean, I wasn't attacked! It's not like someone forced me, got me drunk, and made me do things on a dirty mattress. That would be ridiculous, you see."

She stared at me. I hung my head.

"Relax, young man." She relented and sighed. "Take a seat out there. Someone will be with you shortly."

I went back to the waiting room, but she raced out of the intake room to the emergency ward.

I was deathly afraid of being found out. As a plan of action, I decided if I were forced to admit anything, I would jump out of the window. That plan was frustrated by being on the basement floor, but it didn't matter. I convinced myself I had finally done it! I managed to kill myself. Finally, having done it, I wretchedly regretted it. I begged and prayed to God to give me my life back. After hours of waiting, anticipating my death sentence, I was finally called into the emergency ward. I had to go over to a little curtained area.

I was told to disrobe and put on this frock that was open in the back and sit on the table. I looked in the foreign underwear I was still wearing and there they were, blood stains. I thought I could make it all go away, but the whole memory came crashing back as I saw I was still wearing that dirty underwear. I slipped the briefs off and threw it, and the memory along with it, into the trashcan. Now, with just the smock on, sitting on the examination table, I had to wait some more as I stained the table sheets with the blood of my sins.

Finally, a tall, slender, not unalluring man wearing a doctor's coat and holding a clipboard came into my little curtained cubby hell. The doctor was coming to my rescue; he even seemed like he could have been my knight in shining armor if only I was not in such disgrace at the moment. He contemptuously glanced at me first, then at his clipboard, then looking at me again. This time he studied me with a tender kind of pity. Something inside me felt so grateful that I wanted to kiss him. I was beginning to feel better about this, until another older, grimmer man in a suit walked in. He stared at me hard. My heart started to pound.

"Hello, young man," the doctor said. "I am Doctor Mander, and this is Fred Stuyvesant from Security. He's here just to make sure you're all right." The towering scraggly pill of a man nodded his head severely.

"See, there and there" said the older man, pointing at my waist, then my head.

"I see it. That's not necessarily enough to require reporting on it," said the doctor. Then turning to me: "Say, that's quite a bruise on your forehead." He paused. "May I ask how it got there?"

"No one did it. I fell."

"Why protect him?" Fred demanded. "It just appeared by itself?"

"Wait a second, Fred," the doctor cautioned, then he turned to me. "Just say it. No one wants to hurt you. But in order to treat you, I need to know what happened. Is that good enough, Fred?"

"Let me see his back," demanded Fred.

I panicked. The doctor noticed.

"What do you have to see that for?"

"I bet he's bruised there."

The doctor sighed. "Do you have a bruise there, kid?

I kept silent, heart pounding. There was a right and wrong answer here, but nothing was the truth.

The doctor glanced at his clipboard. He didn't say anything either.

The other man glared at me. I couldn't stand it. I slowly turned around, drew the robe back and showed my back.

"Oh, my God!" said the doctor. "That's quite a bruise."

"Kid, who did this?" demanded Fred. "I ain't

leaving here until you tell me."

"I … fell … I said that already, didn't I?"

"Horse feathers! You're falling all over the place, aren't you? On your head, on your back, and on the crack of your ass."

"Fred, calm down," said the doctor.

"Sorry, Doc. You see it as plain as I do; someone has abused this kid. Possibly his parents."

"Gary," I said quickly.

"Gary," repeated the older man. "Gary who?"

"I don't know his last name," I blurted out.

"Figures," Fred hissed with disgust. The doctor waved his hand at Fred, "Okay, doc, go ahead; finish your exam."

"It's okay, I did it. It's not what I am here for, it's about … you know, this. I think it's over." I pointed to my rear, feeling so ashamed at this public display of my filthy behavior.

The doctor looked at me sympathetically. He approached the table where I was sitting. "Okay, Fred, you have to wait outside."

"Okay, but we're gonna talk before this is through." Fred stepped out of the curtained cubbyhole and out of my life, I hoped.

"Stand up, young man. Put your hands on the bed and bend over for me."

I stood up. A drop of blood was on the sheet. He put on a glove and opened a container of Vaseline.

"Relax, this will be a little uncomfortable." He gently slid his greasy finger into my butt. It was surprisingly comfortable compared to what had been up there earlier. He was feeling around. I tightened as a pain shot through my backside. There. Then with his other hand the Doctor took a small flashlight.

"I see it," he said, "right there at twelve o'clock … oh, yes, and a small one at nine o'clock," he said pulling out his hand and carefully pulling off his glove. "You just have some fissures in your anus, young man. Have you been sexually active recently? Come on, son, you might as well admit it."

"Sexually active? Of course not!" I was offended. I hadn't sunk that low. Had I?

"But you have been with a man?" said the doctor carefully.

"Been."

"And he did this to you?" he repeated.

"Yeah, I guess so."

"Guy should be shot, Doc," said Fred from beyond the curtain.

"Wait a moment, Fred; let's do this one thing at a time," the doctor shouted to the curtain. I wished they would now all just disappear. But the doctor was not done. "You didn't have sex?" I shook my head, not wanting Fred to shout anything. "What did he do to you?" he asked.

I stared at the doctor. I could not do it. He wanted me to think about exactly what I had just decided did not happen.

The doctor stared at me. "How did this happen?"

"Er, he stuck … his … you know … in my … you

know ..." I trailed off, unable to even think what happened, let alone describe it.

"Okay, you don't have to tell me anything else. I get the picture," the doctor replied mercifully. "This happened tonight?"

"Er ... yeah, sort of ... this morning ... afternoon, actually."

"I see. Anything else in your anus besides his penis?" asked the doctor.

"No."

"Rape, pure and simple," rang the dismembered voice of Fred, like the voice of some hellish demon. "Forcing a teenager to perform anal intercourse. Guy's getting the electric chair."

"Fred, shut up." The doctor turned back to me, seeing the shock, maybe hearing the pounding in my chest. "Don't worry, there's no death penalty in Michigan."

"Am I guilty?" I asked.

"No, the asshole who did this to you is guilty," Fred's voice barked.

"Am I gonna die?"

"Calm down, Fred. You're upsetting the patient," the doctor shouted. I wished Fred would just go away. "This man, Gary, inserted his penis into your anus, correct?"

"I guesso." I shook my head yes, completing the humiliation. Then I wondered what this man's name really was. "Actually, maybe his name wasn't Gary. I don't think I really knew his name."

"Relax, you are going to survive." I heaved a sigh of relief. "It can bleed again after a bowel movement. So, you may see blood again, but it should stop by tomorrow. Don't worry; the fissures will heal just fine."

"Am I going to live?"

"Of course you will. It's nothing I haven't seen a dozen times already."

I could hear Fred's contemptuous grunt.

"Oh, yes, you should get tested for VD." The doctor skipped through the pages on his clipboard to the back. "Here, this is a clinic you can go to. Lie about your age like you did here and everything will be anonymous."

I looked at the brochure: 'Free and Anonymous VD Testing, Lik Clinic'.

"VD?" Then I did have sex.

"Better safe than sorry. Get tested after every time you have sex, or whatever you call it, but wait a few weeks," the doctor said. "Fred? All yours, but take it easy."

Fred entered.

"Can I get dressed first?" I asked quickly before the doctor left.

"Fred, wait outside."

Fred reluctantly walked beyond the curtains but continued his interrogation from there.

"Gary? Last name?" Fred's voice demanded. I got dressed quickly.

"I don't know it, sir."

"Description?"

"Last time I saw him he was in a dirty green shirt and ... tight gray jeans."

"What else? Say, you dressed yet?" Before I could answer he walked in.

I broke down and cried. I cried and kept crying, hoping he would give up and go away. Instead I had to recount the whole incident, one appalling mistake after another. To protect Gary, I lied about his address and the way he looked.

"This is a required report. I am calling the police. Maybe they can refresh your memory." Fred left.

The moment I realized Fred wasn't the police, I quickly grabbed my jacket, and clutching the VD clinic brochure, I ran as fast as I could out of the hospital to my parents car.

Chapter 21: Processional II

"That which doesn't kill me makes me stronger," I chanted as I drove all the way home, constantly checking my rearview mirror in case Fred was following me. Heart pounding, after a hysterically cautious ride, I drove up to the driveway of the house.

Stronger, I grabbed *The Nietzsche Reader* and ran into the house. I made an amazing decision, profound for my age. There was no real accurate record of what really happened anywhere.

"Got your book?" asked my mother, fiercely eyeing *The Nietzsche Reader*.

"Yes."

"Nietzsche, of course. Wanna tell me the truth now?" she asked.

"I went to … see a … girl." It was an awkward, clumsily muttered lie.

"Really? A girlfriend?" I struck gold. My mother's attitude changed completely.

"Maybe."

"I worry about you, but why keep this secret? What's her name?"

"Julie."

"She have a last name?"

"Einstein." I was back on my game.

"Where does she live?"

"She goes to Southfield High. She has brown hair, she's left-handed, and has blue eyes. I love the intriguing combination of dark hair and blue eyes. We're reading Zarathustra together." Clicking on all cylinders.

"How charming ... Would that explain the mess our bed was in?"

At that suggestion I was morally offended.

"Ma, can you just leave it alone?" I tentatively offered.

"Way back! Way, way back, and it's gone!" blared the television.

"Woo hoo! Horton just hit a home run! How do you like that!" yelled my dad to nobody.

My mother winced.

"I am very happy for you, Jamie; it's about time." I sighed.

"What happened, Dad?" I asked.

"Willie Horton just hit a home run!"

"That's great Dad! Are we winning?" My mother turned away and sat down next to my dad with her notebook.

"No, but we're only three back now."

"That's great, Dad ..."

I so completely convinced myself about the weekend with Julie that I actually began to believe it was true, that I really did sleep with Julie, my first female date and first home run, ever. Despite my anatomical ignorance of how it happened, this lie successfully concluded this sordid chapter in my life. From that moment onward it never happened. None of it. Not Gary—or whatever his name was—not the delicatessen, not the doctor, not Fred. Only Julie.

There was a hole between the sex book, which condemned me, and the trip to the VD clinic. This hole was craftily filled up with the mythical Julie, who forced me into it. Julie never even existed. Yet, strangely, she became the most important girl in my life.

I vowed never to see her again because for weeks afterwards I felt dirty, and bodily invaded by some VD dirt swimming in my blood vessels, polluting my entire body. It also provided the solid grounds to my mother for why I never saw her again. Impossibly for the next few weeks, I actually sat stewing about whether Julie actually gave me VD.

Chapter 22: Grieving

Ferndale, Michigan, June 1976

Four weeks later, the stew was done. I found myself in the waiting room of the Lik Clinic. The improvised waiting room was already familiar to me. I'd snuck out of the house the week before on the pretense of a phony date with Julie to get the VD test. The clinic was in a run-down old house in Ferndale. I did not know what to make of the clientele. They were mostly poorly dressed or over-made-up men passing as women. Guilty by association. Whoever these misfits were, and I was suspecting that I was a freak more and more every day, only Julie could save me.

"Mr. Neets-che?" announced the Nurse.

I walked into a small room—once a charming old bedroom, now a doctor's examining room. "That's Nietzsche," I corrected.

"Oh yes, have a seat there; doctor will be with you shortly."

I sat in the armchair, which seemed very unclean but perfectly in place here. The gaunt old man, not in a white coat but blue jeans and a disturbingly tight T-shirt, walked in.

"Hello, Mr. ... uh ... Mr. Arnold Nietzsche? Not

often we have so distinguished a visitor." He paused for a smile; none was coming. "Arnold, I am Doctor Fein." He was an older doctor and a bit too informal for my taste. "I have your lab results, but something is not right here. It says you had sex with someone named Julie Aschenbach?"

"Yes." Einstein sounded too silly, so I changed it to something more plausible.

"Seriously?"

"I admit it's a peculiar name—"

"It's not the name, Arnold, it's the gender. A girl?"

"Of course. What else?"

"But we took the sample from your anus, why was that?"

"I was bleeding there."

"Uh-huh. Julie wouldn't happen to be a man, would she?" asked the doctor dryly.

"Of course not. She goes to Southfield High. She has brown hair," I replied. I had no idea what an impossible lie I was telling.

"Okay." The doctor looked at me blankly. "You'll be okay. According to the lab results, you have syphilis."

"I do?" The shame hit me like a slap in the face.

"Yes, you do."

"Can I get rid of it right away, please?"

"Yes, but it also says here on the chart you were raped."

"I wasn't raped, sir. Julie is a nice girl," I said with a straight face, fooling myself but not the doctor, who knew the biological flaws in the story.

"Young man, this is the Lik Clinic. We specialize. We see this more often than you think. It's okay to tell the truth. We have a confidentiality policy here. I can't make you go to the police. Nevertheless, I feel it is my duty to tell you that if there is someone walking around raping young boys, we need to know about it."

Rape seemed like such a condemning word to me. I swallowed guiltily. "I didn't want to be raped. No one … did that, sir."

"Okay." He looked at me contemptuously.

"I got VD," I moaned.

"It's a bacteria, not a sin," the doctor said wryly, adding sarcastically, "You'll need to tell *Julie*."

The doctor sat down on his stool and prepared an injection.

"Roll up your sleeve, young man."

Leaving the clinic, I swore I would skip sex altogether. I made a solemn oath that I would never again have sex. Instead I would return to being a virgin.

I drove the car back home. I tried to sneak back into the house.

"Jamie, I want to talk to you!" I heard my mother yell from the kitchen. I ran to my room as if I didn't hear her. I grabbed the first book I found and sat on the floor and pretended to be deep into whatever it was I was reading. It was Goethe's *The Sorrows of Young Werther*. I was reading for a while, and I thought I got away with it.

Entering my room without knocking, my mom asked, "Jamie, I have to talk to you." I felt my mother's gaze still fixed on me as I read about Werther's hopeless infatuation with Charlotte. "Let's go out to eat. You like going to a restaurant?"

I was moved. My mother was reaching out to me. How desperately I needed that. I looked up. "Sure!" I perked up, in spite of myself.

"I know, let's go to Sam's. You know Westside Sam's. You like that place." I flashed red.

"I don't like that place." I shuddered with guilt at the mere mention of the restaurant.

"Since when?"

"I don't know; I don't want to go."

"Come on, don't be silly."

I put my book down. I felt trapped. I couldn't explain why I couldn't go back there. I was frightened Jake would be waiting for me. Or maybe the waitress would ask me where my funny looking friend was.

"I'm not hungry. I just want to stay home." Was I going to lose this moment for the sake of my own fears? I tried to think of something to say. Mom beat me to it.

"Oh, you do not; you just said you wanted to go." She was losing her patience with me.

"I don't feel like it." I felt handcuffed. How could I explain? My past was catching up with me.

"You just said you wanted to go, and now you don't."

"I never said I would go to that place, and I never will, never!"

"Oh, you are being ridiculous. Come on, let's go. I am doing this for you."

"It's not for me—I have bad memories—" but before I could confess that Julie gave me VD, she lost her cool.

"Honestly, I hope you have children as difficult as you are!" She turned and slammed the door shut. After a few moments, I heard her and my father leave the house and drive off.

I realized I couldn't avoid these places forever. I could not make the whole three-mile stretch of Woodward Avenue forbidden territory. Instead I declared the entire incident forbidden territory for my mind. Even Julie from Southfield High was kicked out of my life. But the damage was done; my mother did not try again to reach out to me, and I was too fixated on hiding to dare to reach out to her. In many ways I felt I lost my mother. I had no parents, so the parenting fell to me, but I wasn't a very good parent either.

Chapter 23: Pure Deceit

Clouds of willful and personal deceit descended so much I no longer knew what the truth was. I kept my forbidden territory promise for the rest of high school, the strip of Woodward from Eight Mile Road to Fenkel was off limits. I even convinced myself I was a virgin again. I never had VD, and even Julie disappeared. My mother never asked why, as much as I wanted her to. Who was I kidding? Everyone—except for a bunch of people I would never see again.

Oddly enough, after my failed suicide attempts, school lightened up. I became very good friends with Dorelle, Brian Germaine's ex-girlfriend. First I met her during a chemistry course. Then we would have lunch occasionally. She was easy to talk to; I was eager to listen to her and understand the world of being a girl and the vicarious world of Brian Germaine, though she did not have many kind things to say about him.

Dorelle and I just liked to talk. I suddenly had a girlfriend. She seemed to know, intuitively, that I was not going to bother her romantically or sexually. I didn't tell her of my vow of chastity, yet she seemed to have just assumed it. Everything was quite innocent.

Except the time we got drunk in Dorelle's backyard and I did kiss her, but that was really nothing and she took no offense. Armed with my newfound pure girlfriend and an absence of bullies, my high school years ended successful if prom-less.

The *coup de gras* was a flurry of college acceptances, my personal favorite being a tantalizing college in New York. My plans for an escape of dramatic proportions, however, were thwarted.

My family's fortunes had soured along with Detroit's. My father was laid off from his job as a construction electrician and my mother's political work brought in less than was paid out. She moved to a string of miserable jobs at advertising agencies, where she was even forced to work on a Republican client's campaign for mayor.

My father finally did get back to work; however, waylaid by a mild heart attack, he receded ever more distantly into my personal horizon. I no longer had the heart to confront the poor man on anything.

Consequently, when it came to the choice of colleges, it was a pure economic consideration. I had to attend a local university, where I had a fifty-percent scholarship—Detroit State University.

From all outward appearances, everything in my senior high school year looked good. Inwardly, life was a little different.

Chapter 24: Funeral Rites—the Carrot

To help prevent myself from thinking about the blacked-out periods, I needed new and improved weapons to ensure that my mind never wandered there. Weapons that would not obliterate male images and sexual thoughts, but would crowd and cloud them out. I honed two very powerful rituals in this new and improved battle.

My first and most significant ritual was the expanded role of opera. If I had dabbled in opera before, now I became obsessed by its fantastical surreal and unreal world. I already had an affinity for Wagner. Then I discovered his overlong opera of impossible love, *Tristan und Isolde*.

Almost accidentally, I latched onto my first complete *Tristan* recording. I found the records, a boxed set, in the cutout bin at Harmony House Records. *Tristan und Isolde* retailed for forty-two dollars and was marked down to three dollars and ninety-nine cents. My eyes bulged at the sight: a complete Wagner recording, not a highlights album but a full-blown opera. A complete Wagner opera had the prohibitive reputation of being interminably long. Did I dare to take on such an ambitious endeavor? Five records and a translated libretto, all for four bucks. I grabbed it. The record store clerk approved.

"Wise move, Goldberg. It's about time you graduated to the whole deal. You won't be sorry." He winked at me.

I liked the sound of the word 'graduated'; I could have done without the wink. I went home and played the music. It was slow, arcane, and long—and by that I mean day-killingly long. One page of the libretto would take almost twenty minutes to sing. The music, a mesmerizing web of short themes called *leitmotifs*, though time-consuming, was not boring. I started listening, and before I knew it, the day was over. In short, Tristan was just the thing I needed to cloud up and overcrowd an already overtaxed conscience.

However, a funny thing happened on my way to obsessively swimming in unintelligible music: My mind latched like a limpet onto the story of impossible love. The music, once slow and overbearing, grew iridescent, painful, joyful, and erotic over time. It was an emotional feast of all the things I never allowed myself to feel. I wallowed in the teenage schmaltz of it all. Alone to devour the music, I wanted to be both the lover and the beloved, to be both Tristan *and* Isolde. To feel what they were both feeling. And I was surprised to find that this very idea of merging, melting souls was in the libretto: Each lover wanted to turn into the other.

My only hope seemed *those* words wrapped in *that* music. It didn't matter which person sang what. I could freely imagine I was both Tristan and Isolde, thereby allowing my sexuality a gender-neutral outlet. Moreover, sex or sensuality of any kind was never discussed in program notes nor displayed in stage photos. Their sexual lives were a blank stage my mind could fill in any way it desired.

Tristan und Isolde became my emotional and even sexual substitute, taking me to a special place, as the words in a famous love duet describe. I added my own special meanings to the words based on the music, intensifying their meaning:

Descend,
O Night of never ending love,
grant me oblivion.
Take me up
into your comforting bosom,
and make me forget I live!
Deliver me now
From deceitful fantasies,
From everything desired
From my unwanted memories
Come, sacred twilight
Extinguish the imagined terrors.
Deliver me into your love's
World-redeeming,
Never-ending bliss...

My first musical love-induced tears consecrated my descent into the emotional world of opera.

Of course, my anti-sex promise had another ritual. I used opera as the carrot ritual; but there was also ... a stick.

Chapter 25: Funeral Rites—the Stick

It would only be necessary, of course, to take some corrective measures when I was overwhelmed with the sexual desires I could not name but also could not turn off. In those moments, I would wait until I could be alone in the house, when I knew my parents would be gone for a substantial amount of time. In those moments, I was drawn downstairs to the basement.

I can remember creeping downstairs like a burglar. Walking quietly, even though no one was home, I still worried about making too much noise, as if I were afraid to awake my own consciousness and reveal what I was doing. Safely downstairs, I breathed a sigh of relief. Downstairs was a mini kind of messy shop my father kept for his long list of half-done projects. Stuff was everywhere. Saws, hammers, nails. Once there, I looked around for ... something. It took some experimentation to find what would or would not work.

On my first descent, my heart started pounding. Oddly enough, my cock got stiff during this quest to arrest its excitement. The erection increased my anger. Eventually I settled on a belt, a sturdy belt with a huge metal buckle. It once belonged to my brother, and I found it in a box of his stuff stored downstairs.

With a religious solemnity, I undressed. It was a rite, after all. I knelt on the cold concrete floor, absentmindedly stroking my twitching cock. Thoughts flooded in, thoughts I had to punish, which reminded me why I was there.

I held the belt in my right hand, buckle doubling for a handle. I raised the belt in the air and with a great force slapped the belt around my back.

Crack!

Pain flooded my body, along with shame for those thoughts.

Again. *Crack!* Again. *Crack!* This time a slap around my ass. *Crack!* The pain started to overtake the shame.

Harder. *Crack!*

The surge of pain rose, purifying, giving penance for my sins. The penance was thrilling, and the excitement kept my cock stiff. That wasn't the object! Harder and harder, the pain began to make its way through my arousal. But not enough. I added a strong dose of loud verbal abuse.

Rearing back as hard as I could with the belt, I yelled, seething with hatred, "You faggot. *Crack* You queer faggot. *Crack* I am going to cure *Crack* you, *Crack* or else!" *Crack*

Not enough pain. I switched to the buckle side, continued the whipping. The sharp cracking traded for the dull thud of the metal against flesh. I continued the assault: words angrier, strikes more vicious.

"You worthless shit, *thud* don't *thud* even *thud* think *thud* of *thud* men, *thud* you *thud* inhuman, disgusting *thud* little ..." I stopped immediately. I felt it: that hallowed penance, the hot liquid on my back. Not a spurt. An ooze. Not looking, I just knew it was blood. The thought of the blood made me so sick that finally, sexual excitement turned to disgust.

I collapsed. Not angry at all, I was exhausted. Finally, redeeming shame would come. The shame felt good. It erased all sexual desires.

I lay in a heap and, unable to control myself, I masturbated, thinking first of *women, women, women, tits, ass, tits, ass*, but I could not keep it up. Toward the very end, at the ecstatic height of semi-unconsciousness, it was *men, cock, ass, muscle, male sweat!*

Finally exploding in a disgust of ecstasy and messy semen, the predominant early chants of women returned. The men sunk back into oblivion.

The throbbing pain blinded me to what had just happened. An urgent need to make it all go away came over me. Fast! I grabbed anything I could find: oil rag, dirty towel, anything. I had to wipe myself off; I had to obliterate the evidence. Bloody towels and shirts into the laundry. Throw in the scum-soaked rag. Add a hundred times more soap than needed; then turn on the hot washer. Wear any unwashed dark shirt.

The memory of the blood overshadowed any recollection of masturbating. Remorse raining in buckets, searing remorse about making myself bleed, was so intense I had the metallic taste of regret in my mouth. The pain, the mental noise, was unbearable, so I convinced myself that my soul was cleansed by something holy: hard-earned atonement—not just a plea for forgiveness, but heroic action. My sick desires disappeared as if by magic. I was washed, cleansed, purified. The rite worked!

I said out loud, "I am pure. I will never do this again." Then I sloppily thanked whatever god or spirit wished to take credit for my deliverance.

Atonement complete.

I quickly ran upstairs. Once in my room, more opera. The music would glorify and blur what had happened. In contrast to sharp angry sounds, now lush violins and erotic woodwinds called to me a chaste sexuality. In German it was this:

o sink herneider
nacht der liebe,
dich vergessen
das ich lebt...

In my mind it was this:

Descend,
O Night of never ending love,
grant me oblivion.
Take me up
into your comforting bosom,
and make me forget I live!
Deliver me now

From deceitful fantasies,
From everything desired
From my unwanted memories
Come, sacred twilight
Extinguish the imagined terrors.
Deliver me into your love's
World redeeming,
Never ending bliss...

Ritual pattern over, an oasis of innocence surrounded me. The washing machine was on, doing my dirty work. I privately blotted blood from my back, not even thinking how the blood got there. It was now all forgotten and forgiven.

Those moments afterwards were among my happiest. The troubling thoughts went away. I was pure. Not purified or cured; that would require an admission. No, this was immaculate atonement.

And it worked ... for a while.

Months of peace and rest would go by. I could bury myself in books, movies, and *Tristan*.

Eventually though, the skies would darken. The dreaded fantasies involving male bodies would come back, returning like unwanted guests at my mental doorstep. I succumbed to the drive to watch men and obsess over them. Then the ritual that could only happen once would begin again.

Third Variation: The Discovery
Early Spring 1980

III Scherzo. Wuchtig.
(Musical Joke. Powerful.)

Chapter 26: Detroit State University

In the fall of 1978 I entered Detroit State University in Detroit's New Center area. The Detroit of my childhood, though mere miles away, was lost forever. Woodward Avenue, once a main thoroughfare, had become a desolate street. The Riots had taken their toll. The city did not recover. Burned out and vacant lots gaped the neighborhoods.

The decline in the auto industry and profound city mismanagement made matters worse. Abandoned and demolished properties abounded. The bound-up homes served for other things than housing: prostitution, drugs, and generally depraved activities.

My mother's attempts to stop the slide were as effective as her parenting. Nevertheless, she would never give up trying. While my confidence in city politics turned lukewarm, her hot-blooded passion for her city never cooled.

As I walked down Woodward, I wondered what she was fighting for anymore. Segregation was settled by the default created by white flight. We were a minority among minorities; my mother and father were the only white people, let alone Jews, living in our quickly declining neighborhood.

It was bittersweet to find myself at Detroit State University. Just a short drive from my house, the campus was another world. DSU was an island of green and safety amid the decay and rot. My parents had promised to pay for my education, but they could not afford as much as they could for Steven. So no NYU, U of M, not even MSU, but rather the good, if cut rate, DSU. Cut rate or not, the tuition would still mean a sacrifice. They would make it—as long as I followed the prescribed course of study: pre-law with an eye to becoming a lawyer, government policymaker, or illustrious elected official. None of these options appealed to me, but staying at home appealed to me even less.

At Detroit State, I bunked in a small double-room in the main college dormitory, a ten-story tenement-like building partitioned in authoritarian concrete blocks. The sixth floor, where I lived, was a place of stained carpets, dark walls, male students, and smells of post-adolescent abuses. The students were not a warm group, unless you wanted to buy or drink alcohol or do other junior-varsity drugs.

The third floor of the dorm housed a small college of public policy, my pre-law program. In the evening the classrooms doubled as study rooms. Downstairs on the main floor was a front desk, a miserable university store, and our cafeteria.

The cafeteria allowed students of the dorm to eat for free. It was the main neutral area of the dorm, the gathering place for all, even my dorm mates whom I quickly learned to avoid.

Still, I managed a superficial effort to fit in, and others obliged, however grudgingly. My tray of fish sticks and macaroni and cheese literally in hand, I often bumped into dorm-mates from my floor.

"Hey, Opera Jim," said one of the thickly torsoed jocks from my sixth-floor dorm. "Opera Jim" was their nickname for me, a welcome change from the outright rejection of high school. Still, I knew it was important not to get too close to people. The closer I got to people, the better the chance they would come in contact with my complicated life. I opted for being nonchalant, warm, yet cool.

"Hi, Tyler."

"Man, how many times do I have to tell you, Tyler is my roommate."

"Yes, yes, I know, Kevin, sorry. What's up, dude?" Sometimes I would pepper my speech with 'dude' or 'man'.

"Did you hear the new *Highway to Hell* album?" Kevin asked, his tray overfilled with fish sticks, French fries, and a few plates of pie.

"No, man, didn't get a chance to check it out. Did you hear the *London Calling* album?" I barely knew the album, but I was well aware that in this dorm, punk music turned people away like a crucifix before vampires. Kevin was no exception; he stepped backwards away from me, signifying I had hit my mark again.

"No, man, sounds cool. Maybe you should check

out some other music though; you've been harping on that for a while now, dude. I am playing *Highway to Hell* tonight; come on over with a couple beers and party with us."

"Far out, man," I said as he slipped away.

I did not go to the party, as I am sure Kevin or Tyler or whoever he was secretly hoped, since he didn't tell me when or where it was happening.

In this environment, with fifty to sixty suspicious fellow students listening for the slightest deviation from the norm, my sexual appetite was easy to manage. I shared my dorm room with a nice, very uptight guy named Tim. Tim was a tall, elegant, if severe, music student. His long bony fingers played a lyrical piano. We had three things in common: a love of classical music, a complete bewilderment about girls, and an almost allergic response to intimate conversation. Tim kept erratic hours—practicing in the music building and reading in study halls to all hours of the night and/or day. The dorm rooms were generally too loud to allow the extended periods of concentration he required. This meant I could never depend on his being away for any length of time; he could show up at any moment or not at all.

In short, with no opportunity for the "ritual" to emerge, unwise thoughts stayed repressed. I interpreted this suppression as success. Unwanted ideas floated in my head from time to time, but as a rabbi once said in a sermon I remembered, "We all get ugly ideas. The difference between a normal person and a murderer is that one thinks it and the other actually does it." I was doing fine.

Until one spring day.

Chapter 27: Sucker Punch

In the spring of my sophomore year there came a blow that struck my most vulnerable spot. Powerless: no rite to purge me of it, no purification to exorcise me, no magic potion to make me forget, it hit me unawares like a sucker punch. On March 21, 1980, at 4:50 p.m., I fell in love.

On March 18, at 4:45 p.m., I saw him for the first time. I gazed up from a study room on the third floor, and there he was. No big deal.

On March 19, at 4:45 p.m., while sitting on the benches outside the dorm, I saw him for the second time, this time up close. This time I could not tear my gaze away. His magical blue eyes, his tufts of blond hair, his sweet thick lips delicately etched across a smooth supple face—his lips could form a smile that could silence the portable guillotines of my mind.

By March 21, my spot on the bench had become an obsession. It was just recessed enough from the sidewalk to afford both a clear view and yet offer plausible deniability. I took a seat at three in the afternoon, studying despite the wind and a light rain. I did not want to risk anyone else grabbing this prime sitting real estate. At 4:45 p.m., when I did not see him for the third time, I knew I was lost. A quaking sense of desperation came over me. Then, miraculously, five minutes later he appeared. *Thank God he's all right*, I thought. Of course, it was love. Love, thanks to Tristan, something so noble and refined it became too lofty to question. Love—something so strong that it became stuck to me, and it wouldn't go away no matter how hard I shook it.

With disturbing—yet unconscious—determination, I planned to arbitrarily—yet systematically—run into him. In a short time, this plan to see him would dominate my life. He would eat lunch sometimes at my dormitory's cheap cafeteria, where residents ate for free. Those sweet—yet twitching—eyes, those lips, would show up early around 11:30 a.m., and choose a middle seat in the middle of a sea of long empty tables. I never dared to take a seat within his view. I always sat a table or two back, but the angle and proximity were enough that I could drink in a gorgeous five-eighths view of his face, allowing me to see the back of his beautiful head of hair and his precious earlobes: soft and delicate. I didn't dare eat from my plate, lest my excuse for remaining in the cafeteria would disappear, and I would have to get up and leave, denying him of his unknown admirer.

At around 4:45 every Wednesday and Friday, he would walk by my bench or, in truly hostile weather, past my dormitory window or study room 368 on the third floor, the one with the right view of the street. Some days I dared to stand up from my bench, pretending to have some serious purpose, and walk behind him for a brief distance. If I was lucky, I could breathe in the magical air of his musty commercial cologne.

With each furtive glance I longed to see some refutation, a denial, a blemish, an anything to dissuade or repel me. It only got worse—or better. He had a delicate yet muscled body, an exquisite but firm curve of buttock. Clothes hung loosely over him, as if the cloth were carelessly draped over his naked body.

Ultimately, he defied description. He was a totality, not just the cutest nose in the world, nor the twinkle or darling little twitch in those beautiful blue eyes, nor even the impossible smile. Could I step back and ignore those well-formed legs? How was it possible to deny the perfectly proportioned torso, the slightly muscled arms, the sweet, cute, egg-shaped head? What about the matted blond hair that seemed to beg a caress? No, it was the disturbing compulsive totality that made me feel transported.

He was a *gesamteliebeswerk*, a German word I invented meaning 'a total work of love.' I loved observing him. I loved thinking about him. I loved fantasizing about him. He invaded my deepest sanctuaries. Operatic images began to bow their heads to describe my beloved. No English word, no spoken word, could sum him up, only a stanza from *Tristan und Isolde* could, especially the German word *erhaben*, not because I knew what it meant, though I did find out, but because it just flew gloriously out of the mouth of the bass solo in *Tristan*:

> *He, whom I dare not*
> *approach,*
> *so splendid,*
> *so supreme,*
> *so sublime (erhaben),*
> *who could not but*
> *refresh my soul.*

Objective beauty survived the harshest of mental interrogations. I watched him; he never let me down. Every gesture, every step, confirmed what an *erhaben*—sublime—person he was, affirmed his endowment with the loftiest virtues, so that to long for him could only in itself be lofty. He was the visual and spiritual *gesamteliebeswerk*. How could anyone or anything deny that?

What started out as a mild fascination very quickly became an obsession, and then degenerated into a compulsion forcing me to ever more ridiculous acts just to be in his vicinity. The compulsion took away my ability to sleep or eat, then my ability to have a coherent conversation. I could be studying and the thought of him would come to me, and I would gaze outside in the hope that he might walk by.

Sometimes I could catch snippets of a conversation, or see a book in his hand. With this more close-range contact it became intuitively clear that this guy was a genius, an intellectual with excellent taste in music and a curiosity for late German Romantic culture. He was someone with whom I wanted to talk and share ideas, a moral and courageous soul, a person who could deliver me out of this mess, if only I could give him the chance.

Whenever I saw him in the flesh—at the cafeteria, on the street, or in the library—my stare would last too long. I had to force myself to look away. *You sick pervert, stop looking at that normal sublime person,* I'd chide. Stop it! *Think only of women, as surely he does.* This was my mantra, repeated over and over again; however, it was by now completely ineffective.

Even as I swore to never look at him again, he'd appear somewhere unexpected. His magnetic force was too powerful for my eyes to resist. Horrified, I found myself desperately plotting to meet him; my descent from the sublime to the ridiculous was sealed. Cost what it may, I was determined to meet this sublime man who inspired me beyond the realms of *Werther, Faust,* and even *Tristan.* How far I was willing to go in this pursuit astounded me.

Chapter 28: Great Lengths

As much as I was tempted to berate myself over my obsession with the stranger, somehow this was different. My intuition told me he wasn't the source of damnation but rather deliverance. I had a path to my salvation. Everything I vested in the healing, delivering, and saving powers of romantic love were embodied in this unknown man. Dr. Reuben's onerous book raised some red flags, but here he was wrong. This guy was not the kind of man to corner someone in a dark alley, just concerned about his own groin. Still, there was this concern about being something I had been resisting. Nevertheless, a deep, deep voice inside of me told my critical thinking to *go fuck itself* and urged me to *just do it*. So I did.

Ridiculously, yet religiously, I followed him into the university library. I saw him reading a book by Henry Miller. I didn't notice the title, but surely this was a sign from God, if ever there was one. Henry Miller was one of the great banned authors my mother raved about, a surrealist and experimental novelist, not an author one reads for fun. I searched all over the library for a logged-in but abandoned computer terminal to the library checkout system. It took a while, but eventually I saw the telltale black screen with a green flashing prompt in the special collections room. I rushed over to the terminal. I looked at the cryptic menu and could not find anything that made sense, so I tried all the options. I may have accidentally checked out a book or two. Finally, I found a prompt with a screen title, "Log Review." I typed in H-e-n-r-y M-i-l-l-e-r, then tapped the return key. Gloriously, every book the DSU library had by or about Henry Miller came pouring onto the terminal display. Unfortunately, there were fifty-five books in the system. However, as far as I could tell, only seven books were checked out, but who had checked them out? I saw the student IDs, not the names. I made a list of all the books that were checked out.

"Excuse me, I am in a terrible mess; I was wondering if you could help me. I am doing some research and I need to just look up something in a copy of Harold Miller's *Tropic of Cancer*. You have a couple checked out already. If I could just get their names, I can contact them and ask them to let me look at the book."

The library clerk blinked her eyes at me. She stared blankly, then reluctantly tapped something into her terminal.

"There is no *Tropic of Cancer* by Harold Miller—oh ... you mean Henry Miller. We still have three copies in the stacks; you can just go and get one of those right now."

"I couldn't find them."

"Second floor, under the M's." She flashed an evil smile.

"I couldn't find them."

"Look carefully. It is amazing what you will be able to find."

"Thank you."

"Glad to be of help."

I could not get any further.

Wasn't this spiritual proof to cease and desist? Yet I could not help but think, with only seven of fifty-five books checked out, no one, except possibly me, would read Henry Miller for pleasure. Therefore, Mr. Wrong must be taking an English course. A Plan B kicked in, and before my mental Robespierre knew what hit him, I went to the English department.

The English department was housed in an old Victorian building. It was as old-fashioned as the stately department secretary behind her enormous cherry-wood desk.

"May I help you, young man?" The secretary eyed me suspiciously through her thick-rimmed black glasses, her face peering above the orderly piles of papers on her desk.

"Yes, please. I am thinking of taking … a course in English—I mean literature, ha ha, and I was wondering—well, a student told me you had a stack of syllabuses for the current semester."

"That's syllabi, young man, and please get to the point."

"Well, I wanted to look at them and get an idea of

the different course offerings and the professors' approach, you know." I smiled broadly.

"Really?" The dubious tone in her voice was clear. "Yes."

"Okay, there, in a pile over there—the third pile." She pointed to the right corner of her desk.

Greedily I looked through the stack. The secretary eyed me as if I were mad. When she glanced away to take a phone call, I could not help but notice on her desk, on pile number two, a stack of what looked like class rosters, names, and student numbers. Returning to my stack, I rummaged and rummaged until I found—what? Was it the path to salvation or the road to hell? Whichever, I found the syllabus for English 328—*The Dawn of the Modern Novel*—taught by Professor Walin. Three credits. On the reading list was *The Tropic of Cancer* by Henry Miller. The course met in room 216, Cavanaugh Hall, Wednesday and Friday, 3:00 p.m. to 4:30 p.m.

At 4:15 the following Wednesday, I went to Room 216, Cavanaugh Hall. Peering into the room through a small window in the door, I tried to find him. I saw a professor; he was young, wearing a beard and a tweed suit. Looking further, there *he* was. He sat in the middle of the room, looking attentive, his head sweetly cocked to the left.

The course let out, and he left the room, his cologne unmistakably, if saccharinely, delicious. I saw the beautiful blue eyes with the iridescent black pupils. I even caught the twitch in his eye as he approached me. I could swear he glanced at me, even made eye contact for a microsecond. My heart leapt. His lips contorted into a pleasantly ambiguous shape, and he walked on. I entered the room, pretending to be in the next class. The flock of people around the professor thinned. I tensed and introduced myself.

"Can I help you, young man?" asked Professor Walin.

"Yes, I was wondering … you see … I found this really nice pen; I think it belongs to the person sitting in this seat, where I sit in the next class."

"I see."

"I'd like to give it back to him; do you know who sits there?"

"That's his pen?" The professor looked incredulous.

"Yes. See, it looks nice; I think he'd want it back."

He wasn't buying the story. He grabbed his bag and turned to go. Then he stopped and turned to me. "Casper Tears, and there is no class in here after mine." Then he left the room.

I looked Casper Tears up in the school directory. I could not find his name anywhere. Then, after greedily scanning the T's ten times, I found it: Casper Tyres. I had a name and an address, but no phone number.

The next thing I had to do was get his phone number so I could dare to call him. That meant going back to the English department to see that roster.

"What are you doing, young man? This is my desk!" cried the secretary of the English department.

I jumped and screamed in surprise.

"I was ... I was ... you see this pen, it belonged to someone in the English department, Casper Tyres, and I was looking to see if I could find where he is so I can ... give it back."

"Don't be ridiculous, young man; there is no one here named Casper."

"No, I mean a student."

"I don't care if you were looking for the janitor ..."

"What is the matter here, Mrs. Staples?" An angered professor walked out of his office, wood creaking underneath his feet.

"Dean, this young man was fumbling around my desk, looking for test answers to ... to some class. What class are you enrolled in?"

"I was not cheating! I didn't know you had the answers to any test," I protested.

"What do you call what's in your hands, young man?" said the Dean, pointing to the rosters I was holding.

"There are answers in here?" I dropped the pile on the desk.

"What's your name? A pen? I have heard all kinds of stories, but this one ... Name!"

"Jamie—James Goldberg, sir!"

"Which course are you enrolled in?" he demanded.

"All of them?"

"Yes, all of them. Come on, quick. Call Security, Mrs. Staples."

"Introduction to Public Policy ..."

"No, what *English* courses. How stupid can you be?"

"Oh … none."

"None?"

"No, sir—I mean … yes, sir. None.

"None, Mrs. Staples? Do we have a James Goldberg enrolled this semester?"

"Actually … that name does not sound familiar, but I could swear I've seen you before," Mrs. Staples said. She grabbed the rosters from her desk and started rummaging through them.

"Dean Richards, what do you need?" asked a security guard who came running into the room.

"Just a moment, Ted. Mrs. Staples?"

"I am looking … James … Goldberg … James … Goldberg … James … Goldberg …" She was scanning roster after roster. "I am looking!"

"Mr. Goldberg?"

"I swear, sir, I am not in any English course this semester. Not that I don't like English. I liked the creative writing class last semester. I thought once of majoring in English. Harold Miller is one of my favorite authors."

"To whom does the pen belong?" the Dean asked.

"A student in course 358, professor Walin told me … I think the student is … Casper Tyres."

"There is no, Casper T-e-a …"

"It's spelled with a 'y'," I offered. Mrs. Staples did not appreciate the help at all.

"*No* Casper anything in 358, not even a James

Goldberg. Young man you're ly— Wait, Professor Walin, you mean course 328, The Dawn of the Modern Novel?" announced Mrs. Staples. "Oh, Casper *Tires*! They are reading *Henry* Miller." She glared at me. "I remember you!"

"Mr. Goldberg," said a seething Dean, "I suggest you look elsewhere for Mr. Tyres. And next time, just ask the department secretaries instead of rummaging around yourself. Sorry, Ted, false alarm. But Mr. Goldberg was just leaving, weren't you?"

Finally, carefully compiled on a small sheet of blue colored paper:

Casper Tyres
(pronounced Tears or Tires?)
Theater Major, junior year.
Telephone 313-376-0902.
3.65 GPA.
From Bad Axe, Michigan.
Casper's mother, Mrs. Thelma Watson Tyres,
is a registered Democrat from the Eighth
Precinct of the Tenth Congressional district.
His father, Jackson Tyres, hasn't voted in
sixteen years (most likely he last voted for
Barry Goldwater, after which time he
became a disillusioned conservative).
Checked out Henry Miller's *The Tropic of*
Cancer and returned it six days later.
Technical assistant for an upcoming student
production of the Eugene O'Neill family
drama, *Long Day's Journey into Night*,

planned for next fall semester.
Applied to Prof. Arthur Nathan to be the set
designer for a proposed production the
following year of a play called *The
Caretaker*.
The Caretaker was written by British
modernist playwright Harold Pinter, a
watershed work in his development of his
own absurdist yet realist style.

Now what? I decided to audition for *The Caretaker*
next year.

Chapter 29: Trouble

May 5, 1980

One of my more tense hangouts was at my cousin Rhonda's studio apartment. Rhonda was my Aunt Sylvia's daughter. Rhonda was studying psychology at Detroit State. She was staying off campus in a very nicely furnished room; she had a fluffy powder-blue couch, a big desk, and a large bed with a Star of David-motif comforter. Her house smelled pinky-nice. She was reading just enough psychology text-books to try to diagnose *my problem*. Even though I had not yet admitted to anyone that I had a problem.

Rhonda's version of 'hanging out' was studying while the television played some horrific film in the background. This evening the videocassette of choice was a nightmarish film entitled *Eraserhead*, during which she was peppering me with personal questions based on her psychology studies. They were personal questions to which I didn't know the answers, questions like: "Do you have performance anxiety?" I admitted to stage fright. "Do you suffer from premature ejaculation?" I admitted to premature feelings of anger. She was as nosy as I was confused, and it was beginning to get to me.

"You have anger management issues, don't you?"

"You mean this desire to throw that book you're reading out the window?" I tried to make it sound like a joke. I got up and plopped down on her bed. "Why don't you just leave me alone?"

"Shithead, I am trying to help you." Shithead was a Rhonda term of endearment for me.

"I don't need that kind of help." I looked up at the ceiling and wondered if I had anger management issues.

"Do you have any hidden resentment towards your father?"

"Not hidden."

"Funny, shithead. Do you fantasize about hurting people?"

"Only when they ask too many questions."

"Hilarious, you're a real Groucho Marx tonight. No suppressed anger?"

"No!" I snapped.

"Don't get so defensive."

"I am not being defensive!"

"But you are being angry, shithead, I think this is bigger than both of us."

"I am not angry at anyone."

"Like hell you're not."

"I am only getting angry because you're insisting I am angry and it's pissing me off."

"See. Told ya you're angry. You're out of control. I am serious. I think you should see Dr. Wire. He's great." Her suggestion took me by surprise.

"See who?"

"Dr. Wire, he coauthored this book. He's great. He is just what you need, kiddo."

"He is?"

"Yes."

"Great at what?"

"Jamie, you're not happy, are you?"

"But I'm not crazy."

"I know you're not. But maybe you should talk to someone who can … listen to you. You're not happy. I am sorry to see that."

With Rhonda my guard was down. "No, I guess am not." It had never occurred to me that being unhappy wasn't normal. "We can agree on that. He can help me with that?"

"Oh, yes, kiddo, he can. And if you're lucky, maybe more." She winked.

"Well, kiddo is better than shithead."

We laughed.

"I like your sense of humor; it brings back the sunshine in you."

"It does?" I asked, gloomy again.

"Yes, it does, Jamie. It's when you let us see the real you."

"The real me?" She got up from the couch and plopped down beside me on the bed.

"Yeah, the real you, not this mask you're always wearing."

"I am not wearing any—"

"Sorry, shithead, that's why you should see Dr. Wire."

I decided to call Dr. Wire.

Chapter 30: Opening Moves

Dr. Wire was apparently intrigued by my case. I didn't even realize I had a case. He offered to evaluate me in three visits. After that I could get a referral for any "special help" I might need. I walked into his office feeling disoriented, like someone lost in a forest. Except this was a forest of emptiness. Dr. Wire himself was ignoring me. He sat hunched over his desk, facing the wall, writing something.

The large desk against the wall dominated the room. The desk formed the room's sole source of life. It was heavy, metallic, stacked with thick science tomes and binders of paper. His large office was cold and institutional, giving no sign of personality or warmth. The room was furnished complete with two uncomfortable looking steel chairs. The chairs had thin black leather cushions that could easily be mistaken for black holes that would suck the soul out of a body. Half-populated steel bookshelves stood against bare white walls. Except for an ugly green Michigan Psychiatric license the walls were unadorned, without anything even as vaguely warm or personal as a diploma or certificate of appreciation. The room seemed more suited to interrogation than therapy.

Eventually, he reluctantly swiveled his chair sharply around. Dr. Wire faced me without a barrier between us. His smile looked sarcastic and cold. His penetrating eyes made me wish there was a barrier protecting me.

At first sight, I thought Dr. Wire was a small, gray-haired Jewish professor … until he spoke.

"Please sit down, James," he said in a harsh Middle-American accent.

With no choice, I sat down in one of the uncomfortable chairs. He had penetrating eyes that stared through thick glasses like a laser.

"You can call me Jamie."

"Not Jim?"

"I hate Jim."

"Not Jim then. You signed the confidentiality agreement?" he asked sharply.

"I have. I gave it to your secretary, sir."

"You understood the agreement?" His angular features were sharp and unforgiving. Even his pointy beard seemed to stick its accusing angle into my face.

"Yes, everything I say will be confidential—"

"You certainly know I am a research psychologist. Your case may appear anonymously in a research paper or scientific volume. No one will know who you are. And of course everything will be confidential as long as you don't report that you are going to hurt someone *or* yourself."

"I'd never hurt anyone." I forced a smile. I noticed he had an off-putting clean smell as if he bathed in talcum powder.

"Good, then let's begin."

It seemed as if he expected me to say something. I fidgeted in my chair a bit. I couldn't think of what to talk about. All I could think of was my overwhelming desire to be friends with Casper Tyres. That certainly was of no interest here. Here we needed to discuss the big, important issues.

He was still staring at me, blinking. I looked around the room.

"There's no couch in the room," I offered.

"I don't believe in them," he said, making no effort to continue the conversation. I sat in the hard chair, wondering if I could stand sitting there for the full fifty minutes, what Dr. Wire over the phone called the "analyst's hour."

I looked behind me. There was a clock on the wall. We had forty-three minutes to go.

"What are you expecting from this therapy?" asked Dr. Wire.

I looked out his window, hoping for some answer. Out there somewhere was a shady university campus, but all I could see was a blinding glare from the bright sun reflecting off the window.

"Nothing," I said.

"Nothing," he repeated.

I tried to look out the window; the glare was still there.

"I mean, I don't know ... I never did this before."

He did not move. I wish he would at least give me a clue to the right answer.

"I have anger management issues," I guessed.

"Oh, are you angry?"

"Rhonda says I am."

"Rhonda?"

"You don't know her?"

"Certainly not. Are you angry?"

"I don't feel angry at the moment. No. Maybe I am not angry."

"Is there someone you're angry at?"

I impulsively wanted to say my father … but that's nonsense; that accident happened long ago. And it didn't feel right being angry at your own father.

"I don't know … I'm not doing very well, am I?" I confessed.

"Relax." Dr. Wire glanced toward the window. His glasses picked up some of the sun's glare and it flashed in my eyes. I flinched.

"Can you help me?" I asked.

"Do you need help?" he volleyed.

"That's why I am here. Yes, of course," I countered.

"What for?"

This is impossible. This is going nowhere! I can't even say "hello" without getting some impossible inquisition.

"You must know … I can't be your only patient," I complained, hoping the desperation in my voice would make him understand. It didn't.

"What is your goal? What is your objective for this visit?" he challenged.

I didn't answer. It seemed like a personal affront to ask me the question.

"You just woke up this morning and said to yourself, 'I wonder how old Dr. Wire is doing?'"

"Don't you see, I have never done this before," I said, feeling like a cross between a cornered dog and an idiot.

"Why, then, are you here?" he shot back.

Why did this question seem so stupid and yet so difficult?

"Can't we just skip it and get on with the next question? Why am I here? It's obvious I need someone to talk to." I sensed I was trying his patience.

"Really? Well, one-hundred and fifteen dollars is a lot of money to just talk to someone. I know some places where you can talk to someone for as little as three dollars an hour, if you're a drinking man," he quipped unkindly.

"I am not old enough," I said. I glanced at the door. It seemed to be beckoning me to walk through it. "You don't want to talk to me, do you, doctor?"

"That's odd, I was about to ask you the same thing."

We were back to square one. His eyes met mine. I looked away.

"What am I supposed to do?" Then, daring to look him in the eyes: "I can't figure it out. It ... you know ... life. Something is bothering me, and I don't know what."

"Don't look at me. I can't read your mind,"

"I hate my parents," I barked in frustration.

"You hate your parents?"

"I don't know why I said that." I panicked. "I

want to stop hating my parents." That seemed even worse.

"You want to stop hating your parents? ... Is there a good reason to hate them?"

I was stunned. "A good reason to hate them?"

"Maybe they don't treat you the way you want to be treated?" He leaned in, uncomfortably close, looking at me as if I was a bug specimen.

"Is that a reason to hate someone?" I shifted in my chair, hoping to find some comfortable position.

"Can you just remind me what you to want to achieve if we decide to go forward?"

I realized I was now precariously balanced on the edge of the chair. I slid back. "I feel I am under a constant state of siege, like this conversation. I want it all to stop!"

"There, that wasn't so difficult, was it?" Dr. Wire said, finally writing something in his notepad. I was shocked. Was the answer he was looking for so simple? "So tell me a little bit about yourself, *Jamie*." He pronounced 'Jamie' like it was a pseudonym.

"What is there to tell?" Dr. Wire shot me a murderous look. "I like opera ... I like philosophy ..." I was encouraged as neither of these statements appeared to draw a negative response. "I am a lefty—in politics."

"I see," said Dr. Wire, interested, but not writing anything. But I was tickled to death when he asked me, "Who's your favorite philosopher?"

"Friedrich Nietzsche. My favorite composer is

Wagner, *Rickard Vagner,*" I offered.

"Okay." He nodded. "Why is Wagner important to you?"

"Well, opera allows me to hide … I mean it's like a social life …" Almost holding my breath, my favorite subject careened off into a dangerous direction. "I don't have any friends … they all think I am weird."

"Are you?" He leaned back, crossing his legs.

"I suppose so."

"What makes you weird?"

I suddenly was unsure. "Isn't it obvious?" I asked, shifting in my chair. He still said nothing. "Opera?"

"My wife likes opera."

"She does?"

"It doesn't make her weird."

"I am sorry, I didn't mean anything personal. But I am weird … I do … stuff … to me … no one knows about." I could hardly talk because I could hardly breathe. Dr. Wire's hostile neutrality was disturbing. I didn't dare share something so personal, so terrible as my ritual. I was hurting myself, so he'd have me committed or worse. I suddenly wanted to do almost anything to stop this conversation. "You hate me, don't you?"

"I beg your pardon?" He leaned further back in his chair.

"Well, you just sit there staring at me."

"I am just waiting for you to tell me about yourself."

"Haven't I answered that already?"

"No, but I can sense your frustration. Don't try to impress me. I'm not your friend; I am your analyst. Just tell me about yourself, and don't worry about what I may or may not think," he said neutrally.

"You mean you don't like me?"

"I mean we have a professional relationship. You can tell me if you kick dogs or pick flowers, whatever is important to *you*."

"I don't kick dogs … Opera is important to me, very important." I looked toward the ground. "I play it and it helps me … forget when I need to … forget." The sentence took a wrong turn; it seemed all roads were leading to the one thing I was avoiding: that ritual. "Forget? Did I say that?" I flashed a smile, kicking myself for saying 'forget'. "What I meant is Gary helps me to live, to feel."

"Who's Gary?"

"What?"

"Who's Gary?"

"I don't know any Gary. I said opera. Opera helps me to feel—"

"Who's Gary?"

"Honestly, opera. That's what I meant."

"And Gary?" he asked. I couldn't think how to answer. He ominously wrote something down. We simply could not talk about Gary; there had to be limits. He was looking at his notes. "You need opera in order to feel?"

That sounded just as bad as 'forget'. "Yes, and it keeps me from—" I suddenly stopped myself.

"Keeps you from what?"

"Keeps me ... from doing things," I added sheepishly. Dr. Wire leaned forward; it was upsetting and intimidating. I could feel every muscle tightening inside of me. "You know ... things?"

"Like doing the dishes?" he asked.

I laughed uncontrollably for a minute. Dr. Wire remained impassive. He leaned back in his chair, penetrating eyes drilling into mine. Then it just flew out of my mouth.

"I do things to myself ... bad things ... like ..." I was horrified to my core that I dared to say this. I had to think of something, anything. I decided to grope for the worst thing I'd ever done, anything but describing my ritual. "Suicide," I shouted to no reaction. "I tried to commit suicide, three times," I whispered.

"You think of suicide often?"

"Uh, well ... I do," I confessed sheepishly.

"Any plans?"

"Not anymore."

"But you did?"

"When I was fifteen." I began to feel sick to my stomach.

"Still thinking about it?"

"Not really."

"Want to talk about it?"

"I thought we weren't supposed to talk about it?"

"Go on."

I didn't know how to get out of this conversation alive.

"Well, let's see," I looked at Dr. Wire. I took a

deep breath. Feeling like I was plunging into the depths, I started. "I was … really upset … with life, you know; I was—miserable. You see, back then I looked at my coming life at school like a child in a theater before the curtain is raised, sitting there in anticipation, in high spirits, and eagerly waiting for the play to begin. Until it starts. Then, I realized I was living like an innocent prisoner, having to watch my unhappy life in action."

Dr. Wire frowned. "Oh, very good, very good, indeed … Tell me who was that?"

"Huh?"

"Who wrote it?"

"Schopenhauer," I muttered. Dr. Wire leaned forward.

"Sorry, I didn't hear you; could you speak up?" asked the Grand Inquisitor.

"Schopenhauer!"

The doctor arrogantly curled his lips, catching me red-handed.

"Opera allows me to feel things like a fantasy, but they are real to me."

"I believe the subject was suicide, not opera. Would you rather talk about opera?"

As a matter of fact, I did. I fidgeted tensely in my chair, as he reclined back and stared his stare.

"Okay, it was this, Nietzsche— he hated pity, but I was wallowing in it … so I tried to kill myself."

His impassive "uh huh" wasn't the response I was expecting.

"I did; I tried to commit suicide," I added defensively.

"Oh, I am sure you did."

"I did. I swallowed pills."

"Of course. What did you take?"

"Some of my mother's prescriptions. Something else I read that could dissolve your liver. Some other random stuff in the medicine chest." My right leg started to shake involuntarily.

"How many pills did you take?"

"I don't remember … a handful of 'em."

"Did you get sick?"

"No." I bristled in shame.

"No?"

"No."

"I see. That must have felt awful, trying to kill yourself?"

"I was afraid of being discovered."

"Really? And were you discovered?"

"Yes—sort of."

"Sort of?"

I realized I was lying. I took a deep breath. "Well, I wasn't, actually. My parents came home. I was interrupted. There was room to ignore it, so they did—I guess."

"How does *that* make you feel?"

"Worthless."

"Worthless?"

"It didn't matter." How did I become tangled up in this conversation? I wanted to say, *Never mind.*

Instead I just blurted out, "Everyone wants me dead."

"Everyone? Everyone wants you dead?" Now it was his turn to wait for an unforthcoming answer. "Who then? Who, precisely, besides you?"

"Isn't it obvious? ... Do I have to list them all? ... Uh ... my parents, for starters ... my brother ... Brian Germaine ... Mrs. Bradford ... well, half the school ... I am sounding like an idiot. They didn't want to kill me; but I think everyone would prefer it if I wasn't around," and then I mumbled, 'You probably wish I wasn't around."

"Oh, you like dramatic statements," he retorted.

I felt cornered, unable to speak.

"You said you tried to commit suicide three times. What about the second time?"

"The second time, what?—Oh, you mean the suicides. The second time I swallowed pills—"

"We've done that one already."

"That other time? Oh, yeah, the pills were the second. I cut my wrists the first time—I didn't do a very good job."

"You did an excellent job; you're still here."

"Oh, right."

"What did you do actually?"

"I took out a razor blade and cut myself ... wrists."

"How did you feel doing that?"

"I felt proud, like I wasn't afraid ... let's see ... it bled a lot. I jumped into the bathtub, but it had stopped bleeding. I didn't cut deep enough ... my parents came home so I couldn't try again. I turned on the shower ... there was a Band-Aid and no questions." I felt a torrent of shame.

"You're looking sad."

"I turn on opera when I can't deal with these things," I said, afraid I was going to cry.

"Slashing your wrist, swallowing pills, you said you tried to commit suicide three times. What was the third?"

"Oh, that," I squirmed and swallowed. "That never happened, it was just ... a plan ... gone wrong. You see, I can't do anything right. I can't even do away with myself without screwing things up. My mom, she loves me very much, because she is constantly worrying about me."

"She worries about you."

"Well, at least it is attention. She shows she cares. Most kids I know, their parents don't worry or think about them at all." I began to feel something was dreadfully wrong.

"Tell me more about your family."

"There is not much to tell." Another flash of exasperation from Dr. Wire. "Okay, okay, I have a mother—she doesn't want me dead. I am sure she loves me—so does my dad and my brother ... I really have a normal family. Really, I do. It's really my fault I am so ... screwed up. *That's* why I am here." I felt relieved, like I was back on firm ground.

"I see. Who exactly are these people, since they love you so much."

I didn't particularly care for the tone in his voice.

"My mom is a political activist, my father is a construction electrician, and my brother is an asshole." I flashed a smile. Dr. Wire was not amused.

"They love me, they really do. My mom really encourages me. She … does." Dr. Wire gave no smile or recognition of a great mother. I panicked. "She's a great motivator that way. My dad is … very principled." Dr. Wire still sat poker-faced. "I guess you wonder what I mean by that?" That remark got a half nod from Dr. Wire. "He really does whatever it is he wants—my dad," I felt an edge in my voice and stopped.

I tried to describe my great parents, yet what leapt out of my mouth made them sound like ogres. "I am not saying it right. I can do whatever I want. I don't live in any kind of fascist, parental dictatorship. They *trust* me to do whatever it is I need to do. My parents are very liberal," I pleaded.

"That's why they constantly worry about you?"

"No, you misunderstand." I was beginning to get out of breath again. I had to fight back another urge to cry. "They are way more hip than any of our neighbors. They are the coolest ones in the entire school. The rest of the parents are square, always telling their kids what to do. I have the coolest parents."

"Really? You said you read the confidentiality statement, right?"

In response to my spilling my guts he only asks a

trivial and administrative question. "Yeah, I did, but I don't remember everything in it."

"Let me remind you. What you say won't go beyond this office." Dr. Wire gestured with his pen like a weapon. I almost ducked. "Your parents will never hear of it. Now, try again."

I knew exactly what he was asking for and my heart ached. "I am afraid." I felt my eyes getting itchy. I wondered what was happening. I didn't know what I was about to say, but it had to be awful.

"Try," he offered softly.

"But you don't understand. It makes me feel ashamed just to think this, so how can I say it?" I laughed, part hoping for mercy, part wondering who was controlling what came out of my mouth. My cheek tickled from a tear's betrayal from my right eye. Then my left eye swelled with moisture. I wiped my right cheek and left eye. Stuffy nose. Embarrassed.

I looked away to the window, the glare now gone. I felt nauseated. Still, I moved my mouth and spoke.

"My mom loves to talk to me ... when I am interested in her work." I swallowed. "She loves me ... She gives blanket praise to everything I do ... At first it made me feel good to have someone cheering on the sidelines ... but after a while, I saw if I just drew ... if I just drew crap or wrote garbage, I got the same response as when I ... so I stopped trying. Schoolwork was perfect, but I couldn't do anything else right ... nothing ..." I hated Dr. Wire for making me say this. "Nothing right, from trimming the shrubs to tying my shoelaces. Nothing. Always something wrong. Is that enough?" I asked, feeling bare naked before this mild-mannered evil interrogator.

Dr. Wire kept on looking at me. I felt awkward and embarrassed. I knew I went too far.

"My family ..." I noticed there was a subtle echo in the room. "My dad ... works. He takes naps. He watches TV. I am not there ... This isn't what I really mean, you know. Sometimes I feel so ashamed. They love me so much, and I can't accept it. I have to want more. I gotta be so fucking self-centered, like a baby— that's what they call me—oh, sorry, excuse me ... I mean, they worry about me so much, and I do so little in return." Then I realized something as if I was just putting two and two together for the first time. The anger welled up inside, overwhelming and scary. I exploded: "They worry and worry because they think I can't do a solitary fucking thing! Happy now? Is that making any sense?"

"Perfectly."

"It doesn't! They love me ... They worry about me ... They really do. I'll send 'em to an early grave, but they'll deserve—" Suddenly I thought of something funny. "I guess I have anger issues." I started to laugh.

"I am sure you do." Dr. Wire even smiled. He scribbled in his notebook. He seemed more intent on writing than listening to me as he kept up his questions.

"I am not clear where your father is in all this."

"Do I have to tell you?" The guilty lump in my throat came back to me.

"You don't *have* to do anything. But you made it this far."

I sighed deeply. Why did I trust this bastard with all this information? I wondered if super-subconsciously I was hoping he'd report this all to the police.

"My father never talks to me. He hates me, he really does. For a good reason. It was a stupid accident, long ago. My dad lied to a doctor. He said someone else did it. The doctor then thought it was a black man—but I said a white guy—I didn't think it was fair to attack blacks for something he'd done. I saw the fear in my father's face as if I was going to tattle on my own father. I didn't. But maybe the doctor knew—Dad separated my shoulder. I think I was eight—no, seven. It was during the riots. And he covered up doing it. That's all it was. But the lie made it impossible for us to talk about anything. Ever since then he doesn't care … about me. Oh, he worries alright, I know that—like everyone else. But we don't talk, unless it is about sports, which I hate. I didn't even realize I hated sports until I found myself watching a hockey game without my dad, and I just wondered, *why am I watching this stupid game?* It's stupid; they fight like children; it's violent and pointless, though I suppose all sports are pointless. But they are important to my dad. Okay. Okay. Gary hurt me once, big deal."

"Gary? Who is this Gary?" Dr. Wire finally looked up from his notepad looking at me like a police interrogator.

"Huh?"

"You said Gary again. Gary hurt you or your father? ... What exactly happened?"

"My father. I don't even know anyone named fucking Gary. Stop bringing him up." I tried to look away from the doctor's locked gaze. "Stupidest thing I ever heard of. I should admit, he didn't mean it—my father!—he's not violent but he separated my shoulder. I was running away, and it was during the riots so he was afraid for me. I ran. He was really concerned for me, not angry or anything like that. I ran away and he grabbed my arm ... and separated it. He feels really guilty about it, I'm sure." I wished Dr. Wire stopped looking at me like a police interrogator.

"You feel guilty?"

"It was an accident."

"Who's Gary?"

"Sorry?"

"Who's Gary? Is that your father's first name? You mentioned Gary when you speak of your father."

"Oh, that Gary. Did I say his name? Silly. He was just a friend of Steven's, my older brother."

"Is he? You remember him now?"

"Yes."

"A father figure?"

"I am sorry?"

"Is he, this Gary, a father figure?"

"Definitely not! Of course not. I said his name? Well, that was just a slip." I forced a laugh. Dr. Wire finally went back to his notebook, scribbling furiously. I felt like I was in trouble. I felt like I had to say something positive about my parents before he stopped writing. "What I meant to say is my mother is interested in me as long as I am interested *in her politics*—which I am."

"Sports and politics," Dr. Wire said as he scribbled.

I couldn't stand it anymore; I had to vindicate my parents.

"But they are not the problem, absolutely not. The only really bad thing about my family is my brother. My brother is just an asshole. He fights with me about anything and beats me up. Really beats me up. That's right. Really. He's eight years older than me, so it's completely unfair. He really fights with me … fists and kicking … he's stronger, bigger than me. *He's* the asshole."

"Mom and Dad ever break up one of these fights?"

"Oh, come on. Be reasonable. They're very busy … don't make me say this …"

Much to my surprise, he didn't.

"How often do you go home?" he asked, as if he doubted I even had parents.

"Almost every weekend … I have to. They pay the bills, my tuition. Besides, they …"

"Worry about you?"

"Yes, they worry about me." I began to suspect

worrying wasn't all it was cracked up to be.

"So tell me a little about your studies. What are you majoring in?"

"I am studying political—I am studying political science," I said, adding with a sense of triumph, "and I have my mother to thank for that."

"You like political science?" Dr. Wire asked.

"Of course; it's fighting the good fight ... I also have a minor in theater." There was that disturbing stare of his. "I signed up for theater just this last week. It's not that important to me. I am hoping to go into politics. I really want to fight for social justice. Most politicians these days are all a bunch of horse traders ... my mom would say. But to be able to fight for what's right, that seems great, and theater helps; it helps with public speaking."

"And dramatics."

"I said theater is not that important. You have to stand up and you have to be able to command an audience; that's why this is really a perfect major combination."

"Worry, pity, self-righteousness—that's quite a cocktail you've got going."

Dr. Wire pulled the rug out from under me. I thought he was on my side, judging my mother too harshly. Instead, he was judging me too harshly.

"I meant politics for the common good, not self-righteousness. I am talking about things like, you know, public policy." I was flailing about now. I was losing my audience. "Righting what's wrong, not what

I think is wrong … Objectively speaking, there is so much wrong in this world, I mean with all the human suffering, poverty, civil rights, social injustice … Come on, this can't be new to you? … My mother is into civil rights, and I picked it up from her, *carrying the torch* … this passion for doing what is right. No one really cares about poverty anymore, that's why this country must move to the left of Jimmy Carter this election."

"You want the spotlight, don't you?"

"It's not like that! It's not like that at all." I squirmed in my chair. "It's not like I am studying political science to preach to the masses or studying theater because I want be some kind of star celebrity."

"I'm not so sure of that," Dr. Wire said quickly.

"No?" I was almost begging. "You don't seem to have a very high opinion of me. You don't believe me."

"One last question, Jamie. Who's Gary?"

"I told you already my brother's friend."

"Did he ever do anything to you?" he asked to my horror. I was stunned.

"Uh … no."

"Ever do anything with him?"

He looked at me; I knew he was looking right through me. It was the worst feeling I ever felt. Because he saw things I could not. There was an awkward silence. I felt a disgusting rush of hostility. I swallowed with great difficulty.

"Never … nothing I can remember. I just had a plain boring childhood."

"Apparently, the two enemies of human happiness are pain and boredom," he pontificated wryly. "What are you thinking right now?"

"I know that's Schopenhauer. I don't think you believe I am any good. I'm a pseudo-intellectual. I'd be a judgmental politician or a terrible actor."

"Oh, I think you are a great actor, Jamie. You put on a real virtuoso performance. I can hardly wait until next week for act two." He swirled around in his chair, dismissively ending our session.

Chapter 31: Tryouts

"These shoes are black. Well, they can do, anyway, until I get another pair. Maybe they'll get me down to Sidcup tomorrow. If I can get there, I'll be able to sort myself out—"

I looked up from my script and tensed. I was shocked to see this sweet female student. She was radiant with friendliness. She was one of those people I just wanted to know. She was dressed like it was still the Sixties, she wore no makeup on her cheery, freckled face. I knew her from one of my classes. She was always with her group of friends.

"Don't let me stop you." She smiled. "You sound great! You had me nearly frightened, 'til I realized you were rehearsing. Go on."

"I can't." I blushed.

"If you are going to perform, you can't be scared. You were great." She smiled at me again.

I froze. I don't think anyone had ever smiled at me before like she did. She seemed to have the attentions of many guys. *How could she want me*, I wondered. I suddenly felt naked. "It wasn't perfect ... You r-really l-liked it?" I stammered.

She was one of a group of students who always

studied together. They were very cool and exotic. We shared many of the same classes that semester. They were older than I was, as I tended to take more advanced graduate courses instead of the childish introductory or survey courses intended for lower classmen.

"You were doing fine," she said.

I was smitten, I hoped this was the longed for sign that I was normal. I had worked so hard to eradicate perverse ideas from my head. Had that finally paid off?

"Thank you … Dara, right? I've seen you a lot in class. I'm Jamie Goldberg."

"I know. I've had my eye on you too." She smiled again. My heart started pounding ecstatic confusion. "Right. Mind if I join you?"

Never was a sentence so loaded with multiple meanings before. I couldn't untangle them but didn't care either. "Sure, I'll just study now. I am not afraid, really, but I first want to know the part well before I show it to you. Truth is, I never tried anything like this before—auditioning, I mean."

"Well, it was good, and a convincing British accent too. What is it?"

"It's a play called *The Caretaker*. It's about an old man who connives his way into someone's house and then tries to take it over. It's strange but really quite moving."

"Moving?"

"Well, it is about hopelessness, striving to make

something of yourself and failing."

"I hope you get the part, Jamie."

She sat down.

"Thanks."

I sat down at the other end of the room from where she was seated. She smiled and laughed good-heartedly at me.

"I won't bite."

Red-faced, I got up, crossed over to her side of the room, and not daring to be right next to her, sat one seat away.

She still looked at me.

I plunged into a sentence like my life depended on it. "I know you won't bite, but I might."

"Then you better sit there; we have to study."

I was thrilled. I had successfully flirted with someone. Well, I flirted before, with Julie, but that didn't count because she wasn't a real person.

Dara took her books from her bag. She looked so radiant, voluptuous, and friendly. I marveled how, without makeup, our faces were more alike than different. She didn't seem to mind my peeking at her, either. I suddenly felt happy. I heard a voice inside me even say, *Oh my goodness, I can be normal. I like her.*

"You finished that Nietzsche thing?" she asked. "It was a real bitch, wasn't it?"

"Uh ... yeah." I squirmed, unsure how much of my love for Nietzsche I should reveal to her. "He's a difficult read ... but I really like him. I actually read the book in high school." I figured one of his snappy quotes might help. "There is one quote in particular: 'That which doesn't kill me makes me stronger.'"

"Huh?"

"'That which doesn't kill me makes me stronger.' That's been a life preserver for me." Dr. Wire would say that was one of my "dramatic statements". "I mean it's been helpful to me in times of stress."

"Has it? 'That which doesn't kill me ...'"

"'Makes me stronger.'" I felt a shudder, remembering a tablespoon of my blood in a bathtub. "It means anything you go through that doesn't kill you makes you a stronger person; it's another thing you learned, another thing you survived; it's a successful day further along your journey. It also means even if you screw up, there's still a good side; it will still make you stronger."

She nodded in assent. "That is beautiful. Maybe you would like to study together sometime with my study group?"

"Sure, I'd love that," I said, suddenly feeling an urgent need to cuddle her. Not just a need, a sneaking suspicion that I could do this and she wouldn't mind. I never cuddled anyone before. But she returned to her book. I looked hard at her. *Would she mind my cuddling her?* I wondered I found myself staring at my book, as if I were reading it. I didn't know what to do or how to initiate a cuddle or a kiss, nor how well I had to know her before I could dare try such a bold thing. Then my eyes shot up in outrageous disbelief.

"Hello, Dara."

It's not fair! I cried to myself. There he was. But I wasn't ready. Worse, I was guiltily thinking about someone else besides him.

"Hi, Casper. What you been up to?" asked Dara.

Casper walked up to Dara and gave her a short kiss on her forehead. Thank God I did not try anything with either of them; they must be a couple.

"Studying as usual. Casper, this is my friend, Jamie."

Dara called me her 'friend', and my heart began to pound. But the overwhelming power of Casper's smile now aimed at me. At last I got to freely look at Casper's gorgeous body. I was also finally free to stare directly at him as he spoke to me.

"Hi, Jamie. Good to finally meet you." Finally! My heart was about to burst.

"Oh do you two know each other?" Dara asked. I shrunk; what was he going to say? *"Yes that's the pervert who greedily ogles my body every chance he gets. He even got in trouble with the English department just to spy on me."*

"Well, you look familiar," he offered in a mild tone.

He looked at me with those eyes, and I saw his lovely etched lips give me the most unambiguous smile I had ever seen. Let there be no doubt about it: It was a smile. And he had a girlfriend, so I could rejoice. This would be a *pure* friendship! All I had to do now was say 'hi' back.

He held eye contact. I could not help it. I smiled too, a broad uncontrollable grin. It must have seemed to him an idiotic leer, which as long as I was pure, didn't matter.

"Hi," I finally managed.

"Haven't we met before?" he asked.

Luckily I didn't have to worry about turning red; my face was already burning hot.

"I-I-I d-don't know …" I had to say something to deflect the conversation. I saw him holding his book. "Oh, I see you are reading Harol—Henry Miller."

"I am?"

I looked closer. He was holding a different book.

"Oh, I thought you were. I have a copy of *Tropic of Cancer*—you know, the one he wrote in 1934—anyway, it has a book cover just like your …" I glanced at the book. "Just like your calculus textbook."

"Odd you should say that; I was reading *Tropic of Cancer*. Dara, you remember that one; it was really trying to be shocking but wasn't shocking."

"Oh, yeah, you read that lame line about the lesbian." She laughed. I was almost sure they were a couple.

"Well, still," I rambled in automatic mode. I had prepared too hard for this moment. "Even its legal significance aside, the book did break new literary ground. It ignored conventional divisions between fact and fiction and autobiography and invention. I think he's great, for what he is. I mean, I could understand when he says, 'I need to ponder my shame in seclusion without conversation, with only the music of my heart for company.'"

Dara exchanged quizzical glances with Casper.

"That's heavy stuff," said Dara.

Maybe I shouldn't have said that. I was wondering what more I had done wrong. I flirted with one, didn't want to disappoint the other. I felt trapped. So I did the only sensible thing. I panicked.

"Oh, my God!" I leapt up from my chair. "I totally forgot about it. Sorry, excuse me. I have to go. How could I forget—oh, time; oh, wow. Great meeting you, Casper Tyres."

I ran out of the room as if I had left a teakettle burning in a non-existent stove. In the hallway I could barely hear him say, "How did he know my last name?"

I stopped halfway down the hall. I'd forgotten my copy of *The Caretaker*. But I did not dare go back. Instead, I crouched down behind a trash container in a side corridor. I don't know how long I crouched there, but my knees started to ache. Finally, I heard their voices pass. I waited a moment, then ran back to the study room. I grabbed my copy of *The Caretaker* off the podium. I realized I was alone. I looked around, then opened the book again.

"These shoes are black. Well, they can do, anyway, until I get another pair. Maybe they'll get me down to Sidcup tomorrow ..."

Chapter 32: Endgame

"That's why everyone should read *The Brethren*. The Supreme Court is really a microcosom of America, according to my mom. But nobody really sees it—at least no one my own age." I still hoped for some kind of reaction from Dr. Wire, but by this last visit I knew none was coming beyond the sort of thing he would fire away next.

"How does that make you feel?"

I heaved a deep sigh.

"I don't know. Politics is more important, you see, I am afraid I joined the theater for the wrong reasons."

"What? What are the wrong reasons, Jamie?" Dr. Wire's obnoxiously clean talcum powder odor wafted through the room. I hated that question. I regretted bringing it up.

"I joined the theater ... to meet ... someone. But I really like the theater. There is one student, though, one of those macho types, Ben Geln. He seems to have taken an instant dislike to me. He's just a bully. He teases me; ridicules me in front of the class for no reason. Do you think I should complain to the teacher?"

"You joined theater to meet someone who doesn't

like you?"

"Yes." I fidgeted.

"I find that hard to believe." Dr. Wire raised his head staring down at me while his beard pointed at me like a weapon.

"But I did."

"Really?"

"Not Ben—and I see what you mean, but maybe not entirely." I backed down. I was reticent to mention my trivial obsession with Casper, which could not possibly interest Dr. Wire.

"What else *could* have motivated you?"

"I don't know."

"No, I suppose you don't. We're running out of time. I need to know more about this Gary you keep mentioning."

"There's nothing to really say."

"All right, then." Dr. Wire put down his notebook in his lap. "Right now, in this moment, how do you feel about yourself?"

"I'm a … I'm a …" I couldn't finish the sentence. I tried again with equal results. "What is the matter with me?"

"What were you going to say, Jamie?" he asked in a voice pregnant with hostility.

He even moved to the edge of his chair, which I had never seen him do before. His eyes seemed to be popping out of their sockets, as if demanding total access to my brain. I didn't know what to say. I was trapped, cornered, as if I had at last landed into the trap he had set three weeks ago.

"Just say it," he ordered. His notebook fell to the floor but he made no attempt to pick it up. His stare, his entire form, was riveted at me. He was clearly telling me, *You're not leaving here until you tell me, you coward!*

Totally ashamed, I said, "I joined the theater ... No, I'll tell you. I'm ... an asshole."

"What? A what? I could hardly hear you," he said, a lion jumping on his prey.

"I am an asshole," I shouted belligerently. "I thought theater would make me better or at least help me cover it up."

"You joined the theater because you're an *asshole?*"

"I want to meet Casper, but I am making an ass out myself, aren't I? I am just a jerk who can't do anything right, aren't I?"

"Meet who? Casper?" There it was: the verbal gut punch.

"No one!" I was almost in tears and in a panic I couldn't control.

"Right. Now to your question ..." He was back to all calmness. He picked up his notebook off the floor. He couldn't reach his pen so I shot out of my chair and tried to pick it up. I accidentally knocked it away. I chased after it, picked it up, and handed the pen back to him. I plopped back down in my chair, hoping he'd forget the whole thing. Dr. Wire sat back in his chair grinning. "You tell me now what your problem is."

"I don't know!" I was suddenly crying uncontrollably.

"You tell me right now what your problem is," he demanded.

"Sitting here with you," I blurted.

Even Dr. Wire chuckled at that. If I thought I was off the hook, I was sorely disappointed. With a deadly serious voice, Dr. Wire delivered, "You *are* an asshole, aren't you?"

"No," I answered defensively.

"You just said so yourself," said Mr. Evil. "Jamie, you have to tell me now what you believe your problem to be."

I said nothing.

"Why did you come here?"

I thought I had shaken off that question a long time ago. No thoughts could come to me. My brain was on hold.

Then, in a flash, I knew the answer, a way out. "Vexation management!"

"Jamie, you have to tell me now what you think your problem is," Dr. Wire repeated.

"Vex ...?" It didn't work. I was cornered prey; death was imminent. Finally I opened my mouth with the only thing that would come out. "I am an asshole? ... Can't you just tell me?"

Dr. Wire looked at his watch and relented. "Okay. It is obvious what your problem is, Jamie. Isn't it?"

"Oh, thank goodness; what is it?"

"You hate yourself."

Check.

I thought I was prepared for the worst: I was schizophrenic. I needed to be committed. I had to take anti-psychotic pills. Electroshock treatments. I was ready for all of that dramatic stuff. I was not ready for something that was just plain disgusting: hating myself. My heart was pierced. Emotional blood spilled all over the floor.

"I what?" I repulsed.

"It is obvious you hate yourself," he continued with a hard, dry certainty. "You just called yourself an asshole; that doesn't sound like someone who loves himself, does it?"

"No."

"Do you love yourself?"

"No!" I was surprised how vehemently I could say that.

"You project all your problems on other people. You can never talk about your feelings to save your soul, but you love drama. You hide yourself in all your intellectualism as your excuse to be alive."

"Aren't you afraid I'll kill myself?" I asked, begging for mercy.

"You won't kill yourself, Jamie; you're enjoying yourself far too much to do anything as drastic as all that, don't you think?"

Enjoying? I was silent. Was he daring me to kill myself? I felt stripped of all self-worth, but Dr. Wire was not finished.

"Every time you are called on to say something honest, you are silent."

I was naked and defenseless.

Realizing I was being silent, I finally protested, "I am not." That didn't seem particularly convincing to anyone, so I tried again. "Sometimes things are just difficult."

"Oh, come on; it is obvious, James. Your mother is always wrong. Your father is wrong. Your professors, students, whoever this Ben Geln is or this Casper or Gary—it is always someone other than you."

Ashamed, I realized nothing had escaped his notice. This interview became very dangerous and I had no exit.

"Not that your mother and father are any great shakes. Jesus, look at the lengths you went through just to get their attention. But it's *you* who are holding on to a dysfunctional family because they reassure you of how odious you are."

My heart sank into an abyss. "I am holding on to? Dysfunctional?" I was too stunned to process anything more. "But dysfunctional? They're perfect if you see how most—" From his look of contempt, he wasn't buying it. "Really, they are! Compare them to anyone else. Dysfunctional? I haven't said that! ... They don't hate me."

"James, *you* hate yourself. You can't escape that fact or pawn it off on your family, why Davies goes to Sidcup, or the sociopolitical economy of Russia. It's you and only *you*." Dr. Wire paused. "Let me put it this way, in words you can appreciate: all the high-minded esoterica will not endow your life with value as long as you hate yourself."

Checkmate. Death.

Dr. Wire was certain and confident. It was not an argument; it was a statement of fact, the guilty verdict

I feared the most, even though I was completely unprepared for it.

"What can I do?" I surrendered.

"I am not going to lie to you and say you aren't so bad; that you should be yourself and be the great person you truly are. I can't. I don't know you. I only know what I see, and I see your self-hatred."

Stop saying that! I thought. "Why?" I pleaded.

"You think you're so great; don't you, James? You have such an unrealistic, overinflated view of yourself you can't possibly hope to live up to. You think you are so smart. But you have to *prove it* in this world with acts, not platitudes. Stop hiding. Let us see who you really are." To make sure I got the message, he twisted the knife in my back. "Take all the senior or graduate courses you want, but they won't hide who you really are, whoever that is. We're out of time!" He scoffed. He swirled his chair around.

And that was it.

I stood up, dejected. I turned to leave the room. I took a miserable step away and turned around. There he was hunched over a notepad, writing about the self-hating chump for his colleagues to laugh about. Then I gazed up at the clock behind my chair; the hour was *not* up. All the pent-up anger, the disappointment in this "therapy"; it all finally welled up inside. I faced Dr. Wire and exploded.

"YOU FUCKING BASTARD, I JUST WANT TO BE CURED!" The viciousness in my screaming voice surprised even me. Dr. Wire swirled back around. I stiffened—immediately regretful tears streaming down my cheeks but not daring to let myself cry again in front of him of all people. Dr. Wire was surprised, but almost smiling, not at all angry at me. "I am sorry," I moaned.

"No. Thank you, Jamie. That is the most honest and decent thing you said in all these sessions. Think about that. Who can cure you of being yourself?"

I was condemned: a death sentence.

He looked at me as if I were a moldy piece of meat.

"One thing I will say …" He hesitated. He took off his glasses. "Whoever you are, you have nothing to be cured of." I suddenly noticed the tired and worn look in his eyes. "You are *not* a disease."

At last, the redeeming message I so desperately needed to hear. Until I heard it, I didn't know how starved I was for this simple judgment. *You are not a disease.*

"No one's ever told me that before." I sat back down, crying into my hands. Dr. Wire did not say anything. After a while I stopped. Dr. Wire sat in the exact same position with the same cool expression as when I started crying. "Dr. Wire, I am sorry I called you a bastard; I didn't mean it." I didn't dare add what I wanted to add, *I am the bastard, not you.* Instead of that I just said, "Thank you." Gratitude to him seemed the ultimate humiliation.

"Pleasure was all mine." He smiled. "Oh, and see my secretary on your way out; she has some Kleenex and something else for you."

"One more question, sir?" I asked.

"Yes?"

"Did I make it into the book … the one you're writing?"

"Good luck, Jamie," and he swirled back around.

Walking like a zombie, my head was spinning. I was so sure Dr. Wire hated me. He didn't hate me; I hated me. I mulled the most important words in my life out loud: "I am not a disease."

Then came the frightening question: *If I am not a disease, well then, who am I?*

Chapter 33: Chasing Ghosts

The secretary gave me a student psychology clinic referral in case I wanted to continue to see someone—the last thing I wanted to do.

I wandered out of his office. Suicide seemed the only path left. Until I remembered, *You are not a disease.* And I realized, the path wasn't suicide, but the death of something else inside of me—or at least the desire to kill something inside of me. At any rate, my life would no longer be the same.

Walking outside of Dr. Wire's office, the sun was shining as if God was celebrating with me. I felt both euphoric and melancholy. Euphoric because I had discovered, for the first time, what was really troubling me. Melancholy because the solution I came up with did not sit well with me: going over to the other side, after fighting it for so long. Do I admit defeat? In my heart—deep in my soul—the words resounded: You are not a disease. But did Dr. Wire realize that if that was true, I was one of *them.* No, he did not know this, I concluded. Accepting the unacceptable. I couldn't do that. The wretched picture of my cousin Harold came before me. No, it was not an option. Rejecting that, I truly understood why I wanted to commit suicide: I hated myself. The underlying reason was irrelevant; all I needed to do was strive to stop hating myself and just accept myself and my struggles.

I walked around the grassy campus. Just as a scant block beyond the trees and grass was a riot-torn city, I walked in the hope of removing my self-hatred without exposing my riot-torn soul.

In the weeks that followed, I made several attempts to swallow my self-hatred and act on being better. *How did I get from a cloak of obfuscation to the blinding clarity around what an unlovable jerk I have been*—but wait, that's name calling, hating yourself. *Will you fucking stop it!* But that was self-hatred too. *Don't do that, how can you be so fucking stupid?* Oh, that was self-hatred as well. The problem was trickier than I realized. How could I stop hating myself? Every attempt to stop it produced a counterproductive effect. Self-hatred stalked me at every corner, yet this self-hatred never seemed to really come out in the open.

I don't quite remember, but I somehow boarded a bus home. Then in a flash, I felt inspired. I realized how to get rid of the self-hatred at once. I felt like an idiot for not thinking of it earlier. At once, it was like hearing my father's voice in a bizarre tirade: How much of a moron could I be anyway? The answer was right in front of my stupid goddamn eyes, if only I would open them! I wanted to cure myself and atone for how bad I had been. The quicker I could get my sorry ass to my parents' house, the sooner I could start with a clean slate.

I ran from the bus. After several blocks, I was out of breath, but I forced myself to go faster and faster, almost willfully torturing my out-of-shape body, urging myself on, *"Get home, asshole!"* Inside, panting and exhausted, I yelled, "Anybody home?"

No one answered.

I ran downstairs, almost tripping all the way down. I caught myself on the handrail. I ran to the wood shop area of the basement. I tugged off my belt. Without any pretense of delusion, I pulled down my pants, and kneeling, started the ritual, savagely beating myself, this time scolding, "Stop hating yourself. Stop hating yourself!" I repeated it louder and whipped myself harder, mindlessly soaking up the pain to purify my soul. As I was whipping myself, I saw a huge blade hanging from the wall and knew I needed something more painful and vicious. I was getting up to my feet, walking to the wall all the while whipping myself. I walked closer to the sawtoothed blade when I heard my own vicious voice saying over the cracks of the belt, "Stop hating yourself, you piece of shit!" I grabbed the blade and got ready to assault myself with it. I stopped.

Panting like a lunatic, at once I recognized the inner voice of my father stripped of everything but pure unadulterated hatred and aimed at myself. The voice I was used to hearing curse the Detroit Pistons, bombarding me. I stared at the saw-like blade now in my hand; what was I about to do? I looked down at the other hand holding my belt.

I saw what self-hatred was doing to me.

The belt dropped to the floor. I quietly put the blade back on the wall. I felt the throbbing pain on my back and ass cheeks. In a moment of self-revulsion, I wondered, "Why are you doing this to me?" I had caught myself *in flagrante delicto*. I felt grotesquely obscene, compounding the self-hatred. Layer upon layer, thread upon thread, I was entangled in a layered web of disgust and revulsion. I sunk to the ground in shock, unable to move or think. There was no forgetting, no clean slate, and seemingly no end to the self-perpetuating horror. I could not stop it. Then I shouted, at the top of my lungs, "NO!" as I ejaculated.

I was kneeling on the cold floor. I coldly reviewed everything I just did to myself—the verbal abuse, the whipping, even the times before, the ones I thought I had blotted out forever. My pants were still humiliatingly down around my knees. Cum dripping on them. My knees hurt. I prostrated myself on the cold concrete floor. At once I knew and confessed to myself that I was some dark kind of pervert, worse than anything anyone could ever imagine. I had to end it and end it quickly. That blade on the wall seemed the best course of action. Then, the thought of suicide revolted me. In frustration, I yelled, "Help me, damn it! God, do you hear me? I am not a fucking disease!" And then in a whimper, "I am not an 'asshole' either."

Awkward silence. I shrugged my shoulders, embarrassed. I asked myself three questions: *Who are you, James Macaiah Goldberg? Do you dare to find out? Can I forgive me for being me?*

I picked myself up off the cold basement floor.

I answered those questions out loud. "I'll try."

I looked at my hands, covered with dirt from the basement floor. I pulled up my pants. I looked down on the ground. I saw my belt on the floor and picked it up. *I'll try.* I put the belt back on. I was searching in a pile of laundry for a towel and a dark shirt to put on, then I laughed. *Take your victories where you find them,* I thought as I realized that since there was no blood, I didn't need a dark shirt or a towel.

Spiritually exhausted, I walked upstairs to the bathroom. I washed my hands and face. I looked up in the bathroom mirror. I saw my face. I hated looking at it. I almost wanted to run back down the stairs. *Self-hatred,* I reminded myself.

I closed my eyes. I tried to empty my brain of all thought. I took a swallow of built-up emotion. Then staring at the ground, "One, two, three, four, five … six … seven … eight … nine … ten." I repeated to myself many times, "I can like myself." Then I opened my eyes and looked at my face again. For the first time I objectively looked at myself. I saw my face staring at me in the mirror. A nose. I looked at my nose. I touched it. I looked at my ears. *Ears look weird just sticking out of a head,* I thought. I caressed my cheek. It felt surprisingly okay. I looked at myself from different angles. That is a cute nose. Those are sensitive eyes. Other people have larger ears than I do. I have a nice full head of hair; a washing would help it a bit. My shirt needed ironing. *I don't look so bad at all ... at the right angle, kind of cute. Could I like myself? Casper would have to be dealt with. I'll try.*

I felt a moment of relief. Then I realized that this wasn't the end of the journey; it was only the beginning.

Chapter 34: New Ways

On the somber bus back to school, the pain was still fresh on my back and my soul. I realized whatever game I was playing, it was over. I made a huge concession to personal charity and admitted I was lonely. I couldn't do this life alone; I wanted—needed—a friend. That seemed a safe goal. Anyone can be a friend. I looked, and suddenly noticed the people on the bus. In the front, there was an old lady with a bag of groceries. She looked old and haggard. A sympathy for her welled up inside. I imagined the hard life she was leading, having to carry a heavy bag of groceries all by herself. A few seats down, there was an old man who looked very frail and sad. Perhaps he was a retiree whose children never came to visit him. Maybe he was a distant father, like my own dad, and still he wondered why his children never visited him. In the back, two kids were eating fried chicken, spitting out bones on the floor and making a mess. I thought of gently asking them to clean up their mess. Reality came back to me as I noticed they were dressed in club jackets and sported rings and gold chains around their necks. They would probably just as soon spit me on the floor as mop up their chicken bones. Even so, these kids didn't get the parental attention they needed, and here in the bus might be their only chance to eat inside somewhere. Then I thought of the old man. I wondered if the old man decried misbehaving children like these boys without thinking how he contributed to the problem.

A strong sense of empathy overcame me: how stupidly I used to feel superior to them. Old people who lived rich lives, young kids happily dirtying a public bus. None of them did anything so gross as what I had just done. I was about to berate myself further, then the self-hatred flag was mentally raised. Behind me sat a thin man, a few years older than me. He looked lost in thought. *Was something troubling him?* I wondered.

"Hi," I said to him.

"Hello yourself," he shot back dismissively.

I felt so alive.

Back in the dorm room, alone, I felt the loneliness even more painfully. The walls seemed to be a cage preventing all contact with the world beyond. Loneliness was a most humiliating admission to myself. "I am lonely," I said out loud. The sound of it was so pathetic and weak. I had failed; I could not attain *this* by myself. *This* being what? Education? Finding a Path? Life itself? All of it? Were all of my efforts to be a better person a waste? Did I waste my entire childhood? The life I led was discredited. That struck me as so sad, as if a beautiful house I had toiled so hard to build turned out to be not only ugly, but also structurally unsound and dangerous. The only thing to be do was to abandon it.

But where do I start? Maybe by undoing some of the self-inflicted damage, I could try and make friends. Maybe Casper? Just give up the obsession and just try to be his friend. First I needed to be honest about my feelings for Casper. All I needed to do was exchange the evil thoughts about Casper for just the nobler and purer ones. *But could I?* I wondered. *Could I make a friend without screwing it up?*

And why would anyone want to be my friend? I wondered. I couldn't think of one solitary reason. I had collected a bunch of worthless, uninteresting interests. True, I was nice, I cared about people, but who knew that besides me? Had I ever expressed it? I had been so afraid of humans that I hadn't dared to show my real me; isn't that what Dr. Wire said all along?

That's when my clumsy roommate, Tim, literally tripped into the room. He fell flat on the tile floor, his dark mop of hair flown into his face. His tall lanky body sprawled awkwardly among a pile of musical scores. His elegant sharp face sporting a silly stunned look, uncomprehending what had happened. I'd found my guinea pig.

Fourth Variation: Fitting In?
Late Spring 1980

IV Adagio. Sehr langsam und noch zurückhaltend.

(Slow. Very slow and even reluctant.)

Chapter 35: First Test

"Let me help you up, Tim." I offered a hand and helped him off the floor. I wiped his clothes trying to get some dust off his jacket. I realized this was a bit of unintentional intimacy. I quickly bent over and picked up the musical scores he dropped on the floor. He almost bumped my head helping out.

"Oh, Mahler," I said, looking at one of the scores. "I didn't know he wrote for the piano."

"Thanks, they're songs," he said defensively. That wasn't the reaction I was hoping for, but I began to suspect it was the one I had earned.

"That's great, Tim, I like Mahler. I don't know him well. I know his Fifth Symphony; the DSO did it last year. I was an usher for the Detroit Symphony Orchestra my last year in high school and saw quite a few concerts." I also spied Schubert among the scores Tim brought home. "You're studying some great music; maybe I can hear you play sometime."

Tim looked at me wide-eyed, then smiled. "Sure, I'd love to do that, get your opinion." He rubbed his chin. "That damn doorway does it every time."

"You're okay?"

"Just my chin. That little piece in front of the

doorway is uneven … I trip.”

“I know; that is so annoying,” I agreed eagerly if not entirely convincingly. Then I wondered how my past behavior as a loner affected Tim’s reaction to me. “I … uh … owe you an apology, Tim.”

“You do?”

“I am sorry I hadn’t asked earlier. I always wanted to hear you play … I’m just shy.”

“I’m shy too, so don’t be shy around me, then we’ll never talk.” He laughed. I laughed. He was as shy as I was. We were going to be friends. I was going to pass my first test.

I hit upon the idea of asking Tim to have dinner with me. Even though we occupied the same room, we rarely did anything together. “Tim, I was wondering …” I swallowed.

“Hey, Jamie, I am going to see a movie tonight with the honors college group. I wanted to ask you something.”

“Oh, I guess you’re not coming back for dinner.”

“No, I’ll be back late. Why?”

“I—I was wondering if you wanted to have dinner with me sometime?”

“Sure.”

“Really?” I tried to suppress sounding so surprised.

“How about sometime this weekend?” he asked.

“Great.”

“Great.” Tim nodded his head. He relaxed and sighed. “That’s over with. Now I have been meaning to ask you a favor."

He wanted a favor from me! That's how you get friends: Do favors for them. Tim's dark brown eyes gazed into mine. I trembled with joy because this was precisely the gaze I wanted from Casper's blue eyes. "Sure. What can I do?" Tim could ask for anything. Even something crazy, like if he wanted me to sleep with him during a thunderstorm, just to calm him and keep him safe. For Casper's sake, I would do that.

"Can I borrow your recording of *Tristan und Isolde*?" He had to be out of his mind. "I wanted to play it for my friends—the parts you played for me the other night."

At first, it was out of the question. I knew if I loaned him the record, he would scratch it in an instant. But I had to be more giving. Tim, anticipating a different answer anyway, took the record off of my desk.

"Just be careful," I said with plaintive eyes.

"Sure thing." He took it and opened the box and looked at the booklet inside. He opened it. "Oh, that's it? The libretto?"

"Yes."

"It's in German."

"Yes, it's one of the best recordings," I said proudly, hoping to instill a sense of responsibility in him. I opened the booklet. "Don't worry, it's only the introduction; the libretto is translated in English, French, and Italian. Just turn the pages there ... see?"

234

I flipped the book to the middle.

"Oh. Okay, see you later. Hey, thanks ... about dinner," he added shyly.

"Me too." I couldn't help but be charmed.

The door shut.

He likes me! This means it is possible that Casper might like me. What an achievement. I heaved a deep sigh. I was relieved, even if I had to entrust my prize possession to such an unworthy stranger.

Again alone, the strong need to atone returned. Atone for what I had just done back at my parents' house. Atone for not trusting Tim, for not befriending Casper, and for still hating myself.

As if right on cue, I noticed a copy of the student newspaper on Tim's desk. It was no accident that the word 'atone' was fresh in my mind. There was an ad for the upcoming meeting of a liberal Jewish student group called Antviklen. Antviklen met on Sundays. Maybe this could be more help on the way. With friends and spiritual help, I could finally throw this nasty self-hatred behind me, once and for all. I could come clean and be a normal person. I was firing on all cylinders.

Chapter 36: Second Test

The next evening, I was studying in a classroom on the third floor. However, this time, in an attempt to be a social being, I picked a classroom with people already in it. I walked in and saw three students huddled together. I entered, very proud of myself.

"Hi," I said to my fellow students.

They looked up begrudgingly.

"Hi," someone muttered.

I sat down, my smile greeting their disgust, trying to non-verbally say I just wanted to be friends. I took my books out of my backpack. Setting *The Caretaker* aside, I reached for *Thus Spoke Zarathustra*, while the others in the room gathered their books, gave me the evil eye, and left.

Nobody's perfect, I thought. After a while, certain they were not coming back, I set my book aside and sneaked over to the podium with my copy of *The Caretaker*.

Standing erect at the podium, and glancing around one last time to make sure no one was in the empty room, I opened the book to where I had left off in the middle of Act One, studying the part of Davies.

"These shoes are black. Well, they can do, anyway, until I get another pair. Maybe they'll get me down to Sidcup tomorrow. If I can get there I'll be able to sort—"

"Hey, Jamie!" Tim rushed in. I perked up for my new friend like a puppy seeing its master.

"Hi, Tim."

"I am so glad I bumped into you. They didn't like *Tristan*. I can't explain it to them like you can. I have your record here."

"What, so soon?"

Tim dropped it on a desk. The box looked torn. There was a small stain on the record cover. "What are you giving it to me for? Can't you just bring it gently back to the room?" *Like you found it?*

"No, they're waiting for me downstairs. Do you mind?"

As a matter of fact, I did mind. "Okay, sure, Tim," I replied, realizing that friendships have their pluses and minuses, though I needed the pluses more than I wanted to avoid the minuses.

"Thank you, Jamie," he said, pursing his lips. *Was he blowing me a kiss?*

I opened poor *Tristan*. I was appalled. The records were stacked on each other outside of the record jacket.

"I'm sorry," I said, as if talking to a small pet. Carefully, I put the bare records back in their protective sleeves.

"Wanna hang out?" Dara's voice.

I screeched in surprise, almost dropping a record on the floor. I turned around and there she was, smiling and radiant.

"Sorry, didn't mean to scare you."

"I was just—practicing, you know."

"Did you want to hang out—study together? Remember my study group?"

"With you? Me?"

"Yeah, you." She chuckled good-naturedly. "I am with a couple of friends in my room. You know them: Ahmed and Niti. Wanna study with us?"

"Sure," I said, trying my nonchalant best to contain my uncontrolled ecstatic glee.

"Great, come on," she said.

We no sooner walked out of the room than I needed to run back. I had forgotten my recording of *Tristan und Isolde*. I was tempted to leave it there: A four-hour German opera would only embarrass me, and who would steal it? Against my better judgment, I went back to get it. I slipped the album under my arm.

"What's that?" Dara asked immediately.

"What? You mean this?" The records almost fell out from under my arm. I made a quick grab that threw me off balance and almost crashed into her. "You mean this … this record? Why, it's music."

"I know, silly. What kind of music?" She took the album out of my hand. I was helpless to stop her. I wanted her to take anything from me she wanted, but not that. She would immediately write me off as an opera-loving square, I just knew it. Cursing Tim, I was already formulating an apology in my mind for carrying something so stupid.

"*Tristan und Isolde?* ... What is it, an opera?" She looked at it. On the cover was an embarrassing picture of an extremely ugly man with a silly beard and mustache singing to an extremely fat woman wearing ridiculous clothes.

"It's not what you think—"

"You'll have to play it for us. Jamie, relax—you're one of us now."

One of us? Oh, if she only knew who I really was—If I only knew. I tried desperately to swallow. I didn't want my first test to cause me to being kicked out of being one of them. I had never been one of anything before, except a loner. I held back the urge to say something lame like, "You won't like it." Instead, I remembered not to hate myself, so I decided to say something insightful and debonair. "Are you sure?" I winced at the wretched words that had tumbled from my mouth.

"Of course." She held on to the evidence.

We walked down the stairs to her second-floor room. I started playing over in my mind a comparison of the 'Tristan chord' and its fragile tonal progression to the Grateful Dead, Pink Floyd, and every other rock band they probably liked. It was a damning comparison.

Chapter 37: Sentimental Education

The door to Dara's room was already open. A bizarre floral fragrance hit me upon entering. The dark room seemed cool and edgy with its non-standard loft beds above and the young with-it faces below. Two students were sitting in lotus positions on a beat-up red oriental rug.

I recognized Ahmed and Niti. They were from my Ethics of a Republic class. Ahmed, as always, looked cool and suave in a formal suit. Niti, whom I assumed was his girlfriend, was quite similar to Ahmed; except that where he was stiff, Niti was elegant and smooth. She had a penchant for flowing floral dresses and wraps. Everything about them exuded exoticism, including their elegant British accents. I looked around with hope and despair for Casper, but he wasn't there.

I loomed from my standing height like a plane not yet landed, overlooking the closed world below, still able to make a graceful exit in case I was rejected.

Then I gasped. My eyes shot up like metal to magnets, and my heart began to pound. Casper walked in from the bathroom.

"Oh, hello … Jamie, right?"

He spoke to me! He knew my name! Oh, rapture!

"Y-yes, it's me." I looked at Casper as I spoke. It was allowed. People can look at people when they talk to them. But I could not think of anything to say. My scheme to talk to him had finally succeeded. In fact, my plot, the one that had brought me shame among library clerks and department secretaries, had no exit strategy. The plan was so far-fetched, I never accounted for actually succeeding.

"Well, hi again," I said hastily, awkwardly, and judging by everyone's reaction, abruptly.

"I won't bite, Jamie, but I am what I am," he said, and to prove it, he did my favorite thing—he ran his fingers through my hair. He winked ambiguously. My heart went soaring so high that it almost seemed like my life was over. I was about to disappear in a matter/anti-matter combustion of longing and reciprocation. I could scarcely think when I realized that Ahmed asked me a question, which I didn't hear.

"I like the theater," I said, hoping that was the answer. "I admire great actors like Marlon Brando, John Ritter ..." My voice started to trail off by the blank faces I was getting.

"Are you studying theater?" asked Casper.

Was he reading my mind? Before I could answer, Ahmed forced a laugh.

"I was just saying, Jamie, so you are the boy who actually likes Nietzsche," said Ahmed in his suave British accent. I was glad someone finally noticed or cared, but this was the wrong moment. I didn't want to be esoteric just then.

"Nietzsche? That's sounds pretty thick," said Casper.

"Casper, liking Mr. Nietzsche is quite an accomplishment," said Niti.

"What can you like about Nietzsche that you can learn much quicker in *Gentlemen Prefer Blondes,*" Casper quipped.

"*Gentlemen Prefer Blondes?*" I was stunned. No, not stunned, wounded. Never had anyone dared to trample on my love of Nietzsche, let alone with an old movie, an old movie I had never seen. Was *Der Wille zur Macht, The Anti-Christ* and *Thus Spoke Zarathustra* so trivial that one Marilyn Monroe movie could subsume it all?

"I'll say it is; that stuff is too dense. There's too much to do in life to get bogged down," said Casper, my beloved-turned-assailant.

"It didn't bog me down," I protested softly. "I mean—it was different with me." Niti came to my rescue, and I suddenly realized I had friends.

"I find this very intriguing, dear boy," said Niti, using 'boy' to remind me I was the youngest person there by a few years, in her own elegant Indian-British accent. Again, I was touched, but couldn't they just drop the topic? I flashed an embarrassed smile at Casper. Niti flashed a welcoming smile of bright white teeth. "Tell us, Jamie dear, what do you see in him?"

"I first saw him when I was—" I had to stop

myself. She meant what I saw in Nietzsche, not Casper. I had waited years for someone to ask me that question, but not in front of Casper. Moreover there was Dr. Wire's admonition that I liked dramatic statements. "He is difficult to read, I admit. In high school, I guess I had a lot of time on my hands. But I have learned a lot." I tried to keep it simple and vague.

"Then tell us something you learned, something that is special to you," said Niti.

I swallowed. I glanced at Casper. Casper was not interested. My eyes begging him for sympathy, I looked around. Everyone else was staring at me. I had to dare to say something. Tim wanted my record; they were going for my heart. I spoke to them, but I knew that what I said would fall deaf on Casper's ears.

"I haven't had the easiest of times …" I was horrified at the words flying out of my mouth. I had no idea where I was going with that thought. My mouth took on its own life. "You know … I felt people pitied me. It's not a nice feeling; no one wants to be pitiable. Nietzsche believes pity is a sickness. He taught me to stand up and do something, or at least try. Failure is better than not trying. So here I am … trying …" My voice trailed away. I looked down to the ground. *I blew it. I blew it. They all think I am weird.*

"I can see that," said Dara.

I couldn't believe my ears. Dara was agreeing with

me. Dara then sat down and joined the others in the lotus position on the floor. It left me dangling, standing up.

"Very articulate, Jamie. I will read your Mr. Nietzsche with a little more attention," said Niti. "Come on, sit down with us."

How did that happen? Somehow I'd passed the test, and just by being me—clumsy, awkward me.

I was alarmed to see the only place available was between Ahmed and Casper. I just couldn't sit next to them. I was trying to figure out how to sit in the only neutral place I could think of, a small sliver of space between Niti and Dara.

"What do you have in your hands, Dara? Is that a record?" asked Ahmed. No sooner had one storm passed than another began.

"Oh, this? This is Jamie's. He's gonna play some in a while," said Dara. My worst nightmare had come true, a nightmare I didn't even know I had, playing Wagner for Casper.

"What is the record? It certainly looks a bit queer," said Niti.

"It's an opera," I squeaked. Casper was looking away at Dara. Dara passed the record to the empty space between Ahmed and Casper. Casper had this position I thought of as 'Casper's position'. The others were all in a yoga-like lotus posture; Casper bent his knees straight out and sat on his heels. It was a stunning posture, allowing you to see the curving line of the hip turning into the thigh.

I dared to slide the record to the center with my foot. I lowered my legs by bending my knees straight out and lowered myself into the circle. It was like lowering myself into a different universe. Below, it was like we were at the bottom of an ocean, in our own private world, a world where I could sit next to a handsome foreigner and my friend Casper. I could savor just being with him. In fact, I felt that by just enjoying his presence I was banking imaginary but finite credits to stare at him. This way I could make sure I wasn't staring at him too much.

Besides, as long as I stayed in the Casper position, I was reminded of his succulent presence without looking. The position felt great, even as my legs tingled and my knees ached. Now, if I could only think of how to slip *The Caretaker* into our conversation, we'd really hit it off. Until then, I snuck the record out of the circle behind me—both of us still ready to escape at a moment's notice.

I hoped my new friends would just forget this opera business. Slowly, my nose untangled the room's mixture of exotic perfume, incense, and the distinctive smell of marijuana. The familiar scent indicated a way out of this mess: the longer I waited the higher they would be. Eventually, they would either not care about the music or forget about the opera entirely. Indeed, Casper started passing around a joint.

"Jamie, perhaps you can settle an issue for us," said Ahmed, running his hand through my hair.

"Oh, don't start that again," Niti whined.

"Niti, why get so upset at me? I just want to know," he said, hands still deliciously entwined in my hair. "Think of it as part of my education."

"Let him," said Dara.

"Good. Jamie? You game?" He pulled his hand away. How I wished Casper would do that to me. "I promise if you don't want to answer, you don't have to, not at all. Casper here didn't, and we love him just the same; don't we, Dara?"

Casper rolled his eyes. How I wish I could engage him, yet as much as he did not want to be engaged, my new friends—Ahmed, Niti, and Dara—were actively engaging me. How could I say no? Yet by saying yes, I felt I was alienating Casper.

"Um-hmm. I am game." I turned red, moving my head like a movie camera to make sure I focused my eyes only on the speaker rather than snapping back to Casper's hip-to-thigh line.

"It's about politics," announced Ahmed.

"Oh, I know what you're going to ask," said Casper. "Boring." *Boring?* I had to keep this short if I could help it.

"Exactly. So, here is the question: What is the difference if Nicaragua was caught spying, as the U.S. alleges," said Ahmed, "if you compare that crime with the meddling your country is currently doing there? I mean, specifically, aiding a military group opposed to the current legitimate regime?"

I couldn't believe my ears; this was going to be easy! My mother's politics had certainly prepared me for this one. I heaved a sigh of relief. I lazily used up a credit and looked over to Casper's luxurious Raphaelite beauty. Then I quickly looked back to Ahmed.

"I see your point. You could even say the Nicaraguans were just trying to protect themselves from American subterfuge, right?" I countered. Ahmed was duly impressed.

"Dara, did you already discuss this with him?" asked Ahmed.

"Not a word," she said.

"Well, the U.S. feels it is impervious to criticism because it always does this as if it was its birthright," said Ahmed.

"Exactly. You know, ever since World War II, in fact, America has been taking over the role of Great Britain as the world's empire. Gore Vidal said so. Did you see his interview in *The Nation*?" I asked, enjoying myself.

"Okay, you pass the test, Jamie. He can stay, Dara." Ahmed smiled and patted my head in a sweet if paternalistic way, reminding me again how much younger I was than the rest.

"Did you know what the U.S. did in my country?" asked Ahmed.

"Your country?"

"Yes, I am from Iran."

"Oh, wow. Really. Well, the U.S. supported the Shah. I mean, that is pretty bad." Ahmed nodded in agreement. A sudden feeling of glee was pouring over me: I was fitting in. As Dara said, I really was one of them.

"But what if I told you it was even worse than just supporting the Shah?"

"What could be worse?"

"Just like in Chile and soon as in Nicaragua, the U.S. government deposed a democratically elected president and installed a dictator: the Shah."

"Wow, really?" Finally I felt like I was having a meaningful conversation with someone. Not just some blah-blah talk about our cafeteria, or sports, or our professors, but something that really mattered: United States policy.

"Yes, and it's not conspiracy theory or anything like that. This really happened—Dara, do you mind? I don't want to bore everyone." Ahmed then turned his sharp intellectual eyes to me, to talk just to me. "They've heard me tell this story so I will keep it short. It was in 1952. Mohammad Mosaddeq was the first democratically elected president of Iran. He was pro-Western, by the way."

"That is amazing," I said.

"He even kept a picture of himself posing in front of your American Liberty Bell in Philadelphia."

"Really, the Liberty Bell?" I was fascinated.

"Yes. He even studied your American Constitution."

"Why did we depose him? What happened?" I asked.

"What happened was Mosaddeq took away the British control of Iranian oil."

"They did? I never knew this—wow." I suddenly realized I was stoned. And Ahmed and I had been talking while the rest of the group went on about something else completely different.

"So the Americans made a pact with the British to help them reclaim their oil," intoned the dashing Ahmed. It suddenly occurred to me Ahmed must need his hair stroked too.

"That seems so silly—and unfair, super unfair," I slurred. I lost my balance and lost my aim instead of patting his head, I groped his crotch and awkwardly jerked my hand away. "Oh, sorry there. Why would the Americans—I mean us—I mean them—why would the American government do this for the British? Of all people, a backwards country with a stupid queen, for crying out loud." Everyone stared at me. But Ahmed was oblivious.

"Oh, no, they did not do it for the British," continued Ahmed. "The new order kept the lion's share of the oil revenues for the Americans. The CIA infiltrated the political scene in Iran and engineered a *coup d'etat*. They replaced Mossadeq with your Shah of Iran."

"Did you hear that, Casper—" I turned to look at Casper using another credit, though by now I forgot how many I had left. But before I could speak to Casper, Ahmed interrupted.

"But before you get the idea I am anti-American, I tell you I am not."

"I can see that," I added inanely.

"I am very grateful to be here."

"Yes, but that certainly puts the Iranian hostage situation in a different light." Then out of nowhere, I blurted, "You know, I'm Jewish!"

"I think I knew that, Mr. Goldberg."

"You know what else?" I regrettably continued.

"Let me guess. I am the first Iranian you ever met."

"The first Arab, period."

"Then I am sorry to disappoint you, Jamie." He affectionately patted me on the head again. His face was so close to mine that for a moment I panicked he would kiss me. "You still have not met an Arab. I am Persian. I speak Arabic, but as a second language." He smiled at me.

"Chaldeans aren't Arabs either … is anyone …" My voice trailed off. I felt a shoe lazily lean against my thigh. Without looking, I fantasized it was Casper's foot inside his shoe touching me.

Casper spoke abruptly. "Let's all agree that we hate the American military-industrial complex. Let's listen to some music."

My head shot back to look at Casper. The reason Casper's foot, or rather shoe, grazed mine is that he had reached for a small tray with cigarette papers. He was now rolling another joint. It helped calm my concerns about *Tristan* rearing its over-the-top head.

"Great idea. Let's all take turns sharing music," Dara suggested. "Niti, why don't you start with that new album?"

"Thank you, I have been quite eager to hear this one."

"What is it?" asked Casper. I wished he spoke more. I could look at him more often and not use up my looking credits.

"Karnatic music. I hope you will like it. This music is from where I come from."

Chapter 38: Music Appreciation

To my delight she put on completely unintelligible music. Music so bizarre it made *Tristan* into a rock opera by comparison. I leaned into Casper's foot, but he withdrew his shoe from my side. I felt a sting of jealousy as he snuggled up to Dara. It was a jealousy I actually enjoyed. I was happy for Casper, even at my own expense. I enjoyed Casper's luck of having so fitting a partner as Dara. I had a higher love for Casper. Higher than the baser desires the couple probably shared. In fact, thinking of Dara touching Casper's naked body thrilled me with delight for them.

"This music is far out," sighed Casper.

"Jamie, you seem to be enjoying this music very much."

"Yeah, you're really groovin' with the music," said Casper.

A lump formed in my throat. *I can really fit in here, and without doing anything more than being myself. If only I could find a way to make them forget about my record album.*

Casper lit the joint and then passed it to me, not Dara. This had to be a sign of true friendship. His hand pressed liberally into my skin. My flesh seemed to soak him up like a sponge. My hand trembled as I dared to put my mouth to something that he had just touched—not just touched, created. I took a puff, knowing the moistness on the tip was Casper.

"Let me get you some water," said Dara as I inhaled too deeply and coughed loudly. The water calmed me down. I closed my eyes, listening to Niti's mellow Karnatic music, feeling the memory of Casper touching my hand. I kept my eyes closed as it made me feel mellow and safe. My eyes couldn't bother me or Casper with their mad desire to look at him. The music was just a single male voice singing an amazingly long, delicate vocal line. The singer was accompanied by various exotic instruments. There were waves of musical sensuality—unsure if the wobbliness was a function of the music or the pot. I found it particularly delightful to think that these sensual musical waves that entered through my ears and thrust into my brain were the same sound waves that were simultaneously thrusting into Casper's brain.

Dara stroked Casper's face. And Niti leaned against Ahmed and pressed her legs against my side, her elegant naked foot against my thigh.

"It's really beautiful, Niti; what are they singing?" I slurred merrily.

"It's celebrating the life of Parvati, the wife of Shiva. He sings about the ritual mortification of her flesh," she said, puffing on the incredible shrinking joint.

"You mean like rituals of purification, atonement?"

"Exactly, Jamie."

"Ah, at last," I sighed. Then I shuddered as unspeakable childhood memories came to me, reminding me I was inexorably different from them. Then I recalled my own humiliating rituals of purification. "Maybe they worked," I said accidentally aloud, though no one seemed to mind. "There are many rituals of purification. There is something … universal there, isn't there?" I wondered aloud.

The songs were very long, the melodies hypnotic. I opened my eyes again to ask Niti a question, but instead my eyes went to Casper. The sound waves were still pulsating in and out of our brains together. It made me laugh, realizing that to talk to him, all I needed to do was move my marijuana-softened lips.

"Casper, I am so glad we finally had a chance to meet," I said gratuitously.

"So am I," Casper said wistfully. He glanced over at Dara, and they smiled, almost laughed. They were definitely together. It made me feel almost ecstatic that they could have sexual intercourse, possibly even tonight.

I swallowed, "Ca—Casper?"

"Huh?"

"Can I ask you a question?"

"This sounds like a trick," said Ahmed. "Do not let him do it." He laughed.

"What's up?" asked Casper.

"I am thinking of changing my major to theater."

"Oh, really?"

"Yeah, I was just wondering if you have any suggestions ... you know, courses I should take."

"Well, you should meet with an academic advisor, but if you want to see if you like theater or not, I'd advise two things. First, get your feet wet and help someone out on a theater production. Second, you should take any class with Mr. Nathan. He has to be the best teacher in this whole school."

"Mr. Nathan?" I asked, picking the safest option first.

"Yeah, Arthur Nathan. You should just take any course from him; he's amazing."

"That's enough of this music for now," said Niti, as she took her record off the turntable. "Ahmed. What do you want to play?"

"I love Frank Zappa's *Over-Nite Sensation* album that Dara brought."

"Oh, far out! Let's liven things up a bit," cried Dara. Casper sat back up to his kneeling position. Niti caused an erection by sticking her foot against my groin as she stretched behind us to switch records; it brought back some strange memory of a foot against my crotch.

I was used to the primitive rock music that issued out of our dorm halls. I was not prepared, especially with a little marijuana in me, for Frank Zappa. The music sounded like rock band meets Arnold Schoenberg. The music was alive and compelling, but the lyrics were accusational, a personal indictment:

I am gross and perverted
I'm obsessed and deranged
I have existed for years ...

I heard the verse, "I am the slime oozing out from your TV set."

"Oh, thank God!" I yelled, laughing. Ahmed stared at me for a moment, then laughed too. "Oh, Jamie boy, you are apparently the only one with even less scruples than I."

"*Casablanca!*" I yelled.

"Oh, I am busted," said Ahmed, "My favorite movie."

"When he gets high, he recites lines from it."

"Oh, that's not true, though there are many exit visas sold here, but you've never sold one—"

Casablanca was one of the movies I would watch when I was avoiding thinking of myself in high school.

I had to laugh. "Wow, we really are alike," I said, disarmed. Together with the marijuana, this made me feel whimsically naked; it was even safe to open my eyes and look at Casper. My head wasn't on the floor, so it was on someone's leg. I was looking at Casper, so it wasn't his. The strange Zappa music was so soothing, it was clearly outsider's rock music. The lyrics wafted in and out:

Give me
Your dirty love
Like a pink donation
To the dragon in your dreams

Dirty love, someone was actually asking for it. *Could I ask for it too?* I wondered.

I don't need your sweet devotion
I don't want your cheap emotion
Just whip me up some dragon lotion
For your dirty love

Chapter 39: Lost in Space

I was oddly relieved when it was Dara's turn to pick an album.

Dara put on an album by Tom Waits, a singer with the most gravelly voice I ever heard in my life, singing sarcastic renditions of the most romantic words. His music was some cross of punk band meets beatnik jazz. I was enjoying this catchy but underhanded music. I was no longer on the floor. I was leaning my two hands behind me, just in front of Casper. In fact, my right hand was in between Casper's legs. If I relaxed a little, my arm could graze the blue denim lining the inside of his thigh. I looked at the bare skin between his sock and pant cuff out of the corner of my eye. It looked so easy to touch. I had no idea how much I had smoked by then, but the leg just stood in front of me as a dismembered piece of a body that was probably lonely and needed touching.

The song was at first a cool jazz tune. At once the music took a very ugly turn.

and then and he leans against
the car doors and feels the blood in his shoes

I had to remember the enormity of touching,

interacting with someone I loved so much. Everything had to be above board. I drew my hand away from Casper. And scooted my body to be a regular part of our circle.

> *and someone's crying in the phone booth*
> *at the 5 points by the store*
> *romeo starts his engine ...*

I felt a sickening peaceful lull when the lyrics seemed to turn to Spanish.

> *andele pues*
> *hey pachuco ...*

"Oh, wow, this is blowing my mind!" yelled Casper, and he stretched out his leg now right in front of the hand I had withdrawn. It was as if his leg were begging to be touched.

"This is killing me," said Ahmed, no longer so prim and proper. "Wow! Spanish in the middle of this fucking great song, what a genius!" The swear words sounding so unnatural in his refined accent.

He stretched out, putting his head in Niti's lap. Casper placed his head on Dara's. Both Ahmed's and Casper's legs wound up right in front of me. This was no accident, I reasoned; they wanted me to touch them.

It was like a miracle struck. I now had two legs that wanted to be touched: one from Ahmed and one from Casper. I became absolutely convinced of their legs' need to be touched. I had to do it; no one else knew. Furtively, but lightly, I first skimmed Ahmed's shin with my finger. His leg seemed to purr, so I stroked it again. I traced a finger down the small exposed shin and his sock. He seemed to purr again, not even caring who was touching it. I was so happy to make someone feel good, just by touching him. I felt emboldened. My heart raced. Did I dare to touch Casper Tyres?

Just then, I could swear the music teamed with an evil voice inside of me as it yelled: "YOU ARE GOING TO HELL!"

I could only manage a silly smile at the thought because I realized, at the moment, that 'hell' was such a stupid word. Hell seemed like a place with soft cushions. What else could it be with a sound like heh-llll. I said the word softly to myself, "Hell, hell, hell." How could such an insipid sounding word cause trouble? I looked at Casper. Hell was worth it. Or at least it didn't seem like anything I couldn't handle. Casper's lips moved. He must have been deep in a conversation I could not hear for the lips danced about in a beautiful ballet.

I looked down. His leg. *HIS* leg. *What could "hell" be compared to the word "his?"* I wondered. Touching Ahmed was relatively easy. What was so difficult with touching—no grazing—*his* leg? HIS. Hell. His hell. Hell his. Hell mine. His mine. Never had a word appeared sexier or more powerful than his. Never was a leg sexier at that moment than Casper's. I knew the act of touch was so powerful that it alone could be the source for the most powerful orgasm, one that would be destructive like a cannon shot.

I lifted my hand. It started a seemingly interminable voyage toward an open spot of skin on Casper's shin. Closer and closer it came, my world narrowing to just this one spot on Casper's leg. The finger finally reached its goal. The music grabbed my attention for a moment. I looked down and the leg was gone! Casper's leg was gone. Vanished. That must have meant that he was gone too, I deduced. *Quick, Harold Pinter!* I urged myself.

"You know, this song, it reminds me so much of Harold Pinter, doesn't it?" I asked. I looked around. "Where's Casper?"

"Jamie, you didn't notice? He just left," said Dara.

Then to make the cognitive dissonance complete, Dara added, "Hey, let's hear Jamie's album."

A new imbroglio.

"The opera thing!" Niti enthused clumsily. She leaned back to get the record. At the same time, I twisted my body to get the record as well. I fell over on top of her. I heard her giggling, and to my horror realized my face was buried right in her breasts. All about me was flesh and flowery scents. I couldn't get out, my face stuck in a valley of flesh. I was truly horrified. Horrified most of all because I was sure she thought I did this on purpose. "Oh, my God, it isn't what you think," I muffled. I could not gasp for air. I was being suffocated by her breasts. Everyone erupted in laughter. It seemed like hours before I was able to free my face from the intimidating bosom. A lock of hair wrapped around a button was my jailer.

"Enjoy your little voyage?" chirped Niti.

"So that's how it's done, I must try that sometime," joked Ahmed.

My embarrassment was only mellowed by the sumptuous *Tristan* chord. Someone had put on the record and the languid longing sounded. It had a mellowing effect on everything. I turned over and lowered my head onto Niti's lap—forgetting Ahmed was already there. We bumped heads.

"Hey, watch it, man!" Ahmed was holding his head in his hands. I didn't even really get what had happened: nuzzled one moment and conked on the head the next.

"What are we listening to?" asked Niti.

Rubbing my head, I said, "Desire, pursuit, loss, searching ..." I trailed off as I saw that was all I needed to say.

"Is this the beginning of the opera? I do not hear any singing," Niti said.

Sobering up, or at least thinking I had, I straightened my posture. "This is the prelude before the singing starts. It sets the mood. A mood like ... desire." Everyone giggled when I said this.

"Yes, I know, little boy." Niti laughed, throwing her head back.

"It's more like longing for someone ... not something," I said, getting carried away by the yearning prelude. "Desire—want him, but you can't; he's not there." I suddenly realized I was using the wrong pronoun, so I kept quiet. Until after a while, carried away by the music, I tried again, this time without pronouns. "You try harder. It makes your desire harder, but it seems the more you desire, the more unattainable ... listen for yearning, closer and closer but not close enough."

The music of sensual desire surged. It engulfed my friends. They listened. They swayed with the music.

"Lovely floating," uttered Niti.

"Very intense," cooed Ahmed.

I wished I could see Dara and Casper embrace to this music. I leaned against something.

At once, I felt a hand on my shoulder. It squeezed. I was being seduced. *Tristan* works! I felt Dara's fragile hand with her sweet fragrance. She was next to me. She put her arm around my shoulder, like buddies do in a movie. I loved that touch so much, I didn't move, wanting time to just stay as frozen as my body.

"Wow, that's very ... intense," Dara whispered, her arm still on my shoulder. I was unsure what to do. Her hand moved to my arm. The mysterious hieroglyphic codes of human beings—how ill prepared I was to interpret them.

Niti, Ahmed, Dara, and I listening to music, how could I be happier? Then a sailor's distant voice sang, pensive and longing.

Westward my glance strays
Eastward sails the ship.
Fresh wind blows us home,

my Irish child, where have you gone?
Is that your sighs blowing my sails?
Pain, Pain to the wind!
Pain, alas, pain to you my maiden!
Irish child,
You wild, loving maiden!

Then came Isolde's furious cry to the sea to annihilate her ship and all aboard. The music became histrionic to the uninitiated, screams and brass made unintelligible by the extreme volume. Dara removed her hand. The spell was broken. The warmth of friendship was at odds with Isolde's furious demand for destruction and annihilation. We listened to the rabid first act, so full of pain and hatred. I was impatient to get to the love and the passion after Tristan and Isolde drink the love potion. Finally the music calmed again, and the group's mood improved. But then, suddenly, Ahmed suggested, "It's getting late; let's go."

It was about then that I noticed my forehead felt like it was melting onto my eyes. I realized I had smoked too much. Time passed and it was said again, "Let's go." But I didn't know where.

We left as a mocking chorus of sailors sang their contempt for Isolde's dead kinsman.

Now his head hangs
in Ire-land
as taxes paid
by Engel-land:
hail to our hero, Tristan,
he knows how to pay taxes!

Unsure where we were supposed to be going, I roamed a bit too randomly and missed the elevator. By the time I waddled down the stairs, they had drifted away. I had lost my group. I was walking alone, unsure if I had just made friends or just made a fool of myself.

Chapter 40: A Redeeming Horse

Mr. Nathan was a short, mustached professor. His looks fell on the wrong side of nondescript, almost a cartoon character of a middling college professor right down to the tweed coat for legitimacy and blue jeans for coolness. The difference being the glint in his eye, it imbued a power to his face that was exceptional. His twinkling eyes radiated the interest or fascination he had with you, while their absence spoke louder than any words of contempt. And when he read from a play, those eyes and his voice teamed to transform him into a jaw-dropping presence way out of proportion to his mild stature.

"I'm stiff! Stiff into the wind." Mr. Nathan's voice sounded as if it was in the throes of an agitated sexual climax. "My flanks! My hooves! Mane on my flanks, like whips! Raw! Raw! I'm raw!" He spoke with increasing visceral obscenity. "Feel me on you! On you! On you! I want to be in you! I want to *be* you! I want to be you forever and ever!" Then out of control and in total rapture: "Equus, I *love you*! Now! Bear me away! MAKE US ONE PERSON! One PERSON! One PERSON! One person. Ha-HA! Ha-HA! He-haaaaaa." Panting, Mr. Nathan looked up from the book.

The entire classroom was in shock. I was breathless. Not just from his reading; the play itself trembled through my body. I didn't harbor any secret attachment to horses, but the tension in the play, *Equus*, of a teenage boy lost in wayward sexual thinking, spoke to me with disturbing intensity.

In a beat, after Mr Nathan finished reading, he switched from orgasmic exhaustion to his usual good humor—even his panting was an act. But I was still shaken. "That's how it goes! That's what Alan Strang is really about." Mr. Nathan looked around the room. "A teenager with the sexual fire to almost burn up everyone in this room." He paused, looking around for someone to raise their hand. "Can everyone see what scares the shit out of Dysart? ... Huh? ... Can everyone see that? ... What is it?"

The old wooden floor of the classroom creaked as people shifted uncomfortably in their wooden chair-desk seats. The sun beamed down through the windows.

"Whatever it is, it scared the shit out of more people than just Dysart," said Eula, a boyish female student in the class. Everyone laughed to relieve the tension.

Mr. Nathan enjoyed the chuckle, a little more sardonically than we did. "Come on, Eula, what is it? ... Anyone guess?"

"Dysart's ... fascinated by Alan's passion," I confessed.

"Fascinated? He's *obsessed!* He is totally obsessed by the boy's love and passion for those horses, a passion that Dysart himself can never feel. Do we get it now, people? And what's the tension here? Eh? Come on."

I decided to try and hide my feelings, and say something safer. "Alan doesn't like his own love for horses."

"Doesn't *like* it? He feels like shit about it!" I shook in panic as I was afraid Mr. Nathan was going to say "he hates himself". Instead he said: "Alan didn't pick it. You don't pick the thing you end up loving, do you? Love happens to you. Sexual attraction happens to you, and you react. The synapses just snap together—as Dysart said. Do you get it?"

No one dared say anything. Though I had no fondness for horses, Mr. Nathan was speaking dangerously close to my soul. Maybe the others felt it too.

"Alec? Nothing? Ben?"

"Well, it's gross, he's having sex with horses, for crying out loud," the class bully Ben Geln brayed.

"It's not sex." The words jumped out of my mouth. Now everyone stared at me. Suddenly I felt I was now confronted with the most important moment in my life. I could finally talk about something that had bothered me, plagued me for so long. I searched, and no atonement, no Yom Kippur service, nothing, was able to put my feelings into words the way this play, *Equus*, did. Expecting ridicule and rejection, I still felt I had no choice but to say everything that had laid trapped inside of me. "It's a ... it's a ..." I almost didn't dare say the word, convinced that everyone would read my mind. "What you just read … it's a ritual. Alan combined sex … with religion, somehow identifying …" *Just say it*, I encouraged myself, "the horse as the … redeemer, the savior from Alan's own personal hell." I heard some students giggle and Mr. Nathan said nothing. "Well, who wouldn't like that? Deliverance from your own … personal …hell." It was quiet and awkward in the room. Mr. Nathan's eyes were closed. I felt I had just stripped myself naked in front of the class. I was again a total outsider.

Slowly Mr. Nathan opened his eyes.

"You know what I love about teaching?" said Mr. Nathan, looking at the class. "You can never say you know it all. Mr. … Mr. Goldberg, that sums it up far more eloquently than I even conceived of *Equus*. A logical extension of your comment is that Dysart is also in his own personal hell—what a great way of putting it—clearly he is, he even says so himself in the very first line of the book, doesn't he?" Again he looked around for someone to speak. I would not be ridiculed. I had found my voice and my audience.

"Jamie, you are saying that Alan sees the horse as the redeemer? Dysart clearly wants to be saved—not in the Christian sense of the word—but as you say, from a personal hell—not the one in the center of the earth, the one that's in the center of our hearts. Christianity as a metaphor for the human mind, mind and soul, Dysart's staring at the very thing he wants most. He looks on in horror at the price it will cost—

that's inspiring. I am not completely convinced of it, but it is inspiring. And combining sex with religion—that is also a very common and powerful theme."

"It's just bestiality, Mr. Nathan," said Ben contemptuously. A few students laughed nervously.

"It is not!" The fury in my voice shocked me. "I never touched the horse's—I mean Alan never did …"

Too late. Everybody broke out into hysterical, humiliating laughter.

"Now the truth comes out, Goldberg" Ben chuckled. I felt my face run hot; my ears seemed on fire. Powerless, I just stood there. Completely humiliated. The laughter finally subsided.

"People, focus. Jamie, thank you. You are making an excellent point; ignore Ben. Go ahead, Alec, what do you think?" asked Mr. Nathan. Alec was the oldest and most respected student in the class.

"Okay … Alan does not have sex with a horse. He never touches or mentions the horse's sex organs. So it can't be bestiality," said Alec. "Alan touches its neck, the flanks. He looks into the horse's eyes. He tries to be in touch with the horse's spirit and connect with a living being the only way he knows how. And yet, just touching a horse like that is so … perverse … it makes it even more sacred. That's why Alan needed a placebo truth serum in order to finally confess. The scene with the horse was sacred, not just dirty. When he does talk about this religious ritual, the confrontation and, my God, the shame must have been … terrible."

When Alec had finished, we exchanged

acknowledging glances. I took a deep sigh. I notice my hands were trembling.

"Thank you, Alec and Jamie. Both of you, that took courage going out on a limb like that." To my relief, Mr. Nathan and Alec understood me—finally someone did. "Get that, everyone? You see that sex isn't that spark that makes Alan so passionate. This isn't pornography. It's not just the horses. It's that combination of sex and religion, the forbidden and the holy, that makes this so powerful, just as it made *Parsifal* so powerful one hundred years ago. For those wanting extra credit, write me an essay about the borders between sacred and sexual ... Okay, everyone, think about it. You're not getting off this easy. Prepare a monologue like Dysart's in the first act, saying something you are jealous of and that is capable of sparking an entire play. Make it something you see in others that you wished you had. Okay, get out of here. Mr. Goldberg, please see me on your way out."

I dreaded going up to see him. I still feared confrontation and shame. I walked up immediately, but he waved me aside while he took other students' questions. Mr. Nathan had these core groupies, which made talking with him almost impossible. Alec, Ben, and Eula were among his main groupies and, as far as I could tell, his favorites. To me, Ben had always been a bully. After bullies in high school, I had little appetite for them in college. I sat aside until Ben left.

The last student to talk with Mr. Nathan was not a groupie but seemed to take forever.

"Mr. Nathan, can you stop swearing in class, that

is so gauche."

"I am sure you were offended, Cindy," said Mr. Nathan, "and you certainly have a right to complain to the dean or to whomever you want. But theater is all about confrontation and tension."

"It doesn't have to be. A play like *Peter Pan* or *42nd Street* ..."

"Cindy, all those plays, however insipid you may think they are ..."

"I don't think they are insipid; they are the types of plays I want to write."

"You think they do not confront people in their own ways? The tensions in *Peter Pan*—"

"Tensions? It's just a decent show."

"If that's how you feel, this is probably not the course for you."

"It's the only playwriting course there is. I'm complaining to the dean. I want to write that decent kind of show. Not these perverted things you're forcing us to read."

"*Equus* is a profound work for the theater."

"It's not just the play that's obscene; it's also your language."

"Of course, I am truly sorry if my swearing offends you, but sometimes it is necessary for me to get a point across, and get you people to talk. Cindy, take my advice; just drop the course. Complaining to the dean is only going to make you look bad. It won't get you anywhere."

"We'll just see about that!"

Chapter 41: Bluff Called

Cindy stormed out. Mr. Nathan watched after her. "Jamie, you're next. Phew! Can you believe her? She's in New York and what does she see? Not Pinter's *The Betrayal*, not Peter Hall directing *Amadeus*—which you could be reading next year if you join the honors seminar—But what does she see?" He imitated Cindy's squeaky voice: "*Peter Pan*, when just down the street is the *West Side Story*. My goodness, I hope she drops—the class, I mean." He laughed.

"So what do you think? Gonna read *Amadeus* with us next year? It's the same author as *Equus* ... I think you should; it will be just a small group—only five others."

"I know, but I don't think Ben would like me in the group."

"Oh, that's right. I forgot. Ben's teaching the class, isn't he? I thought I was. Jamie, we will meet Thursdays in my office. The only requirement is *Amadeus* ... and ..." He paused and looked at me with a critical squint. "And working harder."

"Working harder?" I asked defensively.

"Where is it?" He searched his leather briefcase. "Ah, here's your paper." He handed me the paper I had written on *No Exit* by Jean-Paul Sartre.

"What's wrong with it?" I asked guiltily.

"What's wrong with it? Let me see: good analysis, obviously creative and in-depth. You say the play takes place in heaven, and you make some clever arguments for that. All in all, better than most papers I have read. But I am not going to grade this thing."

"What's wrong with it?"

He shifted to a dramatic voice. "It's lazy! That's what's wrong with it."

"But you said it's better than most."

"All the students in my class, Jamie, have to give the same effort. I don't grade on content. I grade on effort, and you put very little effort into this. And right now I see on your face another lazy reaction."

"I feel terrible."

"I wouldn't be talking to you if I didn't know you were capable of much better. I know you better than you think, Mr. Goldberg."

"You do?"

"Yes, I was Sherlock Holmes in another life. Let me see, by the mud on your shoes, I can tell you floated through high school. You can't write, but they don't teach you to write in high school these days anyway. You were a loner who sat in unoccupied corners of the classroom. In your loneliness, you delved into books and philosophy. Then you used big words and concepts to intimidate your teachers. These teachers were just insecure enough that they didn't want to touch you with a ten-foot pole, so these teachers passed you on. But college professors won't fall for this so easily. If you want me to pass you, you either have to package it up better or just get real."

I lowered my head. I felt like a hardened criminal who was finally caught shoplifting. "How do you know all that?"

"Jamie, other students pick *Peter Pan, A Chorus Line*, Shakespeare's plays if I'm lucky." Mr. Nathan's smile and lighthearted voice had not vanished for a second. "But you, you picked a play by an existentialist philosopher. And look at the pretension in your prose—not to mention the careless grammar and spelling. It shows a lack of respect."

Beet red with humiliation, I blurted, "I didn't mean that, Sir. I respect you a lot ... I just wanted to impress you—"

"I don't mean disrespectful to me. I mean to *Sartre*. And call me Arthur. So try this one again ... and Thursdays, what do you say? Are you ready to get to work?" I nodded my head yes. "Good. Casper tells me you want to transfer and be a theater major."

"He did? I do. But—"

"Good, I think you'd be a natural for it. You show flashes of brilliance; we just have to stop it from being a disco ball to a flare shining up the firmament for all to see."

"You think I can do it?"

"Well, I'd like to see you try."

I was right. I had been stripped naked. He'd seen right through me, just like Dr. Wire had. I had to give up any pretenses and just admit I needed help. I wasn't going to pass for the brilliant wunderkind they thought I was in high school.

"All right. Mr. Nathan, it seems overwhelming to me. How do I begin?"

"Begin by being real. If you're going to tackle a subject like *No Exit* with me, then I want what's in here." Mr. Nathan pounded on his heart. "Not some unsupportable discussion of whether the play takes place in heaven or hell. Shoot, even Cindy's account of discord among the fairies in *Peter Pan* shows more heart."

"You want me to choose a different play?"

"No, I don't. I want you to write about Sartre in a way that shows me you really understand it. I tell you what. I'll give you an incomplete. Finish the paper over the summer. If you need help, try this title on for size: 'Why I am insanely jealous of Garcin—twenty pages."

"But Garcin is a coward in hell."

"You get it already; give it a shot."

"A coward?"

"You won't join an honors group because of Ben Geln?"

"It's not just that ..."

"No, it isn't. Your own plays seem academic while you're reading other plays—look at your analysis of Alan in class; that was amazing. Why isn't that in your playwriting exercises? Don't give me that look; you have the potential."

"How do I write a paper the way you want?"

"Actually, you have already. Just remove the philosophical gobbledygook and there will be your vulnerable spine. All the shame and embarrassment that is turning your face red right now, pour that into this paper." It was comforting that he seemed to be both comfortable with and understand my shame. I felt like I could stop pretending; in fact I hadn't even been aware I was pretending until this decision to stop it.

"I'll give it my best try. But suddenly this doesn't feel … safe."

"Right. You're learning. I am not being nice right now, am I?" I actually thought he was being the nicest person in the world to me. "Theater is risk. So forget about safe and tell me how *you* feel like Garcin."

"In the paper?"

"No, right now."

"Right now? I can't … because …"

"Oh, come on, you know I know already. You just don't dare to tell me; I can see that."

Quickly, I said, "I hate myself." I was horrified. I thought I would never tell another living soul that.

"Thank you," he said enthusiastically, "that's exactly what I am missing. Put that in your paper." Reason became dizzy. What I feared the most is what most impressed Mr. Nathan.

"Can you tell me how?" I pleaded.

"Certainly not. But please remove all references to existentialism and *mauvaise foi*. Just remember, I got your number, so you might as well make it insightful and interesting." He looked at me peevishly. "And lots of fun."

"I'm sorry."

Mr. Nathan at once stiffened, put on a maniacal grin, and spoke with a wild voice. "'I paced my cell. I pried into my heart, I sleuthed myself like a detective. By the end of it I felt as if I'd given my whole life to introspection.'" Then he relaxed and smiled. "That's the line Garcin sums up your past eighteen years. And if I am wrong—well let me see it. If you're sticking with me, better get used to me calling you on your bullshit. Calling people on their crap is what theater is all about."

Had I somehow stumbled on the meaning of life?

"You mean all theater?"

"All of it, Jamie."

"Even comedies?"

"Especially the comedies!" Mr. Nathan changed his voice to an artificially high tenor. "It's a fascinating theory, sir. Does it tie in with the known facts?" Then changing to a deep bass British accent, "That need not cause us undue anxiety. Civilizations have been founded and maintained on theories which refused to obey facts." We laughed. "There, a little Joe Orton can do the trick."

"I get it; but I appreciate Cindy's point now. I hoped theater could help me escape. Hide the bad times, not expose them."

"That's the beauty of it all. We put ourselves on

the line, show ourselves naked on stage. Yet we can all hide behind the saying, 'It's just a play.' We can get away with anything." He had no idea, or maybe he did, how I had done exactly that with my discussion of Alan Strang in class. Mr. Nathan looked at me with an encouraging smile. "You've got heart—and you talk about Cindy!"

"Don't you want some escapism to just relax and enjoy something? Does every play have to mentally exhaust us? Once in a while we need to escape."

"That's not escaping, that's drowning. You're thinking of changing majors. You want to escape? Then change your major to philosophy, if that's what you want. If you want to roll up the sleeves and deal with all that muck in your brain, and then help others do the same, then change your major to theater." Mr. Nathan then looked hard into my eyes with a searing force only Dr. Wire had managed. "If you do change your major, tell Mrs. Gibbons, the department secretary: *Professor* Arthur Nathan has requested to be your academic advisor."

"You want to be my advisor? Really? Thank you, sir." This was getting too much. The emotional exhaustion of my confession in class was now compounded by facing someone who knew me better than I did and he was positive about it, not negative. Why hadn't I done this long ago? "Mr. Nathan, I am thinking of trying out for Davies. Is that a good idea?"

"Davies?"

"*The Caretaker.* You know, the watershed play that devel—"

"Oh, stop it! You may send me to an early grave with that nonsense. Call me 'Arthur'. Pinter's not until next year. How did you hear of that?" I stood there silently shivering. "Never mind, I can guess. You know Dwight?

"Dwight? Dwight who?"

"Dwight Griss?"

"No."

"Anyway, he's going to be the director, and he's holding public auditions, but not for a while. It might even get delayed if I get this gig with the music department that I am working on. Anyway, *Caretaker* is a three-person play, and we have about twenty-five people who will probably sign up for it. But why don't you prepare for the part of Aston?"

"I actually was planning on reading for Davies."

"For Davies?" Mr. Nathan looked at me like a used car. "I think you need Aston. Yes, that's for sure, you're Aston. Give it a try and let me know what you think. I have a good feeling about this. Alan used a placebo and *you're* going to use Pinter. You'll see."

"What?"

Mr. Nathan used his most visceral theatrical voice. "'If he leaves at all, it will be with your intestines in his teeth. And I don't stock replacements.'" Then cheerfully, "See you Thursday, and don't forget to buy *Amadeus.*"

Could I dare do this? Give up my bullshit, as Mr.

Nathan called it, for this kind of truth-telling, this painful reality, this honesty, which I feared so much? Could this thing I hated about myself actually be the real way to Casper's trust. Why, then, was this so scary? I could easily see Alan's problems; why couldn't I see my own? Washing all that crap away, I had no idea what I would see. But this looking in the mirror should be easier than performing my own rituals. And with Mr. Nathan, I felt I had a friendly mentor. It made me feel the risk was worth it.

Fifth Variation: Durchfürung (Development)
September 1980

V Allegro maestoso: Mit durchaus ernstem und feierlichem Ausdruck.

(Majestic: with a thorough, serious, and solemn expression.)

Chapter 42: Friends at Last

Rewriting my paper on *No Exit* proved a thrilling experience. Just as Dr. Wire confronted me with self-hatred, Mr. Nathan was confronting me with something far more revolutionary: cowardice. The paper was writing itself as I realized Garcin's cowardice in the play didn't just separate him from bravery but also self-discovery. The question was whether I was prepared to spend eternity, like Garcin, asking for redemption from the one person whose aim was not to give it—and how this dynamic mirrored my relationship with my parents. Maybe also my dynamic with Casper. Casper had been idealized to the point that I thought he would save me, save me from being me. But who was I? According to Garcin's arch-nemesis, the answer is easy:

> *One always dies too soon—or too late. And yet one's whole life is complete at that moment, with a line drawn neatly under it, ready for the summing up. You are—your life, and nothing else.*

I could feel Garcin shudder with horror. How I was striving for something, but you are not remembered for what you strive for, only what you've done. Reviewing my life since I was four years old, it was a damning thought. I had to take life in a new direction, and Mr. Nathan pointed one way I could do that. I could no longer deny an obligation. I had to confess to Casper that I loved him. What that would do to me or what Casper would do to me was irrelevant. Even if I was not a homosexual, I had to confess to Casper that I loved him.

Looking around, I made sure no one snuck into the empty classroom. I stood up and opened my copy of *The Caretaker.* Unlike the rote exercise of learning the role of Davies, learning Aston was fascinating and confrontational.

"We were just sitting there, having this bit of a conversation, then suddenly she put her hand over to mine and she said, 'How would you like me to have a look at your body?'"

I stopped and turned deep red. Dara, peeking into the classroom, had caught me practicing my lines again.

"Oh, Dara, you scared me."

"Why? I am your favorite audience. Pinter never sounded better."

I blushed. "It sounds better with the pauses in it. I rushed through it."

"Sounds good to me; I see you dropped the British accent."

"Yes, it sounds more natural this way, doesn't it?"

"It sounds more *you*." Sounds more 'me'? I didn't know I had a sound. "Did you get the part?"

I blushed. She was so beguiling. "Not yet. I read for the role of Davies, you know. They didn't like that. Dwight, the director, asked me to prepare a different role: Aston. I am not sure about this. The character is mentally disturbed and really out of it. He lets just anyone take advantage of him. They think I am perfect for the part. But I don't know how I fit that at all."

"But that's good news. He didn't just send you home."

"Yes, you're right. I just wish I didn't have to wait 'til next term for the auditions."

"I thought you did the audition."

"No, it's just a reading."

"What's the difference?"

"I just read for this director and Mr. Nathan."

"Oh, you followed Casper's advice and took a course from Arthur?"

"Yes—you know him?"

"I met him at a school party once. He's real cool."

"He is; I learned so much already," I said, unsure how far I could go with that statement with Dara, Casper's girlfriend.

"What did you learn?"

I wanted to say, *I found out I am a coward*, but didn't. "I learned I like you and Casper a lot. And maybe I don't show it as I should."

"You're sweet. Say, did you want to do something tonight?"

"Tonight?" I was elated. My chance to prove I

was a better person had arrived.

"Another night is okay."

"No, no, tonight is fine," I said. "What should we do? See a movie—my treat? I know this movie *Simon*. I like Alan Arkin."

"How about something a bit more intimate?"

I knew exactly what to suggest. She seemed receptive to *Tristan und Isolde* a couple of weeks ago. My roommate, Tim, was gone for the weekend. We could play the opera excerpts, and I could explain to her the importance and the beauty of the music, just like I did for Tim. Tim liked that a lot.

"Come back to my room? We've got the whole night. We won't disturb Tim, my roommate—he's home for the weekend. We can play mu—"

"Jamie, that's a great idea." She smiled. She took my arm.

Immediately, I understood the misunderstanding. I was about to correct her when I realized, *Oh my god, Jamie, what have you done? You just inadvertently propositioned a woman ... and she accepted!* I looked at Dara. She looked at me. We grinned. Courage! I encouraged myself. She held on to my arm with her hands. Her warmth was so comforting. I knew this would be okay, no matter what happened.

Chapter 43: More Than He Bargained For

Walking to my room, I was so excited. I was about to have sex! Sex! I could kiss the lips Casper kissed. I could be where Casper … had been. I could celebrate the union between Dara and Casper. I was not going to be a virgin anymore!

The gravity of the situation only dawned on me when I saw the door to my room. We were about to go inside. What had I gotten myself into? I needed help, a manual of some kind. I needed equipment. And the room was a mess.

We walked into the dark dorm room. I closed the door behind me. I turned and bumped into her.

"Oops!" I blurted. "Oops," I repeated, softer.

"Aren't you going to turn on the lights?" she asked.

"I don't know if that's a good idea."

She laughed.

I turned on the lights and accidentally knocked books off the nearby dresser. One book fell on her foot. She let out a scream.

"Sorry about that," I said hastily picking up the books. But she smiled anyway and bent over and helped me collect them. She looked at the cover of one of them.

"Of course, Henry Miller," she said, handing me a copy of *Tropic of Cancer*.

I looked around; the place was a mess. Tim had left his underwear in a heap next to his bed.

I cleverly walked over and awkwardly kicked them under his bed.

"This is my room." I made an awkward TV game show gesture.

"Looks nice. Interesting posters; are they yours?" Dara asked. My eyes darted up, realizing those posters of Marlon Brando and James Dean weren't such a good idea. Tim had already asked me about them. She continued to stare at them. "Do you like motorcycles?"

"No!" I panicked a bit. "I mean … I like James Dean." That didn't sound any better. "I don't know why I … I was quite a fan of *Rebel Without a Cause*, when I was … ha ha. Marlon Brando … I am a theater major." That sounded worse still. "Would you like something to drink? I have a bottle of wine in the fridge."

"Sure, that would great," she said.

"Have a seat on the couch here." I scooped up the stuff off the couch, shoveling things over to my upper bunk. A small blue-colored sheet of paper fell like a feather next to Dara. Quickly, I realized it was my little biography of Casper. I grabbed it and threw it into the garbage.

I went to the dresser. Buried under a pile of books

was a small fridge. In the fridge was a contraband bottle of Reunite wine. In conformance with the serving suggestion, I took ice cubes from the small freezer compartment and put them in plastic cups.

I poured each of us a cup of wine. I put the bottle down on my desk next to the couch. On the other side of the couch was Tim's neatly made bed.

Hand shaking, I handed Dara a cup.

"Sorry, did I get you wet?"

"No, only the couch."

I quickly wiped the couch with my shirt sleeve, forgetting I was wearing a white sweater. I decided to ignore the stain. "Well, cheers!"

"Sweet."

"Yes, it is sweet; it's like champagne, except it's red."

Dara laughed. "I meant you, Jamie."

Silently we sipped our soda pop wine. My body began to relax. I thought of dear Casper's face, his eyes with the sweet little twitch. I took another gulp of wine.

I snuggled right up to her. About six inches away, I could feel her warmth, smell her flowery perfume. Her breath was minty-fresh. I was pretty sure mine wasn't. I lowered my face.

I counted to three, then plunged. I placed my arm about three inches over her shoulder, resting it on top of the couch. Then I felt a crane begin to lift my arm to its ultimate goal. Misjudging the distance, the arm landed with a plop. I shivered. I put my hand gently on the soft curve where her shoulder and her arm met.

"I'm a bit strange, aren't I?" I blushed.

"If I got rid of all my strange friends, there would be none left." Dara was radiant. "I'm gonna stay here tonight, if that's okay with you." She put her arm on my thigh, completing the circuit.

"Great! Have some more wine?"

"Thank you, Jamie."

I clumsily pulled away to get the wine bottle. She seemed pleased anyway. This was my day. I could do no wrong.

Still, I wondered, *Now what?* Sipping wine, I began to connect the evening's dots in my mind. *Staying the night. Sleeping in my bed. Sleeping with me. Naked together. Kissing. Foreplay. Preplay. The play. Post-op. Putting my thing into that thing and all the implied laws of thermodynamics.*

I wished I had a map or a guide, as I suspected my sixth-grade sex education would not help me here. There I learned that a male stuck it in the female and just … waited, I guess. Dara came closer to me.

Oh, well, at least I would no longer be a virgin.

This is my dream of all dreams come true, I insisted to myself. I would brook no opposition. Not even visions of Casper could dissuade me. In fact, they even encouraged me. This is what I had wanted all my life: the chance to prove I was normal. That I could be a normal friend and normal lover. If I only knew how.

"Relax, Jamie."

"You know I am too skinny."

"What?"

"Yeah, I am. I am just skin and bones. So if you change your mind ..."

She looked into my eyes and that said enough. I looked at her very closely. I could imagine the soft feel of her shoulders being quite similar to Casper's. Her small ears and freckles, well, Casper had something like that too, and her cute nose. His lips were thicker.

Finally, her closeness intimidated and then conquered me. My body started obeying her call. Suddenly I found she was plastered to the side of my body. I had to move. Then I did the most daring thing I knew: I stroked her arm. Our bodies touched skin to skin, open hand to bare arm. Scintillating. We touched.

Do something to save me! I pleaded to myself. I wasn't sure if I wanted to save myself or Dara.

Dara, almost on top of me, moved her face toward mine. Her mouth reached mine. I braced, my lips pursed tighter than the tightest sphincter. Her lips landed softly on my tensed ones. Mine relaxed. They pulsated together. I start to lead in the movement of the lips; she followed. Her kiss became my kiss. *Hey, this is going to be easy*, I realized. *James Micaiah Goldberg kisses a woman! And it's nice.*

I felt her delicate, small tongue probing my lips. *Okay, two can play at that game.* My tongue crept out of its lower recesses to battle hers. Our tongues touched, a shockingly soft and succulent sensation. It had to be love … wasn't it? What else could this be?

"Shall we go to bed?" asked Dara. *Let the sex begin!*

Chapter 44: Heterofunctional

This is the moment! But wait—what would be selfish or rude? I began to think myself into a frenzy. And then it came to me. "Ah, wait a second, birth control?"

"Dear, don't worry; it's all taken care of. I just need you."

That settled everything. *Buckle up; we're going all the way.*

I fumbled about as if I had never taken off my clothes before; I was far too fascinated watching Dara. She took off her shirt. And sure enough, just like you read about, there was a bra. It looked exactly like a bra looks, too. She started taking off her pants. Pants were the same as mine, but her underwear was much smaller and more delicate.

I was so happy. I could tell from between my legs, I was going to be normal. And although I thought about Casper, I was in the presence of Dara and that's what mattered most.

As our naked bodies were revealed, it became apparent: those old magazines were right. She had a different body than I did. It was curvy and had parts I did not have and missed parts I did have.

Mentally, I wasn't so sure anymore. Physically,

my body was convinced.

"It's not what you think. I don't like you just for—you know, there's also Platonic—"

Dara pulled me toward her. Together we climbed into Tim's bed. Naked, we were lying in bed a good two feet between us, my back against the wall. Getting our bodies together felt like crossing oceans. I was putting off the inevitable, until the time-space continuum could stand it no longer.

We met side by side. She turned to lie on her back, and I landed on top of her. I stroked her face. She smiled. I stroked her body. It shimmered. Her legs parted. She nodded her head. It was time.

It went in. It went in quite easily. You could say it was even tailor-made for the occasion. I tried just putting it there and remaining very quiet, but as suspected, the laws of thermodynamics took over. Because a small movement made my penis feel better. Then moving it up and down made it feel even better. Kinetically, it also made Dara feel better. The first slight thrust led to a compelling pleasure that needed to be felt again and again. The motoric pumping began. It was dehumanizing in a delightful kind of way.

As the pumping activity reached a kind of pleasurable plateau, I realized this was going to be easy. *Straight at last, straight at last, thank God Almighty, we are straight at last!*

The whole matter could have taken care of itself. The problem was I had a good physical feeling, but a bad mental feeling, as if my body were taking advantage of her body. One person using another person left a sour taste in my liberal mouth. Full of confidence and a sense of virtuosity, I tried to take it moderately slow so as not to hurt her. Intuitively I knew a slow start was best, since everything I really knew about sex came from the love duet in *Tristan und Isolde*. Unlike the other perfunctory kind of sex, this man-to-woman love continued: *Without end, without waking, without fear, nameless. No more Dara, no more Casper, I have become Dara. I have become Casper ...*

Not yet realizing there was a symbiotic nature to what I was already doing, I fumbled around for ways to make sure Dara was enjoying herself. Dara sensed what was going on and sweetly guided my hands or mouth on the right journey around her body. With her help I was getting even better at being straight because some of these moves were quite difficult given the continuing motoric activity going on below. It just delighted me to see she really enjoyed my tongue tenderly in her ear. She also particularly liked it when my tongue stimulated her nipples, though I must admit her breasts were disappointingly soft. The taste of her skin was flowery and slightly soapy, but still I managed to do it for her sake. Her smile and other signs of enjoyment made me proud that I could do that. I could already hear myself confidently ask at the end of this business, "Was it as good for you as it was for me?"

Down below, despite a lack of attention, things were going just fine, but being so busy with improvisation, I lost where this enterprise was headed. I was particularly blindsided by the onset of something I had only experienced in private, during masturbation: that animalistic moment. I was about to lose control and consciousness for that final wild moment and I presumed she would too somehow. I fought the urge to yell, "Time out." Instead Wagner's sex duet took over again.

Primal sacred force, free from the peril of waking! Freed from daylight's delusion, cloaked in a holy hiding night. No more Jamie, no more Dara, no more Casper.

I could feel my trepidation being conquered by the slow appearance of the greedy monster who wanted it all. Oddly enough, Dara's body eased into the sudden increase in speed. She began to shift her body with mine. The rush of pleasure was driving us to the heterosexual finish line.

No more consciousness, no more thinking, just a rush of never-ending joy!

Stripped of our humanity, we made groans and movements that seemed involuntary and driven by a compulsive pleasure. With each thrust, I felt so fucking normal. It was ecstasy itself.

Liebeslust! Love's pleasure, lasting forever and ever!

Suddenly I lost all control over thoughts. My brain flooded with wild images of Casper. Casper's fantasized body. But who cared in this everlasting whirl of hetero-sex. Every physical thrust from my body caused mental explosions of Casper: his body, his groin, his lips, his sweat growing more and more palpable until, just as in the love duet, Dara became Casper; Casper became Dara. Then, I exploded: my body wrenched, spasmed; my brain spasmed. Immediately my world shrunk down to Dara's real-life body. She looked in danger, yet she clearly did not want me to stop. The real work began. So I thrust and thrust until her breath was blown out. I saw her spasms had subsided; I could swear she looked disappointed, but then she said sweetly, "Okay, that's enough, stop."

The deed was done.

My body collapsed next to hers. Wagner was right. After sex came the piercing scream of hateful daylight. I was suddenly aware of a whole host of things I had not noticed just moments before. I heard the obnoxious music that had been playing too loud next door. I smelled my own body odor. I smelled hers as well. I suddenly felt the cramps in my body from balancing and stretching in odd positions. Casper turned back into Dara. The memory banks went into a frenzy to erase any thoughts of Casper. Underneath me was my best friend, whom I had just senselessly attacked like an animal. Dara, saving me from any more shame, gave me an exhausted smile. I smiled back.

I fought the desire to turn over, close my eyes, and

weep. Instead I lowered myself to her side and cuddled. I stroked her cheeks. I finally asked, "Was it good for you?" Then I realized I had left out the other part, which I hastily added, "As it was for me?"

I felt tender protectiveness for Dara. Having successfully connected the sex dots, I now could connect the other dots I hadn't thought of: the guilt ones. I had just screwed my best friend's girlfriend. I felt an urgent need to cover up my footsteps of betrayal.

"Dara, I love you."

"Yes, Jamie, I understand."

The act succeeded, but I had failed. My attempt to get Dara to cure me failed. In the attempted cure, I had to betray. Dara turned away on her side. I moved to her, so we were like two spoons lying side by side. I held on for all the security I could soak out of her body.

She fell asleep in my arms. As badly as I needed to sleep in her arms, I could not sleep. My arm fell asleep under her body, with painful tingling. Then came waves of thoughts I could not turn off. Wave 1: Did this work, was I really cured? Wave 2: This act which I bet the bank on, what was this going to cost me? Wave 3: Would Casper find out? Wave 4: I might lose all my friends. Wave 5: But no matter the cost, I proved I was normal. I am a heterosexual. Which set the stage for Wave 1 again. The cycle played itself out over and over again for the seven hours that Dara slept. Sometime late at night contemplating Wave 1, I was so happy not to be a virgin anymore. It was a bold, courageous victory, until hot tears rolled down my cheeks. It took me by surprise because I wasn't crying or weeping. Petting Dara's sleeping skin, sadly and vaguely I remembered I was not a virgin; I was anything but that. I darkened my best friend by what I did. Ashamed and forgetful, I finally fell asleep.

When we awoke, I could tell things had changed. Not for the better. There was some invisible barrier between us.

"I have to go." Dara got out of bed. She was still naked. Her body looked soft and innocent, untouched by the events that had transpired overnight.

"Thanks ... for ... staying." I struggled with my arm, which had lost all feeling since she had slept on it all night. It felt like a lifeless brick attached to my shoulders.

"Are we ... can we ... Don't get me wrong, Dara; I don't want to come in between you and Casper."

"What?"

"You and Casper, I could see you two are together."

"What gave you that idea? Casper is—never mind. Silly. Ahmed and I are seeing each other."

"I saw Casper kiss you—"

"Oh, we may have just had a little fun, nothing serious."

Oh, so that's what this was? I thought ruefully. Then at once I changed; I was overcome with joy. I had not betrayed Casper after all. With a sense of jubilation, I asked, "Is Ahmed going to kill me now?"

Dara laughed. The barrier fell, but our intimacy from last night was clearly over. She reverted to running her hands through my hair. I reverted to being a newly broken-in virgin.

"No, silly. Of course not."

"Why not? I would if I were in his shoes." I was so happy.

"Well, thank you, but Ahmed and I are just seeing each other with no strings attached. At the end of the year, when he graduates, he leaves to go back to Iran, and I am probably going back to South Dakota." Watching her get dressed, I realized I was about to lose something, lose it for the rest of my life, though I was not sure what.

"Really? South Dakota ... and Iran?"

"Well, if he can; he may have to go to Saudi Arabia first. His family is in some political trouble."

"Oh, that's terrible; I am sorry to hear that. Wow ..." *He's really Iranian.* "He'll understand?"

"Maybe not. It'll be better if it's just our secret, okay?"

"Sure."

"You were very considerate, Jamie. Even for a first time." She was fully dressed; I was still naked.

"You could tell?" I was disappointed. I had hoped I pulled it off better than that, but it reaffirmed I was a virgin after all. She walked resolutely to the door without me.

"I'll see you in class?" I asked.

"Absolutely!"

The door clicked shut. She was taking something of me with her. It frightened me a little. But I couldn't suppress a giggle, then the giggle grew to chuckles, and finally crescendoing to a guffaw! Triumphal thoughts of Casper raced through my mind. A flood of happiness swirled around me. I bet the bank on this and hit the jackpot! I hadn't blown it. I am straight, and I still get Casper. I am not going to lose my friend. And to top it all off, I am an official, very considerate heterosexual.

Dr. Wire, take notice: I AM CURED!

My ascent from hell is over, and I survived!

I defy you all!

Chapter 45: Blooming Flowers

"The Lord thy God is a Jealous God. He sees you. He sees you forever and ever. He sees you. HE SEES YOU!" said Mr. Nathan in his most diabolical voice as Dysart.

"Eyes! White eyes—never closed! Eyes like flames—coming!" I cried reading the role of Alan. Then a fury I didn't quite understand overtook me and I screamed, *"God seest. God seest? NO! No more! No more, Equus! THOU GOD SEEST NOTHING!"* I was panting—for real. After a moment, I realized the only sound was my panting. I seemed to have scared everyone in the class, as Mr. Nathan had done before.

"Now *that* reading had fire," said Mr. Nathan softly, and then he winked at me. "You get it, Jamie. You have this deep sympathy for Alan—if this were my acting class, we could spend the rest of the day dissecting your reading."

"But you have to admit this guy is really twisted," said the macho Ben. "I mean seriously twisted, and it takes one to know one, if you know what I mean." Many students laughed. I heard Ben talking to another student and heard him use the word "faggot." My heart was pounding.

"Twisted, Ben?" asked Mr. Nathan. "Next year we'll be doing *Equus.* So you are saying it's too twisted for you?"

"I didn't say that." Ben backed down.

"Then I would stick your judgments in your back pocket if I were you and learn a thing or two from Jamie here," said Mr. Nathan. I was joining another group, not just my friends, but my new major was quickly becoming my new community, Ben notwithstanding. "Jamie's got a leg up on you for that role. He has the sympathy and understanding. It's not twisted, it's insight. So, Ben, what's your take on this scene—from the *playwriting* perspective."

"In the structure of the play," said Ben, "this is the climactic scene."

"Climatic scene? Structure? Come on, what is going on here?" Mr. Nathan grilled him. "Ben, you know this, you're smarter than that. Maybe you don't have the courage Jamie here has." Courage? Jamie? Was he talking about me? "Jamie, I guess you'll have to tell him."

I was afraid he would ask me, but after his "courage" remark I had to go on.

"Well, he's dealing with his own ..." I had to think hard; I wanted to live up to Mr. Nathan's courageous assessment. "I guess, like Ben said, Alan discovers he's depraved—or at least confronted in a way he can no longer lie to himself about. The confrontation of the fantasy world in the broad daylight of disgust."

"Stop right there, Jamie. Everyone write that down: 'The confrontation of the fantasy world in the broad daylight of disgust.' Go on."

"And what Alan once thought would purify him now makes him disgusting. He can't stand knowing … Dara—Jill was his new measure of normalcy. And he couldn't hide this from her … That started a whole journey that was only going to end in this moment, the revelation of his horrible mutilation of the horses. And J-Jill … had to have her own opinion of that. It confronted him; he had to find a cure. He had become a disease for his actions."

"Thank you, Jamie. Actions, which at the beginning of the play seemed so monstrous, we now see in a more human light," said Mr. Nathan.

"Right, this climax shows Alan's own internal Reign of Terror, if you will."

"Oh." Mr. Nathan was not expecting me to continue, but it was too late now to stop.

"How Alan internally punishes himself, that can't help but make us feel sympathy for him. We all have things we hide, and feel guilty about."

"Our own guilty pleasures," savored Mr. Nathan.

"Guilty pleasures … Our first impulse is to kill what makes us … special." My face felt like it was burning. The strange looks from Ben and the other students told me I had talked too much. I went too far.

"Speak for yourself!" quipped Ben. No one laughed.

"How do you see it, Ben?" asked Alec, a senior student in the class.

"Fair question. How do you see it, Ben?" asked Mr. Nathan.

"Mr. Nathan, it's plain. Alan's a sicko and suddenly sees it and takes it out on these innocent animals."

"What is he missing that Jamie gets? Alec, you say it."

"Ben is denying the basic humanity of Alan. Alan has this mix of love and religion for … these horses, and killing them would be killing such a basic part of what he has become."

There was a silence in the class as Mr. Nathan looked around the room.

"I can also see what Jamie means," commented Eula. I turned and saw her. She was looking at me with a grin of approval. "He means something more like an archetype. Like for me, being a lesbian—yeah, you might as well all know it, if you didn't already— you get raised in a homophobic world and at once you realize you're gay; you want to try and kill that part of you, right, Jamie?"

I froze. How did she know? Was she accusing me of being gay? Yet I shook my head 'yes' to her question, unsure of what I was assenting to. To make it clearer, I hoarsely added, "I agree with your point."

"Good. I hope everyone has taken careful notes on what Eula and Jamie have said. I'm not going to kick the dead horse." Mr. Nathan managed a good laugh from the still classroom. "If *Equus* discusses how we can sell ourselves out, next week we're going to find out how we can sell out our fellow man. Have Dürrenmatt's *The Visit* read and digested by next Tuesday."

I couldn't get out of my mind what Eula had said. I know it was meant as a compliment, but did Eula and Mr. Nathan just hint I was homosexual? They probably needed to know that I happened to have just had successful sex with a woman. But who was I kidding? I felt Eula's and Mr. Nathan's horses' eyes fixed on me. Their weight was heavy. But I was not willing to blind these animals. Still, I needed to talk to Dara as soon as possible.

Chapter 46: Heteroimplausible

"The summary of the Federalist Papers is the unique perspective of Hamilton and Madison in recognizing that we have competing interests, competing desires, and competing taste," said our Constitutional History instructor. "They embraced and encouraged these differences to create this foundation of our republic: a foundation not of friends but of loyal enemies. Okay, with that we leave the Federalists. Next week, de Tocqueville."

The class was being dismissed. I tried many times to talk with Dara, but she had been avoiding me. Now was the time to show them what I was made of. Dara got up to leave with Niti and Ahmed. I rushed over to them.

"Hello, Dara!"

"Hi, Jamie. Good to see you," said Niti.

"Thanks—ah, don't go. Dara, please, can we talk?"

"We are going to be late," said Ahmed.

"Late for what?" I snapped.

"Jamie, don't be an asshole," Ahmed shot back.

"Not a very prim British thing to say, is it?"

"Okay, both of you stop it!" Dara directed.

I smiled triumphantly.

"I miss you, Dara. I just need to talk to you—alone!" I was proud.

"Ahmed, Niti, can you excuse us? I am going to speak to Jamie alone for a moment." She looked at Ahmed, who clearly objected.

"Come on, Ahmed, let's have lunch downstairs," said Niti. "Hope to see you around, Jamie."

We waited until the room emptied and we were alone.

"How are you doing, Jamie?"

"Not so good. I really miss you."

"Jamie, what's going on?"

"I want to talk to you, see you more often." I moved closer to her, moving to touch her, but she pulled away. I felt a flash of shame.

"Oh, Jamie, you are a sweetheart. How do I say this to you?" she said more out of frustration than endearment.

"You don't want me back," I pouted.

"I didn't say that."

"Come on, I haven't seen you since we had … since we did it." I totally surprised myself. I tried to put my arm around her. She backed away again.

"That was only a week ago," she said sharply. The rejection hurt more than I anticipated.

"Please don't make me out to be a goon."

"You're not a goon, Jamie. No one would think that of you. I am seeing Ahmed. You know that."

"You told him, didn't you?"

"I am bad at keeping secrets."

"He's not as broad-minded as you thought," I guessed.

"Men rarely are."

"Can I be … friends at least."

"Of course. It's just that I'm gonna be busy." She moved away from me.

"Busy with what?"

"You need more friends, Jamie. You need to try things out."

"Try things out?"

"Look, it's a sunny day. Why don't you just go and see Casper."

"Casper? Why Casper?" He was the last person I wanted to see.

"You're friends, aren't you?"

"He's never called me. He doesn't even know I am alive."

"He knows you're alive."

"What are you saying, Dara?" I couldn't help leave a glimmer of self-defeating hope for his friendship.

"You don't love me, Jamie."

"Can't we be friends though?"

"Don't settle for someone you don't love. It doesn't do anyone any favors."

"But I just want to be friends." I felt the world falling from under me.

"Right, and that's why you yelled at Ahmed."

"He yelled first … I sound like a jerk, don't I?"

I knew I was lost.

"You're not a jerk, Jamie. You made me feel very good."

"I want to do it again for you. Can't I? Is that so wrong?"

"Follow your heart, Jamie."

"My heart?"

"I think you should talk to Casper."

"I should?" A shiver of terror ran through my body.

"Yeah, you should both try and be ... bisexual."

"Huh? Me?" I hated this direction where others seemed to be pushing me. "Eula, did you talk with Eula?"

"Who?"

"What if I don't want to be bisexual?"

"Why don't you look up Casper?" She stood up. "I have to meet Ahmed and Niti."

"Casper and me? Did he say anything?"

"No, but he's asked about you. I see the way you look at him too."

"You do?" I felt the weight of defeat, a kind of monumental defeat. A defeat that could leave one traumatized forever.

She nodded her head.

"Then why did you let me ...?"

"I felt sorry for you." I didn't want to hear that. It was almost as bad as 'You hate yourself.' "Look, Jamie, it's warm and sunny out. Enjoy the weather and just be free. Try lots of things out. I gotta get back to Ahmed. I'll see you around."

"Dara, please, wait." She stopped walking away and looked at me. There was no anger in her eyes. "Please, don't do this. Don't abandon me."

"Jamie."

"I know, but we were good together, weren't we?"

"You were very … good. Now be good to others."

I watched her walk away from me, out of the empty room. I broke down. I slumped into a chair. The seat wasn't where I thought it was, and I crashed to the floor. My butt hurt, my head hurt ricocheting off the chair against a table leg. I cried. I was abandoned. Once when I was this desperate, my cousin Harold told me I would be okay. Well, where was he now? What I had done to Dara was so wrong. What I was thinking about Casper was so wrong. What I let happen to me was so wrong. "I am not okay!" I yelled, unsure if it was in my head or out loud. When someone finally walked into the room, I quickly stifled my crying. Standing up, I wiped the tears off my face. I felt guilty being caught crying like that. I rubbed my head, which hurt from the fall. I put the chair back upright. I was quickly getting out of the room when a brilliant sun beam shone through the window. The light was dazzling. It caught me by surprise. I thought of an art history class I took. Only in a Vermeer painting had I seen sunlight so beautiful. It shone into the room. I couldn't help manage a reluctant curl in my lips. The sun lit up a small flyer tacked to the wall. *The sun* on the flyer. The sun had to be the sign. I walked over to the board to read it. The subject was that Jewish student group I'd heard of, which was hosting Yom Kippur services next Saturday. I needed to atone! Now God was giving me my chance. Maybe this was my cousin Harold speaking from heaven. What I did to Dara, my thoughts for Casper; I could solve this guilt once and for all. Yom Kippur, the Day of Atonement, the holiest day of the year for Jews—and I was surely one of those. I had waited for this moment for so long. The end of the tunnel. A way out. The beauty of the solution was its elegance. Yom Kippur comes every year—so obvious, yet so genius. It solved everything! Just as Wagner's hero Tannhauser traveled to Rome, this sinner would journey to the synagogue and re-win God's grace.

Chapter 47: Yom Kippur

Our father, our king, hear our voice
We have sinned before you
Have mercy upon us
Bring an end to all trouble
and oppression around us
Our father, our king,
Redeem and save us this year
Hear our voice

It seemed out of left field coming to a synagogue after years of absence, but after this prayer, *Avinu Malkeinu (Our Father, Our King)*, I felt my redemption could not be far off. Memories of going to synagogue with my father gave me this hope. However, even in this urgent need for salvation and redemption, I could not ignore the shooting pains of self-recrimination: *Who did I think I was kidding?* But that only made me all the more determined to be saved, to atone, and to be written into the book of life.

"As we recite now the *Amidah* on this day of atonement," our stubbly-faced boy-rabbi preached, "I want us all to keep in mind the words of the prayer: 'Oh, Lord, keep my tongue and my lips from speaking deceit, and to them that curse me let my soul be silent, and like dust to all. Open my heart in Your Torah, and let my soul pursue Thy commandments.' Let's start on page 348 in your prayer books."

"On this Yom Kippur, what is a better sentiment than to keep your hearts open to Torah and above all keep your tongues free from deceit, and while reciting this *Amidah* think also of how you may be cursing yourselves. Dare to be who you are and stand up for yourself and our people of Israel. Daring to speak, to admit to be Jewish, and celebrate Israel's right to exist. There will be those anti-Semites, those anti-Zionists, who will confront you with their hatred, but meet their hatred with silence. Don't let it drag you into any further sin. Let's begin the *Amidah* on page 281. It is customary to stand and then add your own personal prayer at the end."

It was a breathtaking sentiment. Be true to yourself, even if unpopular. But as to small-mindedness, I had suffered greatly from the Jewish community's own small-mindedness, their seeming hatred for the people like my cousin Harold, their smug contempt for those who were not Zionists. My mother and I were not Zionists; my father was a rabid one. I could not accept a theocracy in the twentieth century, even if it was my own religion.

Nevertheless, the rabbi appeared to be encouraging me to just accept myself for what I was ... until I started reading the *Amidah*. The prayers started with their obsequious addresses to a God who must be impressed by emphatic flattery. It went on for so long that it started to bother me, like it always did. I was unsure why this God needed our praises. Was He insecure? Perhaps more than flattery, this God would value loyalty to our integrity, which is what God gave us, after all.

The little Nietzschean voice inside me rebelled and said to me, "Just look at these people!" As usual, during this prayer, I heard people muttering instead of contemplatively praying or meditating. They turned the pages faster than anyone could read, even by memory. I could not help but think of hypocrisy.

I had hoped Yom Kippur would simplify my life. I would atone for what I had done, for what I had thought, and for what I wanted to do. Eula's, Mr. Nathan's, and Dara's words haunted me. Instead, I felt alone. I looked around. The makeshift synagogue was packed with a sea of Jewish faces: faces set on singing the praises of Israel; faces to shut me out, ignore me, or worse, attack me and my reprehensible yet irresistible desires.

I sat on the aisle. Next to me was a rather severe looking student. She had a harsh, disapproving look affixed to her prematurely old-looking face.

At the end of my silent *Amidah* reading, I added my own personal prayer: *Lord, please make me fit in here. I know I have offended people, and I wish to put this aright, but to do that, please chase from me these sinful thoughts I am having.* Surprisingly, it seemed as if God was interested, because in my mind

He asked me, as if he were Dr. Wire: *Oh, what thoughts?*

Dirty ones, I replied.

Thoughts are not deeds. So thoughts cannot be sinful. What thoughts are you talking about anyway? God seemed to respond.

I want, more than anything else in the world, to marry Casper Tyres.

The response made me shudder in shame and hopelessness:

Oh, under-man, that which does not kill you shall make you stronger. Who was replying?

As the service went on, I was surprised by how easily the Hebrew melodies came back to me. But the words did not. I became mired in my old Jewish morass. I was lost in the sea of Hebrew. I muddled my way through, faking the words to the familiar melodies. The service lumbered along, as rote prayer followed rote prayer, one obsequious praise of God after another. I was here in crisis, and this Yom Kippur service seemed to only heighten my need. I had one last hope.

Chapter 48: Yom Kippur Burlesque

We came to a prayer called the *Ashamnu*. To me, the *Ashamnu* represented the most important confession of our sins in the whole service. In confessing all the sins from A to Z of the Hebrew alphabet, I remembered my father would lightly beat or rap his chest with every sin. This was the moment. This was the atonement, the gateway to my redemption, if I ever had one. The ancient Hebrew came back to me, the melody loud and clear. All other prayers aside, this was the one I needed to let my soul breathe once again. We chanted. I lightly rapped my fist against my chest.

Ashamnu, We have trespassed (a hard rap on my chest). How dare you trample on the feelings and aspirations of Jews with your own petty doubts!

We have robbed (another painful rap). Through my baseness I have robbed myself of my sense of belonging, of being just a normal person!

We have spoken slander (another blow). I said bad things about my family to Doctor Wire.

We have done wrong (deep rap). My brain would not stop with the gross and disgusting thoughts that God hates! I hit myself again for good measure and people started to stare. In horror, I realized this was *my* self-hatred speaking.

We have dealt treacherously (deep rap, tears and sobbing). I am betraying the only thing I dared to love.

We have acted perversely (rap so hard the severe lady next to me turned and looked). I wanted to look at Casper; please, just one more time.

We have acted presumptuously (deep rap and tears). Then there is my behavior with Dara.

We have done violence (a slight rap). I think of the violence I have done to myself with belts and sticks just for thinking about Casper. I dare to ask for compassion, maybe for the first time in my life, for my Casper, for someone I love.

We have practiced deceit (deeper rap). The irony: I have deceived myself and I deceived Casper by lying to him, lying and not saying how I truly feel.

We have counseled evil (deeper rap, a resonating knock on my rib cage). I have listened to this religion for too long.

We have spoken falsehood (deeper rap, bitter sarcasm). I cannot help now but think of the hypocrisy of the piety here. But wait, hypocrisy of the pious? What about my own hypocrisy? I am lying to myself! What am I doing here, anyway? Could this congregation magically make me heterosexual, just as I kidded myself that Dara would?

We have scoffed (rap, anger replacing tears). I have been scoffed at. I suddenly think of my poor cousin, Harold. What comfort did he ever get here? The kids who bullied me, how I delighted in their torments because they made me the victim.

We have revolted (no rap). I have been untrue to myself.

We have blasphemed. But maybe not enough.

We have rebelled. What else could you possibly expect?

We have committed iniquity. But I have been wronged! I am not a disease!

We have transgressed. Against my heart!

We have oppressed. I have let myself be oppressed.

We have been arrogant. Who claims to compliment God with rote prayers? Who claims self-righteousness?

We have victimized. My cousin Harold was victimized! I have been victimizing myself.

We have dealt corruptly. You corrupted me to hate myself!

We have committed abomination. I have been outraged!

We have led others astray. NO MORE! THOU GOD SEEST NOTHING!

The atonement vanished, as ephemeral as the air. The *Ashamnu* turned on me. The prayer meant to atone for my transgressions only called up more transgressions.

"Oh, God Almighty, what path have you left for me?" I muttered aloud.

"You are a deeply spiritual person," whispered

the austere woman next to me.

This was not what I was signing up for on Yom Kippur—a full-blown crisis. The crisis spread from my head to my unsteady knees, which started to shake.

The service got grimmer.

Just before the *shofar* would be blown to signify our atonement and start the joy of the new year, the rabbi stopped. "We have come to the concluding service," he said. "I look up and outside I can see the sun has set. I realize this has been a long but beautiful Yom Kippur. Now that we have atoned," and then the rabbi made eye contact with me, "I see the earnestness and humility with which we have prayed." He held my gaze, then looked away. "May we all be inscribed in the Book of Life. Now it is time to celebrate, bring the joy we have absented from our lives, for this moment of atonement. And upstairs I hope you will all join me in the celebration, as a wonderful spread of our favorite break-the-fast foods awaits us. And I mean plates of lox and bagels, challah and whitefish, and of course, some wine and juice. And we should be joyous and have a good time. But lest we forget ourselves, we must not have too good a time. First, remember in our joy that we should not transgress. So here, our concluding prayer before the *shofar* is blown, is a little reminder of the bad ways to celebrate. Turn your books to page 817."

As I turned to the page, a sentence leapt out at me.

"Man shalt not lie with man as with a woman for

it is an abomination."

Eula's words came back to me. She frightened me when she said them, but now they were the blessing I was searching for. "You get raised in a homophobic world and at once you realize you're gay; you want to try and kill that part of you, right, Jamie?"

I stared again at the offending sentence in the High Holiday prayer book.

"How could I be such an idiot!" I exclaimed. Everyone around me stared at me. It was at this moment, on Yom Kippur, that I had the epiphany. I was hunched over and feeling sorry for myself just like Zarathustra! Pity for myself! Is that what I'd sunk to? Is that why I studied Nietzsche since childhood? Nietzsche who hated pity beyond all else?

For the first time, I saw myself as I truly was. Nietzsche wanted me to shine! Wagner wanted me to love! Follow your heart, Dara had said. Follow my heart? The evidence was now so overwhelming that even a jury would be convinced.

"Has the jury reached a verdict?" asked the judge in my mind.

"We have, your honor," answered my jury of angels.

"Defendant, please rise. How do you find the defendant, James Micaiah Goldberg?"

"We find the defendant homosexual."

How could I be such an idiot!

I knew why I hated myself. It was obvious; it *had been* obvious. I needed Casper's image during Yom

Kippur to wake me up. I was in such a fierce rage, I scared myself; I put my prayer book down. I pulled on my jacket, the severe woman next to me looking at me as if I was crazy. I marched down the middle aisle during the final dramatic prayers and left the building. I stormed outside into the twilight, the rim of the sun still a blazing bronze sickle, then at once it disappeared and I heard the *shofar* blowing.

At first I was furious. *How stupid could you be, you dumb fucking asshole. You fell in love with a fucking guy, for crying out loud!* But I decided not to think those thoughts because that was self-hatred. I hated myself and now I knew why.

I hated myself because I hated homosexuals. Unfortunately for me, I was the homosexual I hated so much. 'I saw the enemy, and it was me.'

No longer! I would not hate homosexuals, though others clearly did. These others I would not conspire with any longer.

No matter: Bowling alleys, toilets, s&m crazies— I was throwing my lot in with all of them. Let that take me wherever it must.

Wherever? It was clear. It was taking me to one place, to Casper!

Chapter 49: The Label: Homosexual

I had spent the weeks after Yom Kippur in the reference section of the library, desperately looking for some objective information on who I was. I waited until I was alone to turn to the damning pages. Homosexuality was still a great target of McCarthyism. Just being caught looking up the word made you suspect. I knew that from all the years I spent on the other side.

I looked with great trepidation. I was expecting to find a definition like these:

Homosexual—Sexual crazies better off dead.

Homosexual—Degenerates who have sex in bowling alley toilets.

Instead what I found was usually a variation on this theme:

Homosexual—Someone attracted to members of the same gender.

The big controversy among the definitions was whether the definition included someone who actually practiced this attraction or not. A practicing homosexual sounded like a practicing clinician. I had visions of a licensed homosexual.

Nevertheless, I had to think of the horrible life of the homosexuals I had once read about long ago and accepted as fact—homosexuals performing illicit sex acts in very unromantic places. To that I had to just shrug my shoulders. I tried fighting the unpleasant implications, and could not any longer. Still, as long as I didn't think about it too long, I felt a resurgent pride in myself. If it led me to a gross sex life, well, I could cross that bridge when I came to it. In one book on sociopolitical definitions, I came across this definition:

Homophobia—Morbid fear of homosexuality in the form of both prejudice and discrimination based in social perceptions using stereotypes of moral, psychological, and biological differences in homosexuals.

The definition was surprisingly similar to the same book's definition of racism. Racism, sexism, fascism, ageism, nationalism, religionism, xenophobia, prejudice, closed-mindedness of all kinds—these were the sworn enemies of my childhood. To the list of enemies I had to add retroactively and incongruously a new word: homophobia.

In homophobia, I recognized myself in two ways: both as perpetrator and victim, predator and prey. The concept and the definition of homophobia made objective sense to me. Subjectively, this word was devastating, even more devastating than the word homosexual. Even politics was turning on my former life, a life that was caving in on me. Adopting the label homosexual led to the destruction of so much of what I was doing. The Reign of Terror, the self-inflicted pain, the fear of my own sexuality—all that was now a thing of the past. It had its bad side, however. I went from something deep and complex to something that sounded rather banal: a person attracted to someone of the same gender. It didn't quite pack the wallop that the passionate romantic or the tortured loner did. Still, enlightenment was certainly worth the price, and I would later find out this word, homosexual, carried considerable knockout power.

It hurt more than I realized that sex with Dara proved nothing. I really thought it would be the cure. I could have sex with Dara, but I needed something more. As Dara herself said, I needed to follow my heart. Despite my genuine feelings for Dara, my heart was leading me to Casper. I went to the synagogue to atone for being a homosexual, and instead I ended up atoning for being Jewish.

Since my heart was still leading me to Casper, I resolved to tell Casper I loved him—no matter what it cost me.

To begin with, I was going to do something I had never done before, something I had never even thought of. I walked into a flower shop. I had never stepped in a flower shop in all my life. I had no idea what to expect, how to behave, what to ask for, or how much anything would cost.

I walked in and all was foreign, everything so

strange and yet so familiar. Flowers bloomed all around me. There were bunches upon multicolored bunches of the stuff. I had always thought of flowers as banal and bourgeois, but the moment I stepped in this flower shop, flowers became glorious and absolutely radical and revolutionary. I said my life had to change forever. This simple act, buying flowers, was about to do exactly that. Standing there, I could not help feeling I did not belong. I was frightened but completely exhilarated.

"May I help you, young man?" asked the woman behind the counter. My heart pounded.

"Yes, I need some flowers." Every word seemed accompanied by bombastic music. "What are the most romantic flowers you have, the ones that shout 'I love you?'"

"Nice to see such a happy young fella. You'll want roses. We have these lovely pink ones." I had to brace myself. I now had to get used to this for the rest of my life. From now on there would be a million-and-one confrontations I was now and forever going to face. I tried to speak as calmly as possible to face confrontation number one. "I need some more masculine-looking roses."

"Oh."

"They're for a man." I couldn't help myself.

"What? ... I see ... or I think I do anyway ... Dark red?" she asked me. I had a blank look.

"I don't know; you're the florist."

"Yeah, but you're the customer. Okay, young man,

dark red. Red. Dark, dark, dark red, yep, that's what you need. Dark—red. Wrapped?"

"What?"

"Wrapped? Do you want them wrapped? It costs extra, but the right answer is 'yes,'" she said somewhat acidly but with feeling.

"How much extra?" I asked. She rolled her eyes. "I am still a student."

"Lord have mercy, for you it's free. That'll be twelve dollars," she said as she wrapped the flowers into a cone of plastic wrap, first adding some austere green twigs between the flowers.

"Thank you, they look really nice. The green is a nice touch," I said, trying to cheer her up a bit.

"Yeah? That's twelve dollars, young fella." I handed her the money. She counted out the change and then looked in my eyes. "You done caught me off guard, fella. But you're happy, and your kind are some of my best customers." Welcome to the world of mixed signals and mixed victories. I loved the sound of 'your kind'.

"Thank you. Before I knew who I was–I wasn't alive."

She smiled and added ambiguously, "Well, you're a live one now."

I walked outside, suddenly realizing, how revolutionary this act was. If I met anyone I knew from school, any teacher or student or administrator or even my mother, they would ask me who I bought the flowers for. The confrontation would result in some possibly negative outcome I could not predict, but I also could not shy away. It was hard to get used to a life where almost everything you do is an overt act.

I brought the flowers back to my dorm room. How to get them to Casper was the challenge. I fished out Casper's little biography. It reminded me that Casper was the technical assistant for a student production of Eugene O'Neill's *Long Day's Journey into Night*. The dress rehearsal would be at 7:30 p.m. on Friday. All I had to do was go, flowers in hand, to the Theater Arts building early on Friday afternoon and wait. Sooner or later he would show up.

"Can we have a cup of coffee?" I asked Casper in the mirror. "Oh, hi, Casper; can we get a cup of coffee? Now, about that cup of coffee? Let's go for a coffee."

"Where did you want to go?" My roommate Tim had walked in.

"Oh, sorry about that, Tim. I didn't hear you come in. I was just … rehearsing for my audition."

"Who are the flowers for?"

The confrontations were coming fast and furious to such a susceptible rookie. Lying was out of the question, but so was the truth.

"Flowers? Oh yeah, those … uh …" In that split second I learned what every gay person has learned since, that there are shades of the truth. Most people ask for a very superficial shade of it; if they dig in instead, they get what they deserve. So with that plan in mind, I ventured forth. "Tomorrow is the final dress rehearsal of *Long Day's Journey into Night*, and I bought these to give to the technical crew. Everyone gives flowers to the leads or the directors, but no one ever gives them to the technical crew, so I think it would be a very kind gesture, don't you?"

"Very kind. I just never saw anyone get flowers before."

"Oh, in the theater we do it all the time—on opening night—or the final dress rehearsal."

Really? Good for you." Tim's smile told me he thought it was kind. I felt a genuine sense of affection and friendship for Tim, maybe for the first time for anyone.

"Hey, I am going to a recital, Jamie. Do you wanna come? Nina and Dorothy are singing Schubert's *Lieder*."

Nina and Dorothy were two graduate music students Tim and I had come to know. Nina had a beautiful voice. Dorothy, on the other hand, sang with pure overwhelming will.

"When is it?" I asked eagerly.

"Friday—oh, you can't go—couldn't you skip the dress rehearsal and give the flowers on the opening night?"

"I can't really; I have to—I mean I offered to help out at the dress rehearsal. Just some ... guy ... Casper Tyres, Tenth Congressional District, he's in the theater department and one of their top set designers; I have to help him. I promised I would. But the recital sounds great. I love anything Nina or Dorothy do."

"Well, Nina will be disappointed. You know, she asked about you."

"She did? Then, tell her I said 'hello.' We should all do something this weekend or something like that. Maybe I can see them rehearse?"

"Cool. Great idea. I will ask her."

Chapter 50: Forgotten Flowers

Friday night after classes, I skipped dinner and ran as fast as I could to the Theater Arts building. The theater was adjacent to a recessed park, placing it away from the busy streets just behind it. The park had a small concrete bench just perfect for waiting.

The pseudo-neoclassical building housed two theaters: a large one for major productions and a smaller one for student projects. *Long Day's Journey into Night* was on the small stage.

The prospects of what might happen made me very nervous. I never told anyone, except myself, that I was homosexual. What if Casper was one of those who hated people like me? Would he hit me? Would he tell everyone? Yet it seemed as if people knew already. He might hate me. He might hurt me or damage my reputation. He might think I was asking him to have sex in a toilet. I didn't want him to think that. I had to make my feelings clear. I would confess how I felt. He'd react disgusted. Then I'd explain how much I love him and he'll take pity on me and be my best friend. That's all I needed.

I couldn't sit still on the bench, so I paced back and forth. Then I saw Casper in the distance and realized I had forgotten the flowers. I felt a flash of anger. Instead of letting the flowers do the talking, I'd have to do it myself. I needed to prepare some line. A pickup line, I suppose. "Casper I need to tell you something"—sounds like an apology. "Casper, I love you." Too abrupt. "Casper, you know the opera *Tristan*—" I'd be out of my mind. "Hi Casper, want to get a cup of coffee? I want to say something very important." Too late, he was approaching, so coffee would have to take the place of the flowers.

"Coffee. Do you want a coffee?" I muttered, hiding myself behind one of the neoclassical pillars. I peeked out to see him approach. *Oh rapture!* I thought. *He is still standing and hasn't run away. Play the coffee card! It's all I have left!* As if ordering a torpedo strike, I shouted in my head: *Approach and load the coffee line! "Coffee, may I buy you a cup of coffee after the performance?" Approach!*

I stepped out from the pillar and pretended to nonchalantly walk past Casper. Then I would stop and say, "Hello Casper, may I buy you a cup of coffee?"

That didn't work out quite as planned. I hadn't factored the rate of acceleration correctly, nor the mass-to-velocity ratio, and my hand swung and jammed right into Casper's hip. I stopped and tripped onto him. Poor Casper didn't know what hit him.

"Sorry, Casper, I just wanted a cup of coffee—with you."

"What the hell?" He looked up at me. "Jamie!"

He smiled, getting off the ground. I hadn't blown it—at least not yet. "That's quite an entrance."

"Sorry, are you all right?"

"I'm fine. What are you doing here?" intoned the silken voice of my beloved. But he wasn't supposed to say that. It wasn't in my script. Did he hear my coffee line? I had to improvise something.

"Yes, sorry, I just wanted to—I mean, do you want to—" Uuh-oh—what? How was I suppose to ask?

"Relax, Jamie," said Casper, still smiling at me. My heart felt even more intimidated by his smile than the anger I was bracing for. "I was wondering … you know … *Coffee!*"

"Jamie, I am on my way to the theater. I have to TA for my friend Dwight." In DSU theater-speak, TA meant Technical Assistant; helping him meant I would get to spend the entire evening with him if I helped too. He was happy to see me!

"Oh, Dwight, that Dwight … he's your friend. I see. The director."

"Are you doing anything tonight?" he asked me.

"No!" I snapped.

"Did you want to help me? Get your feet wet with some backstage work?"

"I'd love … that—that—that would be great. Youknowthisismychancetoreallygettolearnsomethingt hanksforthechance."

"Good, then come along, I'll show you around and you can help with the light controller."

That sounded important. "What's the play?"

"*A Long Day's Journey into Night*. You know it?" Casper asked. I couldn't believe my good luck. My life was turning around. I felt truly redeemed.

"No, I never saw it. I'd love to help out. You mentioned about getting my feet wet in theater; this is a good way."

"Excellent, you follow instructions very well, my boy," he smiled. I was so happy. But would he be so happy when I told him how much I loved him?

"Come on, it's gonna start in less than an hour and we got lots to set up."

"Great! It's Eugene O'Neill's family drama masterwork—"

"Oh, you do know it?" he asked me.

"Know it? Well, I've heard of it, of course."

His eyes did their sweet little twinge. I erupted in joy. *I did it! I did it! All the world, just stop all of your whining; everything is okay now! He's my friend!*

"Well, you're a bit overdressed for the occasion— you have a T-shirt underneath your shirt?"

"Oh, uh, no, I don't, as a matter of fact."

"It's okay. Just be careful." He sounded disappointed. I realized he was dressed scruffily, a windbreaker and jogging pants. Apparently it did not matter, because before I knew what hit me, I realized I was walking together with Casper, just like I had seen him do with so many others, only now it was *me*. As we were walking—and talking—I wondered whether there was someone head-over-heels in love with him staring at him right then, at that moment, wishing he was in *my* shoes.

Casper asked me if I had TA experience before and whether I could help him. I have no idea what I said, but it got me in the theater.

"Hi, Casper; can't let that guy in until seven," said some blond-haired jerk at the door.

"You know Jamie?" Casper asked. I smiled.

"No, I don't," said the flunky.

"Anyway, he's helping me TA tonight in the back."

"Oh, you have help. Well, you've done very well for yourself, Casper. Go right in, as I am sure you will." He winked. Casper seemed to at least exchange glances with the jerk. But who cared, I was in.

Chapter 51: Long Night's Journey

The small theater seated maybe seventy-five people. The theater was an improvised space created by combining rooms together and stealing some space from the hallway. While the large theater looked resplendently neoclassical, the smaller theater was dark and unimaginatively rectangular.

"Jamie have you been to this theater before?"

"No, this is my first time to the small stage. But, I saw *The Homecoming* last year."

"Did you like it?"

"I loved it. I have to admit I didn't understand all of it, but it was really moving."

"Good—hmm—I need you to put the stage together. You think you can do that?"

"Of course," I lied completely, beginning to feel a queasy sense of doom inside. "Ah, Casper, I just need to—"

"I have to set up the lights, Jamie. You just take those wooden boxes piled up off to the side there and put them in front of the stage. You take four boxes from back to front; you should have enough for five across. If not, give me a holler."

"Casper, just one quick confess—" But he had already

run off before I could tell him I loved him.

I wish I had my flowers; they would have spoken volumes. The stage, meanwhile, was more of a challenge than I thought it would be. The boxes looked square, but weren't. There was a definite top side and front side. I placed one row together and then saw my mistake. When I put the next row back, they slightly mismatched. I had to play around with them for about twenty minutes until I discovered a small black arrow on the top side pointing in the right-side direction. Then it was a piece of cake. Eventually this fuss was all irrelevant because Casper directed me to put a huge sheet of cardboard over them, which masked any mismatched blocks. I stood on the stage to see if it was stable. It seemed okay. I looked out at the stage and felt a shiver. I looked out at the empty old movie-house seats, which created empty rows—yet I could easily imagine them filled with people eagerly waiting for me to speak my first lines.

"These shoes are black. Well, they can do, anyway, until I get another pair. Maybe they'll get me down to Sidcup—"

"Hey, Jamie! Knock it off. Plenty of time for that next term! Help me put the sets together," yelled Casper. I wondered if he knew what I was reading from. They hadn't even started the auditions yet for *The Caretaker.*

The sets were minimalist by necessity, and putting them together was easy. The Tyrone family home was defined by single pieces of furniture: a table, a bench, a counter. The positions for the furniture were easily identified by taped markings on the cardboard floor. Casper positioned the lights to help define the spaces. The cast also trickled in, and irony of ironies, the person playing Jamie Tyrone was Ben Geln, the class bully. I was in a good mood, and I thought I would just reach out and make friends with him.

"Hey, Ben, I saw you were playing Jamie; that's funny."

"Yes, hilarious. What are you doing here anyway?"

"I am helping Casper TA."

Ben looked contemptuously at Casper and then at me.

"Yeah, I bet you are. How stupid can you be?"

"I see you're still spending all your money on charm school."

"Just don't fuck up—ha, ha, ha—great pun; don't mess up my spots. Watch for it in the fourth act, my confrontation with Mama. Butt boy." Ben walked arrogantly away, leaving me at first very angry until I realized I had to get used to that kind of reception. But I could not imagine how Ben discovered or guessed I was homosexual—as Eula also seemed to know. The prospect didn't frighten me. Just knowing about me and the word 'homosexual'—it sounded so fresh, new, perverse, but beautiful. This whole situation made me feel incredibly fresh and young. I felt like the embodiment of spring.

Behind the theater seats was the narrow tech booth. This would be the world I inhabited with Casper once the play started. A glass wall separated the booth from the audience. On the far side of the booth was a ladder to access the overhead lights. In the center of the glass booth were two control panels, one for the lights and one for the sound. The room was made even more narrow as flats for sets of plays, future and past, were stacked against the wall, along with junk of every variety—from tools and buckets to props from a circus to a royal wedding.

The booth was a very intimate space to share with Casper. He had a magnetic masculine odor I would have found repulsive before Yom Kippur. The narrow passageway meant Casper had to brush up against me. Something I could swear he was doing on purpose. His chest slightly rubbing my back gave me a tingling thrill and an explosion of split-second fantasies. Then I tried to think of reasons to pass in front of him, daring to let my butt softly glide across him, imagining sparks flying as fabric rubbed against fabric.

Casper stood close to me, explaining the lightboard. I could feel his warmth. He was so extremely kind, I was in heaven in a tech booth. I had to pinch myself not only to remind myself this was real, but also to stay focused on Casper's instructions.

"It's easy, Jamie; I'll explain one more time," he intoned patiently. "Follow along the script here; it's on this stand." He pointed to a music stand with the script mimeographed and marked in the margins what lights went on and at what strength. "You know which ones are the mains?"

I could feel his breath, could even smell its tantalizing staleness. "Sure, the middle two." I looked up into his warm eyes. We were a team. The team I so longed for.

"Right. The main thing is that at the end of each act, Dwight wants a slow fade for like five minutes so that no one notices. Got it?"

"Sure, whatever you say, Casper. Casper—just like it was done last year in the last act of *The Home-coming.*"

"How observant." Casper smiled at me. "When it's lights out, you kill the sound system.

"You can count on me." I trembled. Out in the audience I saw Dwight, the critical and obese director of *The Caretaker.* Along with Mr. Nathan, he thought I was 'too nervous' for the role of the old man, Davies.

"You see the red mark." Casper showed me a red-marker asterisk in the corner of a script page. And then he put his arm on my shoulder. I was in love; it felt so good admitting that to myself.

"Yes, I heard you, Casper. That mark indicates the start of the fade-out. Every ten lines or so, take it down. Casper, can I just—"

"Good boy!" That must have been a sign he loved me too. The touching, the gentle reproaching, the encouragement.

Throughout the play, I could actually watch Casper all I wanted to, as I had the excuse that I was learning the technical side of things. Plus, he seemed to enjoy my looking at him. I saw him fiddling around with the soundboard. I had to pinch myself, realizing that he was mentoring me. I was actually in his gorgeous company. He had such incredible good taste in clothes. I would never have matched a sleek green T-shirt with purple jogging pants.

I just couldn't believe my good luck. Just wanting to hear his voice, I asked a question I already knew the answer to.

"What's that green button for on the soundboard, Casper?"

"That's the power switch. If we don't turn that on, we can't hear anything."

At one moment, Casper hugged me from behind. "Excuse me," he said. He actually wasn't hugging me, he was reaching over me to adjust the lightboard, but it felt like a hug, so maybe it counted.

"Casper, I have to tell you something."

"Jamie, you have to focus. We got work to do." My heart was about to explode.

"Got it." He meant for me to focus on the play. He went up front and talked with the actors and Dwight while the crowd filed in. There was a sprinkling of attendees for the dress rehearsal.

I positioned myself in front of the soundboard and Casper came back in and took his spot up among the lights. He waved at me. I turned on the green button on the sound board and faded the lights up carefully and slowly. I could not wait for this play to end. I would buy him a coffee and we'd be able to really express ourselves. I could finally tell him how much I had loved him from afar. The lights were on.

Casper gave me a thumbs-up.

Tyrone and Mary entered, both young students made to look old by putting talcum powder on their skin and hair to make it looked parched and aged. Tyrone was hugging Mary the same way Casper almost did.

> MARY: Why did the boys stay in the dining room, I wonder? Cathleen must be clearing the table.

"She flubbed her first line," I whispered.

"Shh," Casper cooed.

> TYRONE: It's a secret confab they don't want me to hear, I suppose. I'll bet they're cooking up some new scheme to touch the Old Man.

Chapter 52: Final Curtain—Dress Rehearsal

The dress rehearsal started off boring and stiff, especially as heard through tinny speakers in the tech room. Nevertheless, Eugene O'Neill's story of his dysfunctional family could not help but grab me—especially since the most preyed upon character in the cast was also named Jamie, even though he was being played by a homophobe, Ben Geln. At least he could act: his portrayal of Jamie was much more likable than he was in real life.

Throughout the play, the lies, the self-deception, hit a familiar chord. My mother was no drug addict like Mary Tyrone, yet there was the familiar dysfunctional self-delusion.

EDMUND: Listen, Mama! You haven't asked me what I found out this afternoon. Don't you care a damn?

MARY: Don't say that! You hurt me, dear!

EDMUND: What I've got is serious, Mama. Doc Hardy knows for sure now.

MARY: That lying old quack! I warned you he'd invent—!

EDMUND: He called in a specialist to examine me, so he'd be absolutely sure.

MARY: Don't tell me about Hardy! If you heard what the doctor at the sanatorium, who really knows something, said about how he'd treated me! He said he ought to be locked up!

Like most things this fall, I got more than I paid for. I was so engrossed in the act that Casper pinched me—painfully—and I almost screamed in surprise. I stared at him.

"Red asterisk," he whispered sharply.

I missed my cue to fade out the lights. I started the fade-out a little late. At the end of the act, I turned to Casper.

"I'm sorry, Casper, I got a little caught up in the play." I felt the heat radiating from my face.

"It's the only cue you had the entire act." He looked angry and then softened. "Don't sweat it; I'm sure no one noticed it. Jamie, you're doing fine. The fade-out, once you started, was smooth. You stay here and don't let anyone in."

"Okay, Casper, and just one thing—"

"Oh yes, after most of the audience clears out, go out and remove the bench on stage and replace it with a couch off in the wing."

"Put the couch in the same place as the bench?"

"Exactly, and just come back here afterwards. Got it?"

"Got it!" It felt so great to help Casper; he seemed to really appreciate my help. Casper then disappeared and didn't reappear until I finished the couch task. I saw him talking with Dwight, who was sitting in the audience along with Eula and Ben.

I wanted to talk with them, but Casper shooed me away. "Go back to the booth, Jamie; I need to talk to you in a moment." I could not resist him, especially since he was being so affectionate, even if it was to tell me to piss off.

There was something I didn't like about Dwight. There was something suspect in the way his pudgy face would stare at me, almost like a sneer, sometimes a leer, and other times a gawk. It was disturbing to me. It seemed so unfair that a fat, oily-haired moron got to talk to my Casper.

In the last intermission, I couldn't stand it anymore that I couldn't tell Casper I loved him, so I dashed to my dorm room and fetched the flowers. I raced back, completely out of breath. I put the flowers in back of the booth. I would hand them to Casper as soon as the play was over.

I walked out of the booth and saw Casper was again chatting with Dwight. I walked by them.

"Where were you?" Casper asked me.

"Oh, I had to get something, something I want to

show you."

"Aren't you at least going to say hi, Jamie?" asked Dwight, as if I were slighting him somehow.

"Hi, Dwight. I didn't want to interrupt you guys." He grabbed my leg. I didn't like it. "I hope you are preparing to read Aston for us," he said, but in a way that rubbed me the wrong way—as if he was inferring something else. But I didn't want to be unfriendly to my potential director or Casper's friend. I swallowed and pretended I liked him.

"Of course I am studying, very hard," I said, hoping Casper heard me. "I want this role very badly."

"We'll see." He turned to Casper as if I weren't there. "I didn't think he was the right type for Davies, but I think with the right effort we can make him a good Aston."

Dwight let go of my leg, finally, and I just knew he was a homosexual. Not a good one; probably one of the toilet sex guys. The creep patted my butt as he walked by—how did he know he could do that? He was gross, but still the touch gave me a secret thrill of affirmation. *I am gay, dammit. And apparently attractive too.*

"Come on, let's go inside for the last act. You ready?" Casper asked.

"Yeah, ready and willing," I enthused.

"That's what I heard."

"Huh? What?" I didn't understand what Casper meant by that.

"Come on, kid," He patted my back. After coming

out, I noticed my backside was getting all kinds of attention. Was it always like this, and I never noticed before?

Walking back with him, I wanted to hold his arm.

"Hey, Casper, can we get a cup of coffee sometime?"

"What?"

"I was wondering, can we get a cup of coffee sometime?"

"Of course, Jamie."

"Great, because there is something I just have to tell you—"

"Don't forget, whatever happens though, don't miss your cue. Think of us as actors behind the sets. If you get into the play, follow along with the script; you'll see the cues. You got three of them this time."

The last act, the entire cast came alive. For most of the act, Casper stood close to me.

JAMIE (TYRONE): But to think when it's a question of your son having consumption, you can show yourself up before the whole town as such a stinking old tightwad! Don't you know Hardy will talk and the whole damned town will know! Jesus, Papa, haven't you any pride or shame?

I noticed a tear crawling down my cheek.

"My dad wasn't like that, but it still hurt me to see a father's callous unconcern," I whispered. Casper's arm went around my shoulder.

"You must have a screwed-up family like mine," Casper whispered.

He liked me!

"Ben's doing a great job," said Casper.

"I hate to admit that, but he is. Why can't he be like Jamie Tyrone in real life?"

"It takes all kinds," whispered Casper.

After what seemed like an eternity, finally, the red asterisk appeared on the script signaling the final descent. I looked at Casper. I smiled and he smiled back. Casper smiled at me just like Dara did. Casper, the one I loved.

"Don't rush; she's going to talk slowly. Time it so you go to dark five seconds after she finishes, okay?— and she's stumbling, so take it extra slow."

"Got it," I said softly.

The script was on a stand like a musical score, so I could follow Mary Tyrone's descent into darkness.

MARY: I had a talk with Mother Elizabeth. She is so sweet and good ...

As the lights started to dim, they emitted a rude kind of hum.

MARY: It may be sinful of me, but I love her better than my own mother ...

The lights were a quarter of the way to dark.

"Follow her speech," admonished Casper. I was rushing the lights, so I let up and slowed the descent.

MARY: ... and then if after a year or two I still felt sure, I could come back to see her and we would talk it over again ...

"Good job," Casper crooned in his lovely tenor voice.

MARY: ... I never dreamed Holy Mother would give me such advice! I was really shocked. I said, of course, I would do anything she suggested, but I knew it was simply a waste of time ...

I shot a glance at Casper. He was watching the play, allowing me to view his sweet profile. Up close, not from afar. This was flesh and blood. Could he possibly, really be a homosexual like me? Or would he evaporate when the lights went dark?

Then came the curtain line. But the student playing Mary stopped, like she forgot her lines. In character she looked distant. I looked at her; she seemed so vulnerable. Then she got it, and for a moment I thought Mary was talking directly to me.

"Count it!" Casper uttered softly

MARY: ... Then in the spring

something happened to me.

I counted: *One-Mississippi,* dim, *two-Mississippi,* a little dimmer.

MARY: Yes, I remember. I fell in love with James Tyrone and was so happy for a time.

Ever dimmer, *four-Mississippi,* dimmest, *five-Mississippi,* dark.

Chapter 53: Homoperfunctional

Applause trickled from the small gathering attending the dress rehearsal. I set the lights back up so the cast could take their bows. Then it was over. I felt a huge sense of relief. Judging by Casper's smile, he did too. Then he did something dazzling, so perfect and beautiful I would have prayed to God to end the night right there. He grabbed me and hugged me.

"Great job, you little wonderful thing!" He messed up my hair. It was breathtaking. Dwight pounded on the glass and gave us a thumbs-up.

I walked out of the booth happy and full of confidence.

"You were amazing, Ben!" I said, in a generous mood. I walked up to the student playing Mary Tyrone, and I wanted to say "Good job" but she seemed to collapse in my arms. She was hanging on my shoulders. I had no idea what to do. "Great job," I said.

"I made so many mistakes, Jamie." Jamie? I didn't even know her name, how did she know mine? I held her; she was almost crying.

"I know, but no one noticed them, they were all in character. It made your character more believable. I'd even think of putting them in on purpose."

"Really?"

"Really, you were great."

"You are amazing."

"Thanks—I have to strike the set." No one told me to do it, but I needed to extricate myself from her. Still, I was feeling warm and happy with the world as I put the sets to the side and restocked the blocks of the stage platform.

"Hope you are joining us for opening night," said Dwight. "You've been a real help. Thanks, Jamie."

I realized we were going to be friends, like I had once inherited Dara's friends. I was about to enter Casper's circle.

I returned to the tech booth to clean up with almost everyone gone. I felt like jelly from the mental exhaustion of the play and Casper. But it wasn't over yet. The flowers. I had to get the flowers.

First, I helped finish the props in the narrow tech booth. I was in the booth to turn out the lights and fetch the flowers. By then everyone else had left. It was now safe to risk a scene with Casper.

"Wait a sec, Jim," Casper said, blocking my way from getting the flowers.

"It's Jamie."

"Of course, Jamie."

"Casper, now I have to tell you something. Let me first get something."

"Sure, but wait a minute. I have something I want to tell you too." That took me by surprise. I suddenly was afraid of him. I wasn't so sure I wanted to hear what he had to say.

He stood at the door to the booth.

"Stay here a minute." Casper walked past me and closed the door to the tech booth. My heart beat quickly. The only reason he could possibly do that was to kiss me. We would kiss just like Dara and I did, except this would be the real thing.

Suddenly afraid, I asked, "Did you wanna go for a cup of coffee?"

"Thanks for helping out … sweetie." His voice crooned with a little tremble in it. Hearing the word 'sweetie', my heart began to pound. A swelling in my heart and between my legs. At once I felt overflowing with a desire at once so pure and so right.

"You're … welcome … Casper," I whispered. "Shall we go … for coffee?"

Silence.

"Come here."

This is what I so longed to hear, so why was I afraid?

He gestured with his hand, at once distant and serious.

I walked over to him. Heart pounding. I never felt the power of a presence like this in my life. Casper seemed to grow ten feet tall.

"Don't worry, Jamie; we're alone. I am glad you came to see me. I know why you came."

"You did?" I basked in his uttering that word I so longed to hear. But I didn't know what to say back.

"Your eyes were on me for a long time, weren't they?" he whispered.

I knew then I had to say it, I had to say 'I love you.' I summed up the courage. "Yeah, well, Casper, I am so glad to see you, and I have to say something, Casper." I loved the sound of my voice saying his name out loud for the first time. "I hope you aren't mad at me, but I—"

"Why would I be mad at you?" asked Casper

"The way I stared—before we met, I mean." My voice trailed off. The booth was dark and small, yet as vast as an ocean. *Just say it!* I shouted at myself.

"What?"

"The time I … Oh, never mind." We were so alone, yet I also felt so lost. Casper came closer to me. He was so larger than life. Like my deliverance from a long-lived hell was finally at hand. A redeemer of religious proportions. "The only balsam for eternal grieving," Wagner wrote.

Casper whispered, like it was a special secret: "You know, I thought we better see each other now."

He smiled. There was nothing else, just this booth and Casper. Softly, my mind played the undulating love theme from *Tristan*. I could clearly hear the sonorous tenor sing:

Descend,
O Night of never-ending love,
grant me oblivion.
"Now?" I pleaded.
Take me up

into your comforting bosom,
and make me forget I live!

"Yes ... You little sweetie ..." His voice trailed off. He called me his little sweetie again! The pureness of desire came back. How much more love could I take in a night. I had to say it; I'd never told anyone I loved them before. I realized now it was not just words. He looked me right in the eyes, my eyes, studying them for some sign.

"Could you help me?" he asked.

With those words, the music of *Tristan* started to play in my head:

Deliver me now
From deceitful fantasies,
From everything desired
From my unwanted memories ...

"Yes, what can I help you with, Casper?"

Come, sacred twilight
Extinguish the imagined—

"My jogging pants ... are tied in a knot."
Extinguish the imagined terrors?
He looked at me with an irresistible shyness. "Can you untie them?"

"Huh?" The record stopped.

"Yes, sweetie," he said the 's' word for the third time. How could I not help him? My long unfocussed desire now all seemed to find a home in Casper's presence. I was happy to help him.

I couldn't see so well. It was dark. My hands fumbled a little. My dream of love was shaken awake with the administrative task of untying a knot. Casper put a heavy hand on my shoulder and he pushed gently downward, indicating how I could more easily untie the knot. I could feel a slime underneath me as I knelt in front of him. I felt some horrid slime pouring over me, tainting me with the old taint. It smelled something like a burned out house would smell. I looked up at his face. He was looking down, grinning at me. My heart was pounding. I looked down at his pants. He was right. There in front of his pants I saw it: a tight knot.

"Oh, that triple knot will get you every time," I said. Thoughts of love started to curdle and evaporate. Sweetie didn't mean sweetheart, it didn't mean love, it meant something so horrible ... The most wretched feeling came back to me: I am no virgin, I am a joke of a virgin. My brain told me, *You know full well what you are and what you are supposed to do.* I felt so sad. Bitterly I thought of the word 'pure'; how dare I ever feel that? Then at once I remembered what I had dared not to remember so long ago. I didn't feel pure at all. It all came back to me: Gary. Not one but two Garys. One I had met when I was seven years old. My brother's friend, who used to take me to his house. The other, the male prostitute, whose name I suddenly realized I didn't really know. Both made me do things I knew now I had to repeat. They both confronted me loud and clear.

I knew what I was.

I knew what I had to do.

There would be no love, not imagined or otherwise. He was priming the proverbial pump—me. Trying to untie it, my hand shook. My fingers fumbled.

"Yes," he said in a damning whisper.

Shame came crashing down on me. I somehow had convinced myself I was still a virgin. As if Gary never existed, or even that Dara didn't count. But, then this came, and I could not escape it. The worst is that it was in front of Casper. Suddenly came an unpleasant feeling of *deja vu*. I had no idea what to do, but somehow I knew exactly what to do. He knew to expect it from me. I felt an uncontrollable sadness. It welled up and flooded into my throat. Sobless tears started leaking from my eyes. Self-hatred, the power of which I had not felt for a long time, seized me and refused to let go.

Too quiet for Casper to hear, I whispered, "Please don't make me."

He did. He had to. I was sentenced to it. As the knot came undone, his pants fell to the floor.

There it was. An erect penis. So normal. So plain. So simple. I couldn't look at it. I closed my eyes.

But maybe this is all a homosexual gets. I'd been warned.

I felt suddenly like the lowest animal on the planet. What happened to my beautiful dream of love?

Perverse self-hatred took over. An inner voice said,

This is all you are good for. My mouth dropped wide open. He stuck it in. I went too deep and gagged. I suddenly started sucking on Casper's cock, wildly and desperately, as if my entire life depended on one and only one thing: keeping Casper with me. But it didn't work. He disappeared. All that was left was a cock. If I did a good enough job, I knew he would stay. The pulsating of my head against his cock was leading to a gag reflex I somehow ignored like the pain in my knees, pleasing him being way more important. This greedy need grabbed hold of my head and slowed me down.

"Take it easy, sweetheart," it whispered.

'Sweetheart' falling on my ears like a sarcastic death sentence, I slowed down in exhaustion. What happened to the face I loved so much? Where was the body I dreamed about? If I could see him again ...

The thoughts of *Tristan*, with bitter sarcasm, taunted me.

> *Deliver me now*
> *From deceitful fantasies,*
> *From everything desired*
> *From my unwanted memories.*

Suddenly the speed came back. This lizard could stand it no longer. It held my head firmly. With greedy gyrations, he pumped his cock. Finally he got into his animal phase, his desire for a climax overwhelming. It was a brief incredible frenzy. It was marked by his pushing my head to him too far, and I could feel a gag. We both became subhuman.

He gave out a groan. I went down harder and harder, wanting him to explode and be done with it.

Then at once the feared throbbing, and my mouth filled with the taste of betrayal. His cock slid deep into my throat for another pump of cum.

My mouth swelled. He pulled away, a drip or two hitting me in the face. Each drop felt like tainting slime.

Then the worst, most evil thing happened: Casper reappeared. I could look up and see him. I was this vile thing, but he got back his beauty. He got back his sweet little twitch. Casper was suddenly anxious and looking around. Slowly, I realized his cum tasted sour and obnoxious. Unsure of what else to do, with revulsion I swallowed. The taste's familiarity condemned me far more than Casper's sudden reappearance. His behavior seemed only logical given what I was. I could only blame myself. I could feel his cum sliding down my throat. I swallowed again. I wanted to stay in this position. I wanted to beg him to stay, to finish the job: kill me. I sat still, even as pain shot from my knees, while I trembled with shame and a soreness in my jaw made itself known.

He let me go.

I looked up at Casper's grinning sweaty face. He was smiling at me with a beatific satisfaction, then looked up again anxiously. He pressed my head against his damp groin. I can't remember what he said; I couldn't hear it. It was something soft. His soft penis against my face, moist cum wetting my cheek.

A painful cloud of penance came back to me from thoughts long ago. I knew this was as close as this homosexual was ever going to come to love. A book I read as a child returned to haunt me. Greedily, I caressed those gorgeous legs I desired for so long. I hungrily squeezed the buttocks I had seen from a distance, the curve of his hips and legs. I could not possibly get to know Casper's body more intimately.

He reached down and picked up his jogging pants.

I tried to think of something to say. All memories of any Gary vanished. A sense of purity violated returned.

"Can we get a cup of coffee, Casper?" was all I could think of.

Casper muttered, "Thank you, Jamie. That was great; you're a real pro." I cringed at how 'sweetie' was replaced with 'a real pro'.

He bent over and lowered his gorgeous head. His eyes twitching, puckering his beautiful lips, he kissed my forehead. It took a while, kneeling there stupidly.

He retied his drawstring in a knot.

"Gotta go."

I heard the door shut. Casper's voice still haunted me: "That was great; you're a real pro."

I remained there on the floor. I felt broken, completely broken. I was still kneeling on the ground.

I spoke out loud to no one in particular, "Casper Tyres, I love you."

My self-hatred laughed back.

"Let it lead me wherever it must, but not back here!" I cried to the empty booth. "Damn you!"

I cried bitterly. After a while, exhaustion quieted my tears. I heard someone else leaving the building. I snorted up my sniffling nose. I realized I could not escape myself. I was putting off what I had to do.

The self-hatred I thought I had beaten returned. I thought it was gone and here it was back in the worst possible moment in my life. I didn't know what else to do. I had to atone. I took off my shirt and lowered my pants and underwear to around my knees.

What else could I do?

I unthreaded my belt from my pants. I held it in my hand. It felt like a gauntlet. I raised my hand. In the corner of my eyes, I saw the flowers I never gave him. I put the belt down. Crawled like an insect over to the roses. They still had their thorns on. It was just what I needed.

Sixth Variation: A Label's Price Tag
Late Autumn 1980

VI Finale. Im Tempo Des Scherzos.
Wild Herausfahrend —
Allegro Energico — Langsam.
(Finale. In the tempo of a scherzo. Wildly inexorable —
Energetically fast — slow.)

Chapter 54: Intense Ambiguity

Early the next morning, I was freed from my prison when a janitor unlocked the building. Cuts from the thorns—mostly on my hands—had closed. Flowers made for poor whips. My back ached as I put my shirt back on. My jacket would cover any blood drops that might have stained my shirt, if any. I didn't look.

During my walk home from *Long Day's Journey into Night*, I did the only thing I could do: forget.

I talked myself into believing this was a great introduction to my new homosexual lifestyle. Casper gave me exactly what I wanted or needed or both. He was the one I had desired for so long. What else was there from these kind of people—my kind of people?

Arriving home, I wished I could wake up Tim and talk to him about Casper (my purified version of him, which I had regained through mortification of my own flesh). But I didn't dare. I needed someone to turn to: a cousin Harold or a gay friend or mentor or someone, anyone.

All night long, I tossed and turned on the couch in the small theater. My back stung from the scratches I inflicted on it. I was trying to make sense of what happened. In one moment, I felt a flash of joy: Casper and I finally connected. We even had sex together. But then the joy diminished. I questioned my own behavior. He gave me sex, but I wanted love. It wasn't really enjoyable, or was that what sex really meant? Without so much as a 'hello', I started sucking his cock. He was satisfied and walked off. He said I did it like a pro, and I never did it before that I knew of. I just did what came naturally, the satisfaction ephemeral, the pain everlasting.

But even so, Casper put his arm over my shoulder last night. He mentored me. He called me 'sweetie': that must mean something, even if I didn't know what. Plus, I made him smile. *Relax and enjoy the moment you had with the most gorgeous man in the world,* I told myself. You could brag that you went all the way on the first date. But brag to whom? Besides, I already knew that homosexuals only cared about their penises. I was the lone exception apparently—so I had to get over it and treasure it, be thankful for what I had.

So many incompatible thoughts coursed through my overworked brain.

Everything was clear!

Everything was muddled!

I did it exactly right!

I screwed everything up!

But one thing was certain: I'd followed my heart. I just didn't realize where it was leading me.

Chapter 55: Withered Flowers

It really was love, or as much love as I would ever get. I couldn't deny that. I had fallen in love with him. I bought him flowers. Last night, I shivered at the ugly site of the withered flowers on the floor after I tried to whip my back with them. There were two roses I hadn't destroyed. With a trembling bloodied hand, I took them home with me. Still, I knew Casper was the only one I had ever truly loved. That love had to be worth something. That made things simpler; I could not lose this battle without a fight. I had to get help from Casper.

I remembered I had his phone number. He said he would have a cup of coffee with me. If we met, I could clear everything up. I got out of bed. Tim was still sleeping. I fumbled around, looking for the scrap of paper with Casper's life history. I looked and looked, trying not to wake Tim. I went through a pile of papers on my desk, then the garbage, and there I found it! I picked away an old banana peel; I could still read it.

I put on a pair of jogging pants and rummaged around and found a greenish T-shirt. I ran downstairs to a phone booth in the lobby. I stepped inside the pay phone booth and sat down. I took a deep breath. I looked at the piece of paper. I prayed to a vague deity for guidance.

I dropped in the quarter. I dialed.

His phone rang!

And rang.

No one answered.

I tried this many more times. I had no idea how many more.

Finally someone picked up.

"Hello, Casper?" I asked.

"Hello. Do you know what time it is?" came a groggy, vaguely familiar male voice.

"Oh, early. Sorry. This is Jamie, a friend."

"Yes, it's early ... Jamie?"

"Yes, and I have to talk to him."

"Wait a second ... Casper isn't here anyway ... he left last night for home. Got it?"

"Can't you tell him it's Jamie? I need to talk to him!"

"Weirdo, I said he wasn't here. Don't call back."

Click.

Weirdo? Who was that on the phone? It almost sounded like Dwight. That would be ridiculous. And did he say Casper left? Left? There were still two months left in the term. *Long Day's Journey into Night* run had not finished, hadn't even started. Everything seemed confused. I racked my brain to no effect: I now had no idea what had happened.

A door was kicked open. I went through that

door. But I still had no idea where I was. Casper didn't stay? Had he left Detroit? For good, or just for a while? Was he in Bad Axe? When had that ever happened—someone makes love to you and leaves? What did I do to my love? The fog came and my once positive thoughts seemed evasive. Could Casper have redeemed me? Could I have redeemed Casper? Why was that all lost now?

Two months passed until I finally gave up on a letter or a returned phone call from Casper. I never saw him in the theater building, so maybe he had gone. The two remaining roses had long since wilted. I tried to salvage them by drying them, and pressing them into a book. It was a trick I once learned from my mother. Unfortunately, the roses were too thick and only ruined the book they were pressed in.

I eventually learned that Casper did not leave. I had gone back to see *Long Day's Journey into Night* and spied him in the tech booth with another student. I left after the first act. Then, I dared to wait a few times for him, both before and after the play. Each time, he saw me on the bench, waiting, and quickly walked by. I acclimated myself to the polite cold shoulder from Dara and Ahmed. My only friend now was Tim. As close as we were, I didn't dare broach the subject of the love that dare not speak its name or anyone else's.

Soberly, I realized that sex can be divorced from love. And if someone does that, do they divorce *themselves* from love? Perhaps the answer was 'yes', because I am a faggot, and I had read that's all we were about: the prick and not the person. I had nothing against pricks; I just didn't want to be one.

Tristan and Isolde never have their love consummated. Their final moments end equally bizarrely. Tristan, so deliriously happy to see Isolde again, tears off his bandages and bleeds to death before Isolde sees him. Isolde, from some glorifying apotheosis, dissolves or commits suicide. Maybe this opera was closer to the truth for homosexuals.

Of course, I could just be a garden-variety freak. Maybe I only needed to be broken in. I loved Casper now. Maybe the next time I would seek out someone who reminded me of him, a Casper facsimile. The facsimile would start out being someone with the same beautiful nose in my theater class. Then I would meet someone with the same smile out on the street. After that, I'd settle for a guy with the same build in the park. Then in a men's bathroom, I'd look for the same penis, and then eventually any penis. Probably about then, one started taking drugs and wearing women's clothes, and would soon appear dead in the local newspaper.

Then I remembered, crisply, like it was yesterday, my Aunt Louise once saying to me in a whisper: "He was depressed, you know. It's not what you think." Maybe my cousin Harold did not die because he was homosexual. Everything was becoming confusing. I was in over my head. What was I? What did Casper and Dara make me? A wayward heterosexual? A homosexual? A bisexual? I had lots of questions and no answers.

I suddenly realized I knew nothing about being anything.

Heterosexuality couldn't just be sticking your thing in a woman. It had far greater consequences than just that. Plus, I had stuck my thing in a woman, and it didn't get me anywhere.

Bisexuality? Dara suggested I should be one. But what did that mean? 'Bisexual' sounded weird, but not as bad as homosexual—in fact, fifty-percent not as bad. And homosexuality, did I really ever know someone who was a homosexual? I mean a real one? My cousin Harold, but now I was not sure about who he was anymore, or why or how he died. I was out of the closet and didn't know who I was. I had to find out. But I had to find out discreetly.

Chapter 56: Searching the Library

I awoke early, the Sunday before Thanksgiving. I had scoped out the library on many occasions looking for a time when few people would be present. I hoped that Sunday morning would be the perfect time to go to the library to research this forbidden love. I figured no one would be there early. Getting up, I decided to put on some inconspicuous clothes. Luckily that was all I had. I put on faded dark pants and a once-black shirt, now a dull charcoal gray. I topped it off with a pair of sunglasses and a dark green parka.

I walked to the library. There were, in fact, very few people out and about on Sunday morning. I walked to the card catalog. A few more people milled about there than I would have liked. Some beady-eyed pervert was already at the H's. I knew what he was up to. So nonchalantly I walked over to the B's. I opened the drawer. I couldn't see anything. I had to take off my sunglasses.

Bisexual … bisexual … I kept flipping through cards, occasionally looking around me to see if anyone was looking. I saw the pervert was gone. I moved abruptly over to the H drawers. A generic human in a formal suit stalked nearby.

"Homer ... Ho*mer* ..." I muttered as I kept flipping cards. Eventually, the man passed by, and I went to the titles and subjects under the forbidden word 'HOMOSEXUAL'. The books all appeared to be on the third floor. My mission was now clear.

There in the third-floor stacks were books with large screaming titles: HOMOSEXUAL this and HOMOSEXUAL that. I grabbed as many as I could. Then I hid deep in the reading cubicles to look them over. Placing them in the cubicle next to me if they weren't worthy of reading. Very few were.

The True Nature of the Homosexual Pathology described homosexual mental illness and some grisly cures that were "at least better than leaving the poor patient a homosexual." Toss.

The Homosexual Question referred to the "sickness of homosexuals." The author spent a lot of time on something called "homosexual panic." At first I thought that was what I could be suffering from. What the author actually meant was how "homosexual panic" was a valid defense for any person who murdered a homosexual in reaction to the homosexual making unnatural advances. Toss.

Homosexuals and Society proved to be a hopelessly complex book. But I looked at the index and I saw an entry on Tchaikovsky, one of my favorite composers. I glanced at the chapter. I came across this quote:

Tchaikovsky was of course one of the most famous of the homosexual composers.

Schubert, Handel, Brahms, and Britten are other composers we think were also homosexual. There is even strong evidence that Richard Wagner was a bisexual.

Richard Wagner! My Richard Wagner? It mentioned nothing else. I went on and the only other thing I found was another entry on Tchaikovsky:

Tchaikovsky's diary, however, leaves little doubt. He mentions, for example, how his Fourth Symphony is his celebration of accepting his homosexuality ...

I was angry because I was all too familiar with the Fourth Symphony and the liner notes on my recording of it. According to the record company, the Fourth Symphony was his "symphony of fate". That was clearly a lie. Moreover, I had no idea that these other well-known composers were also homosexual. With a conspiracy of silence, it was no wonder it was so difficult to discover more about homosexuals. And with '"homosexual panic", no wonder homosexuals were afraid to be seen.

None of these books seemed to be very enlightening of just who or what a homosexual was, or at least could give me a clue as to how I was supposed to behave with other homosexuals. I worried about my integrity; was it dead? How does a homosexual behave with integrity, or is that just not possible? Do I have to give up on love and just go for sex?

Fascinated about Wagner, I went to research him.

Sure enough, I had the confirmation I needed. Almost every book on Wagner mentions a trite rationalization for his close friendship with some well-known homosexuals, most notably King Ludwig II, with whom he had an ongoing love letter exchange. I could add more certainly the Wagner opera about forbidden love, about the vice of erotica, the lofty chaste romantic love. I dared to combine it as he did. We both seemed to be varying degrees of bisexuals.

I walked back to the homo-stack to see if I could find anything else.

Just then, I spied some students from my dorm floor. I shot out of the homo-stacks and ran into a random book section. I landed among Medieval History titles. One thing caught my eye: *Tristan* by Gottfried von Strasbourg. I was leafing through it, enjoying the echoes of the Wagner opera, when an obese student tried to get by me. I had to turn sideways and press into the books to allow him to pass. Just as he passed through, a word on a book caught my eye: Homosexuality. I looked again: *Christianity, Social Tolerance, and Homosexuality*, by John Boswell. This seemed perfect. A history book full of plausible deniability. I could be reading it for information on Christianity or social tolerance. More important, it was a book that might address some of the concerns I had about homosexuality and religion. This was the book I would take home.

Sensing the need for discretion, I did not take the book right away. I first grabbed the *Tristan* book, and then another book on Percival, sandwiching the homo book between the clean ones, then added a book on the medieval political economy of Aix-en-Provence for good measure. I turned the contraband book so the spine was discretely against my chest.

Sunglasses back on, I hurriedly walked to the checkout counter, avoiding any eye contact. I had to wait in an interminable line, which included some elderly lady who was checking out a dozen books on anthropological studies in Africa. Finally, it was my turn. I slid the books cautiously over to the check-out clerk. She grabbed them.

She scanned the political economy book. The machine emitted a beep.

She scanned the Tristan, beep!

Scanned the third book … no beep.

Scanned the Percival, beep!

"It helps if you put them all facing the same way, so I can scan them," she lectured me.

She tried the third book again; still no beep. Now she was looking at the cover. Then she immediately glanced at me. I turned red. She looked around and shouted angrily to someone sitting at a desk across from her with a large computer on it.

"Herb, here is a book you forgot to put a code on. I think it's brand-new." Herb did not answer, so she yelled, "SOMEONE MUST HAVE FORGOT THE CODE—AGAIN."

"Well, then it shouldn't be on the shelf," Herb snapped.

"Can you just look it up for me?"

"Oh, gawd, can't be left alone a second. She sees I am busy ... Author?" he asked. "AUTHOR?"

Why was this happening to me? Everyone who had been minding their own business was now entranced on these two adversarial colleagues.

"Boswell," she shouted much louder than necessary, "Boswell ... John."

"John? Well, that makes a big difference, doesn't it! ... Boswell, John... Title?"

"Christianity ...

"Christianity," repeated Herb.

"Social Tolerance ..."

"Social Tolerance," repeated Herb. "Jesus, how long is this title anyway?"

"And Homosexuality."

"And what?" cried Herb.

"HOMO-SEX-Uality," she screamed, adding under her breath, "How stupid can you be?"

Everyone was now staring at me.

Herb typed this into his computer.

I wanted to melt away. I wanted to say, "Never mind, I don't need it; it's for a sick friend who just died." Then Herb shouted back petulantly, "THREE, ZERO, SIX, SEVEN, SIX, SIX, B-O-7."

"That wasn't so hard, was it? ... Was it, Herb? You know, I am still not going out with you," said the clerk, seething with contempt.

"Ha! Round three to you," sneered Herb.

She handed me the book. "Ignore him, more like

round three-hundred. Have a nice day."

Thoroughly humiliated, I grabbed the books, walked outside, turned the corner, put the other books in the return bin, and kept the Boswell book.

I immediately realized that was a stupid thing to do. I was now holding this naked homosexual book. I looked around. On the ground was an empty fast-food bag. I put the book in the bag. And then what? I didn't know what to do.

I didn't know where I could go now. I couldn't bring the book back to my dorm room. My roommate would flip. I couldn't read it in public, certainly not out in the open. I wandered about, not knowing where to go.

Chapter 57: Good Book Successor

I went back to my dorm room study floor. There were people cramming for exams in every room. Holding the book to me like a bottle of contraband whiskey, I snuck into my room. Thankfully, Tim was gone. I climbed on my top bunk, taking a few other books with me in case Tim came in. I would keep the book hidden in my pillowcase or zipped up in my backpack. That was safe, as I could hardly find anything in that mess of a backpack let alone someone else doing so. It wasn't so much a backpack as an archaeological dig of my college career. I vaulted myself and my backpack onto my bunk bed. I took out the book and started to read.

Heart pounding, fearing discovery, I read the book that changed my life. The book claimed to show that homosexuality was tolerated in Christian European society until the 12th century. But in order to do so, the book had to prove that the Bible had not condemned homosexuality. It had also to discuss homosexuals and homosexual couples who were "accepted" by society. It also had to prove that early Christian writers had nothing against homosexuality. Of course, in making the claim, it was also showing the Old Testament had nothing particularly homo-phobic in it. This was more than a book; it was a spiritual sign, a sign from God/it/him/her/themselves! There were even gay couples back then, just like "normal" married couples.

The door was being unlocked. I stuffed the book into my backpack and took out another study book. I leaned in against the wall in my bunk to hide. Tim came in. He didn't know I was there. I knew that because he stared at himself in the mirror and talked to himself.

"I don't look so bad. I wish I looked like Jamie." I blushed. I didn't know anyone wanted to look like me.

I could barely see an arm out of the corner of my eye. He was taking off his shirt. I was horrified and astounded. I heard a pants zipper unzip. I was scared to death. But to prove I had turned into a real homosexual, I started fantasizing that he was going to masturbate, and that he would then notice me and get angry and start fucking me as punishment. I could hear him removing his pants. A drawer opened. I heard him throwing clothes, heard them landing on his bed. My heartbeat lowered. He was just changing his clothes.

I lay perfectly still. He finished changing clothes and left the room. I peeked at his bed. A pair of pants and a button-up dress shirt was lying on it. It occurred to me that these clothes were right next to Tim's skin, that Tim must have a body that filled those clothes. I reached down. I couldn't reach. I climbed halfway down. I took his pants. I didn't know what I was supposed to do then, but it seemed so sexy to have his pants in my bed.

I opened the book again, with Tim's pants next to me in my bed. Not knowing what else to do, I smelled them. Disappointingly, they smelled like laundry detergent. I put the pants on my lap and read.

One by one, Boswell attacked the stereotypes. Sodom and Gomorrah had nothing to do with homosexuality. Even Christ allegedly preached that the story was about inhospitality to strangers, not sexual perversity. Later in history, the crime of sodomy referred to rape in general, not to male-to-male sex. And so on. The Old Testament bans on 'lying with a man' were, in context, shown as more general prohibitions against prostitution than something specifically homosexual. Stereotypes were dispelled. Prejudices I never knew existed before collapsed as a house whose foundation was eaten away. Lastly, I was suddenly confronted with, as impossible as it sounded, but nonetheless unequivocally, that there was heavenly permission to be homosexual. I felt so excited and happy. I was going to unzip my pants but then the door opened.

Chapter 58: Searching Tim

Tim came back. His pants were still in my bed.

"Hi, Jamie." He looked up at me. "I didn't know you were here?"

"I was sleeping."

"What are you reading?"

"Just a book for my ... Medieval History class."

"Oh, I didn't know you were studying Medieval History."

"Well, actually, it's a self-study. I am fascinated with the formation of early republics, and in the Middle Ages you can see these early roots."

"Really? I didn't know that."

"What's that got to do with theater?"

"Well, these small city-states started to form, and they formed the kernel of the republics like in Venice and Florence. Those were the areas where Greek drama had a kind of revival ... sort of." I felt sick to my stomach; I was lying like there was no tomorrow. "But I am tired of reading; you want to go with me to the record store?"

"Sure. I hear they have the new Horowitz recordings."

I rushed Tim out the door and hurried along to our favorite record store, Harmony House, wondering how I was going to get back to the room before Tim in order to get his pants off my bunk bed and hide that book.

At the store, Tim and I usually split up. He would go to the solo piano section and I would go over to the opera section. But first we would look at the 'new releases' bin together. I was surprised how close I had to stand next to Tim to look at the records together. So close I could smell this Tim smell. I could even casually graze his body with mine as I moved from one record to the next, which felt very calming. I wondered whether looking at records was always this intimate.

"Hey, Goldberg!"

No record store is complete without an obnoxious salesperson trying to get you to buy recordings you don't like.

"What is it, Todd?"

"You're gonna love this one!"

"What is it?"

"Come over here and let me show you."

Tim and I exchanged glances. We both had our experiences with this pushy clerk.

"Can't you just tell me?" I walked over to Todd.

"I told you I was getting this in. It's a European import, much better quality than any you can buy locally."

It was a legendary recording of *Tristan und Isolde* conducted by Wilhelm Furtwangler. It supposedly had the dream cast and the dream performance.

"Come on, just listen to it in our listening room."

"I'll be right back, Tim." I was sure this would be quick, as I hated old tinny recordings.

The music started, and I was taken by surprise. The sound was tinny, but the performance was very intense. "The voice of Kirsten Flagstad is amazing."

"Told you. Wait 'til you hear the love duet, just a sample. Let me see where it is." Todd fished around for the record. Then he put it on. It was sinewy and seductive. Time seemed to stand still. The music just brought it back to me: Casper's thighs. Tim's breath—Tim! I ran out of the listening room. The store was empty.

"Where did Tim go?"

"I don't know. I was in there with you, Goldberg."

"I have to go—amazing recording. Thanks for sharing it."

"Sure, no problem. I'll hold it for you."

"Yes, thanks. Bye!" I ran out of there as fast as I could. I ran back to the dorm room as fast as my legs would carry me.

Chapter 59: Searching Myself

I'm dead, I'm dead, I'm dead, I kept repeating to myself, urging myself to go ever faster. I ran up the stairs, skipping every other step. I ran up to the door. It was locked! *Oh, thank you, God. Thank you. I will go back to the synagogue. I'll become a rabbi just to thank you for this.*

I opened the door.

Tim's pants were no longer on my bed.

Oh, thank you, just fucking thank you! For crying out loud, I asked for one simple, solitary thing! Just thanks for nothing. I have a memory too!

I checked for the book. The book was closer to the edge of the bed than I remembered leaving it. But I wasn't sure. Did Tim look at it, or was he just looking for his pants in his autistic way? Just saw the pants on my bed and sighed, "Oh, there they are; thank goodness. I thought I lost them."

It was either that or he saw them on my bed and thought, "What a fucking pervert."

Or he saw them both and thought, "What a dead fucking pervert."

He had the perfect alibi: homosexual panic. I was at his mercy.

Or he saw the book on the bed and his pants and thought, "Of course, there's my pants—oh, he's studying medieval history.

I just didn't know.

A new nightmare began right were the old one left off.

That evening I saw him in the cafeteria. He seemed to avoid me. That night he did not come back. *What could I do to save myself? What story could I fabricate?* I saw them, folded on his dresser—the pants.

I climbed back into my bed and hid the book under my pillow. I felt so guilty for having been so happy to be a faggot. That's when I realized, I had to just face the music. I worked too hard to be here. Lying in my life had to stop. I would just admit who I was: a homosexual—okay, gay—it sounded happier. My mother used to say when she saw a particularly bad driver, "There goes a gay one." I know she didn't mean its new definition.

I climbed down and took out the *Tristan* record. I didn't feel like listening to the love duet. On an impulse, I played King Marke's monologue. It takes place just after the *coitus interuptus* of the love duet. The king catches his wife and his best friend, half-naked in each others' arms. With the libretto over my lap, I listened to the dreary betrayal monologue.

King Marke isn't angry; he is sad and despondent. Tristan, his closest friend, whom he loved more than any other, betrayed him. Reading along with the music from the libretto, I was sad—and feeling oddly guilty. I had betrayed someone. Somehow, I had sunk to the depths Tristan had sunk to. "Struck with the most enemy-like betrayal." I read the libretto with the music; it seemed so deeply sad. Yet as I was reading, the words seemed to change their meaning. To me, they became a non-ending list of my faults, my errors.

King Marke: Why wound me where I hurt the
most?
Now, with my heart
open to pain more than ever before,
Most vulnerable and exposed
There you attacked me
without hope
that I might ever be healed.
There, with the weapon
of tormenting poison,
searing and maiming
my senses and mind
so that my trust and love
to my friend is destroyed,
my open heart
now filled with pain suspicion,
so that I, a king, creep around
like a slithering spy
in the dead of the night
And here I find you and see
my honor destroyed?

Did I destroy my friendship with Casper? Did I betray Dara? Was I planning to betray Tim? Was there no one I could talk to about this, to help me untangle this mess.

Did I betray Casper or perhaps myself? Why did I feel this musical betrayal so deeply inside of me? I couldn't answer, but the king's lament sounded in my heart too.

King Marke: Why did you do this,
Why put me through this
hell!
No heaven can redeem it
No misery can atone for
this disgrace?

The king's most poignant, angry, and desolate question to Tristan went unanswered.

Tristan's reply made me at once understand the musical symbolism:

Marke: Can't you at least
tell me the unknown
mysterious cause
for this betrayal?

Tristan: O King,
I cannot tell you that;
what you would ask
you can never know.

Am I too ashamed to admit I am gay? Is there anything wrong with that? Is there anything wrong with not telling people? People don't understand who I am. They are mistaken, unknowingly.

Tristan: Wherever Tristan now goes

> will you, Isolde, follow him?
> To that land of which Tristan
> spoke,
> where the sun's light does not
> shine;
> it is the dark
> land of Night

A land of hidden secrets and clandestine truths. The nights of alleys, men's rooms and darkened tech booths. No, I can shine a light on this. The betrayal was to me. I betrayed myself. I knew my journey was over. My voyage to the other side was complete. I was one of them now. The fags, the queers, the fruits had transformed like butterflies into gays, lesbians, transsexuals, and bisexuals. Once the enemy, now my tribe. The struggle was over. They had won. Part of me still didn't want to give up, but the fight was already decided. "Struck with the most enemy-like betrayal." I had abandoned my struggle to be what I wanted to be for so long: a normal person.

They had won, but they were generous in their victory, as now the self-hatred, the tensions in my life—all that would be over, too. Over, because I finally found the root cause of it all: I was homosexual—no, I was gay. All my problems were solved! All the hard knocks, the emotional turbulence, and the self-flagellation, they were all traceable to this single fact. It would be downhill from here. I couldn't wait to tell my parents. Being liberals, they would understand, I thought.

The king's last unanswered question—"Can't you at least tell me the unknown, mysterious cause for this betrayal?"— still rang disturbingly on my mind. Even as I left for home on Thanksgiving weekend, the question haunted me.

Chapter 60: Miscalculation

My mother took the mound of chicken out of the paper wrap of the kosher butcher. She was putting her first chicken leg in the shake bag. Sunday dinners with my parents were always a little early because my father would have to give me a silent ride back to the college campus afterwards. Dinner was tenaciously the same—even after an overdose of Thanksgiving turkey: shake-and-bake fried chicken, powdered mashed potatoes, and canned green beans with canned fried onions on top.

My father was already at the dining table in our kitchen, watching the news on our small black-and-white television set. Steven had flown the coop, his room converted into my Mom's home office. She was calmly preparing the chicken. I thought this was the moment.

"Mom?" I asked.

"Yes?" she answered vaguely, as she shook the bag, coating a chicken leg.

"I've been thinking a lot lately," I said, trying to introduce the subject.

"Yeah, well don't overuse it," she said wryly as she shook another piece of chicken back and forth in the bag.

This wasn't going to be easy. I took out a book from my backpack. I thought the book would help the discussion. She placed the coated chicken on a baking sheet.

"Mom, I read this really interesting book the other day—"

"Really? You know what I am reading? I am reading *Sophie's Choice*; have you read it?"

"Uh, no, I haven't."

"Oh, you have to be kidding me! You *have* to read that book. Everyone must read *that* book. Everything you need to know about what really matters is in *Sophie's Choice*. Really, I can't believe you haven't read it, Jamie. If you read *it*, you'd understand a lot of things that are wrong with this country. Not just the civil rights struggle, but anti-Semitism. You know, you don't do enough in this area. I don't see you doing anything about anti-Semitism." She shook more chicken pieces in the bag.

"I do ..." I said, trying to stall to think of what I was doing for anti-Semitism. "I do a lot ... but it's just that ... I think civil rights is a more pressing issue. You know, I am planning to join DSOC again—"

"Screw that. I can connect you with a volunteer job at the DCC. Then you can *really* do something." She was a member of the Wayne County Democratic Central Committee. She put more bread crumbs and more chicken parts in the bag and started to shake it again.

"That would be great; it would really help my political science degree," I said, thinking this was not the time to share the fact that I was now majoring in theater. "And my poli-sci degree touches everything: anti-Semitism, civil rights, *human* rights …"

"Yeah, but you have to put it into action," she said, placing the coated chicken pieces on the crowded baking sheet. She was making enough chicken for the ten people who might show up.

"Yes, but you have to admit, civil rights is important."

"Of course," she said. I had her full attention as she mindlessly shook the bag with yet more chicken pieces.

"But you have to see civil rights in a broad perspective. I put anti-Semitism under that."

"Good for you. If we can help redefine civil rights in a broader context, it can stay alive."

"That's exactly what I wanted to talk about," I said, finally seeing an inroad. "Expanding it to everyone who is oppressed."

"Absolutely," she said, putting the chicken in the oven.

"You've always taught me the importance of being o—pen, li—beral, and uh … tolerant, right?" My stuttering, set Mom's parenting radar on red alert.

"What's the matter?" she asked, regretting the words the moment they flew out of her mouth.

"You really want to know?" I asked, hoping to make it her fault.

"I am not so sure." She wasn't biting. She looked at me, very cross. I suddenly realized this might not go my way. I looked for an out. I relied on her parental cowardice. But in that she let me down. "Okay, tell me what these shenanigans are all about," she finally said. The train had left the station.

"I think I might be, I actually know I might be," I stammered, "gay."

No response.

"Or homosexual." Finally I produced the book. "Here, I just wanted you to read this." I handed her a book I had borrowed from the university library: *Now That You Know Your Son is Gay.*

She looked at it as if someone had just given her a handful of dog shit. It sunk in.

"You're *what?*" my mother said in utter disbelief. That's when I learned that her tolerance was not a blank check. Her liberalism had its limits. Its limit was me. What would I do now?

Desperately, I glanced over to my father for help. My father was still watching the small television, acting like he was oblivious, but I could tell otherwise.

Don't lie to your mother, my conscience told me.

"I'm gay—"

Unexpectedly, she dropped the book. It landed with a loud bang. My father looked up. She put her hands to her mouth. I'd stabbed a dagger through her heart; I could see that. She was clearly struck with the most enemy-like betrayal. The person I loved most, I destroyed her. But I was destroyed and finally put back together; how could I explain that to her?

"You are not a *faygela*!"

"Look, it's not that bad—"

"Not that bad? Being a pervert is not that bad? Irv, did you hear that, our son thinks he's a *faygela*! Is that what I did all this for?" My father pretended to be intently watching television.

"Look, just read this book; it will explain everything." I picked it up. She moved away from it like it carried the plague.

"I will do no such thing. You are not ... that, and that's the end of the story. We'll do what we need to do to get your—brain—unscrewed." Her voice trembled with contempt.

My dad looked up, said nothing, but looked physically ill. At least he stopped watching television.

"I can't do anything about it, Mom. I am ... gay."

"Stop! No, they can cure this now; I know that. I read about it. We'll get you the help you need." My mother started to go into worry mode.

"Don't worry about me!" I really surprised myself.

"Of course we worry; we love you. How can you possibly think you're a *faygela*?"

"Mom, you don't understand. I thought we were always so liberal ..." That was the wrong card to play.

"Don't give me that bullshit. I know full well; I saw what your cousin Harold did to your Aunt Louise. And I am gonna stop and watch you degenerate in front of my eyes? I'll call that Dr. Wire immediately; he'll set you straight."

"He's the one who helped me."

She looked furious. I knew she wanted to say something she did not dare to say.

"Look, Mom, just read this book; you will see." I offered the book again.

I thought I had gotten through. She took the book. She looked at it. But instead of opening it, she reared back and impulsively threw it into the living room. Glass crashed as a framed Diego Rivera print fell to the ground. My mother put her hands to her face, shocked at what she had done.

My father got up from his chair.

"You're—" she stopped herself.

"You better settle down," my dad said to my mom. Lest you think he was taking my side, he then turned to me. "You better go. Leave us alone before you give your mother a heart attack. And don't come back until you're cured."

But I am not a disease, I protested to myself.

"Careful, Irv, *you'll* get the heart attack," she yelled at my father.

No Plan B, I went quietly. I grabbed my jacket and backpack. I left them alone, my mother crying in the comforting arms of my father.

Chapter 61: Harsh Realities

The self-hatred returned. I staggered out of the house, holding back the strong desire to smash my head against the brick wall of a neighbor's house. The haunting image of my father comforting my wounded mother stuck like a fishhook in my brain. I walked several blocks before I realized I was holding a useless can of green beans.

Walking to the bus stop, I passed happy children playing in front of their houses. I felt a nostalgia—not that I was ever a happy child, but with no chance of experiencing any such delight, I'd hoped I would have been cut some slack. Vain hope. Wretched longing. Terrible, futile dream. I put the can of green beans in my backpack.

Feeling numb on the bus back to school, I took pragmatic stock of the situation: I had no one to turn to; my family was gone. I had nowhere to go. At the end of the term, I had no money to stay in school, let alone the dorm. I would soon be homeless, a homeless man with a fifty-percent scholarship. Life suddenly looked unreasonably ugly. Getting off the bus, I arrived at my new home, at least until the end of the term, one month away in dark December.

Desperately, I found myself walking to the Theater

Arts building, sneaking into the building, hoping to see Casper. In mad desire, I envisioned him waiting for me at the scene of the crime, in the hour I needed him most. I snuck into the small theater by a side door. It was dark.

"Where are you?!" I screamed. "Why leave me alone for so long? Come on, right now! I need you," I demanded. No one answered.

An abyss opened wide and long before me. Life never seemed so desolate.

I'd made a big mistake. It was such a profound mistake. I wanted to believe I had never made one of this magnitude before. But some God-like presence in my mind reminded me: long before "coming out," I had committed a much more serious offense. One that so offended God that this crime preordained my destruction. What that crime was, I could not think; but still it hung over me like a prison sentence even heavier than the condemnation of my own parents. Suddenly, I thought Casper might be in the tech room.

I walked toward the empty tech room. On the way there, I tripped over something and fell, bumping my head on a chair's armrest. I crashed to the ground, my body slammed with pain and I cursed my stupidity. I felt angry at myself for being so careless, scolding myself the way my mother would. It was the perfect catalyst. Cue the unrestrained crying. Comfortable that no one could hear me, I bawled outrageously and for a long time. It seemed to be my new favorite pastime.

Hoarse, exhausted, and wet from crying; tortured

with a mind-splitting headache; humiliated by the collage of my evening's behavior, I put my head down on my arm and dozed on the floor.

I awoke in a fetal position on the floor. I felt a pain on my right hip from lying on the hard floor. My shirt sleeve was wet from my open mouth sliming it. My arm tingled with numbness. I opened my eyes. I was disoriented. I forgot where I was. In a sad panic, I thought I actually missed Casper, who had come while I was asleep on the floor. I tried to get up. It was harder than expected. The arm and leg that had fallen asleep were momentarily useless. I fell back. Finally I stood up. I walked outside into the dark night. The campus was silent. Numbly, I stiffly strode through the empty campus back to my room. It was late, late enough that I could sneak into the dorm room with scarcely anyone seeing me.

I stole into my pitch-black dorm room. By my bed, a little moonlight seeped in from between the window curtains. I saw Tim's face in the dark. He seemed so peaceful, so ignorant of what I had been through. I wanted to climb into bed with him, innocently—though I bristled at the word innocent— just to cuddle his ignorance for a little while.

Instead, fully dressed, I climbed into my bunk bed. I felt the weight of my body sink into the bed. I felt such a contemptible conflation of self-hatred, pity, and outrage that my overworked brain finally shut off into sleep.

Chapter 62: Help Wanted

December 1, 1980

The next morning, I had a coming-out hangover: guilt, insecurity, self-righteousness, relief, giddy joy, and pent-up anger all combined to concoct the most exquisite—if paralyzing—headache I'd ever had. Even though I was up hours before him, I stayed in bed pretending to be asleep until Tim left for class. No longer sure who I could 'come out' to, I thought silence was the best protection. Moreover, I wanted to keep my parents' reaction a secret until they changed their minds, which I naively thought would be sooner rather than later.

Bitterly, I remembered that just the day before, I thought being gay was going to solve all my problems. I had no idea it would actually cause so many, so painfully, and so quickly. Instantly, just because I was gay, I had a parent problem, a college problem, a tuition problem, a life direction problem, and for my troubles, I also had the self-hatred come back for offending my parents. I could not think who to turn to. I pulled clothes over my body and walked downstairs. I skipped classes. I was unconsciously walking outside. Where was I going?

I felt lost and desperate. I was wondering who I could turn to? Who did I know who could give me good advice, if they discovered I was erring? I suddenly remembered Dr. Wire. I was even standing right in front of his office.

The secretary lowered her glasses and pointedly asked, "Do you have an appointment, Mr. Goldberg?" I was taken aback by her belligerent tone.

"No, no I don't. But this is kind of an emergency. I was wondering if Dr. Wire was available, just for a short talk?"

"He's very busy, of course. I rather doubt it," she said, as she picked up her phone. "Hello … Yes, Dr. Wire … Jamie Goldberg is standing in front of my desk—oh … oh." She again peered at me through her glasses. "I'm so sor—yes, of course, yes, he's right here. I will send him in." She looked at me with a newfound sensitive look, different than the one I was used to. I wondered what she was told. "Go in; he seems to be expecting you."

"He is?" I asked. Then I realized my mother must have called him.

I walked into his sterile metallic office. It looked softer now than it used to. It seemed to have lost the edge of danger.

Dr. Wire spun around. I also saw a difference in him. His contemptuous, rather challenging posture was gone. He looked at me, and for the first time, I felt like he was on my side. Again, he knew something, but I was unsure what.

"Please sit down, James, but I don't have much time."

"I was hoping," I was contrite, almost begging, "that I could see you again, doctor."

"James, I want to be honest with you; you can't afford my visits. Your mother still hasn't paid for the ones we already had—"

"I'll pay you. I am having issues with my parents," I said, fighting back a lump in my throat.

"Sit down, James." I sunk into my usual chair. "I can't say I am surprised."

"Did she talk to you?"

"I am not at liberty to comment on who I have or have not spoken to. But more to the point, you have spoken to me."

"I am breaking apart."

"What happened?"

"My parents hate me."

"I can't say anything about that, Jamie." His tone was surprisingly soft and empathic. "Just tell me what happened."

"I told them … I told them …" I was suddenly not so sure this was the right thing to say. "I am gay."

"They didn't particularly care to hear that, did they?"

"No, no they didn't … But you don't understand; they threw me out—disowned me or whatever. I have nothing to live on. They hate me." Far from feeling any pride, I was overcome with shame.

He looked at me with a winsome sadness. "I can't

give you the acceptance you need from your parents. You need to think whether your parents are capable of giving you that acceptance."

"But being homosexual, that's bad, isn't it?"

"Good or bad is out of my line. It's not a disease. I told you that."

"But you didn't know."

"Come on, Jamie."

"You knew … of course. Everyone but me."

"That's how it usually is. Look, there is nothing wrong with you; just go to the clinic, here." The doctor wrote on a slip of paper. "Ask to see Doctor Jones. He'll be a good resource for you. And look, whether you see Dr. Jones or not, be prepared. You are going to grow quite a bit and in a very short time. For what it's worth, it's my considered opinion that you'll be okay."

"I wish you had told me that before."

"You're not my patient now." He smiled.

"I'm still not a disease?" I asked.

"I'm a man of my word, okay?"

"Okay. Thank you."

Then Dr. Wire swirled around in that familiar gesture one last time.

Leaving the office, the secretary already had a Kleenex waiting for me.

"Why doesn't he have these in his office? Am I the only one who's ever cried in his presence?"

"No, you're not," she laughed. Then she looked seriously at me. "What's the matter, Jamie?" she asked with such sympathy—more than my own parents would show me—that I just wanted to cry.

"I need a job," I said, breathlessly.

"You need a job?"

I nodded my head 'yes.'

"Badly?"

I shook my head again.

"I might know of one, if you don't mind working in a bagel factory."

"No, not at all." I had no idea what that entailed.

She wrote on a card. "Here. Call my friend Sheldon Kaufman. He manages the Brooklyn Bagel Factory; it's not too far from here. He's always looking to hire someone."

I looked at the card. Baking bagels hardly seemed like a glamorous job. It was probably a minimum-wage sweatshop kind of job. I put the card in my pocket. I would rather not work there. Surely with my skills I could find a job in a bank or an office somewhere. Still, I was grateful for the help.

Chapter 63: Abandonment

Back at the dorm, I knocked on Dara's door. After a moment, it opened. She was surprised to see me.

"Can we talk?" I looked pleadingly into Dara's eyes. "Please?"

"Jamie?" Her initial smile faded when she read the misery in my face, and then she looked behind her. "Look, maybe it's not a good idea; I don't want you to be disappointed again."

"Dara, just talk with him," said Ahmed, walking up to the door dressed in his typical formal suit. Dara heaved a sigh, looking plaintively at Ahmed. "Look, let me leave you two alone. I'll come back tonight, after dinner. I have things I have to do anyway. Good to see you again, Jamie." Surprisingly, Ahmed gave me a warm hug, as if he knew what happened.

"Thanks, Ahmed, I hope everything is going okay?"

"They've been better Jamie. We missed you. Take care of yourself." He walked out the door.

"I am surprised," I said watching. "I didn't know he still liked me."

"Of course he does. He is just a bit sensitive right now."

"How come?"

"Because I am leaving."

That was the last thing I wanted to hear. I thought we were just being friends again. "You're leaving? ... Really, when?"

"Next week."

"You aren't even going to finish the term?" I feebly protested.

"It's arranged." She was clearly tired of defending herself and her decision.

"Well, don't be surprised when people want to talk you out of it. I'll miss you."

"You are sweet, Jamie. Come on in." I walked in her room. Together we stood on her familiar Persian rug. "I am glad I came by then. I am gonna miss this rug."

"You want it?"

"I don't have any place to put it ..." I didn't know what to do with it, but soon I would be homeless and it would be nice to have something to put on a floor. "Can I? You wouldn't mind?"

"Of course not. Come get it this weekend."

"Where are you going?"

"I am leaving with a women's theater collective. We're touring a play called *Women's Rights in Argentina* around the U.S."

"Really? I didn't know you were into theater, too."

"Well, it's more a political thing. I've gotten involved in politics and the arts."

"Cool, can I see the play?"

"Only if you want to go to Urbana, Illinois."

"I can't go to Urbana, Illinois."

"Oh, Jamie, what's the matter?"

"Is it that obvious?"

"You don't hide your emotions very well. What's the matter?"

"I hurt my parents, hurt them really bad. You, Casper, everyone, everything … "

"What did you do?"

"I'm just so inconsiderate … self-centered. Unnecessary …" I cast my eyes into Dara's. Thoughts were raining down—disorganized, painful thoughts. "You must hate me."

"Of course I don't."

"But you never talk to me anymore. You didn't even want to talk to me just now."

"Jamie, what did you do to your parents?"

"It's not just them. I don't know where to start. It's all gone wrong. I thought everything was going so right and well … now you're leaving."

"Jamie, I have to—" Dara glanced at her watch. "Okay, sit down. Take a deep breath and start at the beginning." I dropped to the floor, crossed my legs. She wanted to sit on a chair but she joined me on the rug.

"I'll try and keep it short." I heaved a deep sigh. I looked around the room. I thought this was going to be a second home. Now it was probably the last time I would see it. I looked at Dara. She was supposed to have been my girlfriend or at least my female savior. "I don't know where to begin. Oh shoot—when I realized I was attracted to men, I tried to fight it." Dara didn't flinch. "I tried to stop thinking about it. When that didn't work, I tried faceless ideas, then faceless musical voices, but then finally I saw a person I could not ignore, or did not want to … Casper."

"I know."

"Casper was different from everything else. It was really love at first sight. My feelings for Casper I swore were something different. I told myself, it was a noble love. I fought the sex and thought I won the battle, when I …" Looking at Dara, I suddenly feared what I was about to say would be very hurtful to her. I wanted to say it in a way to show I knew it was wrong. "I thought I won the battle, when I …violated you—"

"You didn't *violate* me. Come on. I seduced you, Jamie."

"Really?" That winded me for a moment. "Seduced me? Why?—Anyway, after we … were together, whatever it was I did, it was bad enough that you didn't want to see me anymore."

"I'll admit things got a little screwed up afterwards, Jamie, but I enjoyed being with you. That was a fun night, wasn't it?" It was such a relief to hear her talk positively of our night together. I hadn't realized how badly I felt about it until she said that.

"It was a very special night, Dara, almost sacred to me. But I hope I wasn't taking advantage of you."

"Definitely not."

"Afterwards, you said I should see Casper … anyway, I *saw* him." I felt my face blush.

She nodded knowingly. I didn't want to know what that nod meant or how much she knew from Casper just yet. I hurried my story.

"He was glad to see me … I guess. I helped him on the set of *Long Day's Journey*. I thought we were just being friends, but … he *seduced* me …" the word seduced sounded weird on my mouth. "I guess that happens to me more than I realize … but I was in—" I hesitated to finish the sentence. "Love … I was in love with him, and the love I felt intimidated me. He could … intimidate me … whether he knew it or not … and he did, he intimidated me to—" I looked away from Dara, "kneel in front of him."

"Yes, I know." Again I had to ignore what she heard, but it hurt knowing Casper was bragging about dominating an idiot like me.

"Still, I let him, or I forced myself to do *it*. I don't know why it happened. I wanted to be elevated to the heights and instead knelt to the ground. Ugh. All I know is instead of love, he hates me now. Like you do. Like my parents do. Like Tim will in a moment, when he finds out about me."

"Aren't you being a bit unrealistic? I doubt any of these people hate you. I certainly don't."

"You don't?"

"No, of course not."

"Why not? Okay, you said that already … You

may not hate me, but you don't love me."

"No, I don't."

"Casper doesn't love me."

"I can't speak for him."

"My parents don't love me."

"Look, before you start feeling too sorry for yourself, you should know I like you, and I hold you in a … high regard."

"Oh, terrific, great, let me just take that to the bank and cash it in for—" Frustration and pain were getting the better of me and my ability to control events around me.

"Jamie, you're hurt. Listen. I didn't want to build your hopes up about being with me. You needed to find out who you were, and I think you have. That wasn't easy."

"Easier than you think. Dealing with the aftermath is the real bitch."

"I understand your bitterness."

"Am I bitter? This is what bitter feels like? Well, I don't like it. Great, I am bitter about being bitter. Errgh!"

"Jamie, please. I am sorry I wasn't there to help you. Casper wasn't too kind, was he?"

"Did you know? What, is Casper bragging what a pushover faggot I am?" I asked, realizing I had to face what Casper was saying sooner or later.

"Actually I heard from someone else first … then Casper told me."

"Everything?"

"He left out the gory details." She laughed. "I didn't really piece it together until just now."

"He hates me."

"Jamie, we've just been through that. Calm down. He didn't say it was you. Casper did say the one he talked about had more experience than you. So maybe it was someone else."

"More experience? Maybe I am a fraud; did you ever think of that? Maybe I am the sickest person you ever met."

"I know you're not. Calm down."

"How would Casper know anything about me anyway?" I couldn't think how he would think I had more experience. He could not have spoken to Julie Aschenbach from Southfield High; she didn't exist. What other ghosts had he spoken to? I panicked. "I am freaking out! How can anyone tell me to calm down? My life is fucked. I am screwed. I am royally fucking screwed, and I did it all to myself!"

I felt as if were on the verge of hysteria when she grabbed me. The grab turned into a hug. We got up and continued our embrace, sitting on her bed.

I felt stupid, embarrassing myself by behaving like a seven-year-old child. I lay my head peacefully on her lap. I remembered her floral smell. I felt nostalgic for her, like a lost life, a lost chance at simplicity. Impetuously, I kissed her. She let me. But it was just an ephemeral dream, never a concrete possibility. At that moment, I understood why some people don't go see the doctor when they're ill, as if through sheer ignorance they could escape a fatal diagnosis. Had I just not known I was gay, couldn't I have kidded or lied to myself that I was straight? Don't some people do that for an entire lifetime? Knowledge isn't power; it can be a prison. A death sentence even—especially for innocence and naivety, these were the very things my life depended on. Having bitten the apple, I certainly couldn't go back and un-eat it. You could spit it out, but that isn't the same thing. Once the onion is peeled, you can't unpeel it. "I am so totally fucking screwed," I said, my head lying in her lap. "I'm sorry, I behaved like an idiot." I got up from her lap. "You're trying to be nice, and I am just freaking out like a child. I'll go." The full weight of my misery crashed down on me. I felt depressed. Too much had happened.

"You've been through hell, haven't you?" she blessedly asked.

"Dara, my life is destroyed, and I don't know how to put it back together. I counted on you." I looked in her eyes. "Maybe it wasn't fair, but I did. I counted on you. I counted on Casper and I counted on my parents, and you're all gone. I chased you all away. I chased you away by making love to you; I chased away Casper by falling in love with him; and I chased away my own parents by telling them the truth. How could I do so many nice things and yet chase everyone away, unless I am some evil, terrible—"

"Don't, Jamie."

"Don't you see? For the first time in my life, I

thought I understood life and could be true to myself. I thought I would first celebrate myself with you, then with Casper, and then my parents. I just tried to be honest with others; and I have nothing, just nothing to show for it. No friends, no love, no parents. I won't even have a place to stay at the end of the term, let alone money to register for classes. My life is ruined, fucking messed up, destroyed, devastated." Dara put a hand on my arm. "In the name of the truth, I blew up my whole life just because I wanted to be a FUCKING FAGGOT!" I panted as if out of breath. Dara kissed me on the cheek. I calmed down. "Sorry, I didn't mean to yell. There was just no one to turn to …. And I have never … I have never been so sad and angry before in my entire life. I don't know what to do with this—this rage and sadness. And yet I am happy, too. I did feel happy with you, even with Casper. That night was so beautiful until the way it ended. I don't know myself anymore. But I don't like it, and I was supposed to."

"Sounds like you know yourself better than ever before. Oh, Jamie. There is a lot about you I do love. You know that." She stroked my cheek; how I adored that feeling. "What will you do?"

"I don't know." I looked her in the eyes. I saw such a welling of, I don't know what in her eyes, but it was beautiful. I had to admit I did have a friend, after all. I could not help but smile. It seemed wrong to smile after such horrible things happened. But there it was. She stared at me softly. I just knew it was okay.

"At least I don't have to go around pleasing people who are unappeasable. I can stop trying to do the impossible and do what I want."

"There, good for you."

"It seems so comfortable to feel sorry for yourself. I want you to pity me. But I won't drown myself in that darkness. I've come too far, haven't I?"

"It'll be okay. Let's take it one step at a time. We'll put together a plan. Okay? Let's see, the first step?"

"I need a job."

"Right."

"Then, I need to find a place to stay."

"And you have until the end of the term."

"Yes."

"And through the dorm, your food is taken care of too?"

"Yes, it is, actually. I'm not in such a bad spot."

"Not at all; in some ways you're lucky. You've got time to find a job and start saving for next term. You can take a lighter course load next year and move off campus. Finding a job will be easy; you'll see. You're bright. You make a good impression on people."

"I do?"

"You do. I shouldn't have left you alone like that. I didn't realize I had. And Casper has his own issues, too."

"He does?"

"Yes, he does. But I don't know about your parents."

"They kicked me out of the house."

"You told them?"

"I told them I'm gay."

"I thought your parents were politically liberal and everything."

"I thought so too."

"I am sure they'll come around."

"Just be patient," I said bitterly.

"Yes, unfortunately, just be patient. Until then, you're gonna have to be self-reliant."

"Self-reliant." It seemed so final. It really happened. I was really cut off from the lifeline I always assumed would be there.

"Can you do that, Jamie?"

"I have to."

"Getting a room to rent is really easy and much cheaper than the dorms. Look at the student news and you'll see a hundred rooms for rent.

"I've seen the ads; there are plenty."

"And you have a scholarship, too, don't you?"

"I almost forgot about that. You're right; I do."

"So your tuition is almost covered anyway."

"Half of it, anyway. You're right. A job, a room, how hard can that be? You know, someone just gave me a lead on a job. But working in a bagel factory."

"What's wrong with that? The next time you see your parents, they'll be looking at a full-blown adult."

I laughed involuntarily.

"That wasn't the comfort I was hoping for. But I should stop blubbering and get on with it, huh?" There was a fear I didn't dare to mention to Dara.

Without my parents, I felt I was no longer protected from someone. I even knew his name: Gary. I'd have to face this Gary guy on my own. I didn't know him or who he was, but he seemed frightening to deal with all alone. He had to be dealt with; he seemed to have spoken to Casper somehow.

"Turning the page is never easy, Jamie. I wish I could help you. But I know you're a survivor. I don't need to worry about you. I trust you will do well."

"This is surviving?"

"Believe it or not, this is surviving. I know what you are going through. I was kicked out the house when I was sixteen."

"Really? Dara, how could they do that to you?"

"Sometimes you have to stand up for yourself, even when the consequences stink. Like you did with coming out of the closet. I know something about coming out of closets."

"You do?" I looked her in the eyes. "You know, I was raised thinking the whole world was heterosexual. It was so common it was never mentioned by name— it's so assumed to be the one and only true way. Anything else had to be wrong."

"I was raised that women didn't go to college; they didn't have careers. We were just passive supporters of men," Dara said.

I was surprised. I realized she and I had more in common than I thought. "And then, at one moment, you realize that mold isn't right for you."

"Exactly, Jamie, I realized I wasn't made for that life."

"I wondered what was wrong with me." We both smiled at the recognition.

"And I wondered what was wrong with *me*. And yet, everyone thought we were crazy for thinking anything different."

"And no one encourages us to dare to stand out."

"It was even the opposite." Dara laughed. "You get punished and ostracized if you so much as hint at going against the norm."

"Exactly, until you either give in, break apart ..."

"Or break away. Tell them to all go to hell. You matter."

"Yes! Go to hell! We matter! Ah, but the next thing you know, Dara, you've lost everything and everyone."

"Eventually, you get to be yourself. Being different, isn't so ... different, Jamie."

"I can't control being different. I tried, and look at the result." That seemed a happy thought to me and we both laughed. I started feeling good, which triggered a guilt impulse. Guilt, because I sensed my parents were suffering on my account. "I can't control my parents, so they can't control me," I interjected, wondering if I really believed that. It was comforting to say. I relaxed for maybe the first time since I left my parents' house. "I am glad I saw you, Dara."

"I needed this too. Ahmed was right. We needed to talk. I was probably as afraid of this as you were. Thanks for doing this. It took courage. I should have done this first."

"Wow." It seemed she was the needy one all of a

sudden. I folded my arms around her. "Well, thanks. Things aren't as bad as we thought they were. I hope we can be friends again, when you come back."

"We sure can, Jamie."

Kissing her was more like kissing a memory of Dara than the flesh and blood before me, as she was kissing the Jamie she walked out on.

"Bye, Jamie."

"Bye, Dara. I know what to do."

"I know. I trust you, remember that."

"Dara, I know you do … and I know you love me."

"Well, I am in good company, because you love me too."

"Break a leg in Urbana."

"I'll try not to."

Sharing a last laugh, I left. I walked out of the dorm and into the shining sun. The sun's warmth made my face feel aglow. I reached into my pocket and there was a card: Sheldon Kaufman, Brooklyn Bagel Factory.

Chapter 64: Oak Park Deliverance

December 3, 1980

Brooklyn Bagel was near the DSU campus, but I needed to go to all the way to its administrative offices in Oak Park, a northern suburb of Detroit, to apply. In a nondescript faceless strip mall, there was an equally nondescript bagel shop. Around the back entrance of the store was the small office with a receptionist and two levels of little box-like offices.

A middle-aged receptionist was seated behind an old gray metal desk. She was wearing what had to be a tall blonde wig and metal-framed eyeglasses the size of tennis balls on her strong Roman nose. She had thin lips tinged with white. In her hand was a mound of cream cheese supported by half a bagel. More prominently than any of the work papers on her desk was a big plate of yet more cream cheese and multicolored bagel halves. As I walked in, she looked up at me with a quizzical look, as if she was unsure why anyone would be walking into the office.

"I am here to see Sheldon Kaufman," I told her.

"Shel? Shel ain't here; he's in Murderers' Row … ain't he?" She seemed to ask me, as if I would know if he was recently convicted of murder. I shrugged my shoulders. Then she startled me by yelling, "IS SHEL IN THE DETROIT STORE? HEY, SID, IS SHEL HERE?"

"HOW MANY TIMES I GOTTA TELL YOU, USE THE FUCKING PHONE."

"DON'T SWEAR AT ME. I TOLD YOU, I DON'T LIKE IT WHEN PEOPLE SWEAR."

"I BOUGHT YOU THE ... FRIGGIN' PHONE—"

"THAT'S BETTER."

"—SO USE IT."

"WILL YOU JUST FUCKING TELL ME IF SHEL'S HERE?"

"OH, SO *YOU* CAN SWEAR, BUT I CAN'T?"

"*YOU'RE* BEING A MORON."

"USE THE PHONE! AND DON'T GIVE ME THAT *MISHEGOSS*."

"Oh, yeah? *Gai kakhen afenyam*." She was shaking her head and looked at me. "Can you believe this?"

"Incredible."

"This is what I gotta put up with all day. He doesn't even pay me. I DO THIS FOR FUN!"

"I PAY YOU!"

"YOU HAVE EARS WHEN YOU WANNA HAVE 'EM! AND YOUR VISITOR AGREES WITH ME. I'M UNDERPAID!"

"THEN HE'S STUPIDER THAN YOU ARE!"

I wanted to melt away while she waited for a response. There was none, so she picked up the phone. "Okay, Mr. Executive, is Shel there?"

"I AM HERE! IS IT GOLDBERG? SEND HIM UP!"

"SEND HIM INTO SID'S OFFICE?"

She started nodding into the phone while rolling her eyes.

"Okay, but get your own pastrami sandwich. I have to answer the phones." She then looked at me and smiled. "Welcome to Brooklyn Bagel, Mr. Goldberg. Please sit in room number 118, just behind me. Someone will be with you in a short moment. Can I get you a cup of coffee while you are waiting?"

"No thanks."

"Water?"

"Yes, please."

"Well, I have to watch the phones, but if I get a break, I'll get ya one."

"Thank you."

I looked behind her. There were only two rooms: one marked 'Lunchroom', the other marked 'Room 118'.

I sat in the small room. Past the solid white plastic door, the windowless room was barely big enough for the two swivel chairs on either side of a gray metal desk with an adding machine and stacks of papers.

I was feeling a little uneasy, unsure if I was the Goldberg that Mr. Kaufman was expecting since the receptionist didn't even ask my name. I couldn't possibly be the only Goldberg in Oak Park, a predominantly Jewish neighborhood.

Eventually, in walked a large man holding a sheet

of paper—my application. He closed the door after him. He was tall, with a prominent mustache, his head like a large reddish egg draped on the sides with dark gray hair. Based on the rest of his body, he would have been skinny, if not for the balloon-shaped protrusion of his belly.

"Hi, I'm Shel," he said, offering his hand. After he sadistically shook my hand, Shel edged his way into the chair behind the desk. His belly hung over the top of the desk.

"Hello. I'm James Goldberg."

"James?"

"Uh … Jim."

"Right, Jimmy. Have a seat. I heard from Marjorie, you want to work at the bagel factory?"

"Well … if you have an opening."

"As a matter of fact, I don't; but maybe, for the right person, we'd make one. *Kapeesh?*"

Unsure, I nodded my head anyway.

"I have your application here. You're a good student," he glanced at the paper, "studying political science?"

"It runs in the family. I come from a politically active family." I tried to cover up being in the theater, thinking it was too fey for bagel work.

"I see. You certainly volunteered on a lot of political campaigns. Have you ever baked bagels before?"

"No."

"No … bakery experience?"

"No."

"How about … er … food service?"

"No."

"Okay, how about any job at all?"

I didn't dare say anything. I was seeing the job slip through my hands. I had to say something more positive.

"Let me see your hands."

It was embarrassing enough that this interview was not going my way, but now he had to get personal. I showed him my hands.

"Have you worked a day in your life?"

"I had a newspaper route once!"

"A newspaper route!" He was unimpressed.

"And I helped out as a stock boy in my uncle's shoe store when I was in high school."

"And why exactly should I hire you?" I thought of my empty job experience, but then also of my near-empty bank account.

"I need a job, Mr. Kaufman."

"You need a job? And call me Shel; I don't like that 'mister' crap. You need a job?"

"I do. I need a job, badly. I am a quick learner, and I'll do good work."

"Oh, you will?"

"I'll do whatever needs to get done."

"You will?"

"I don't know how else to say it. I need this job."

"Whaddya need it for?"

"I have to support myself through college. And

I don't know where else to turn. I need the work. I learned to be a good worker. My father is a construction electrician in the IBEW."

"Really? My brother Sam is a member of that union too; maybe they know each other. It doesn't matter. The guy's a bum, anyway. You want to bake bagels?"

"Yes, absolutely."

"It isn't fun. Those pretty hands of yours will get calloused."

"I can learn fast." I relaxed; I felt like I had some chance.

"I am gonna spend all this time teaching you to make bagels; how do I know you just won't turn around and get a job at a ... well, like a bank or some sissy sit-down work."

I internally bristled at the 'sissy' comment, but outwardly trudged on in pursuit of this job.

"I hate banks."

"You do? Well, don't hate, it's a moronic thing to do, but you're in good company." Shel glanced up at the ceiling.

"What kind of commitment can I make to you?"

"It'd be nice if you hung around for six months. But I can't stop you from ... you'll be out of here at the first chance, I know. The pay is lousy, Sid up there is a cheapskate—I love the guy, but he's cheap. Gives us Jews a bad name, *kapeesh?*"

"*Capisco.*" I felt this was beginning to go my way.

"Huh?"

"Yes, I understand."

"I don't know. I got your application. I'll see what I can do for you, young man. I can't make any promises." He stared at me long and hard. "Why do you have to support yourself all of a sudden?"

"My parents stopped supporting me."

"What, you've been a moron to them or something?"

"I suppose so."

"Yeah, well I don't like morons. But maybe you're okay."

"Do you think I can get the job?"

"Hard to say. You have no experience. It would be a huge risk. But it isn't every day a stray walks up onto your doorstep. You need a chance. Maybe I got one for ya. I'll talk to Sid and let you know. I got your phone number." He winked, then leaned over, grabbed the door handle from his chair, and threw the door open. "HEY, CANDY!"

"WHAT IS IT, SHEL?"

"JIMMY HERE IS JUST LEAVING; THINK YOU CAN MAKE HIM A BAGEL AND CREAM CHEESE TO GO?"

"LOVE TO, BABE."

"LOVE YUH, CANDY!"

Chapter 65: Jackpot

I was sitting in the library, hidden in the cubicles reading up on homosexuality. Once my source of terror, it was now my only source of comfort. I had found the few library books that were positive about it. They were suspect comfort, since they were written by homosexuals. It seemed with homosexuality, the more *objective* the author, the more prejudiced the book; while the more *subjective* the author, the more tolerant the book. Homosexuality and impartiality apparently did not mix.

I still would occasionally look around in paranoia, in case anyone would catch me reading the books. But reading about the ins and outs of gay culture was so fascinating, I could not help being engrossed by them. Especially since one book would completely contradict the other. With the seeming exception of the John Boswell book, there seemed little inclination of authors to substantiate anything they claimed. This would usually amuse me, though every once in a while there would be an author—usually a homophobic one—that would hit a raw nerve. There was one particular sociology book which claimed the 'urban homosexual subculture' was a breeding ground for criminals, even though he cited no evidence. Another book, on the homosexual and the legal system, mentioned that in many states, Michigan included, homosexual activity was illegal. Consequently, this otherwise crackpot sociological tome was in fact right that the 'urban homosexual subculture' was by definition a breeding ground for felonious criminal sexual behavior, as spelled out by the Michigan sodomy laws. These facts struck me as quite depressing. I was facing more opposition—and structural opposition—than I really cared for. I even started doubting if coming out was such a good idea after all, when a voice frightened me.

"Hey, you."

I screamed. My face shot up in fright and I tried to hide the book under my lap—but I had many more homosexual books on the table. Then I looked up.

"Sorry, I didn't mean to scare you," said a voice with a light Southern accent. The possessor looked handsome and well dressed. He had gorgeous thick black hair and a well-groomed mustache, smart-looking glasses, and his clothes were pressed and sharp. Though he had just scared the daylights out of me, I could not help but think of the word *debonair*.

"Hello," I said defensively, not knowing if this person would be friend or foe.

"Interesting book you got there," he said, again with a charming intellectual Southern lilt. I took the book out from under my lap. I had a sickly feeling I was being busted. I knew this guy.

"You can read the title from there?" I said as neutrally as I could manage.

"No, I recognized the cover."

"Really?" I asked, wondering if that was comforting or not. Was he friend or foe? He hadn't played that card yet. Luckily, I was reading one of the homophobic tomes, so I could still claim some kind of tacit innocence.

"You look surprised? Maybe it's my nice suit coat? Or my clever little bow tie? Not what you were expecting?"

"I wasn't expecting anything. You surprised me."

"You don't recognize me, James M. Goldberg—Jamie to your friends." Luckily he spoke long enough that I recognized flashes of his voice.

"Mr. Devlin." I remembered. The teaching assistant for a course in medieval history I had taken. But he never behaved like this, and he did not speak with a Southern accent.

"Mr. Divine to you." He flashed a friendly smile, and I knew I was safe—but not to what extent. "But we're out of school, so you, my dear, may just call me Jack."

"Hi, Jack."

"But you didn't recognize me at first, sugar, I could tell. I remembered you all right. You're a hard one to forget."

"I am?"

"You're a meek little guy in class, but on paper you're ... surprising."

"I am?"

"Yes, and it is lucky for you I grabbed your final exam instead of Professor Sykes. He would have trounced that cute derrière of yours."

"Is he … gay?" *Are you gay? Why are you talking to me?*

"Oh, dear child," he lowered his voice to a whisper. "He is as *homo*-phobic as it gets, and you wrote about that John Boswell's book on the Bible and Sexuality—"

"*Christianity, Social Tolerance and Homosexuality.*"

"Please." His tone turned quite mean at once. "Not so loud here."

"He wouldn't have approved of it? It was published by the Yale Press."

"Honey, that's all the more reason he would hate it. Professor Sykes is not your modern medievalist. You should know I am his only graduate student—well, the only one of consequence. Anyway, we have to look out for each other. I had to give you a three-point-three on that exam of yours. The trusting professor insists on reviewing anything I give a three-seven or higher. I took you down a few points just to be safe. Had he looked and saw I gave you a four—mercy. Well, that wouldn't have been pleasant for either one of us. So why are you reading that horrible book there?" His smile was allusively disturbing. "I didn't have you pegged for a Christian."

"What?"

"The book there." He pointed to a book on Christianity and homosexuality I had placed in the corner of the cubicle.

"I was just reading about—" I looked around to make sure no one was listening, then whispered, "*it* ... and redemption."

"Redemption? What do you care about redemption?"

"Yes, I thought for the longest time about redemption ... in general, but there wasn't anything, at least there's nothing in that book about it."

"I can teach you all about redemption, because we are going to hell." He flashed his disturbing smile.

"I'm not Christian. I wasn't thinking about that kind of redemption."

His smile sagged noticeably.

"What other kind is there—what, you're not ... then .... you're what, atheist? Oh, let me guess; I do know ... Goldberg ... you're Jewish?"

"Yes."

"You know how I know? Your paper had a propensity to talk about food and you Jews love your food, don't you?" I squirmed. It wasn't anything too negative, but it was the strangest observation of Jews I had ever heard. Besides, I don't think I discussed food in my western civilization exam.

"I guesso."

"Ah well, at least you don't look Jewish," he said, as if it were a compliment.

"Thank you," I said, trying to sound wry.

"Oh dear, I put my foot in my mouth again, didn't I? Trust me, dear, I don't have anything against you Jews, or blacks for that matter. I just can't say some of you are my best friends, because I hardly know any. That's why I am always sticking my foot in my mouth."

"I guess I have to go."

"You'll just have to educate me. I wouldn't put too much store in that Boswell book, though; he's so full of it."

"He is?"

"He has an evil agenda. Take it from me; I should know all about it. In addition to studying medieval history, I am also Catholic. There's nothing redeeming about men having sex with each other."

"Oh."

"Well, you don't see fags leading very normal lives—even the good ones were, what's the word ... exceptional."

"The good ones?"

"Da Vinci and Michelangelo."

"Or Tchaikovsky."

"Exactly, James." Somehow he had been inching closer to me because now he was right on top of me, his thighs touching my side as I sat in my chair.

"I think I should go."

"I am scaring you away?" He looked hurt.

"No, not at all." I started putting my notebook into my backpack.

"Good, then you'll have dinner with me?"

"No, I should go back to the dorm. I should eat there, but I need to go before they stop serving dinner." I stood up.

"Well, can you at least tell me what your book's about? I was thinking of reading it sometime." His dubious smile returned. I sat back down. He moved a chair from the adjacent cube and sat down so our thighs were again touching. I moved slightly away. I couldn't get away fast enough—part of me. Another part of me thought, *Here is an intellectual homosexual; we could have an interesting talk about it.* I didn't know any other gays and he seemed a more typical one: He didn't wear women's clothes or speak in too feminine a voice—or at least didn't at work. I wondered if I would have to talk like that too in order to fit in.

"I understand, James. You're not feeling so comfortable—out here. Come with me." He got up and beckoned me with a wave of his fingers. "Follow."

Chapter 66: A Gay One

The next thing I knew I was following him toward the back wall, where a series of doors were. He took out a key.

"I have the keys to the good professor's carrel." He opened the door to a small room the size of a cubicle with two chairs. It was stacked with books. "You see the books; he keeps them here so he can have them as reference ... and also assure no one else can check them out. He's a pig. But they all do it." He waved me again into the room. "Come on, I won't bite." True, he wasn't wearing jogging pants. At least he was not going to ask me to untie them. Still, I wondered if he were a serial killer, a self-hating gay who kills the thing he loves.

He closed the door. My heart started pounding.

"Sit down. Relax. No one can disturb us now." It was not a comforting thought. The chairs were next to each other. He pushed them together even closer. We sat. He moved his leg closer to mine. His groin now exposed, yet safely draped by zipper-secured dark wool pants. He put his hand on my thigh. I knew he was going to rape me, or at least intimidate me into sucking his cock.

"So here we don't have to worry about being disturbed or undesirably spied upon." He lifted his eyebrows on the word undesirably. Here it came, the moment I was dreading. How could I escape? He squeezed my thigh again. He removed his hand. I leaned forward in the chair ready to try and jump away from him. But before I could let out a sigh of relief, he put his arm around my waist and squeezed it. My heart was pounding. I was ready to run, but I wasn't sure whether he had locked the door. Thankfully, he withdrew his arm from my body. "So tell me about this terrible book you are reading."

"Of course," I swallowed. "The book talks about why gay people should be more focused on sex than … others. Because they have no social support to keep relationships together."

"Well, that's true."

"It says because of that we're more liberated and don't need to do what he calls 'aping the straights'. Meaning pretending to get married and behaving like they do. We can make up our own relationships."

"He's got that right; we faggots fuck like bunnies. It's all we can do. Fuck like bunnies, but nothin' to show for it—except a sore behind and the clap."

"But that's not the way I see it. If the right two people can get together and support each other, they can have a loving relationship, don't you think?"

"I wish we could. I do. For your sake I wish we could. But, no, we can't; because God will just tear it down."

"God? How so?"

"Ever see two guys owning a house together? Ever see two guys living together—not students, that's normal enough, I mean two old guys? Never. Because who would sell it to them? Who is going to let them live in their neighborhood? It's just like being a nigger, except you can hide it." I bristled as he spoke the word 'nigger'. "You know what I mean; because you don't look Jewish, you can pretend to fit in."

"I don't pretend to fit in."

"What are you so upset about? Oh dear, did I put my foot in my mouth again? I am sorry."

"You can't talk like that."

"Like what? Oh, I see, you are sensitive—I like that. Just don't take me too seriously. I know, I used—"

"Don't say it again, please."

"I don't mean it like the way you are thinkin'. I grew up amongst some backward crazy Baptists, and they just say 'nigger this' and 'nigger that.' It's terrible, let me tell you. They still treat ni—coloreds—like slaves. I am not like them. Quite the opposite. I see how they suffer—we can hide our perversion; they can't hide their skin color."

"Okay, but I think they prefer to be called 'black.' And I prefer to be called gay."

"Yes, yes … I am not prejudiced *at all*. But I need to learn to be more sensitive. You'll forgive me, dear, won't you? You'll help me out? Please?"

"But you can't say that—word."

"I won't. Scout's honor." He crossed his heart and

held up two fingers. Then he looked into my eyes and softly added, "We need to stick together, you and me, because we have something in common."

"We do?' I swallowed again. *Here comes the assault.* I braced.

"We do indeed, sugar." He put his arm around my back again and held it. It stuck like it was plastered there. "How about we go have a cup of coffee together?"

"I gotta eat before the dorms close."

"Don't be such a prude. I am not suggesting we play strip chess—"

"That's not funny!" I just about screamed in frustration.

"Don't bite my head off, I was just ... oh, I see I hit the jackpot, didn't I? Who played that with you—come on?" He laughed.

"Fuck you!" I barked, shocking myself with how angry I had become.

"Touchy, touchy; never mind, I'll let it go. Well, how about just a coffee?"

"I need to eat something."

"Cool, let's go grab a bite to eat. On me. My treat. Least I can do to make it up to you. I am not a horrible person. Please?"

"I don't think you're a horrible person. I just have to go. I promised my roommate, Tim, I would meet him for dinner."

"Well, why didn't you say so? I am holding you back. I hope we can meet again sometime? It's good to have friends like us. We can confide in each other."

I was so relieved; he just wanted to be friends all along. "Yes, of course," I said.

"We all need friends. I surely do, dear."

"I need friends too, very badly."

"Oh, why is that, dear?"

"It's a long story. I can't tell it now. I gotta go."

"Well, do you need help now, like this minute? Maybe I can help you?"

"No, it's not like that. It's just … I came out to my parents, and they threw me out of the house. They won't even pay for my school anymore."

"My goodness, how terrible! How simply awful" He hugged me, though this time, mentioning my parents, I involuntarily hugged back. "How can they do that. You poor dear. Do you need a place to stay?"

"No, no thanks. I can stay at the dorms at least for this term, but then I will have to move out."

"Oh, you poor dear. Well, if you need a place, you just let me know," he said as his hug soon turned into hands caressing my back and sliding down to my butt. I stiffened.

"I have to go see my friend." I pulled away.

"Oh, right. You and … Tim."

"That's right."

"Is it *that* kind of relationship?"

"Oh no, we're just roomies. But I like him a lot. He's just a bit distant."

"Are you sure? I bet he's eager to have dinner with you."

"Well, we're roommates."

"I am willing to bet he's in love with you."

"In love with me?"

"You are too adorable, James. I know people very well, as you will *soooooon* learn. Take it from me."

"But you never met him."

"I know the type. Believe me, I do. And of course, you are so charming and sweet … Let me give you an example: I bet he doesn't have any girlfriends."

"Actually …. no, as a matter of fact, he doesn't."

"He has never dated."

"No, he hasn't."

"But he likes you. Likes you very much."

"Exactly."

"It's pretty clear then, isn't it?"

This sounded too ridiculous for words. "But he's never hinted anything to me."

"Are you sure?"

"Well, nothing physical."

"But something *intellectual*?"

"Yeah, we like to share things; we seem to be getting closer—that way, but not like you're thinking."

"See, I told you. I know people so well; I am simply clairvoyant. I just knew it."

"But it doesn't mean anything just because he doesn't have a girlfriend."

"Oh, I am sure it does. Has he ever dated a girl?"

"Well, no."

"Maybe he's mentioned … them … you know, an interest?"

"Yes, yes he has. We share two friends, Nina and Dorothy—both singers. He's a music major."

"And let me guess, they're older. Has he taken either of them out?"

Even the idea of dating Dorothy was ridiculous. She was more the portly mama type.

"No, he hasn't taken them out."

"Oh, you have a little closet case on your hands, and I am sure he just has the hots for you."

"You think so?"

"Oh, I know so … say, what time does the kitchen close at your dorm?"

"Seven-thirty."

"Why not let me join you for dinner; I'd like to meet him."

"Oh no, I could never do that!" I said a little too quickly.

"What's the matter? You don't trust me? You think I act like this all the time? You know I don't. We'll be straight as an arrow. Believe me, it's a sad sorry person who even hints to anyone outside our perverted little circle that I might be queer. I won't embarrass you in front of your darling." Jack looked at his watch. "Oh dear, you missed your dinner. I am sure poor Tim already ate and left. Say, come eat with me. Come on, we can go to a Chinese place I know about. They've got real Chinese food, not just this Chinese-American crap Detroit usually has. They have something called Szechwan food; it's really good—a little spicy, but I think you like it that way. Come on. It will be my treat. Besides, those zipper-heads can cook up a storm."

"Jack—"

"Oh dear, I fear I've put my foot in my mouth again. I am so sorry. You would think as often as that foot's in my mouth, I'd never be hungry; but I am famished. Let's go eat."

"No thanks. But look, if you are so worried about appearance, I was just wondering, what would you have done if Dr. Sykes burst in while we were here?"

"Oh, ha-ha, this isn't his carrel, it's someone even naughtier. Sooo, we'd have nothing to worry about. Let me see here. Yes, here it is." He picked up a magazine between two books. "Modern physique. Soft porn by any other name. You'll be safe with me, dear. Let's go stiffen our wrists and get something to eat."

"Thanks, Jack, but I really have to go, he's ..." I forgot whether I said Tim was waiting for me or Casper. "He's waiting—gotta go!"

Running back to the dorm, I vowed to avoid Mr. Jack Devlin as much as possible. Yet, the more I thought of it, the more unfair this snap judgment seemed. He was the first gay person I met with whom I could talk. He didn't mean any harm. He was charming in a queer kind of way and not bad-looking either. He certainly used a language I did not approve of. But he was kind and seemed teachable. He invited me to dinner. Maybe I can finally have a boon companion.

Also, Jack seemed to understand Tim better than I did. Tim and I were indeed becoming very close. So close that I myself began to wonder about him. I decided to watch Tim a little more carefully. If he needed me, if we needed each other, I wanted to make sure I was available.

Chapter 67: Dried Flowers

Tim was becoming the center of my life. He was filling a vacuum left as others abandoned me. Unreturned calls and returned letters told me my parents had not forgiven me. Casper avoided me. Dr. Wire was played out. Dara gone. Alone.

There were now just three people intimately in my life: this gay yet obnoxious friend, Jack; a theater class bully, Ben; and my kind considerate roommate, Tim. With Tim, I felt I could just be myself—no mask, no pretense.

But could I afford to trust Tim? Emotionally needy, I had nowhere else to turn. Could I dare to tell him the truth about me? If I did tell him I was gay, I risked losing him. Because I learned that for this transaction, there are no returns. All sales were final. I was gay, and he would have a definite opinion about it.

Tim had already learned I was not getting money from my parents. I was debating what to tell him when the phone rang.

"*Mr.* Goldberg?"

"Yes, speaking."

"James Goldberg?"

"The one and only."

"Good. This is Shel from Brooklyn Bagel."

"Oh, hello, Mr.—I mean Shel. How are you doing?" I just knew this had to be good news.

"I am doing just fine. Look, I'll make it short and sweet: Welcome to the team. Against my better judgment, I decided to hire you. Can you start at six a.m., next week Monday?"

"You mean next Monday morning?"

"No, I mean next Fourth of July. Next fucking Monday morning at six a.m. Look, don't give me a reason to change my mind. Next Monday, *kapeesh*?"

"Yes, yes, that's great news. You won't be sorry!"

"Oh, yeah, we'll start you off at three-fifty an hour."

"Wow, almost a dollar over minimum wage. I'll be there! That's the best news I've heard all day!"

"Thrilled you're happy. See you next week, *Mr.* Goldberg." Click.

If I worked enough hours, I might even save enough money to stay in college part-time next year.

I couldn't wait to tell Tim. I could concentrate on the good news without delving into the bad news and murky waters. Part of me did not want to become too close to Tim. Yet the bond between us grew stronger and stronger, as did my dependence. He was quite gentle and understanding. He sensed my problems at home. He looked the other way when I cried myself to sleep on those days when the pain I inflicted on my parents, mistakes I made with Casper, or the lost chance I had with Dara were too much for me.

Tim was very giving, and I was very needy.

Despite myself, love was creeping into my feelings for him. Love completely different from my love for Casper. It was a physical love for him. Not for Tim. Tim was gently beautiful, while Casper was irresistibly sexy. Tim's tall delicate body, by contrast, was more vulnerable. If I longed to be held by Casper, I could see myself succoring Tim.

Tim and I had much in common. We were not popular. We stuck to ourselves at school. We never dated women. We loved classical music, theater, and serious movies, which he called 'cinema'.

I have to admit I experienced some familiar symptoms of love. Alone in our room, I'd think of him and our arms sexlessly around each other. Alone, in the cafeteria, I did not feel like eating at all. Studying, I only wanted to think of him or Casper: Casper the love, Tim the need.

But Tim was a difficult person to read. He was always rather stiff and cautious. He spoke in a soft basso profundo voice, sometimes barely audible, making me all the more hanging on his every syllable. Even his soft smile seemed to have a trace of reticence. His idea of exciting music was the rather tepid composer Felix Mendelssohn. My love of Wagner offended his penchant for emotional equilibrium. Still, I felt bound to Tim. Tim's advice, Tim's company, Tim's intimacy, Tim the only game in town. If Tim minded this dependency, he rarely showed it.

Tim seemed as starved for intimacy as I, for when we started talking, we often stayed up half the night. All night long we would discuss which was a higher form of art, theater or music. We'd play music or read excerpts to defend our points.

If Tim came in when I was playing music, it was always a great conversation starter. I had been listening to my latest passion, Schubert's song cycle of unrequited and rejected love: *Die Schöne Müllerin*. The music moved me and helped me to process some of the sense of rejection I felt, not just from Casper but also my own parents. But when Tim walked in carrying his usual stack of musical scores and study books, I was eager to avoid those topics of conversation.

"I got a job!" I blurted out the moment he walked in the room. I pushed a lever of the phonograph and lifted the needle—leaving Schubert's music, like the needle itself, in midair.

"Oh, congratulations. You'll stay in the dorms next year, you think? Maybe we can share a room again."

"I hope we can." Tim looked down and looked at the spinning record and the needle suspended in mid-record.

"I see you're still listening to *Die Schöne Müllerin*."

"It's just so moving, like it can read my heart," I said, hoping he would either take the hint if he wanted to hear more or ignore it if he didn't.

"Okay, tell me more about these songs," he said, taking the hint. "Nina and I were playing around with some of them. See?" He grabbed a score from his book pile and showed me *Die Schöne Müllerin*. "I was accompanying her on some of these. They are quite nice."

"I can imagine, especially with Nina's voice." Nina was a graduate voice student we both admired.

"So, tell me your interpretation of them." With that request, blue skies rippled through me and I shivered. I could make it. I had a new job and a real close friend. This all seemed to confirm Dr. Wire's assertion that I would grow quickly.

"Okay, sit down next me." I touched the couch. "Where do I start? They're so beautiful. It is about someone, a young wanderer—could be you or me." I looked tenderly into Tim's eyes, and those eyes greeted me warmly, or so it seemed. "He is looking for someone to love. Then he sees the Millers' daughter. She is so beautiful, noble, and pure. First he is afraid to approach her, but the attraction proves irresistible. He convinces himself he has finally found the one, the one who really loves him. But it turns out to be his illusion; he's deluding himself, just seeing what he wanted to see, but not what was actually there. The words are passionate, but the music tells us his fate will be quite different."

"Really? Very interesting."

He made eye contact with me. I thought I could sense the mutual affection. It seemed unmistakable.

"If you're interested, sit here with me, and we can go over the text together."

"Why not start with the song that was playing when I came in? That was so Schubert to me, so simple and elegant, but with lots of depth."

Only a small reading lamp lit a spotlight on the couch. The couch was full of stuff: books and clothes. I lifted the books gently off the couch and put them on the floor. I set the clothes on top of the books.

Tim sat down next to me, a little closer than a casual acquaintance might. I could not help but think, *Could this be my "mullerin?"* He took his winter coat off and laid it on my pile of books and clothes. I took the score from Tim. I looked for the song, *"Die Trockne Blumen,"* and draped the book over our laps. To keep the book balanced, I held my leg at an odd angle, balancing my leg on the balls of my feet to make the surface level. Downward our two faces joined, eyes focused on the musical score. Then I placed the tone arm at the start of the track. The late hour meant we had to keep the stereo volume low and speak in hushed tones.

"This song, coming up, is really moving. See this text here?" As I pointed to the book, my arm brushed against his arm; his flesh felt so soft and emotionally tender. "The song is titled 'Dried Flowers,' because someone he once loved gave him a bunch of flowers. He pressed and preserved them as the only proof that his love ever existed." I lowered the tone arm. We looked at the score, the music started, and we began to listen.

On the recording, Benjamin Britten played the piano accompaniment softly and sensitively.

"Tim, hear the sad introduction?"

"What a chordal beat."

Then the singer on the record, Peter Pears, sang with his raspy love-shattered voice.

All you little flowers,
That she gave me,
You shall lie
With me in my grave.

"The longing and sadness, yet a sense of hope," I said.

"Like a tonal tug of war."

We were sitting so close, I could feel the warm whisper of his breath.

Why do you all look
At me so sadly,
As if you had known
What would happen to me?

"The sound of pain ..."
"Nice. E-flat minor dominates."

You little flowers all,
How wilted, how pale!
You little flowers all,
Why so moist?

"Now just this hint of light."
"Amazing yet simple chords."
The music seemed to shimmer.

Ah, these tears will not create
The green of May,

Nor can they make dead love
Bloom again.

"It brightens because even an echo of love ..."
"Oh, he's toying with the keys."

And spring will come,
And winter will go,
And flowers will
Grow in the grass.

"So sad and fragile but—"
"What key will win?"
Peter Pears sang as if he, too, were unsure which key would triumph.

And flowers will lie
In my grave,
All the flowers
That she gave me.

"But just this crumb ... of love ... is that all ..."
"Chords perfectly misplaced."
Peter Pears's coarse dry voice seemed to caress every word.

And when she wanders
Past the nearby hill
And thinks in her heart:
At least his feelings were true!

"A stunning rise of hope!"
"A triumphant rising figure."

Then, all you little flowers,
Come out, come out!
May has come,
Winter is over.

"Spiritual optimism." My eyes seek his.
"E-major wins." Tim smiles!
The triumph in Pears's voice was magical, Britten's accompaniment soaring.

And when she wanders
Past the nearby hill
And thinks in her heart:
At least his feelings were true!

"Spring comes, but the sadness returning … "
"Back to the eerie funeral march."

Then, all you little flowers,
Come out, come out!
May has come,
Winter is over!

"The victory retreats, as if Schubert himself were afraid of hope."
"The final chords slip down."
Tim slid away from me.

Then, all you little flowers,
Come out, come out!
May has come,
Winter is over.

"Maybe it won't turn out right."

"Of course not, we're back in E flat-minor."

Transfixed on the music, the piano coda's final notes were walking away from us.

"There is this modicum of hope."

"Ritardando."

"But hope seems to linger ..."

"... diminuendo ..."

"Yes, it dissolves to nothing."

"Yeah, nothing."

Acknowledgements

The author would like to thank those who have suffered along with him and/or materially assisted him: his husband the late Dr. Morris Taylor, Michael Arent, Lawrence Brown, Susan Dray, Barbara Evenson, Nancy Reuscher, and David Siegel. Lastly, I tip my hat to Peter Paulus at ArnoLand Press.

About the Goldberg Variations

Although *The Rites of Passage* is intended to stand alone, this volume comprises the first installment in *The Goldberg Variations* series. This series follows its main character on a journey of self-discovery through an odyssey of trials, errors, and the occasional moment of grace leading the main character Jamie Goldberg on his elusive journey to forgiveness and redemption. This journey takes him to many places around the world while meeting a quirky cast of characters along the path to his own surprising, quirky self-discoveries.

About the Author

Jonathan A. Taylor is a San Francisco-based writer and designer. He is a leading designer for creating user-friendly technology and has worked for companies such as Google, Nokia, IBM, and GE, as well as for the Dutch design bureaus Informaat and Stroomt Interactions. Jonathan has published two books on software design. *The Rites of Passage* is the first installment of a multi-volume series, *The Goldberg Variations.*

As this book will show, Jonathan's passions include theater, opera, travel, social justice, and cooking. All of these passions figure prominently in his writing. A leader in the community of alternative sexuality, he is the title holder of the 2013 International Master/slave education title, which he earned with his recently deceased husband Morris Taylor. *The Goldberg Variations* is Jonathan's first work of fiction.